C000089841

Quality fiction is imagined reality

For Thou Art with Me

~

Robert F. Jackson, Jr.

Cover Illustration by

Sonia J. Summers

Always for Maria

Dedication

Richard A. Cataldi, Commander USN (Retired)

United States Naval Academy

This book is a work of fiction, and any similarity or resemblance of any character or person in this story to any actual person, living or dead, is purely coincidental. Events, situations, specific locations, or specific businesses portrayed within are fictional and set in a fictional future. The same can be said for organizations and agencies.

Any copying, retrieval, storage, or transmission of the material in this book by mechanical, electronic, photocopying, digital, or any other means is strictly prohibited, unless written permission is received from the author.

Limited short excerpts for promotion and review purposes or for educational assignments are allowed.

ISBN-13: 9798655013377

Copyright © 2020 Robert Jackson
Cover Illustration, Copyright © 2020 Sonia J. Summers

Contents

Preface

Acknowledgements

Various people have been helpful with historical, technical, and other types of information and advice. Some of them have done so on most of my books. Often it is verification of what I already knew or had forgotten, and other times new information. For example, I have learned that, growing up right after the War, I used many of the slang expressions of their day and the decades before because that was the slang of my parents that I heard every day.

Richard A. Cataldi, Commander USN (Retired)

Ron Dominy .... Historical

Greg Martin .... Technical, historical

Martin Sykes .... Firearms

Maria Jackson .... Medical

Margy Jackson .... Medical

Charlene Rossell Mitchell* .... American Slang

Brenda L. Moore, Phd. Associate Professor of Sociology, University of Buffalo; *To Serve My Country, To Serve My Race*[1] [pg. 83 this novel]

*Author of: 1930s SLANG DICTIONARY
(And others)

Preface

The inspiration for this story is my mother-in-law, Doctora Natividad Corrales Taboada, who, as a young woman, insisted on becoming a doctor when few thought women should in a country and culture (the American controlled but Spanish influenced Philippines) where it was considered even more not to be a woman's place. She went on to graduate on the eve of the war with Japan, an enemy that redefined evil in those days. Often, I try to explain slavery (which I abhor) in my American South by saying slavery (as bad as it was, and then dying out) was still accepted in that era. The military behavior of Japan toward captive combatants and conquered civilians in the Second World War era was not acceptable in any era past the most ancient barbaric times, and should never have been even then.

Standing near the pillars holding up the roof above at Cebu Maternity Hospital (or clinic) because that was the safest place as the Japanese bombs fell on Cebu City, she may have decided then to suggest to her new husband, a law graduate from the same prestigious University of Santo Tomas, the same year she she received her medical degree, that it was time to head for the hills. That they did, in his car, the generator of which, attached to a water wheel of his design and construction, charged batteries throughout the war for them and some of the Cebu Guerrillas. They themselves were not guerrilla fighters but often in danger from nearby Japanese. Surviving harrowing moments, she provided medical care for civilians and guerrilla fighters alike, and he provided electricity for themselves and the guerrillas as he protected the valuable doctor and the two children born in hiding during the war. More than once they were in danger of capture, and numerous accounts have proven that capture by the Japanese often, almost always, meant death by beheading, while children were stabbed. For women, things could be so much worse before a violent death or forced military prostitution.

The Cebu Guerrillas went on to fame, acquiring and sending to the Allied commanders in Australia the plans of the Japanese defense of the Philippines, allowing Gen MacArthur and others to plan around that. After the War, she and her husband went on to found St. Vincent Hospital and San Vicente School of Midwifery. St. Vincent Hospital lives on today as one of two medical centers of the University of Cebu.

One might ask, "Why not write their biography of their war experiences or a novel about them instead of the story about an African American doctora and her white male companion, a friend from youth?" The answers are simple. I do not know enough details and general information to write of their wartime years, and I do not make up fiction about real people. Secondly, I am a poet and novelist. I deal in writing as an art. When I place my stories in history, I keep the main historical points accurate, and the smaller plot 'fictional facts' remain within the realm of that which occurred, probably occurred, or logically could have occurred in that time and place. Thirdly, I may even have a real historical person appear in a story briefly, a cameo if you will. Such characters may even reoccur or their presence just off stage may continue, as several novels that include the Navajo woman Johónaá-eí 'Sunny' Jefferson reveal her friendship and correspondence by mail with Theodore Roosevelt. But I will not write fictional stories about real people. To me that is disingenuous. It would be writing made up lies.

My themes are always courage, the Christian faith, and egalitarianism, the latter encapsulated in my hate of racism and healthy obsession on an intellectual level with the theme of miscegenation. I find that for men and women to marry people of other ethnicities is commonsensical and adventurous on many levels, none negative. I did so, and bonded comfortably with **her** family and with friends and new acquaintance as I was a minority for more than three years in her homeland. So, it was not just romance, not just the woman; it was an embracing of the other people that was colorblind other than seeing the obvious attributes of the other people. I find the same to be true with any ethnically mixed marriage entered into with an open mind by both parties. The fictional Dr. Carolyn Ann Davis and pilot and adventurer, Allan Allison represent all those elements and struggles just mentioned in this paragraph above and those of my mother-in-law.

~

One might wonder: Why another war story of the Great Pacific War, the Pacific Theater of the Second World War? As well as any crisis can, the great worldwide conflagration can teach us about ourselves. Isn't it obvious that the largest event in history effecting the most people, except the birth and sacrifice of Christ, which is history's greatest event, should garner as much respect, attention, and educational opportunities as any other lesser occurrence? Don't worry, reading this, that the novel will preach to you. It is not a novel of the Christian genre per se. As a son of two people who were members of America's Greatest Generation, their momentous era is close to my heart. Knowing my Filipino wife's parents of that same generation, American subjects who suffered the Japanese occupation of their homeland, has enriched my interest and connection to that time as well.

Still, some might ask_ why bring up the atrocities again and denigrate the Japanese, our allies now in our own place in time on the planet? The answers are several: That it happened and it is important history now being slowly diluted and evaporating from our race memory . . the human race's memory; that it is a lesson in the evil people are capable of, showing the barbarism that can arise, even in modern times; and that its truths blunt and deaden the criticism of America's Atomic bomb attacks, revealing to the world what actions perpetrated such a response. The defenses and denials that can be found of the Japanese behavior during that war are almost sickening, and the ignorance of the truth by many today is saddening. That some younger generations hold some reverence for the Imperial Japanese war machine is disturbing.

Japan was ill prepared to take on the British Empire and the rising American superpower. Only a greater lack of preparedness of the isolationist and peace loving Americans and the preoccupation of the British with the threat to them from Hitler's Germans gave little Japan a chance in the beginning. Nipponese equipment wasn't always the best; personnel served out of blind loyalty and were harshly trained and disciplined; and battle techniques were not always refined. Storied Banzai charges were blind obedient rushes into death from the tactics of a more barbaric time, not bravery or initiative, and flawed carrier airplane operations were glaring during the moments of their greatest defeats in battle. Besides an archaic warrior culture, and racism born of a sense of superiority even over their fellow Asians, perhaps the need to terrorize to make up for industrial, military, and technical weaknesses was a strategy of the Japanese military. The populace at home supported the efforts out of blind loyalty and obedience to and reverence for a strong brutal archaic culture that indicated their emperor was a God. They knew it was a war of brutal conquest and they learned some of the atrocities in their newspapers. Japan and its people, great people now, were simply stuck in a time warp, stuck in the wrong century. And when their time of defeat came, when the roll call was called out, their leaders did not have the courage . . and their culture did not have the flexibility and intellectual sophistication to facilitate a surrender . . and thus, those big bombs.

This book is a love story. A story of romantic love for another, in this case between two somewhat dramatically different but very similar lovers; of love for one's fellow man and woman; of love for one's duty; of love for one's country; and of love for all that is good, while the world is being blown apart . . a kind of love that can still see the good while the embers of the conflagration still smolder afterward. The evil perpetrated by one fictitious Japanese officer herein, who represents the thousands who emulated his actions and worse in the real world, is only part of this story. As *quality fiction is imagined reality*, and all the more so in historically set yarns, the events in this book are real, and the people involved in them are simply fictitious representations of people that were probably real (in some form) or could have been real. Within the broader historical events, these minute specific events are not true, but they represent ones like them that happened and were true. The atrocities that happen at the hands of the Japanese military herein are true and occurred in other real-life moments and scenarios, and perhaps in slightly different ways each time they occurred over and over. Not only has this author researched them, but he has been told of some by people who were actually there and witnessed them firsthand.

People

The events in this novel occur during the same time period as those in the life of Chief Petty Officer Jake Pierce USNR and his younger friend Sarah Willowood portrayed in the novel *For the Duration*. Allan Allison in this novel and Jake met and became friends before the war as expatriate Americans and pilots in the Philippines. Jake and Sarah appear briefly in this book, but the reader does not have to have read their story to understand their role.

The characters in this book commonly refer to their **Japanese enemy in Asia and the Pacific** as 'Japs' and 'Nips' (Nipponese). It would have been a logical short slang term without the anger and resentment caused by the sneak attack and military misbehavior of the enemy. That the words were also used to denigrate the enemy is easily understandable, given the general methods of abuse perpetrated on captive peoples by Japanese forces. This author has heard firsthand eyewitness accounts from relatives in the Philippines, and there is plenty of photographic evidence. The novel's narrator, in attempting to indicate the feelings of the characters and their moment in history, sometimes uses 'Jap' and 'Nip' too. This is **not** intended to denigrate or insult Japanese people today. But at the historical moment, when directed at the active foreign enemy and his behavior, it seemed appropriate.

Except in the case of broader historical actions, campaigns, and events, military units, people and operations are fiction in this book; but, for the sake of realism, they are similar to the operations that did take place during World War II. As an example, the hospital ship, *USS Refuge AH-11* was real and her general location and movements in the story are as well.

For Thou Art with Me

~

Even though I walk through the
valley of the shadow of death,
I will fear no evil;
for thou art with me;
thy rod and thy staff,
they comfort me.

Psalm 23:4

Africa, June 1941

Just north of the Twentieth Parallel South, quite a ways above the Tropic of Capricorn, in a small patch of savanna surrounded by trees, they sat under a portable awning of light canvas that blocked the sun but not much of its heat. They were drinking scotch on the rocks, the latter having survived the long flight in an ice chest due to the abundance of cold irregular chunks of frozen water, the quality of the chest, and the coolness of the unheated Aero's cabin. Watching the girl work with the bearers in the shade of the plane's wing, Allison and the Frenchman had chosen the awning under which the shade was more stable and less mobile, as the sun moved through its daily routine.

It wasn't the sweltering region one would expect in the African tropics but an expanse of grasslands near the convergence of the little Nata and the Gwabadzabuya on the borderlands of Southern Rhodesia and Bechuanaland. With bearers actively working, pack animals standing here and there, equipment and supplies scattered on the ground, and her movements, the industrious dark woman hadn't the same luxury. Wearing a light khaki short sleeve shirt and nearly knee-length shorts of the Western adventurer style in Africa and elsewhere in the tropics, she calmly supervised the appearance of disorder and chaos, guiding matters into a reasonable semblance of a real expedition. Allison noted the rich dark coffee brown skin of her legs and arms that was different from the darker Africans who surrounded her. It wasn't the latté of the East Indies girls, it was a deeper, richer brown, a dark mahogany or coffee light on the cream.

"She eez a beet short for most Africans I have known," commented the Frenchman casually.

"She's not African; she's from America."

"Nevertheless, she eez of these roots."

Both watched the woman move to her tasks, as the safari was staged and her instructions were followed. There wasn't a white man or woman among her group of apparent companions. It was a warm day, but there was a breeze. And there was the scotch . . and the rare ice.

"Well, here the lady comes. I believe you are een for eet now, my friend. Though deliciously petite, she walks with a command of herself that ees not of a colonial. I mean to say a local."

"Well, here goes," Allison commented with a different source of angst than the Frenchman was poking fun about.

Standing and hiding his stretching as much as possible for the formality of the moment, he met her gaze, as the dark brown woman with shiny, slightly coarse, yet gracefully flowing, straight, black hair approached with a look of concern. She would often put the hair up off of her neck in the heat of the upcoming trek.

"Mr. Allison . . Captain, some things are missing . . the most important..."

"Don't worry, they're here," he stopped her complaint with the gently raised palm of his right hand. "I wanted them safe with me in the cockpit."

"How so?" she responded, expecting some subterfuge, a scam perhaps and higher charges.

"It's Africa, Doctor . . or shall we say, 'the world' . . one must protect one's valuables."

"I see," she responded with a lingering suspicion in her voice that he didn't miss. She had a soothingly deep, soft, velvet-like, rich voice. In the right moment and atmosphere, one might say 'sultry'.

The two walked toward the hatch at the middle of the Aero's fuselage, as she followed his lead. When he had gotten out of Czechoslovakia with it, he had made many modifications. He reached in where he had moved the small crates containing her instruments and medicines after landing. There had been passengers on the first leg of the flight and only he and Beaumont to watch things up to Pretoria.

Turning with the smallest one, he said, "This is light."

As she took it, they were close now, face to face, and he said, "I've wanted to talk to you, Doctora," using the Spanish way he had learned on the border and in the islands. And as he said it, he locked in on her face, unconsciously staring, . . and it unnerved her a moment and she looked down. He realized the rudeness, but his mind had wanted to refresh his memory and then hold it, molding a new one.

"I'm sorry, I hadn't meant to stare. It's just that it has been a very long time."

Looking up and smiling inquisitively, the seemingly young Doctor Carolyn Ann Davis said, "Yes, we've met, haven't we? Where was it?"

"The last, most recent time was a year ago. You had just come to Africa. I flew you down from Cairo."

"Oh, yes, and the British fighters escorting us part of the way over Egypt and all . . a bit tense. 'Most recent'? There have been others?"

"Our fathers knew each other, our families mixed a little . . uh, I mean ah . ."

"Don't worry; I know what you mean. Go on, I remember. Your name, I thought about that a year ago and wondered. You've changed so much."

Allison was embarrassed by his word choice, but strengthened himself and continued. "Those . . what seven or eight picnics . . And then your father was so proud of you and asked Dad to come to your graduation. You didn't see us because we weren't sitting with your family. We were in the back. I heard your salutatorian speech."

"You mean high school . . !" said with a girlish surprise as if she were back there . . "in Knoxville?!"

"Yup. But I would 'uv made it to Paris for your med school graduation if I'd 'uv known."

"Oh my, well then, this is just like old times . . or something. I remember the picnics. My graduation? And you didn't get beat up?"

"You know, East Tennessee was never that bad. But then from your perspective, well, I don't know." He again felt he'd put his foot in his mouth.

"Well, now we've met again, but I've got to get going. Perhaps we can talk in six months when I'm back. You'll pick me up out here somewhere won't you and take me to Durban?"

"Why Durban?"

"I have to catch a ship to Singapore; I've a position there."

5

She was remembering the scrawny, yet wiry and athletic boy now. He had been nice, and they might have become closer, but the picnics were few and far between and both were shy_ shy as teenagers can be at first and shy because of the racial issue. She knew then that he surely knew why the outings were so private and always on his or her father's private land. He looked now nothing like the boy she remembered from back then. It was the parents who were close and very careful with it, the friendship. She supposed some people knew and didn't care to make an issue. The boy's father wasn't wealthy but had a significant business, was strong in many ways, like her father, and had a presence about him. No one messed with Allan Allison, Sr., the local hotheads, the small local Klan . . nobody. She wondered if the boy . . the strapping, strong, handsome and tanned man before her was like his father.

"I just wanted to say . . ," and pausing he had taken her hand, the left one in his right and took the small instrument case from her with his left. She looked down at it, the hand he held, and he felt she might be offended but thought he better not be weak and didn't drop it. "This is Africa. What you're doing is dangerous."

"I'm African American," said with that typical sort of softly incredulous sarcasm.

"But you weren't raised here, you're not African. There's so much to know. I've been here on-and-off for a while now. The people where you're going are tribal. They have rules different than ours. And different from each other, their neighbors."

Teasing a little, because she could see his concern, which shocked her within, Carolyn inquired, "Are you saying my people, these Africans, are not civilized?"

Looking seriously now and straight into her eyes, brushing off the renewed embarrassment from the spot she had put him in with her words because it mattered so, Allan replied, "I'm saying it's Africa; and, if the native people here were white, the world would still call it the Dark Continent, for its mystery, lingering tribal ways, and jungle, the black mamba, lions ... and I'd be just as worried."

"Well, the rain forests are north of here. I'm not going into the Congo yet, not this time. I've picked a small tribal community to work with and see what I can do for them, what they might need on another trip, you know. They're known, friendly, and neglected as to modern health. But of course, they are active people and eat rather healthy. And they have their time-tested cures. I want to learn from them. It's all very informal. I don't have a lab with me. . . One microscope and some slides."

"Well, be careful. I know them. In the world political environment, they are a good group to target with some subterfuge to get close into British Africa. You know, for sabotage and spying. Just south of here is old Dutch Boer country, easy for the Germans to pass themselves off as Dutch."

"I doubt the Germans would get down here."

"Doctor, the South Africans didn't want to support the Empire. If Smuts hadn't gained control, who knows? And the Italians are on the Horn. there's fighting there right now."

"That's hundreds of miles, Captain."

"I know, but we live in a new age of mobile war. Look at what the Krauts did in the Low Countries and France."

As he talked and she took in the deeply penetrating gaze of his blue gray eyes, she could read his feelings a bit, and it warmed and unnerved her. He was taller than her and handsome, and he was an adventurer. She had always known, when her wealthy parents sent her abroad after high school to get away from it all, that there might be white men in her life. She just figured they would be doctors, and imagined herself ultimately wedded to a doctor of African origins like herself or just wedded to her work.

For Allan, the woman was the adventurer and it scared him. In general, it scared him, but on a personal level it did as well. On the flight down from Cairo the year before, he had realized who she was and absorbed her beauty and charm. She was taller than the Malayans he had been around so much in the Indies but noticeably shorter than he was. Her hair was full and pretty and framed a face with high, round cheeks, large, dark brown eyes, lusciously full purplish lips and a flat, somewhat petite nose. Her nose and her slanting eyes, like those of many girls of African origin were reminiscent of the Malayans.

People who, unlike the Captain, didn't look closely enough at the world's beauty never realized that most ethnically brown girls had lips that tended more toward purple than pink or red. It was just another alluring thing about them, and made them look odd sometimes when they wore bright red lipstick. One could look and suppose that when God said 'dark'_ by golly, he meant it.

But then, Allan had seen many of the world's beauties now, especially the darker ones down across the southern swath of the Old World, from the tip of Cape Engaño on the shores of the Philippine Sea all the way west across three massive continents to Morocco and across into Andalusia where Iberia was washed by the Mediterranean. And what he liked was that the last thing they needed was makeup messing up God's work, breaking a natural, romantic mood or making for unnatural kisses. And he had also noted that Africans could have exotically slanted eyes like Asians. Ann's face, which mesmerized him, was that of a classic natural beauty . . the natural woman . . somewhat typical of Polynesians, those

9

Malayans he had spent so much time around, and African Americans of who could know what mix of origins? . . but Ann, . . . with those luscious lips and those eyes and the intelligence he knew rested behind them . . .

The accomplished woman, still so early in her career, had now locked into her own, perhaps embarrassing gaze upon the face of the other; and, breaking it with a blink of the eyes and a slight instance of her own self-consciousness, Carolyn inquired, "Where will you be in six months?"

"The Indies, flying between the southern Philippines and Singapore. Or business could keep me here, between here and India."

He didn't say, because he couldn't, that as he flew cargo, he flew for others, making double money, nor that the sideline was more important and paid better, sometimes making triple the money. There were people, during the building world tensions of the late nineteen-thirties and into 1941 and especially in Asia, who couldn't fly commercially, take slow ocean liners and tramp steamers, or wait for military transport (or even want to be seen getting on or off of the latter). The commercial airliners of the day were small and crowded, and far from private. He had a fine, reasonably new, long ranged transport that he had acquired cheaply through the confusion and luck of war. He still wondered at how he had been blessed that day near the factory airfield at Vodochody, north of Prague. He purchased the prototype conversion A204 that was about halfway between commercial plane and bomber as the Wehrmacht was only kilometers away rolling through Eastern Europe. It seemed something that was being experimented with, and he was told that it wasn't even officially on the company's records, as a 204 or the 304 warplane . . just what he was looking for. It was better than the common Ford Trimotor others flew. He had an official looking bill of sale, yet wondered if the man from whom he had purchased the plane was who he had said he was or just some company employee trying to get cash with which to try and survive the storm that was rushing at him from the west, riding on Nazi tanks.

For Allan's important passenger clients now, alone among the crates in the back of his prized Aero was much more suited for whiling away the monotonous hours of a long flight feeling free to confer with each other, especially when there were several and they could compare notes and plan, undisturbed and unheard. The two pilots must have eventually been unknowingly honored with some type of informal security clearance because as the war in Europe, China, and North Africa heated up, the special passengers would occasionally ask to use the plane's radio, right in front of its small crew.

"To relieve you with some proof of my survival, I'll look you up in the British 'Fortress East' then," revealing her knowledge of the current world situation.

"No, I'll get back and pick you up. I'm concerned, Doctor."

"'Carolyn' just 'Carolyn' or 'Ann'."

"Call me 'Allan' then. And handing her a piece of paper, he added, "You have a radio, don't you?"

"No, Allan, They're expensive, and really not very available. I thought about a receiver, but . . then, all that weight just to hear depressing news from far away." She said it with slight mock disgust at the obvious and placed her left hand on his right arm near the elbow, as he had moments ago dropped the hand he had held, to benefit her comfort in the warm, sweaty climate.

He set the small wooden instrument case down in the plane and asked, "Did you get the extra horses I suggested in the instructions about the shipment?"

"Two, what's that about, for me or you?"

"You, I'll reimburse you though. Here, come in the plane."

"Swell, you know, I'm in a hurry."

"Nothing worthwhile is ever rushed, unless you're running from gunfire."

Smiling sardonically, she took his offered hand and preceded him up the portable steps through the hatch and into the plane.

As they bent down in the confined ceiling area nearer the tail, Allan knelt; and, as she followed, he said, "This is for you free of charge."

Watching as he tossed back the tarp in the dimmer light, Ann inquired, "What is all that?"

"It's a two-way radio from Australia. Just between you and me, the Aussies are equipping people in the Solomons and elsewhere as coast watchers. They're getting worried about the Japanese. Keep it quiet . . and this is the new equipment. It's heavy, and there's several pieces, so I made you a little two-wheel horse cart out of aircraft aluminum big enough for all this and two people. If you get in a rush due to some danger, hitch your best and smartest horse in front of the two. It's set up for that. There is a foot pedal charger and a gas one with a Briggs engine, and a five gallon can of gas. Give me an hour and I'll set it up for you."

Ann was speechless . . from the shock of it, the new, obviously expensive equipment, and his concern and proactive manner. This old friend and near stranger (on some level) was very concerned, but not trying to stop her plans like everyone else, . . trying to help her achieve success.

"This must have cost..."

"Don't worry about it. Just give me the hour."

"Is this top-secret stuff?"

"Not exactly, but if you have to flee for your life, try to have one of your men destroy it."

Turning to look at him, there was no smile on his face, and Ann started, "How did you…?"

"I know people; they're clients. Now, look at this. This is a little 12 pound unit that's been used for a while in Canada, the Yukon and such. An engineer named Don Hings at a mining company made it for distant emergency communications in the wilds. It doesn't get much more desolate than Western Canada in the winter. Now, look at me Ann," and he took both of her hands in his, "it's pretty much okay right here. You're near civilization. But where you're going, surprises can happen. Things can get serious really quick."

He wanted to say that he wished he had time to go with her, but he knew that would sound presumptuous. "The manuals are here, and someone like you can understand them easily. Learn how to use both of these quickly. I know the frequencies and have a radio that can receive them all. The big set transmits on three, and the little one on two. If you have to leave the big one and have time, destroy it. Just set the gas can in the middle of it all and fire a couple of rounds from a distance. I've seen you shoot on the farm."

Pausing, he looked in her eyes, and maybe a certain, controlled subtle shock was there, and he continued, "Keep this little one near you and the batteries charged. There are extras in a sealed package to protect them. If at all possible, without risk, make sure it goes with you in flight from danger. I'm only a radio call and an hour or so in the air away while I'm in Africa; and, when I leave to go east, I'll get back within six months."

"How much did this cost?"

"Forget it . . a labor of love," and he said it casually, as he rose from his crouch, not even thinking about how he had said it in the oft used term of endearment.

"An hour," the woman said as she followed him down the four steel steps holding his offered right hand with her left.

He had assembled everything possible before it had been loaded on the plane; and now, after off-loading, only the wheels had to be attached, the hinged sides folded up and locked in place, the bench seat bolted in, and the tailgate attached. Then the radio units and small engine were bolted into place and the gas can placed in its rack that had been bolted on one side. In one half hour, the doctor's expedition had a first class, strong, light weight, two or three-horse cart for up to three people. It could be driven with the radio and/or its

15

gas-powered generator in operation, as well as with the peddle powered one. It was truly mobile.

Forty-five minutes after the two had ended their talk and left the plane, they stood by the waist hatch again, and Allan handed her a small leather, semi-hard shell, rectangular case with a handle and a shoulder strap.

"Here's the little radio. In an emergency, if the big one must be abandoned, this is your lifeline. I had an overseas conversation with the inventor, and he sent it through a courier service. He said he's tested it in the bush at over a hundred miles."

"I appreciate all this, Allan. I don't know what to say. I think this cost you a fortune or it was payment for services rendered, your loss either way."

"We're old friends. What else could I do. I can afford it. I want my new old friend back in one piece so we can catch up on old times."

With that he again offered her the container of surgical instruments that had never left the plane.

Taking the small wooden case and walking away with a wave and a wistful smile cast over her right shoulder she said, "Durban to Singapore then in six months and a week. I've a job interview there at the modern hospital in Johor Bahru. I have to pick up my things in Durban."

Three of her bearers appeared; and, as he handed each of them one of the small crates of instruments and medicines, he called after her, "The underlined ones are the two I monitor the most. They're most often clear." Then calling after her again, "Did you hear me?" And she waved acknowledgment with an arm and hand raised high without turning or looking back. Still concerned, he added, "The top one offers reports and the broadcaster's signal is the strongest. That fellow's an old Boer and broadcasts news of what's going on in clear English and Afrikaans."

As Allan sat back down and poured another scotch and water over what ice was left, the Frenchman teased, "You appear to have returned with your manhood intact, een spite of the wild leetle chéries dismissive wave. But I don't know, perhaps it was a bloodless castration."

"Don't talk about her like that, Beaumont. She's a lady. . . maybe she's French."

"O-Ohh, a low blow, mon capitaine … and a damn courageous lady, I theenk. She eez like these natives in that way."

"I've some good friends here, Beau. You're not the only one. Two years of my business were here . . colored friends . . some of 'em."

"...and thees dark continent will devour a man . . or woman, an outsider een a mere momeent, as well . .

and you know eet, Captain. That eez why you are
worried. You are in love weeth the girl."

"Interested," Allan corrected.

"'Een love with'. You better keep your business
here for a while, close to her. What eez she tryeeng
to prove, anyway?"

Allan didn't know the answer to that, but he mused
on it. Was it to make her mark and gain respect as a
Negro woman challenging a mostly white man's
career world, a men's only world for the most part;
was it just to do some good and learn the land of her
ancestors; did she think herself just that good, to
challenge herself like this; was she that good?

The Aero took off quite some time before the
medical safari or expedition set off. The little band
of good Samaritans were far from real danger, and
the presence of the two pilots unnecessary. To stay
longer would have invoked lack of confidence in a
friend and unwanted influence if not control, as an
older brother might have. He set up shop in Durban,
flying cargo from that coastal port and others to the
interior. As he flew, as always but now more
intently, he monitored the radio. Knowing he had
commitments in the Dutch East Indies in the late
Autumn, he wanted to know of her fate before then;
however, keeping himself busy, he knew that vague
deadline was well before the six-month medical
mission would end. In the Aero, the flight east
would be long and arduous, though she had the

range to cover the miles with only a few fuel stops. He had made it both ways more than a few times because of his more important, less public clients, who trusted him in an underworld defined by distrust, and because of his well-maintained plane. No one serviced and repaired a plane more meticulously than Allan and his friend Jake Pierce, both the product of good upbringing. Parents taught that, and it had nothing to do with flying or other dangerous careers. Trust and good habits were life lessons that Jake had learned on a mountain farm in the California Sierras and Allan had learned on one in the Tennessee hills and an uncle's ranch on the Rio Grande, during his Texas year and a couple of hot summers.

~

Before leaving Africa, the two expatriate Americans occasionally communicated by radio, talking in a manner somewhere between warm acquaintances and somewhat closer but not warm friends.

"Hello, Carolyn Ann, uh Doctora. Is everything well with your work?"

"Why yes, my dashing Captain, but I miss plumbing."

"I'm afraid that's one thing I cannot supply." And he wanted so much to ask if she wanted an early extraction from the wilds, but to do so would offend her.

And then he left, as business called. It was a long haul to the Indies and he arranged to carry a few things to partly pay for it. But he was also just being paid to be there, to be available. The plane's cargoes called for stops in India and Lahore. The long trip around the edge of the Bay of Bengal and the Indian Ocean sometimes included equipment treated with secrecy and sometimes firearms. Big things were brewing and Allan bad possessed the luck to meet the right people with a healthy concern about it and a source of money. Once in Singapore and Jakarta alternately, for the next couple of months, shipping missions were flown here and there around Indochina and throughout the Indies. Still, long lingering days were filled with more angst than the tough adventurer would admit but were mitigated by The Frenchman's companionship and work. He really couldn't have stayed in South Africa longer because even his ordinary contracts were important. He was dependable, trusted, patriotic, and quiet. Flights were long and only tense over certain terrain, not necessarily for the topography but for who might be watching below.

In the cockpit, when the Frenchman was asleep in the back, there were long periods of quiet. And in his quiet was Ann, the fact of her race never consciously entering his mind. Oh, it had, once or twice before he saw her last. But now, with each widely spaced meeting, spaced literally years apart and including childhood, it had melted away. Carolyn Ann, the girl from back home, with whom things would have been very complicated back home, . . Ann was simply the finest person he had ever known. Allan now, in retrospect and knowing the strength of will his father showed and the respect in the white community his dad commanded, . . Allan now wished his dad had pushed the family relationship between their families even more, and to hell with any criticisms. He remembered watching her in youth and realized now the attraction, even longing had always been in him. Maybe his late realization was for the better. Even in confused, historically Confederate East Tennessee, where half the people had sided with the North during the War Between the States, things could have been difficult, maybe even, at some point, dangerous.

Through it all he had to keep shutting his imagination down. Wondering about what could be happening to a young, petite, pretty woman of any skin tone in the African bush would keep a man up all night and age him into uselessness. Surely Ann, the modern, westernized black woman, would seem exotic to some tribal chiefs and elders, with power she might not realize until it was too late. A pretty, strong-willed woman of their own race, commanding the eminence due one with the knowledge and skills beyond that of a powerful witch doctor, might seem to more than one powerful man to be a woman they must wed, own, and control. In weaker moments he imagined small, local tribal wars erupting over who would possess Ann. He drank slightly too much at times, just to get to sleep; and, noticing it, Beaumont would try to maneuver his and Allan's duties so that often the latter would collapse in exhaustion first. Airplane maintenance was paramount in their work and area of operation, with many long flights and a Czech made plane from a nation now under Nazi dominance.

"Eet would be better if we could land on water, like your friend Jake."

"It would in these islands," Allan replied as Beau lined the plane up for a tightly tucked field on Sumatra.

"I think it ees hard on an air frame, though."

"If they set her down too hard, it surely jolts 'em, and a hull has no shock absorption like landing gear. Water's like concrete. People don't realize that."

"The suicides who jump off bridges do. Jake never sets a plane down hard."

"Pierce has a gentle touch for a whipper snapper."

Jake Pierce, who Allan met and befriended in the Philippines, was only twenty-three to Allan's twenty-nine.

Awakened very early one morning as the year of 1941 waned, Allan sat upright, knowing it was important. The Aero was dutifully parked in an assigned space far at the end of the rustic airfield in

Jakarta. Most aerodromes around the world were airfields; the globe was not yet ready for very many airports. The field served as a home base for Allan and Beau when not in Durban or Pretoria. But Allan had put the valuable, irreplaceable spare parts in secure military storage in Darwin. The particular of the two phones ringing at that moment was provided by the Australians for the mutual use of several agencies which had the number. Java had been chosen because it was Dutch, not identifiable as British but in allied Dutch territory. The pilots were American and French, a conscious non-British choice as well. The other phone was for the company's general commercial cargo customers. Both groups of customers had drawn the two adventurers away from the American Philippines.

Answering quickly, Allan recognized the owner of the British accent on the other end and inquired, "Austin, you're up early. This can't be good for my general health, but perhaps my pocketbook. Where's Simpson? What can I do for you?"

The line was as secure as any could be in those days, and the British agent was on the same island. There was some certainty that the line was not known so as to be physically tapped in the style of that era's technology. Thus, the man responded, "Yes, Austin here; George is in India. We've an important cargo. I've taken the liberty to cancel all your contracts that would eat up the next month. Compensation will match the loss and more. You said you needed to be in Africa at the soonest. In

23

case you're back later and need the work, I told all your clients this was a medical emergency for one of our health agencies that George Simpson heads here. It's our cover; so, should they feel put off and do some digging, they will believe it."

"Who, what, when, and where? I know the 'why' is none of my business."

"We'll have them there as soon as you say, you've got time to prepare the ship and eat and such. You can have the whole day, and we'll have them off under cover of darkness then. They have no luggage, got out with the clothes on their backs. We've fake medical crates that will not count toward your weight and fuel, but load them as if they did. Make Beau struggle a bit."

After midnight and thus the very next morning, in the final months of ominous '41, the Aero lifted off into darkness to begin a long clandestine return flight from the Indies to India and Africa, hopping around the rim of the Indian Ocean and crossing India, with stops of course, carrying operatives from French Indochina and Siam, where the Japanese had become dominantly influential. The transfer of these agents, both male and female, was hush-hush, and certain British military men knew the one civilian pilot they could trust. All the air carrier corporation, meaning Allan and Beaumont, had been told was that their passengers needed to be debriefed by British authorities in India and South Africa after having already been thoroughly quizzed in Jakarta. What the two knew because of Beau's delicate hearing ability and French language, was that there was some threat to Southern Africa, a member of the British Commonwealth of Nations not totally supportive of Britain in the war in Europe.

Aboard was Elaine, a stunning multilingual Oriental, really as pretty and graceful an Asian woman as Allan had ever know in more than five years there. She had an unassignable mystique of a Eurasian, without the European blood. The other agents smiled knowingly as the two pilots chose to talk to her often during their rotation out of the pilot's seat. For one thing, it was obvious that the girl and the Aero's crew were acquaintances. She had long been in the Annam region of central Vietnam, living dual lives for the greater good. This flight was the next leg in a never expected tearful flight from home. And with Allan's first off duty moment he embraced her.

It was a long tight embrace, and with a sigh he released it, mostly, and leaning back and looking at her, he seemed to breath the words out heavily with a sigh of relief, "Thank God you got out."

They looked at each other and said nothing more for a long moment, and he added, "I kept hoping the Brits would pull you, but feared you wouldn't go. I was so torn whether to come up there myself or wait."

Tearing slightly yet significantly, because of the moment, the seemingly delicate Southeast Asian flower said, "You had two to worry about. I think, 'til now, her risk was greater."

"Are you prepared, Elaine?" he asked, it seeming as if the capable woman in French Indochina, might be a dangerously frail and delicate flower out of her garden.

"I have funds, in universal currency," Elaine replied through tears generated by his familiar embrace from long ago.

"Others could seek advantage of you and your stake."

She calmly, out of the sight of the others, opened her Vietnamese jacket, revealing the knife he had given her two years prior. Then both smiled together as she pulled back the fold of her overlapping skirt to reveal an expensive, thin, light, long dagger strapped to the inside of her pretty thigh. And the two gave out a soft chuckle together, making the friendship ever more obvious to the other agents in her party, some of whom had worked with her and some not.

Standing there, with her delicate yet strong right hand in his, the pilot said, "I have to sleep; our stops will be quick and only for fuel, food, water, and a plane check." And he bent over and kissed her gently on the lips. He knew he had permission as long as neither was yet married.

Four hours later sitting in the left seat to take over from Beau in the right, he took a deep breath.

"Ah, oui merci, she is always worth at the very least a sigh. That leetle Annamese weel break many hearts, I theenk."

"She only lets people think it, Beau."

"...theenk she is sensuous and beautiful?"

"No, she's that . . pretty more than beautiful."

"Oooh, you are mistaken, mon Capitaine."

"No, I put the one above the other. The former has more class."

"And her deceit?"

"Both, she's Laotian and not a casual lover."

Easing from his seat, the Frenchman paused in a state of surprise. He was no dolt of a companion or sideman to Allan's leading man appearance at times. Out of the work environment, he was a worldly, suave European who had broken a heart or two. He knew of Allan's long, close relationship with Elaine. He had chased the good food and ladies too many times alone in Đà Nẵng, while the pilot and the school teacher had spent days alone in her apartment catching up on lost time together.

A woman with unique strengths when just a girl, Elaine had, on a whim and with great angst, left a crowded mountain farm family in Laos across the Annaman Range. She had afterwards, once briefly been a novice female Theravada Buddhist monastic, a *bhikkhuni*, had aspired to the Catholic convent, and had then become a Catholic school foreign language teacher. As promised, she managed to find a way to send funds back home to her peasant family and make sure they got there. Truly, she was material to have become the person she was in her other life working for the British.

She had also, for over two years, been the romantic partner of Allan who made many trips by ship across the South China Sea from Cebu, in the Philippines, to Đà Nẵng, in Annam, or flown up from Singapore. Coming from wholesome ideological backgrounds that neither rebelled from, they had never made love, never really consummated it completely, though restraining with great difficulty on some occasions. Many a visit was spent in each other's arms. She was exotic, and very pretty, not glamorous. Laotian, Elaine's family had moved into the Annamite Mountains that formed the backbone of the Annam region of central Vietnam. A dirt poor peasant at birth she was the exact opposite in her refugee status at that moment, leaving her part of French Indochina, now on the coast, with her grace, faith, education, experiences, the knowledge of a spy . . and enough jade to get along just fine.

Before sleeping, Beau talked with the unique agent. They knew each other. Off duty later, Allan renewed their ties, talking longer. It had been over a year.

"Well Allan, you see to your pretty African Americana. This world is growing dangerous. You see. I told you I would never leave Indochina and look at me now. I want to meet the girl who won your heart someday."

"Look in the mirror."

"You know you love her more."

"That's not why we aren't married."

"Perhaps, but it is best we are not. Now your suave French copilot . . hummm . . ."

"This may be the time to let him know that."

She looked at him with a wry subtle smile that perhaps shared his evaluation that she wasn't making jest.

"You would be a match. We all grow older, though some wear it well," he finally said, tilting his glass of bourbon and water, toward her. "Old age will be lonely for the single person."

"This world will not be good for marriages for a while."

"You may not be needed anymore and you could teach and work with us. Your knowledge and skills were best there where you can no longer be for now. The countries that will be allied in some way against Japan can use your language skills, training and such. You're only rivaled by Rizal, and he's dead."

Elaine, not her given name at birth, looked at him in thought.

Allan added, "If I'm pulled into this in some way, which I expect, you two could run the airline. Stay in South Africa where the war would not gobble up the plane."

"You seem to know too much."

"I just have eyes and can guess the results down the road."

Looking around almost imperceptibly, one of her wily skills, the sensuous woman regarded their placement, private from her companions, and she responded, "You extrapolate and summate very well."

And of course, with every word, her accent flowing through those lips and from that face would have melted most men into a puddle on the Aero's deck.

With every passing minute, as they conversed, he was more secure in his feelings for Carolyn Ann. No greater test could have been presented, and he was passing it, . . barely, perhaps.

Days later, on the ground in South Africa, in a bar in Pretoria, leaning as close as he could get to be heard only by Allan, Beaumont spoke out suddenly though softly in a public place full of ears.

"You better see to her . . your little black angel. Maybe they did not know I am French. They spoke freely back there . . the two men from Saigon. Pretty Elaine, the Annamese, spoke with you, I noteeced. We have not seen these other people before. Maybe, they do not know me. The ones from Indochina said there is a plan to raise up disrest . . uh, I mean..."

"Distress?"

"No, uh 'un' . . 'unrest' among the African people. We brought those people here for debriefing by the locals, the local authorities because of the many details they had gathered in Indochina. They were talking in my beautiful French about a threat to Allied Africa. The Germans weel come in pretending to be old Dutch colonists, like Boers . . People coming back from Europe to get away from the Germans. Eet will be down here near the Cape. I'm sure of eet. But they weel infiltrate down from where the fighting with the Italians is on the Horn. That young American woman doesn't need to be

31

down here een this out een the bush alone between here and there, the Horn of Africa. Africa herself brings weeth her enough to deal weeth."

"She's Laotian you know, her roots. I told you."

The Frenchman stared back curiously and Allan elaborated . . . "Elaine. When you have a chance, talk to her more, Beau."

There ensued another lingering stay on the great continent. As soon as the sun rose after the late night talking with Beaumont, spent because he couldn't sleep 'til the night wore him out, Allan got on the radio and didn't give up until he reached out to her successfully.

"Ann here. Hello Captain."

"So formal."

"Twas in jest, Darling."

His eyes opened a bit wide with her choice of words, and alone in the cockpit with mike in hand he said, "Ann, I'm aware of new risks; it is best you wrap things up."

"What's up?"

He couldn't say and replied suggestively, "Unusual storms from the northeast," the 'from' connoting southern mobility. He hoped that, since he was unknown to any enemy entity and her mission was innocent enough, any enemy agent listening in would not read the deeper meaning.

"I'll stay in touch more now, but I have to go . . medical emergency, a child. Over and out, Bye, Love."

And there was just the silence broken immediately and softly by subtle static. It scared him within with its sense of an end, like the end of an evening's last radio play as the station went off the air or a station at some lone outpost going off into oblivion in defeat in some conflict with man or nature.

And his last thought before seeking work to occupy his worried mind was to wonder about her use of the terms of endearment.

Allan couldn't bring himself to leave, and working beside the unusually mellow Frenchman was a blessing. Nothing riled Beaumont as long as you treated him fairly. The only angst the man suffered was the lack of love. For, having been a bit of a careful carouser in youth, destroying hearts but not lives, he seemed to want true love at this time in his life, rather than just more of the significant fringe benefits.

By radio, Allan begged out of previously set normal cargo jobs back in the Dutch East Indies and sought any work in South Africa to be able to stay. The emergency transport of personnel to Africa was helpful in that he could tell people that a job had caused him to leave the Indies, and getting back was difficult. It was quite far, after all, several thousand miles in a plane with a fuel range of just over seven hundred. How much of his angst was a clearly felt bond of compatibility and friendship with a girl from back home, where the 'girl' part was incidental, and how much of it was deeper, he wasn't sure yet. And perhaps the taboos of his day were in his mind as well. Perhaps Allan, being an insightful man for one to have not sought higher education, even wondered at the idiosyncratic nature of a modern Western culture that still possessed taboos. One thing was clear in his mind, if not readily spoken in the 'usually' one-way conversation that is stream of consciousness thought. That was his attraction to her all the more after meeting again twice in two and a half years. It was an attraction to the whole woman: physical, mental, personality, and yes, to her racial makeup, one he could not know the details of. Long back through her familial history, romantic encounters and abusive ones created a woman of two different African neighboring ethnicities plus Portuguese, Spanish, and indigenous Caribbean from long ago encounters in early colonial Africa and similar events in the old colonial West Indies. As someone in her lineage had fled slavery to hide, like others, among the tribes along the thickly grown and storied Natchez Trace, Ann possessed significant Natchez Indian blood.

Having lingered in Pretoria as long as he dared, Allan sat in the cockpit of the Aero late one night, which always meant the wee hours of the next day's morning. He was thinking of whether he should contact her and wondering why he had heard nothing of her. He was parked near the hanger and reading war news from Europe in the latest local papers out of Durban and the Cape, as he alternately checked things here and there around him. A meticulous flier, the twenty-nine year old adventurous rambler was among the best at what he did. A dashing, casually well dressed, yet rough edged adventurer, he was well spoken and knowledgeable on many things. It came out of his early and secondary school education, his reading on long flights when not in the pilot's seat or asleep, and his observation and thinking skills.

The radio was on, running off of one of several spare, readily charged batteries he always had aboard, and he laid the latest *"Cape News"* down and started going through a check list of weapons and ammunition. And, as if he had been running on the reserve power of a premonition, the communication device crackled and a distant voice was heard through intermittent static.

"Mayday . . Is anyone there? . . ," crackled in the air, and it was Ann.

Withholding a childish angst, not to appear cool but to keep her thus, he calmly, yet firmly replied, "Yes, this is Allan."

"Allan," came over the air with a palatable, telltale sigh of relief. "Danger here, we need extraction!" her voice said with strained urgency through the crackling airways and across the miles, using medical lingo that would eventually become a common military surgical tactical term as well.

He further suppressed the angst in his voice, and simply inquired, "Location?"

"East and south of where you dropped supplies. Five of us with six horses and the cart. Only weapons and ammunition . . . glad you made me take weapons."

"And your problem is?"

"A chief, sub-chief . . renegade . . Dutch too, Germans, maybe Germans. The claim they are Dutch."

"Stay off radio 'til I call back, move toward clear area, monitor frequencies, and call only if you must."

"Yes, Love."

"Radio can be tracked . . use if you must, only brief messages to me and answer my calls, by all means. Are they close?"

"We're ahead of them, Southeast . . a couple of miles, maybe."

"Total horses?"

"Nine."

'Good' he thought, she had the cart rigged for speed.

"Can you call again in twenty minutes? Just say my name and say 'Roger' when I answer, this frequency. But listen, stay on 'til I say 'Over.'"

"Yes."

"Bye."

Jumping from the seat behind the copilot's and checking his watch, 3:30 AM, he wondered at her familiarly affectionate term as he rushed to awaken Beaumont who was sleeping off a minor hangover.

"Beau, Beau, Beau!" . . in the hanger and shaking the man, Allan exclaimed with suppressed, almost whispered urgency, not wanting to draw attention.

"What, what, mon Capitaine?!"

"As quietly as you can, go to that boarding house where all your old buddies here flop and get the most trusted four you can, and shooters . . and keep it quiet. If they've got personal arms, bring 'em, but

37

we've got the Tommies and rifles. And Beau, don't draw a lot of attention."

"What's up?"

"It's Ann, Get going, Beau!"

"What eez it, Allain!"

"A warlord."

He wanted the second call from her to establish location and started to rush to the airport tower to triangulate her signal location, but then he decided he did not want the authorities alerted. Things could go south fast and bad things might need be done. He had received from the British the best new version of the radio signal directional location equipment they had, and thankfully it was a little smaller than before.

The dim gray glow of early sunrise found them nearing the supposed location in a general sense if the group had proceeded to travel at earliest dawn or never stopped during the final darkness. He was flying the vector discovered earlier and estimated her logical, general course to adjust off that line. On the flight up those many months ago to supply her mission, friends of Beaumont had identified the African leader of her trek and described him as a man of impeccable honor and skills in the bush. Thus, Allan relied on that now, knowing that if, among those still alive, he would guide them properly to remain safe from discovery as they moved and remained safe from animal predators too. She would have passed on his hint that their radio could be tracked if her adversaries had one, and surely, they did. With other friends nearby, they could even triangulate her position. Really, her expedition's adversaries only needed direction, which one radio could give them. They were close enough to estimate distance. That she was the one on the radio hours earlier and had sounded so normal underneath her slight angst, made it clear she was not under the control of anyone, the enemy or her trusted guide possibly turned sour.

There began a tense, sporadic call of, "Ann . . Ann." It was said over and over on the primary frequency he had given her, the one she had used earlier first and foremost.

"Allan! . . . . they are behind us and pacing the same, maybe a half mile, maybe less. I'm not good with that. Our native scout went back and saw one group of three whites and a war party of ten."

"They're closer than you think. The warriors will spread, but cannot out run your mounts. Whites? What whites?"

"Dutch, Germans? . . . pretended friends, seemed sinister . . maybe."

There was an unsaid question in her voice. The languages sounded similar, and the Dutch were a conquered people now as well. Surely in conquest and even before, the Nazis had discovered sympathizers in the Netherlands. The old Boers hated the English who drove them out or assimilated them in a small, brutal war. Sir Winston Churchill, the British Prime Minister, had fought against them.

At that moment, on the radio, Allan needed to give instructions, then he needed her off of it.

"I'll need a visual sign soon. Not yet. Signal when you see the plane. Send smoke or a flare if you have it. Just toss a burning cloth and keep going use oil if you have any. Move now! After the signal, change direction a little to the south."

They were moving slowly, thus she could use the radio. Perhaps there had been a chase, but both group's horses tired at approximately the same time. With tired horses from an initial chase, both predator and prey could only take breaks or move continuously slowly. Ann and her surviving companions were not being chased at the speed of racing horses but tracked and followed in a steady way. This facilitated the use of the heavy radio in its three horse cart. A visually oriented thinker, he saw with his mind's eye the strength, wisdom, and courage to do that, to make sure she brought the radio, and he was instantly, immensely impressed. It was a military like decision to do something difficult because you had to.

"Allan, smoke north of where we thought, and there's a flare . . . It's a trick. They're monitoring our radio."

On a gamble, he took a chance on the smart little doctora's intuitiveness and messaged short and succinctly, "Change quickly."

In a moment, as he dialed it in, the other frequency popped with her breathless voice, "Allan?"

"Quickly, the smoke is theirs. Tell me your location from it. Then switch to number three and move due west."

After a pause, she replied, "About 200 yards southwest, open savanna ahead . . see you now"

"Go! Southwest! Stay in the cart if your speed is good."

Turning to Beaumont, he said, "Get us as close as you can and put me down. Then turn this into a gun ship. Maneuver to avoid rifle fire. They'll try to bring you down. Have two Tommy gunners on each side, in the doors and tethered. Rake them one way and then another, but make unpredictable approaches to avoid a lucky shot from the ground. Accuracy with the Thompsons will be a problem from up here."

Allan became concerned she would worry about destroying the radio and called again, "Ann, Ann, . . Ann . . . Ann …."

With no answer, he quickly switched back-and-forth between the frequencies of the small portable radio and finally heard her, "Allan, Allan ..."

"Roger."

"The cart wheel came off, I believe tampered. Horseback. The radio?!"

"Get going, forget it, get going."

Ann abandoned the radio cart, having seen the direction of the plane. About 350 yards from the position of the small group of refugees, Beau put the big Aero down, and with engines idling, Allan jumped to the ground with a pistol, a Tommy gun, and a rifle, his 1903 Springfield from his father.

Allan was west by southwest of her, and she was coming straight at him on horseback, having seen where the plane had landed to drop him. The pursuers were closing fast from her right, Allan's left, from the north. And, as Beau took off with a roar, Allan turned and dashed toward the impending action that could soon burst, as the locals and the European intruders sought to prevent the escape of the small remnant of the medical mission.
As he ran across the savanna through the high yellow grasses, Ann did the same on the little horse.

The others had suddenly been fired on, and two horses and three riders were no longer with her. It was now only Ann and the experienced guide astride the last two mounts, racing side by side. To his right, Allan saw that the ground rose, and he dashed there for a better view. Just as the girl saw him on the slight high ground, he heard the war whoops and knew the primitive visceral fears they drew from a man and would from her. She was alone now, save for one companion equally at risk, and against the primeval world that still sometimes showed its face in 1940s Africa. And incongruously, the evil chasing them at that moment emanated as much from the primitive instincts of a white European nation as it did the native war chief and witch doctor also following. It was a cold sickening fear, knowing not what would happen if captured other than it would not be pleasant and that for a woman it could be so much worse and lingering, perhaps for a lifetime.

Allan saw her head and shoulders bobbing with each stride of the horse and the nodding head of the steed. And, seeing the warriors now and the white rifleman chasing them on horseback, he wished she could dismount and run less visibly in the grass of the savanna. But he alone could not stop them all unless he got closer with the Thompson submachine gun. He saw the European rein in and stop his mount and aim the rifle, and before he could react, the guide went down and the gun's loud report reached him. He stood tall and quickly aimed his rifle at 150 yards and killed the man without a moment to marvel at his unsuspected ability to do it. It had to be done, and he did it. The Nazi was obviously an excellent shot and she would have been dead with the next shot. More likely her horse; for, as much as they did not want her testimony to get out, the racists probably wanted her to torment for their pleasure and as their doctor. No other stood, and it appeared the other whites might not be in pursuit. But just then he saw her disappear into the tall grass and knew not the cause, a horse's stumble, a spear, her choice to run? Dashing, Allan was truly worried now . . and at that moment, the Aero roared over low and in front of him . . skimming the treetops from the right and lowering still, over the high grass . . like a landing but much too fast, and much lower than he had ordered . . the handheld machine guns on the planes other side, facing the enemy chattered so loud he could just hear it on the back side of their muzzles and out the hatch behind them and open in front of him as it zoomed past. All four men were firing out the opposing one door, again defying orders, chewing up the grass, dirt, and flesh that was behind the woman who now ran like hell toward the safety that was hopefully somewhere ahead for her. Beau had disobeyed and done it his way, and, as usual, that was just fine.

Somewhere in the grasses he found her, having adjusted his long strides to the rustling noises . . and they embraced ever so firmly and longingly . . and he didn't kiss her, they weren't lovers, he held her head against his like a lover would. Then a shock

44

went through the woman, flowing over the terror already coating her insides, as Allan kissed her nearest cheek in a way that could only be interpreted as one of the deepest of emotional feeling.

Suddenly the Aero roared over again, lower with guns blazing, the plane turning as it passed a little in front of them, heading away from the couple toward and out flanking the renegade chief's warriors still giving chase, the Thompsons firing at close range into the African soil and any who failed to flee.

All was quiet, and the plane landed near. Allan picked her up in the classic bride across the threshold manner, also common for the simple rescue of a smaller person of either gender, and walked to the hatch placing her in. He followed her in. It was caring and affection. She could probably have walked. But his was a woman, a friend who had been on the very edge of death and worse. It mattered.

He looked at the men among the friends of Beau and found the one he knew would be the unofficial leader. "Rock, can you go destroy that radio? I don't want that to get captured in very good condition to be reverse engineered, though the Krauts probably have better."

The gentle giant and fearless warrior replied, with his signature gravelly rough voiced, "Get 'er close, the Aero, and we'll lug it in. The parts might be as incriminating or useful to the wrong people as the whole thing. We loaded 'er up before. Captain, we got 'em all. We better put those two fires out. If they catch, it'll be bad for folks around here."

"Take the men you need, but leave me a gunner. We'll get up and locate 'em for you and cover you, but watch it."

Everything completed and, in the air, again with Beau at the controls, he sat and held her for the beginning of the flight, giving her water, then coffee and biscuits. Ann had not only endured the tense escape over several days, but had seen her mission destroyed, ultimately becoming the only survivor and bearing the loss of companions. If desiring such a life, it would steel her or destroy that path. The guilt she might feel for that (though not her fault), and the depression for a failed mission that he expected would follow went through Allan's mind and he steeled himself for it, starting, even then, to plan how he could help. The adventurous pilot had been in the East Indies, India, and Africa for many years while the woman from back home had been in school. He had seen people hurt in various little conflicts, particularly those involving the Philippine Moros and other Muslim pirates that valued women cheaply except for their labor and sexual favors. And he had been in China in '37. He would tell her sometime later . . would console her, that her medical mission failed not through her own fault but just because it happened, history and uncontrollable personalities happened, dangerous personalities, and that it was not a failure in the broader sense . . for she had learned and she could share that with others.

He left her then and took his turn flying the plane and talking with Beaumont. Then Beau went back to eat, and he could hear them talking in French long into the evening.

On the ground back in Pretoria, and having received immediate sustenance in the form of biscuits, water, and coffee on the plane, Ann took a shower and slept. Allan paid off Beau's companions and saw to all their needs. He told them to be generally quiet about all that happened to avoid any political or legal problems for any of them. The Aero was serviced and the tanks topped off, just in case. Allan was always looking ahead. A former Boy Scout, his mantra was 'Be prepared'. He had others. Then, cleaned up and rested (he really couldn't sleep), he took her to diner at the best place he and Beau knew in Pretoria. Beau was invited as well. It wasn't intended to be romantic.

"How did it happen?"

"The chief, he was sort of a warlord, more criminal than chief, and he held those people . . he and his men, they held them to their own demands and wishes. He was anti-white and anti-foreigners, for good reason, I supposed, and I told him I sympathized with that. I think at some point he identified me as a kindred soul and a companion in every way whether I wanted it or not. Then these intruders arrived. We weren't intruding, simply offering medical care."

"And?"

"I believe the Germans had always been nearby befriending him, advising him, and encouraging him. I mean even before we arrived. Unluckily, I just picked the very worst location to operate in. The chieftain said I couldn't leave, that I was their tribe or band's great healer now and must become his wife to seal the bond and rule together. Luckily, I had told everyone to conceal most of their weapons before we encountered any local people. Those were our ace cards. It was for a crisis such as this and to appear in the peaceful manner we intended. We remained, on my instruction, near our own camp more than mingling, though the latter was of course necessary. We slept and operated in our own casually laid out zone."

"Impressive, Ann. Perhaps I worried too much about you."

Looking strongly at him from across the small round table, perhaps a look containing love, he thought, the capable yet still traumatized woman said, "I would be dead or their whore now if it weren't for you . . both of you."

Then she continued the account, "Those are good people, good people, and I left them with that, those

48

men and their anger now. When they approached us aggressively after my refusal, we pulled the Thompsons and fired at the ground. One warrior approached from the side, thinking to grab me, but I spun around in time and killed him." Looking down, she said softly, "Doctors don't do that. . . 'do no harm'. I . . I was so scared."

"Yes, they do. They have always had to, on frontiers and in war. We rescued you during your flight, but you saved yourself, too. You'll probably be safe in that big hospital near Singapore . . where is it, Johor Bahru . . north, northwest just a bit, a good little walk, safe working there for a while, because we're about to be involved in a big war."

"What?!"

He was thinking about the story she had just told, of her actions under the terror and weight of fear, the blanket fear can become. "You know the Japanese are in Indochina now, what with the French defeated in Europe. They control things there and have strong influence in Siam. Surely you don't think they will ignore Singapore forever?"

"Wow . . swell. When will my life settle a little?"

"… or anyone's. This is the big one and it's about to get bigger. I just don't know when or how. You know, I've heard that up in the Ukraine, the Russians have gals about your size driving tanks. A friend of Beau's who was up there, an Australian correspondent, met a petite little T-34 driver. And her gunner wasn't much bigger and a woman too."

"My God, . . what they must have seen?! Those poor girls."

"...defending the homeland, Mother Russia."

"Imagine those Ukrainians, defending their homes while fighting against people they hate and for people they somewhat hate. They don't exactly love the Russians who rule them, but I've heard a little news too. I had heard the Ukrainians were fighting as well. I guess they have to."

"So, you know the lay of the land a little it, too."

"I do."

With a comment or two, Beau generally let them talk, and then the three companions returned to the hanger where the plane was parked. Sensing a need for care, Allan suggested they all stay near to the plane. He wondered if the small battle in the hinterland to he north would jump up and bite them. When he answered Ann's questions concerning his request that she sleep in a fold down sleeper bunk that was one of several that had been installed for long flights, she became a bit more depressed, feeling almost like a fugitive.

The wily Frenchman and the now very experienced American adventurer simply had a bad feeling, knowing how such events could be read the wrong way or, in the wrong hands and minds, twisted the wrong way. And in the hour before sunrise they prepared for flight. Acting on the spur of the moment and trying to diplomatically clamp the lid on her concerns, the two men got the Aero in the air just at the earliest break of dawn without a flight plan properly filed.

"It's like we're running . . I'm running . ." she had reiterated as she was getting ready to board again after eating such an early breakfast and washing up. Only her trust in him now allowed her to.

Standing by the waist hatch, he took her by the arms, the shoulders, and looking in her eyes, said, "You have to understand, this is generally the commonwealth around here, but a lot of folks in these parts aren't all that loyal. It wouldn't be the same game afoot right now if Smuts hadn't come to power. Once airborne and on our way, if anyone contacts us, we can have a reason for leaving, your job for example. You can file a report about the loss of the expedition at another port of call, saying that urgency of travel and the personal trauma prevented it sooner. I needed you out of there because these colonial investigations can become nightmares, what with the government trying to keep the lid on things by appeasing everyone. There is always the chance some tinpot official responsible for that region could try to implicate you or all of us in some way. It is how they always try to deflect from themselves any feared blame that may not even exist. My hope is, my belief and my hope are that this is discovered in a week or two and even more time passes before they remember us. Then, with the German evidence, if any remains, they'll only want us for information. I wasn't prepared back there to have you charged or held for questioning in any way. This world is about to explode, and we all need to be free and on our toes. I Have to talk to someone in authority first, someone I know well. This is my bailiwick, Ann. You're the heroine in this story."

"I'm not a heroine. What's going on Allan?"

He looked at her, still softly gripping her shoulders, as he processed everything in his mind. They were going to be together for a very long flight and now bound in danger and intrigue as the world faced bigger things to come, and he decided to be open with it.

Looking intently at her, Allan said, "Do not repeat a word if we're apart when we get to Singapore. When you get there, you're simply Dr. Carolyn Ann Davis, with a dangerous, partly successful, partly failed medical safari mission under your belt. By then any fault on your part will be erased by my friends, so you shouldn't face too many questions."

Ann sighed, and he added, "Listen Carolyn, you didn't hear this. Okay. I don't want you to be endangered for something you don't even need to know, not yet anyway. I fly for special people. I was in Pretoria when you needed me to be because we knew of a possible risk that Beau heard from some of our special passengers. When we get airborne, I will contact someone who will handle everything, even make you look like an even bigger heroine in this. Then when we land in India, we'll report it all to the big-shots I sometimes work for. They don't care who we've killed as long as it isn't the good guys, and they'll squash any civilian legal whoop-dee-doo."

As he stepped away, Ann slightly raised her voice and inquired, "Who, Allan? You owe me that if you want me to leave with you now and want me to believe you. Yeah, we knew each other. We were kids then, and not that close. We couldn't be."

"I think our fathers wanted us to be," and he paused as he turned toward the cockpit and they looked at each other from a few feet apart. Then he said quietly, "British Intelligence. And I think others I don't even know I work for, maybe the Americans."

After lifting off and getting to cruising altitude, just after they approached, the coast, Allan asked Beau, "Have you got it?"

"Yes, Mon Capítaine, go make love to her now."

Slapping and then pushing gently on the other's shoulder as he got out of the pilot's seat on the left, Allan went back into the cabin.

The woman was sitting in the seat he had suggested on the starboard side, leaning against the window frame and looking out pensively with a hint of melancholy. And, as he walked back, the sunlight through the window lit up her brown face like a smooth wooden carving by a master artist, and highlighted the petite flat nose and made her eyes glow, even in their sadness. Her high, exotic cheeks appeared in the light not unlike those of a young cherubic African American child, and the thought passed through his stream of thought that the very things he admired about her physical beauty were things other men of his race would ignore or even perhaps joke about. She was wrapped in the canvas jacket he had given her. Her flight from danger hours before had left her with nothing but the clothes on her back, and the military fatigue style clothes he had given her were two sizes too large. Lose clothing did not make for warm rest. Breaking open a large duffle bag just behind the last seats he brought her a soft thick blanket he always had aboard for female passengers. It had been cleaned since the last use, as he ran a tight ship.

"Here, you might take off those work clothes to wrap up in this. It's softer than they are."

Ann stood, slightly shivering and, taking off the oversize fatigues, returned to her bush shorts and shirt. Turning, she allowed Allan to drape the large enough blanket over her shoulders, and he wrapped it around her, stealing a brief embrace from behind as he completed the operation. As she sat back in the seat he suggested, he knelt and wrapped it around her legs.

"Lie in the bunk and I'll help you prop up. There're plenty of pillows and such. We're prepared for a long haul. We do it a lot."

The bunk had a small bulkhead like partition on each end for support and a dash of privacy. Allan had put profits into maintenance and modification as the plane, bought with investment help from his parents, was fairly new and in good condition.

Allan brought a case over and opened it, sitting in the seat across the narrow aisle from the bunk. He knew she couldn't read, sleep, or think clearly . . or anything else.

"Here, Carolyn, this will help," as he handed her a scotch on the rocks. They had reloaded their cooler of course and the liquor case was never empty.

"Thank you, Captain, but it's like eleven in the morning." she followed with a smile and then made a slight face at the first sip.

"Not used to it?"

"Sweet."

"I agree, but most don't seem to. Have some bourbon. I'll drink the Scotch."

"I'm a bourbon girl," she said as they exchanged drinks.

Carolyn Ann took a slow long sip, and sighed, relaxing, and he saw a tear in her eye accompanied by a look of longing. He was careful to not be too aggressively comforting. She was an accomplished strong woman in a world not yet ready for that and he was just the fellow to recognize as much and know how to handle that at the moment.

"Ann, what's going on is bigger than you and me. You can't blame yourself for any of it. You fitted out a mission and did your duty. Crap just happens, uncontrolled crap, and we get caught in it."

"We? Do you think there's going to be a big investigation of us both, what with your rescue?"

"No, they'll squash that. I mean if it was Germans there. This is about to get bigger. Europe, the Continent, North Africa. You know that you just got out of France in time."

"France, Morocco, Egypt, South Africa and now Singapore. I'm an expatriate vagabond like those poets and musicians in the twenties in Paris. Well, some of them are famous now. I just read *A Farewell to Arms*, you know . . at night in my tent."

"There's a movie with Cooper. I've heard they're friends."

"They're never quite right, you know . . movies, even the good ones."

"Well, you might be surprised that I read too, and I agree. Together they can be enjoyable, but the book is sacrosanct. Every word counts."

"Right, you get it! Every word matters. And the scenery so carefully described by a writer is just a blur of background and a few items in the foreground in the cinema."

She was off of the worry in her mind, and he knew it wouldn't last and thus he knew he must draw her back to reality with a new concern to worry about, but not spilled milk . . rather something they could deal with ahead. But now was not the time . . next time.

Allan sat quietly, with her just across the narrow isle, and they said no more. There was an exchanged smile and then both were off in thought and he let that simmer. She had lost the angst as was his goal. It wasn't manipulative, the man shielding the girl. She was a woman, and he knew . . somehow knew she was a woman to be reckoned with, and he liked that. They had one more drink, Alan dozed, and then as if with his own alarm, he awoke and strode up to the cockpit.

He and Beau had worked out a system for long hauls like this, often flown alone with only cargo. Each would fly a four hour shift alone that overlapped a little when the other came on duty. Both were flexible. If one had trouble sleeping in only four hours, if one was really tired or needed a drink stronger than the watered-down ones Allan had just taken, the other fellow could easily handle a longer shift. That both men could sleep quickly and get refreshed in four hours of sleep made the system work.

"Mon Capitaine, you must sleep when off duty."

"I did."

"Yes, three hours of four, and I heard no passion no moans, for the loss of the longer rest."

"You've got to let up Beau; she's a lady."

"Exactly, . . so..."

Alan just smiled and took his turn, as eventually the Frenchman went back to his bunk. Refueling, in spite of the plane's ability, was decided upon to prevent doing so later more often than they wanted, so they stopped on the southern coast of the Arabian Peninsula and took a long-needed stretch of the legs and rest on land. No one had connected the events in the African hinterland with the Aero's takeoff without a flight plan, and Allan would argue if necessary that he had filed one and that those country bumpkins way up in dusty Pretoria must have misplaced it. Later, the a three sat at a small table at a small airfield eating the local cuisine available there. All three had come to be able to eat whatever was available, with some exceptions.

"Beau, I could leave you to this cargo business and escort Ann to Singapore myself. But you might not see me until the is war is over."

"Eet ees a long-haul Alain, but I do not want you and Mademoiselle Carolyn Ann torpedoed by the U-boats."

"We can take the coasters. You can fly cargo here for the duration of whatever is to come, my friend."

"They weel not have the accommodations appropriate for her. This way we transfer our business to the Indies weeth all those café latté mademoiselles."

"I see, you have an ulterior motive."

"Not so much. I have an honorable marriage een mind to one of those leetle brown Dutch chéries."

"You had better choose wisely, Beau. Most of them in the Dutch East are Muslim," added Ann to the conversation. "They will probably not be a good match for your free-wheelin' spirit."

"Beau left his best bet in Africa. Sometimes we can't see the forest for the trees."

Both looked at him, and it was as if he could feel their eyes as he concentrated on the food on his plate.

After a long pause, the Frenchman inquired, "Elaine?! . . . . . but she, you and her?"

"Yes?" spoke Ann, "Please go on."

And Allan thought that tease was interesting.

Cutting in before Beau could tease too far, Allan explained, "We were sweethearts, completely on the up and up. She almost became a nun."

"When was this?"

"'37 and '38, before I knew where you were. We cut it off then . . mutually."

"Wow," Ann said softly with his comment and, perhaps with double meaning, as she looked at a very good photo of the girl Beau had reached over to her.

Taking it in her hands, the woman analyzed, "This is a woman who probably cannot take a bad picture. What is she?"

"Laotian"

"A nun?!"

Ann might have been a bit unusual, a Southern black Catholic girl.

"Try Buddhist novice before that."

"Wow, again, and now?"

"Refugee, we brought her over from the Indies coming back. Language teacher, agent. I suspect more."

"So?"

He trusted her, and elaborated, "I'll let her tell you of her interesting youth. She was a peasant. They got her out surely because of some risk to her and that she is valuable, vulnerable and valuable. I'm not sure the Brits care that much about every asset once they become useless where they are embedded. Maybe no one does. I think Simpson does in a fatherly way," and he dropped the name of his main contact, which meant little to Ann beyond the obvious that she could extrapolate. "Well. I don't think it is a common thing, and don't look down on her, but she might, on occasion, be an assassin."

That chilled the moment, but not necessarily dragging down their collective view of the now overwhelmingly interesting beauty, and after the longest of silences, he added, "Beau, if we get separated by duty, you try to see her. She spoke of you quite kindly."

"What?!"

"You lummox. She and I joked about us, and she indicated an interest . . simple as that. Elaine's dead serious when she says things like that."

"We'll continue on," stated Allan. "There's a lot of business there, and they may need us badly. But I'll tell you both: I have a bad feeling about the Indies, Malaya . . all of it."

He had introduced it to her, as he had wanted. Now, he could talk to her about it later on the flight.

Allan continued, "This will be a long flight."

"I left my things in Durban. . . Well, . . actually, you did 'Mon Capitaine,'" the woman said, smiling at the Frenchman as she borrowed his lingo.

"What was there?"

"'Is' there, still is, that's the point."

"And?"

"Just clothes. I sent some books home and some to Singapore, to the hospital."

"What else?"

"A couple of medical books; some personal instruments, you know the old black 'doctor's bag'; and other clothes."

Allan replied, "I tell you what, we'll go shopping in Singapore, and I'll help you pick some more things out. I'm paying, and I won't take 'No' for it."

Tired of refusing his help, which she could always do later, by refusing to have the time, Ann nodded ascent as she mulled over his attitude, the attitude of a man, a nice guy, acting like a boyfriend.

They finished the little meal and took off in the afternoon. Once they were in the air and headed for the next air strip Allan flew the first leg for a straight six hours, and the other two both slept the tension of now distant Africa off in the cool cabin. The two pilots had decided that they would fly the longer shifts, longer than the Navy's four-hour watch, without overlap to allow for more sleep and relaxation time for each. When Beaumont relieved him, he went back for another watered-down drink and relaxed discussion with Carolyn Ann.

They were flying eastward into night, and as he sat down, she said. "The coffee was great, but I'll take one of those bourbons now. How do you keep it here? Is it easy to get?"

"A few places. I also have some American friends. A lot of our products are in the Philippines. Have you been there?"

"It's as if you knew I was coming, you know, like you have someone over for dinner." Then sipping from the glass he offered her, she paused to let it sit on the tongue and then slide down. "No, I went straight across the big pond to Europe, then down here from there, partly by your efforts from Cairo of course."

"Just luck I guess . . and coincidence . . the bourbon."

He wouldn't tell her that he always kept some since the Morocco flight because he knew she was in Africa, and she was of course a Southerner like himself. It was an educated guess. He had tested it that night out of Pretoria, and he was right, she rejected the Scotch. She was such a Southern girl, with all the grace, beauty, and class of any other, and he sighed at the inopportunity of the times for him to have been able to know her better or become involved within the subculture that was fortunately and unfortunately her lot.

Now, he had poured himself a bourbon and water, and Ann said, "Oh, not your scotch."

"I'm from Tennessee too, you know."

And she did know . . knew now he had bought and saved the bourbon for her, as she said, "Well, understandable, Kentucky's just north. But our sippin' whiskey is just as good, don't you think?"

64

To that he raised his glass and nodded, as both leaned back and sipped just a taste. He had made hers half and half for the flavor and his a tiny bit weaker, He wanted a second and would fly in a few hours. He had time if he was careful not to indulge too much. He heard her deep sigh releasing tension. It hadn't been the first or would be the last. Finally, he broke the silence.

"You need to know you can't be in Singapore long. It won't be safe."

"Did you hear that from you friends in intelligence?"

"Listen, what happened back there was out of your hands from the beginning. You couldn't know because no one knew except the bad guys. And there is nothing you could have done and no way you could have prepared better. The risk didn't exist as far as you were concerned, other than general watchfulness . . Now, the Brits don't realize it, but they're gonna lose Singapore."

"So, you've worked with these people how long? . . and now you're second guessing them. They're professionals."

"British people are very proud, and rightly so, although they've made some of the same racial mistakes we Americans of my complexion have. Singapore's guns point seaward to prevent an invasion and bombardment. I see them when I take off and land and fly over. The British have mostly only cruisers and destroyers in the Indies. Japan has been occupying Siam and also French Indochina since the fall of Paris. All the Japs have to do is march down through Malaya."

"'Japs' . . that sounds pretty pejorative."

"I was in Nanking."

"Oh. . . . Want to tell me?"

"Another time perhaps."

"I'm a doctor."

"Not this, Ann. Not now. It needs more whiskey and I have to fly in a few hours. Look, Ann, I've been listening to the chatter on this plane for two years now. They talk freely because I guess they've been told to trust us. I did a couple of dangerous things for them. One in China when nobody wanted to be in China. Beau's quiet and the ones from Indochina may not know he speaks their language. Japan's coming south and that means Singapore. I don't know if the intelligence guys are listening, but I have been. Look, don't worry. We're safe now. Singapore's a safe place now. But we have to talk later."

"Why south. They're embroiled in China? That's a big place."

"Roosevelt knows. He caused it, but he had to. He cut off the oil and steel they bought from us. Japan has no resources like that. The Dutch Indies has oil. Where else can they go?"

"So, it will stir up a brawl down there."

"England and America aren't likely to stand by right next door in the Philippines and Malay and let the Dutch take it on the chin. The Nazis have already taken their homeland."

"So where will you go from Singapore if it gets untenable as you claim, to the Philippines?"

"I don't know, Ann."

"This all sounds crazy. It's a little country."

"We'll know soon enough. The people I've overheard think Japan is going to do something soon, very soon. Just think of it logically. They tried Russia some few years ago and were beaten back. It's not the same Russia they dealt with many decades ago. Their navy is better, but the Russian Army handled them okay. They're in China now. They more or less control Siam and French Indochina. What is left? They take the Philippines or they attack Malaya."

"The Philippines!? Attack American territory? I wonder what naval forces we have in the Pacific. I haven't been home in years or seen an American paper in months."

"I've heard we have some significant ships in Hawaii. The British will have some in Singapore. I saw a meanness in China, Ann. I can't talk about it now. Maybe I can tell you someday."

She looked long in his face and eyes as she held the glass in her two hands out in front of her. She sat on the side of the bunk and her two elbows rested on her knees, covered by the blanket.

And looking back soulfully, Alan said, "I sleep pretty well most of the time. If you ever see me otherwise, tossing and turning, that's why. I want you far from them."

And he said it like a man spoke of his woman, the one closest, the one that mattered. Ann didn't miss that nuance and wondered. He was a man form back home, from the shadows of memories from childhood. He was apparently unattached now, so maybe she was the closest thing to family he had near at this moment of potential world upheaval. Maybe it was just that. She was in the same boat.

He slept right there in the chair with the help of the drink and a slightly smaller one. In the middle of the four hours, after the one and a half they burned up with talk, she was awakened to his restlessness and at one point he was saying emphatically yet in the softness of sleep, "No, No! . ." and his arms were pushed back as if held or bound behind, and he wriggled as if seeking to pull free from the nothingness that restrained him. The memories had been jogged loose that night even if skipped over in the discussion. She got out of bed and eased silently closer, knowing in her doctor way to not awaken him if possible, and she saw eyes damp with tears. Later she did wake him from a quieter slumber when Beaumont called from the cockpit.

The cockpit and cabin were quiet on the flight through the day, and little was said at lunch in New Delhi, where they refueled the plane and themselves. The whiskey did its work and with only a slight shot. When back in the air the tired doctor slept a lot and, at other moments, sat forehead almost against the glass and elbow on the sill looking sadly, longingly out the window. They took short three hour stops when they refueled, eating and stretching their legs, and the next pilot on duty for takeoff would try to catch a few winks. Allan had checked in earlier with his British contact in New Delhi after he was airborne over the Arabian Sea. The man was off duty and Allan had left a vague message and called it urgent.

Across India, at the beautiful port of Trincomalee, on the northeastern coast of Ceylon, an airport official came up to Allan and said, "I am looking for Captain Allan Allison and Monsieur Beaumont Chastain. Would that be you?"

"That depends on whether we're in trouble or not," Allan replied. "Is anything wrong?"

"A mister Simpson is calling from New Delhi . . well, called sometime back. You are to contact him at your soonest opportunity."

The call was made to the British agent, probably the best person to have to own up to. The voice on the other end of the line was British of course, and the man stated that George was out but would call soon and Allan needed to be available by the phone.

So, the three sat and waited in the small airport office having an extra small meal and some tea. They were bored from the monotony of the long flight legs and of so much tea, as good as it was, and would drink more American and French coffee during the legs ahead. Wine was out of the question because neither pilot, during their turn to rest while in the air, wanted that long, deep, welcome sleep it would bring or the foggy effects on their general constitution when their shift came, Allan would drop the whiskey as well. That had been to share the moments with her and to help her relax.

The call came through, the third in the hour and a half they had been stuck there, but the rest for man and machine may have been a good thing. Finally, it was the voice of British agent George Simpson.

"Yes, George?"

"Hello, Allan. Were you involved in the rescue of Doctor Ann Davis? I was told you scrambled out of Pretoria for some reason, and the airport there recorded receiving distress calls from up where she was."

"Yes, Is there a problem?"

"A field full of bodies has a few local authorities in a dither. Why didn't you report?"

"Honestly, the doctor has a job interview in a week."

"That's not it, Allan?"

Well, George was an agent. Suspicion was his game. But Allan replied, "Sure is, George. The woman has to eat, and she's recovering from the threat to her."

"There's more. Were you not going to report to me? There's intrigue in this you know. We found some gear," the agent said, not mentioning any names. Thus, someone listening on a tapped line at either end of the call might think a simple crime scene was being discussed.

"I called **you**, George. Didn't you get my message. Do you want to debrief her on the phone?"

"No! I don't."

"Honestly, George, I wanted her out of there. She went through something that no one should emotionally, psychologically, and she wasn't prepared for it."

Ann was listening, and he minded not. Allan felt that he wasn't criticizing her, maybe he was even elevating her.

"You were afraid this would tie her down there, maybe even implicate her, and her a Negro. I know. But you need to fill me in. I can cover for it. But you knew that. I know you were hoping for me to call first. On the hush hush, I'll make this all an unofficial official operation, but you've got to cooperate."

"Of course."

"You can trust me. You know that. Where's your next stop, Lahore?"

"I know . . I know I can. Yeah Lahore if you need me to. But I wanna get her to Singapore."

"We need her debriefed and it's my bloody butt if we don't. You better have a safe trip. That girl disappears with what she knows, the information out of her failed mission, and the only way to keep my position is to blame you, her, and Beaumont. If you don't make it to Fortress Singapore, you might all be dead from a crash but you'll be dead fugitives. Your reputations will be ruined. If you refueled in Delhi, you should have all been debriefed there."

"Fortress Singapore? You know the Japs aren't sailing into your big guns pointed out into the Strait. they'll come down through the Malayan jungle, and you know it. You didn't answer in Delhi."

"Maybe. Maybe they aren't coming at all."

"You better get over there and straighten the rest of your Limey friends out. You and me, and Beau, are gonna lose a lot of good drinking partners."

"Listen. Call my man, Malandy, there at the soonest in Singapore. Fulton Malandy. I don't want to hold you up anymore, what with the time these things can take. You've got a good plane.. too good for a seat of the pants barnstormer, as you Yanks say. If anything keeps you from getting there, call me from wherever you're mucked up. Tell the doctor that this whole thing, her trip and all, was her sacrifice for country, for your American country and for Britain ..that she was there to look around and to see what help she could bring to the native locals out in the bush . . and that it went sour because of foreign interference. That's at least half true. Now, at the soonest, I have to have someone debrief her face-to-face. Tell her."

"… as soon as I hang up."

"Allan . . Allan . . tell her not to talk to anyone. Use my name . . if you have to. Say that you all, every one of you answer to me . . that I told you to leave and to speak to no one about this. Listen. Your navy has a man there who works in conjunction with us, Buck Shaw, a Lt. Commander. If you run into him, introduce yourself. He'll recognize your name."

The pilot said nothing in the ensuing silence as if he was processing it all, and adding to clarify, the agent continued, "We don't want her to have to meet the press there in Singapore, or wherever and say the wrong thing. Then we cannot fix it later. I can make her look good on this, it having been her show and all."

"Thanks."

"Of course. After all, your position in this is a bit too obvious. Uh, Allan, our little Indochinese friend is headed for Trincomalee. She wasn't needed out of her environment and has friends there. We may yet need her."

"Don't put her in danger, George. Is she going by ship? The U-boats you know."

"We're flying her, when we have a plane going there, and we will. We owe her that. You could have done it if you hadn't left like your tail was on fire. But then the Aero might have become crowded." Simpson said the last as if he knew something and didn't realize Ann could be listening.

"George, if you can, just use her to teach. And Beau and I may need her contact number. Make sure she has all of ours."

"Do you still use Lim Chou's when you are out of Jakarta?"

"Yes, but give the Darwin numbers too. Who knows where we'll be and when."

Hanging up, the plane's captain turned to the other two and said, "We better get airborne, and Ann, listen a moment."

Ann walked up to Allan and he took her two shoulders gently as was his style and said, "This wasn't your fault and they know it. More importantly, they care about how it looks for you. We're to say nothing if asked about the breakdown of the mission and the attack on you or our rescue mission. British intelligence has got this under control. And that is what we say to anyone who asks. Your mission was attacked and the proper authorities are investigating. And we or they will speak about it when we can. That's what you say to the press; that's what we say to any British authorities. If they push, point them to me and I'll drop the proper names. If they come and pick you up when I'm not around, drop George's name and say no more 'til I show up."

"But, what …?"

"This will be seen as an attack by foreign agents that couldn't have been predicted or dealt with, a learning experience for everyone. You're the victim heroine, not the fall guy . . er, gal."

"Those I left?"

"It just happened, victims . . you speak for them now. You're not to blame, no one is."

She looked down and it was apparent, as a doctor, her heart was heavy, and Allan said, taking her hands now and holding them together in front in his, "If you are going to seek this, this adventurous life, steel yourself Ann. I've not yet been in real combat, save moments like days ago, brief flashes of violence and gunfire. There's a big war on, and it is gonna spread across this globe. I doubt you will be close to it, but you could end up in a rear area hospital putting broken Humpty Dumpties together. Who knows what you are about to experience. The last thing you can do is personalize it, make it your fault or your problem to solve. No individual soldier, nurse, doctor, sailor, or anyone else can accept blame for what's happening or about to. Remember when we were kids . . the Great War? This is it times ten and everywhere."

The intrepid three spent a day and a half in Trincomalee, resting, showering, eating well, and sleeping. Airborne again, heading up the east coast of India over the western edge of the enormous Bay of Bengal, he flew a stint, had tea with her, slept and flew another. At one point, Allan awoke early for his next duty tour and sat with her and talked, as dawn slowly lighted the inside of the cabin here and there as the plane and sunlight passed each other going in opposite directions.

"Where did you get a Czech plane?"

"You're a linguist?"

"I recognize some languages in print."

"I was in Czechoslovakia just before the Germans came in. Looking for a plane and seeing a bit of Europe. I was in the right place at both the wrong and right time."

"Did you get a deal due to the neighborhood going down so quickly?"

"Something like that. They were building these 304 bombers out of a transport design. I couldn't find anybody. And then I saw this one in front of a hanger near the company's hanger; and, when the owner must have realized what was gonna happen, he cut me a quick deal. He said he had bought it from them and was customizing it for a cargo business; but then, what could he do? He said his family was in hiding because of the Germans, and he couldn't just leave them by themselves. This one was probably originally gonna be a *Aero A 204.* It wasn't all that militarized yet."

"You'll not get follow-up service."

"He hated the Germans. Course he knew they would take the factory or dominate it and he wouldn't get service or be able to use it anyway. He let me load up all the spare parts I could haul, and I knew what to look for."

"And what do you look for?" She was holding a cup of hot cocoa and sipping it.

The cabin was cool and they sat together in one of the wide seats he had installed. It was almost a bomber made out of a passenger design, which he used for cargo and passengers. Allan had added what seats he wanted where he wanted them.

"I know what parts wear the most on any plane. I found a company man and asked what they had seen in their trials. Of course, they were all the standard maintenance items. I paid the plane's owner for his two spare engines. The plane was gutted and empty, there was a lot of room. Such things are easy when you buy a boxcar and locomotive in combination. I looked around the company warehouse, with their man's blessing, and found the parts that looked likely to be hard to fabricate in a machine shop. Everything's in a warehouse in Darwin and insured. For anything else, Beau was a machinist."

"A machinist, pilot, . . what else?"

"He trained with the Legion, but it was for something else. He won't talk about it."

"He's refined beneath the joking."

"I know. He broke one princess's heart. An Indian girl from some historically important royal line. It wasn't cruel, just not meant to be."

"And Elaine?"

"Meant to be."

"And you?"

Carelessly, he replied, "If not for you..."

She wanted to express sorrow for the Czech whose business and life had collapsed, but she remembered his dreams before and kept it light, saying instead, "My goodness but you're prepared. I thought you adventurers flew by the seat of your pants in all walks of life. You take after your father, as described to me by mine."

"A compliment, Thank you. I believe the air frame will hold up, and I think certain other engines will mount easily enough if necessary. It's not unusual for companies to try different engine options and even sell them that way, different engines in different models of the same plane. It's just the different design and manufacturing culture that could make adaptation of things tough in this case.

With the extra engines, that may never be necessary."

"Were you walking around with that kind of money? Even in the political circumstances, it must have cost a pretty penny. And you did say you went there to purchase a plane if you could find one."

"I had heard there were some good designs being made in Eastern Europe: little transports and such with reasonably good range. Better than Ford Trimotors. I had heard about this one, but they weren't making them as transports anymore . . never really did."

"And the agreement? He couldn't finance it for you."

"Well, I got a deal, that's for sure. And I had made some good money flying a leased hauler after a couple of years flying for someone else. With my prudence, frugality, and success, my parents backed me, but I increased my deal making ability by purchasing some gold coins and precious gems."

"Universal currency. If you had waved pound notes or dollars, he might not have cared to deal at all. Was it a close call? . . . and carrying all those valuables."

"Like in the movies. We had heard the Nazis were nearby. He said he would not be around when I took off, so as not to implicate himself and make them mad at him for the loss of the plane. When I was airborne, I saw a German staff car coming up the road to the field. A chill went up the spine for sure. I just wanted to put some miles behind me before any German aircraft got posted nearby. I paid about a third of what it's worth. The thought crossed my mind: What if he was the janitor? Well, there had been a guard on the plane who he dismissed. A janitor couldn't have done that."

Beside him and laughing after her next sip, glancing up at him, Ann smiled and said, "My hero."

It was a casual joke, perhaps not even a strongly conscious thought on her part, but it warmed him slightly. It carried that sense of ownership of possession that young men who look at girls seriously and not as prey think in terms of . . not just possession of the woman, but possession *by* the woman, as well.

"You took that shot, didn't you? You killed him."

"In Africa?"

"Where else would I mean?"

"Yes."

"I saw . . felt him go down . . my guide beside me. The horse fell too, with it, but I think it was alright. He was a good man, a true blue, trusted guide." And she said it as if she had led a half dozen safaris at least, and he could see her capabilities . . the way she matured through things and moved on . . been there, learned, done that.

And she continued, "I waited for the shot and pain in my back and rode, pushed the horse like hell, all I could do was ride . . and I saw the puff of smoke from the knoll. . . . What did you use, it was like 180 yards?"

"One fifty, I think, or thereabouts. I used my Dad's Springfield, from the war. He managed to keep it somehow."

"What is it?"

"The 1903, like your dad had that day at the farm. I ran into Mr. Hemingway in '33. You know, the author. He told me to never let it get away. He was big game hunting with one at the time."

"Did you fly him in or something? We were pretty young then."

"No, just had the luck to run into him. I was a copilot, third pilot, just a kid getting experience. It was just after we left home, you and me."

"Have you been back, Allan?" the woman asked, unable to mask the sadness of a longtime expatriate.

"Once on their dime, and once I was able to wrangle a job on a clipper, but not as a pilot. I can't leave the Aero now. To risky. The Brits or the Americans may take it. At least if I'm here I can bargain for something."

Airfield hopping was required due to the range limits of the Aero, though its 700 plus mile range was significant during that time. The Douglas DC3 was the star of air travel then and would become the military C47, the primary air cargo warhorse of the Second World War. It would drop paratroopers as well. State of the art then, the DC3 was narrow, crowded, sat at a steep angle high in the front, had a narrow aisle and padded seats that would seem small and rustic to any modern traveler. In such a crowded environment for long periods of time, passengers became friendly acquaintances fast or had unpleasant trips. That was a lesson learned occasionally, as exemplified by two African American WAC officers (Women's Army Corps) who were assigned on a cargo plane flight to England with a group of white, male Army officers and found the trip a friendly one.[1] Perhaps, because it was a worldwide struggle against common foes, people accepted that everyone, of every ethnicity and gender, was in it together.

Covering a long leg across blue water, Ann looked down at the enormous Bay of Bengal below. They refueled in Burma, topping off again in Thailand. Excitement of the traveler drew her from the depths of her depression as the ports of call creeped ever closer to the East Indies, a scattered complicated smorgasbord of delight for the tourist or overseas worker. Americans and people in general did not travel outside their homelands as much then, and overseas travel was still an adventure. And the Indies offered cultures and experiences to be savored, as a mix of peoples from Southeast Asia and the Southwest Pacific had been joined over decades by immigrants, conquerors, and colonizers, each bringing their own culture. And, though the natives wanted the colonial powers gone, the latter had not destroyed but accepted the native ways, and the former had begrudgingly accepted the colonial ones that were beneficial. And thus, a state of at least temporary coexistence and peace existed. In a culturally romantic region, surrounded by the ever-present romantic feel of the sea and its salty air. Marriages happened and soon there were certain numbers of mixed people, Siamese (Thai), Annamese, Filipino, Malaysian and various Europeans all mixed, the whites less so. It required a socially adventurous spirit beyond what it took to just be in that exotic part of the world in the first place.

The East Indies

Hopping around the the coast of the great Indian
Ocean because the Aero hadn't the range to cross it,
the travelers landed in Singapore, and it was the end
of the first week of December. Of course, there, it
was hot, sticky, and often breezy right there on the
Strait. It was a mystical land of exotic peoples,
colors, and smells, religions, and sounds, and bells,
and names, of volcanoes, and tsunamis, and clear
blue skies and azure seas, . . . and sunsets to make
lovers swoon all the more. White British women
and others of the Empire, Aussies and New
Zealanders wore lightweight light-colored dresses
and pants suits with big brimmed hats and
sunglasses. And the ubiquitous small brown women
of Southeast Asia and the scattered Indies were
everywhere: Muslim Malays and some Indonesians
looking beautifully reserved in their head scarfs as
if there was a convent somewhere flowing with
native nuns in colorful habits; Chinese in their silk
dresses when dressed formally; Tonkinese and
Annamese in their pantsuits overlaid with a long
dress; and western style dressed Filipinas. Except
for the Chinese and most of those from French
Indochina, the Tonkin Gulf, and thereabouts, most,
the vast majority were the various shades of rich
coffee lightened with sweet cream and, unless
angered, appeared cheerful and as delectable as the
drink itself. Probably many a Britisher who was
single and passing through sighed that the social

norms of the time prevented him from taking the time to find a petite wife to bring back home to England where, months later, the words of Kipling's *Mandalay* would ring in his ear all too truthfully, and he would wish to be in the East again.

The men were industrious, though often small, and many were handsome enough blends of mankind to attract a daring white Western girl, as one had Cheryl Vasquez (born Cheryl Richards), the friend and former sweetheart of Allan's uncle George Allison. Her first husband, Charles Cable died on the Cagayan Valley expedition in 1907 in Luzon. The widow married a handsome Filipino planter. Allan had seen his uncle in Cebu the last time he was in the Philippines long enough to go around a little. Former Army Capt. George Allison was married to the half Navajo legendary adventuress, the former Sunny Kathleen Jefferson, known as the *Jaguarundi*. Together they had bravely aided many people in danger around the world during the last three decades; and, in their sixties now but seeming much younger, had written two books together on native peoples and one that focused on their rescue operations in Armenia and during the Great Smyrna Fire.

Allan saw Carolyn Ann to the proper authorities, which was easy as a car and an agent awaited them at the airport after Allan had radioed Fulton Malandy his estimated time of arrival many hours before. Things being less strictly formalized in that era, and Allan and Beau having been very involved in both the supplying of the medical safari and the rescue, all three friends were interviewed and debriefed together. There was none of the grilling in separate rooms to make sure stories matched. British Intelligence knew they were questioning the good guys.

In the morning, the next day after arriving, Allan, Ann, and Beaumont went down to the docks, just to see the lay of the land. A British guard started to shoo them away from the particular area they apparently had poorly chosen.

"Why the security, soldier?"

In a recognizable Cockney, smoothed out and decipherable due to a few years in the King's service, the young yet weathered British man said, "Yaw hāven't heard Sar?"

Expecting war, yet still surprised at the timing, Allan looked strong to his face and had the glare the great actor Wayne of that and later eras turned on in his greatest angst and anger on the cinema screen . . A look you never wanted to be on the front end of in real life.

"The Japs have bombed your fleet in the Sandwich Islands, Sar. Destroyed it we think."

"What?! . ." and speechless for a moment, he looked to her, and she was stoic, yet had tears in her eyes. And he turned to the man and inquired, "When? . . Pearl Harbor, Corporal, in Hawai'i?"

"Yes Sar, arely your time yesterday, Sar, a dawn air raid from carriers, Sar. On a Sunday morning."

Scanning the harbor just for the relief, for something to distract his mind, suddenly Allan pointed to the harbor waters and said, "We're here to meet that plane, the little flying boat."

Looking, the guard saw a Grumman Goose anchored just out enough to need a launch, as there was no ramp near to pull the amphibian up out of the water on. Allan said, "That's the O'Brian Company's Goose out of Cebu in the Philippines. My friend flies it, and I haven't seen him for two years."

Turning to his two companions he said, "I checked by radio with them in Cebu. Luckily, I got through. They said Jake was probably here."

Just as they were trying to figure out whether to seek a ride out to the plane or to try and signal it, the Grumman's engines came on and the plane began to move closer. They walked around the area to follow the Goose with their eyes and see where it would dock, then met the boat bringing the crew to shore. They saw the wounded man lying in the low flat vessel and a Malayan girl bending over him. She wore a colorful sarong but no head covering of the Muslims.

"Jake, Jake Pierce," called Allan.

"Well, the man of the world, Allan Allison, the man with the poetic name. What were your parents thinking? Good to see you."

"What's wrong, Jake?"

"It's young Jon, my copilot, you know, Tommy's nephew. We got in a bar fight to save some girls from being prostituted, good girls, and Jon got shot. We have got to get him to the hospital or I could talk."

"Let me grab transport." Looking around Allan saw an empty lorrie coming in from some delivery and flagged it down explaining as they stopped and he ran up to them. Refusing pay the stevedores swung the vehicle over to the group and helped load the stretcher.

The Malayan girl, a woman, but young and pretty, told the driver, "We want to go to the hospital at Johore Bahru, the new one. I'm in nursing there."

"It's a bit of a drive north, ma'am."

"You are correct, sir. Well, the one here then."

Due to the emergency nature of things, no further introductions had taken place, and Ann offered, "I'm a doctor. I'll ride with you." And reaching her hand out she said, "I'm Doctor Ann Davis."

"I am Maya," the other replied with only her first name and a warm smile while taking Ann's hand.

As Jon was loaded gently and all got aboard, Jake said, "Can he make that long drive?"

"Yes, it is best there, but perhaps these men are correct" replied Maya.

Ann had been looking at the patient and said, "He is stable. Johore Bahru will be fine."

Everyone ended up on the flat bed of the truck.

About a week after landing, Allan walked out onto the sunny patio near the big modern hospital at Johore Bahru in the late afternoon. It was the 11th. of December in the region and thus the morning of the 11th. in America, four days after the American naval base in Pearl Harbor at Oahu, Hawaii had been bombed. The Japanese were already landing in Malaya, along the coast, but Allan did not know how much the people of the city knew. The British battleship HMS Prince of Wales and the battlecruiser HMS Repulse had arrived in Singapore and had just recently sailed up the coast on a northerly course to interrupt the landing of enemy troops on the Malayan shores of the South China Sea. At Pearl Harbor a large portion of the United States Navy had been destroyed or damaged, but they were, of course, in port and unable to move and maneuver.

He had called Ann on the evening of the tenth of December, and they had discussed the bombing. Over the phone, she had seemed a bit tearful. He couldn't tell. He told her he wanted to see her again, and she agreed to meet at the hospital the next afternoon. He had more news of the world and the local situation but did not want to talk of such things now to her, and certainly not over the phone at a distance. He had let the Pearl Harbor thing sit with her for three days now and thought it might have been a mistake, even wrong of him, they being close now and countrymen and expatriates in a now embattled foreign land. But he wanted it to be her thoughts when they finally talked, and he wanted her to have time to form them. Such matters required depth of thought and honesty.

The patio wasn't crowded, but many staff were there having an afternoon snack (what Filipinos called merienda), late tea, or an early diner, perhaps due to their hospital duty shift. Allan had met a few of the young doctors at a recent men's club he had been invited to. He was around the same age as the younger doctors and slightly older than the younger nurses. That was because medical school was about twice as long a registered nurse's course and then doctors had to intern for a year or so. Alan was no intellectual professional like them, but the air of adventure that surrounded him, the knowledge he exuded and his handsome charm had been his ticket. He was more intellectual than some doctors who read little beyond their field and specialty. The now almost thirty year old flyer had been quickly welcomed in with whatever was the 'in crowd' at that time and place.

Walking across the patio from the stone archway through which he had entered, the flier caught a glimpse of her at the farthest table sitting alone. She was peacefully engrossed in a magazine and a Singapore Sling, not being in uniform and thus not on duty. An exit through a small stone archway was just behind her, diagonally. The largest most boisterous table held a menagerie composed of mostly British young medical professionals and one or two a little older. There was also a newsman with his big Speed Graphic camera, the standard of the day. Either the man was well off or his paper was, for around his neck he also had a little Leica III on a strap. It was the portable camera that would soon see duty in battles around the world in the hands of brave souls who photographed the war for the Allies. Ironically, it was German made.

As Allan had just adjusted his path to walk to her table, one of the younger doctors, and Australian, quickly stepped over and caught his arm, "Join us, mate. We've a big party to plan for the holidays."

"Thanks, uh, . . John?"

"Jack."

"Sorry, Jack, I met so many of you yesterday."

"That's awright, mate, but come along now."

Pointing to Ann, Allan said, "I'll drop over, but the doctora there is a friend. We traveled together. It would be rude otherwise you see."

Looking perhaps with a mild disdain at the 'colored' doctor, the Australian replied, "Well yes, that is proper. Well, we'll await you then."

Allan walked up to her. He had left her to her plans and needs for a few days, knowing where he could find her. She was employed, or promised such, now but not yet working.

Perhaps to defuse the closeness that had grown between them, she said with a pleasant smile, "Captain, join me, please."

He sat down and said, "Thank you. Are you well?"

"As well as can be expected. Is there news?"

"George Simpson says we should have a meeting with the press and make a statement. He sent the guidelines, but we cannot discuss them here. Let's relax. It is almost Friday. You'll like the outcome."

"Well then. I will follow your instructions without argument for a change. I suppose I seemed so belligerent recently, especially at first."

"No, quite the opposite. Your concerns and emotions were very normal, all things considered, and many a woman would probably not have been as composed. I imagine it is your training, and if I may be so bold as to suggest, your upbringing as well."

The two then launched quietly in to a comparison of their experiences and impressions of Singapore and Johor Bahru. Ann teased him, evaluating her observations of Malaya over the week and alluding back to Elaine, twisting the knife just a bit as they had long ago occasionally sarcastically dared to do as teenagers.

"Given your taste in women, Captain, now, after these few days, I don't see why you are not already married with a brood, or . . just headquartering your cargo business here and enjoying a different cherubic brown smile each weekend for variety's sake. A different kind of brood, so to speak."

It was strong comedy and what would come to be called 'roasting'. Wrongly exercised it could be cruel and damage a friendship. But with a true friend it was just entertainingly fighting dirty.

He didn't smile, just to worry her, and replied, "Most of these Malayan girls aren't like that . . only the ones drawn into that life."

"I see. I never thought for a minute that would attract you, so I suppose flying and adventure keeps your hormones under control, old man. You're bumping into thirty, you know."

She had known his family as decent, yet not prudish Christian folk, just like her own. It was common in years prior to the Second World War in East Tennessee, where they grew up, but their two families set the standard a bit high. She trusted that was still with him, but would not have looked down on him if he had faltered there in that beautiful paradise of overtly pretty women. The weird youthful relationship, distant yet warm, was such that she had realized during the long flight that she knew him deeply, even if she had thought otherwise. At least she knew his core, the original Allan if that was still there, and it seemed to be.

Jabbing back less aggressively, Allan suggested, "Well, if events allow you to stay here, you will have your pick for domestic bliss: British, Aussie, Kiwi, and some exotic Malaysian doctors to add a little color."

Ann smiled in a droll sarcastic way.

As they were talking, the larger party at the other table across the way was somewhat jovial, but distracted also with their interest in the mixed couple sitting alone. It was not unlikely however, for the two newcomers carried an air of adventure and mystery about them. For the others, seeing them together after the rumors of their adventures just increased the mystique. The professionals at the nearby table knew now a little about Ann and Allan's travels and recent adventures. They were moderately interesting news locally, overshadowed a bit by the war. Her mission had been, upon its beginning and was even at the moment, a news story. And with its untimely and unsuccessful end, it was all the more. And of course, she was soon to be their colleague. The two seemed even a bit more exotically interesting in a mixed-race friendliness openly displayed. He had resisted the urge, yet had pulled his chair closer to hers as he had sat. Prying judgmental and accepting eyes did not fail to catch that.

Furthermore, it was an age in which air travel was not yet out of its adolescent developmental years, when most overseas travel was by ship. Planes were nowhere near as long-ranged as the present era, and restricted in capacity as well as distance. Added to that, big airports around the world were not as common as today until after a really big war would require them. The great international commercial passenger aircraft of the day, the late 1930s and first two years of the '40s were the big flying boats, Pan Am's Boeing 314s and the Short Empire flown by British Overseas Airways Corporation (BOAC), Quantas, and a few others. They were the flagships of Pan Am and the others, and most people couldn't afford those somewhat luxurious long sleeper flights, with sleeping compartments, small dorm-like sleeping areas, lounges, and dining rooms.

To travel as Ann had on a plane like Allan and Beau's required hopping across whatever lands required on moderately long 500 to a thousand-mile legs and experiencing all the beautiful scenery, exotic cultures, and sometimes shocking natural and cultural behaviors thrown up into one's face. Thus one might see the burning of the dead in open funeral pyres on the streets of Delhi or Calcutta, or the still occasional free love on a secluded beach in the Marquesas or elsewhere in Polynesia, or Elephants in British Burma doing the work of big steam-powered equipment in New York or London, 'piling teak' as Kipling described in the poem *Mandalay*. Allan's luck at acquiring the converted Aero 204/304, generally out of his price range had blessed the three travelers with longer flight legs of slightly over 700 miles in the extreme. Still the experiences were the same, if farther apart.

And, for those who dared travel around the globe from their comfortable culture on the continent, the United Kingdom, North America, or pockets of civilization in Sydney, Auckland, Christchurch and elsewhere, there must have been, within the young and vibrant bodies of the doctors, nurses, businessmen, officers, and even their spouses a realization of the visual, sexual, intellectual, and personality allure of the darker peoples they met. Yes, there were the average masses of average workers laboring as washer women and construction workers or taxi cart engines and everything in between. And they were less appealing because they were dirty, had not time to allow for primping in mirrors, and often were ill fed and scrawny. No less noble, even more so, they would not be expected to attract the Westerner, no matter how viral or down right horny the white newcomer might be or attractive or sensuous the native laborer might be. But among the smells, bells, colors, exotic spicy menus, uniquely alluring music, religious devotion and all else as a theatrical backdrop, God had placed a cast of attractive, dark often alluring women and men in various shades of coffee, chestnut, and teak, depending upon their particular racial, ethnic, and familial origins. At some point such things can only be ignored by an avowed racist.

Moments into their discussion, which, despite her aggressive teasing and because of it, was ever so comfortable for Allan, another doctor came over. The Britisher requested, "Captain, please come over, there are some young ladies who would like to meet you. We don't have a lot of you Yanks here. You're somewhat of an interesting and pleasant distraction."

Now it all may have seemed so normal a request, even with the subtle teasing about the single females among the larger party. What was off base was both what was not said, the error of omission, and that what was said was so openly spoken. The average Caucasian Westerner of any skin color might not have even caught it, though most darker ones surely would have. Quite obviously, Ann was a new colleague of these doctors and nurses and a Yank as well. Secondly, Allan was already talking quite privately with a young, attractive, single lady.

"I'll step over before I leave. We'll all be here a while, I suppose. Much has occurred." With the last comment, Allan referred to the Pearl Harbor bombing and attacks on British Malaya and the Philippines of course.

About ten minutes passed, and then after some burst of laughter that perhaps made members of the group even more certain that the American fellow should be in their revelry, the Aussie, waved a big 'come over' motion with one arm while looking at Allan, and said, "Com'on, mate!"

With a deep intake of breath and pursed lips and looking down toward the table but with his eyes closed, he triggered her response, and she said, "Go join them."

Looking up and into her eyes with the intensity of past days when he had consoled her and distant days when he had warned her months ago, the strong man from back home said to the woman with a shocking air of honesty, "I want to be with you right now."

Her dark eyes widened almost imperceptibly, and she said, "Its almost turning into a scene, though."

"They're off duty and getting drunk . . and rude."

"I know," Ann said softly, with an equally soft right hand placed on top of his left.

"Give me a moment," Allan said, pushing his chair back and standing up. As he turned to walk away, he looked back and requested, "Please don't leave." The woman nodded affirmatively.

Allan approached the table and stood there to be introduced and to pay his respects. There was a stunningly pretty blonde American nurse just to his left named Jenny, he learned almost immediately. With equal immediacy, she exuded a natural sensuousness and charm. It was as if they were qualities that she couldn't turn off, and their arms were accidentally touching, his wrist to her shoulder as she sat there.

"Si'down, mate, pull up a chair."

"Yes, join us, Captain," a British doctor echoed the other's invitation.

As he had come across the floor and up to the table, the American had decided to be friendly, gracious, yet brutally honest if necessary. "I'm sorry, but I'm with the doctor over there." And of course, it carried with it, '...so why didn't you invite us both.'

Everyone except the blonde in some manner or another glanced toward Ann. Perhaps the nurse was the most aloof or conversely maybe she had the best manners of all and knew better.

There was dead silence very briefly and he added, "We're very close friends."

They were easy to tell apart by their accents for the well-traveled pilot; and, in that era, nurses were women and doctors were men, so there was that, and an Australian nurse asked, "How so?"

"We are from the same hometown and we've traveled and faced death together."

Well, Allan thought, that ought to sober them up a bit, people who dealt daily with death . . struggled, grappled with it as it were . . and knew what it was.

"How?" asked the pretty blonde beside him.

"Her rescue, it was touch and go and right out of a Hollywood movie. It was only two and a half weeks ago, but such things are about to become commonplace."

"She led a disastrous mission. Such things aren't for women," a doctor said. There were about four doctors and six nurses around a circular table just big enough for them all.

"Actually, she did quite well. I helped outfit it, flying in supplies and all. Circumstances beyond her control defeated it . . Africa defeated it."

"Still, a woma ..."

"She hired the best local guide in the southern half of Africa. I watched him die as I shot his killer at a hundred and fifty yards before he could kill her. It has nothing to do with gender. It was Africa and our enemies now. There had been an infiltration in the area."

Allan couldn't help but look down at the generally quiet nurse beside him sending electricity through his arm. They smiled, and she said, "You suggested such dangers were to become commonplace?" with an interrogative tone.

"This war. It will touch men and women indiscriminately."

"There's no need to scare these girls just to show your manliness, Yank."

"I was in Nanking. I take issue with your inference. I just bear warnings of hard things to come. The Japs are in Malaya. I really don't see how you folks can sit here and plan parties now."

"What do you mean? We're fine here. That was back in '37."

Ann sat patiently. She had said she would, and the second Singapore Sling was as good as the first. She could tell there was slight heat rising from the discussion.

"What I mean is the Japanese are in Malaya. They have been in Siam and French Indochina for some time."

"Oh, you just got here. We have brought in new aircrews with their fighters and the pride of the fleet went up the coast two days ago to shoot up those Japanese landings. Those two beauties will get it done. The Prince is almost brand new!"

Allan looked straight at the man with just enough of a pause to unnerve him, and inquired calmly, "You haven't heard then?"

All eyes turned to him, and Allan reported, "*Prince of Wales* and the *Repulse* went down yesterday off Malaya, east of the Kuantan River's mouth, mercilessly bombed by Jap planes. You may be getting survivors in here any moment. The destroyers are bringing them in."

There was a gasp, and the blonde looked up in a way that revealed calm and nervousness at the same time, and inquired, "Why did you mention Nanking?"

"It was very bad there."

"We heard a little in the States. You were there?!"

"Yes."

"Why should we worry about that here?"

"It really isn't the subject for here, . . and now. It was very bad, and . . because of *H.M.S. Prince of Wales* and *Repulse*."

103

"You don't need to scare these ladies, Yank."

"She asked; they're nurses."

"They are hospital nurses, not battlefield medics."

"They will soon see the worst of it and be heroic nurses. Don't shield your women so."

Standing up, the British doctor who had become the most adversarial and was obviously slightly drunk, said strongly, "Look, just because you want to spend your time with your little Negro …"

"Watch your mouth!" said so strongly no physical gesture was needed or presented, and the table froze in silence for a brief moment.

Ann finally stood at her chair, but not to leave. It was as if to assist if needed.

The blonde looked up and said, "Captain?"

"Not here."

"Then at your table perhaps, if I would not be interrupting."

Another nurse, an Australian, put in, "Tell us, Captain." Her land was nearby and she was feeling the threat with the news of the two ships' fate. The hot breath of Japanese conquest would soon be felt on many necks. The woman was alluring with the interesting accent, scattered soft, pale freckles, and beautiful red hair that he knew would have been longer if her nursing hadn't prevented it.

Reaching in his left breast shirt pocket, Allan removed the small clear envelope containing the one picture he could not forget, wanted and didn't want to forget, and his hand wanted to tremble as he handed it to the American girl beside him, feeling the connection of country.

An audible gasp emanated from the pretty face and she drew her hand to her mouth to cut it off, her eyes were as wide as saucers as if she had seen a flying saucer from another world. All eyes were on her in silence, and the Aussie nurse stood and walked behind her chair so as not to wait. She reacted similarly, hand to mouth in surprise and shock.

Jenny looked up, and there were tears in her eyes, and she asked, "Is this real?"

"I was there, I saw it as it happened. I was standing with the photographer."

"And you did nothing?"

"I was restrained by friends and a Jap soldier who all knew I would be killed and could not stop it. There were a hundred Japanese soldiers around us."

"And the child?"

"A similar fate, . . with the same stroke."

Jenny was crying silently now, and the nurse who was standing asked, "Why would they let this out? It is incriminating."

"I actually think they were proud of their work. They may want to intimidate us all. Some of these things make it home and into their newspapers. I'm a serious amateur and took some too, from hiding. Some of mine are blurred from trembling hands."

The photo, taken by a journalist friend with Allan at the time, showed a kneeling, naked, young Chinese woman holding a baby. The young mother was just too pretty for one to imagine in such circumstances as she awaited the stroke of the samurai sword held visibly above her bent neck. It was not unlike a famous photo or two or hundreds available in history books in the modern era. Such victims await their fate unrestrained, resigned to their fate and that of their child, seeing no escape. And, when the adult was killed first, they would never know, unless in an afterlife, the fate of their child, dying left to wonder.

"How many?" asked the visibly shaken attractive Australian, still standing behind Jenny's chair.

"Untold thousands, all ages. The Yangtze river flows through that city and turned red. I saw it just before we flew out. We flew over it."

Not even having seen the image, the belligerent doctor reacted, "The bloody hell, these young women shouldn't …"

"These 'young women' are nurses trained for these things doctor," stated the Australian nurse with a firm expression and staring down the other. "We don't need your help telling the Captain what we think."

"What were you doing in Nanking?" asked Jenny softly, composing herself.

"I went to pick up a plane for our . . my employers' company. A Chinese businessman had sold it to us because he was fleeing by steamship and needed cash. The freelance journalist went with me, partly because he knew he had a quick way out if need be. We did our business in already devastated Shanghai, then went up near Nanjing for the plane and flew east to Nanking on a dare to see the real story. I own my own company now. There's a man there, a Nazi heading the German Siemens Company. He's a hero. It is said he saved one hundred thousand of them, the Chinese. Many more died."

"How could he do that?" a doctor, who had remained composed, asked.

"I know no details, but the Japs may respect Hitler. But I do know the story is true; I just don't know the true numbers."

Allan looked down at Jenny, red-faced from crying, and she looked up with a soft, quick smile and returned his photo gently. Looking at the Australian nurse standing behind her, who had made the strong statement about her profession, and knowing the strength of the Aussies, he said, "In Ukraine there are girls just out of their teens and as delicate and pretty as you manning T-34 Russian tanks against the Nazis." Her mouth dropped a little, and he sensed a reaction from the others just out of his sight, and Allan continued, "My copilot, a worldly Frenchman, has a journalist friend working for one of your papers from Down Under. He met two very young girls, the driver and the gunner for a T-34. This is growing and it will be everybody's war."

Turning to the standing doctor, Allan added, "You brave men here for the Empire . . you make preparations for these 'young ladies', your colleagues. They assaulted every girl, every female in Nanking . . . of every age, even little girls. Those new aircrews and planes? That little Jap fighter will fly circles around them and sweep them from the sky. Then Singapore will be bombed mercilessly. Then they'll swarm out of the Malayan jungle and across the causeway. Your big guns are fixed permanently toward the sea. They aren't coming from there, and airplanes will rule in this war anyway. Those of you who do not get out or die here better steel yourselves for several long years of near starvation in prison camps. And steel yourselves for watching each other struggle with death there with none of your medical tools and supplies. We, America, have to rebuild our navy to come back and rescue you, and your own men, your Commonwealth forces are locked in a death struggle with Hitler."

Allan then nodded a good day to them all, looking at each of the nurses, and he turned and walked over to the standing Ann, and they both sat back down.

"That appeared to go well," Ann said jokingly. "You brought them to their feet."

Nodding and smiling wryly, Allan replied with a forced cheerful smile, coming all the easier because it was her, "Let me take you to dinner somewhere."

"All right."

"Well let's go then."

"Not 'til I see that picture, or do you believe in shielding your women, too."

Looking at her in slight disgust, not directed at her, at her need to see it and his requirement to show it, Allan reluctantly and tentatively handed it to her, as they rose to leave and stood now face to face about two feet apart. As the other two had, she reacted with the hand not holding the image rising to her mouth to smother the requisite, reflexive gasp, and her eyes were also wide.

With not another emotion or expression and looking down at her purse, as she reached down and retrieved it from the table . . not looking at him . . Ann handed it back, saying, "Let's go."

As the two stood to leave, the American nurse, Jenny was saying her farewells to the larger group nearby. The activity was drawn out a little as she was not working for a few days and wouldn't see them, and was of course getting teased about an impending lazy break. The whole table of course was surrounded with a new atmosphere after the heated discussion, the images effect on the two nurses who had seen it, the news of the two ships, and Allan's harshly educating comments.

Walking out the small, more secluded archway that accessed the patio right near Ann's table the couple started down narrow, turning cement stairs, and as they turned he suddenly stopped and pivoted in front of her, blocking her way, taking her left hand gently in his right but then as quickly dropping it as he put that arm around her waist. Then looking softly and deeply into her eyes, he said, "Forgive me this liberty . . I really can't stand it any longer." Then reaching his left hand up behind her neck he pulled her to him firmly in spite of the heat, mitigated slightly in the cool stone and concrete passageway, and kissed Ann gently and extremely affectionately on those beautiful lips.

After a long few seconds, he leaned back to face a shocked expression tinted with an ever so slight, wry smile. Just as the relief that she hadn't slapped him crossed through his mind, they both were surprised to have Jenny turn the corner they had before and bump into them. "Excuse me," escaped her lips, as she had not only interrupted but collided with them. Then revealing a sassy sense of humor, not unlike Ann's, that they would see more of, Jenny said, "Well, this is cozy, just the three of us." Allan replied, "Well, my secret is out."

"We were just going to dinner. Join us," invited Ann.

"Are you sure?" Jenny asked, thinking herself invasive, but really wanting to talk to them.

Looking at Allan, Ann asked, "Allan?" The doctor in her was concerned about the young nurse. She had seen the emotion, even from a distance. Jenny was a countryman as well, apparent to Ann from her accent.

He nodded assent to her and turned to Jenny saying, "Definitely. Are you coming with us or shall we choose a place and meet in a while?"

The nurse was in uniform and replied, "I'd like to change. You go ahead and I'll meet you. It seems you two may have things to talk about. I'm sorry. I really have questions."

Ann replied, "Your welcome with us. I really want to talk with you. Whatever we have to discuss won't

take long. You've been here a while. Where should
we go?"

"Here," replied Jenny, presenting a card she had in
her purse. "I was here a week ago. It's nice, classy,
not too expensive, Captain, and everyone is
welcome. it's cozy too."

Her comments about inclusiveness weren't lost on
either of them and seemed not to be a hidden insult,
and he replied, "Just call me 'Allan' and this is Dr.
Ann Davis."

Jenny handed him the card and offered her hand to
him and then Ann, who said as she took it, "Just call
me 'Ann', except on duty together of course."

Some few minutes later, in the restaurant, which
Ann noticed he had walked rather quickly to, the
adventurous man, now a hero to her in a way, sat
next to her at a small round table that left only room
for the new friend they awaited.

He sat close to see if it mattered to her and inquired,
"Are you angry? Jenny didn't give you time to
react,"

Not moving away, a millimeter, she asked, "Why
should I be?"

"Some would call my behavior inappropriate . .
even think it cheapened the girl, even if sincere."

"That wasn't a cheap kiss. We know each other now."

"So, you're okay with it?"

"With what? You must also use words like 'Love' or it was a cheap kiss. You haven't proposed anything yet. I assume you want us to see each other, which even here might require local geographical gymnastics unless there are a lot of places like this."

"What I want is more. I would like more," he said, looking steadily into her eyes, discernible even in the romantic and adventurous atmosphere of the darkened room and constant music played moderately loud.

The woman looked back as steadily and with a certain twinkle that seemed always in her somewhat large, subtly exotically shaped eyes.

Then Ann laughed casually and perhaps playfully, saying, "Well, maybe it was a cheap kiss."

"Not that way . . the whole kit and caboodle."

She looked at him more intently, searching. They had never stopped looking at each other since they had sat down. The kiss and embrace had insured that.

"I'm asking you to marry me, Ann."

"I understand that . . . now. . . . . Wow, Swell, that was quick. Is it a pilot thing? Does living at over a hundred miles an hour get to a fella eventually?"

"It's a war thing, and a about your ethnicity a little," he said using the more scholarly term to reference her race for the sensitivity of it.

Weathered now by trials and failures as well as success, the accomplished woman looked at Allan, and said, "That **is** an issue, you know."

"It doesn't have to be."

"But it is."

"I didn't expect it to be like that for you as much as me."

Looking sarcastically serious, combative but subtly so (maybe a little angry?), Ann replied, "So the dashing white guy decides to cross the color line, snaps his finger and the little colored girl comes running? Sort of a hierarchy type of thing."

Her hands, touching each other, were laying near his on the tabletop as they were beside each other close and turned toward each other. Bravely, given her last response, he took them in his and said, "No Ann. Not like that. Come on . . you don't believe that."

The doctor turned her head down, leaving her left hand in his and looked down at the table placing her right elbow on the table with her closed hand against her right cheek and supporting the weight of her head. And Allan continued, "I only meant I might have to worry more about the reaction of my people."

"Apparently not your father."

Both paused in thought, and then she said, "...or was that just a guy thing, talk among the boys?"

"You don't believe that?"

"No, I don't. I'm sorry, Allan. I didn't really mean it. I'm just taken aback . . surprised. I always thought . . you know, I'd marry another person of African descent, a, uh, another Negro."

It was a correct term and the common one of the day, common to her, the term of record in the news, and business offices, immigration . . but it was almost hard to say between them, as if all that had gone on, all that was going on, the history, the struggles for her people only just beginning again, reviving . . affected him . . And it felt like it was a softer version of the harder, meaner word. It wasn't the same as if a guy went off and married an Italian or Spanish girl and those names rang musically and spoke of the exotic to the folks back home. But to him it was. She was exotic to him, and he didn't

115

need words, didn't need labels. He didn't even need for her to be exotic. She just was.

And he started to speak, stumbling with the first word or two, "You're just a girl to me, Ann, a helluva girl. And a heavenly gal. I guess your look and color appeal to me, but its only because I like you . . what's inside you and your look too. It's not because you're African. I'm not asking you so I can make a show of things, of our marriage. I just love you. That's all. I love you, and your people happen to have come out of Africa like mine did Europe. These are troubled times ahead. I want to protect you. You know, I never had another girl back home. I never dated much, just prom and such with some good friend for a date. We were always on the farm in the country, hunting and fishing, and sometimes you were there. Any other girls around our family were cousins. But to be honest, I love the way you look, too. You wear the look of your people so well. I ached to be with you all the time you were in the African bush. But mostly, . . the way I feel . . you are the girl from back home, the important one."

She had the college degrees, but the man was no dummy, and he had chosen to use what he perceived as the more attractive ethnic descriptor, not the word she had used that spoke more of race.

"You know, in Knoxville, if we were walking down the sidewalk together, we'd probably have to step in the gutter if a woman of your tint came toward us, step in the gutter to let her pass because of me,

because I was with you. How would you like that?"
Then smiling she said, "We're not even in the deep
South there."

"Together, they might not expect that of us."

Ann looked at him and his innocence, knowing he
didn't get it. You had to be there, to have been there
to get it.

"So, I pass, barely . . with you."

He looked back with a blank, weak smile, and she
knew he had no answer and that it hurt him . . her
words, however true, and that he couldn't respond.

"Yes, Allan . . . well, not exactly like that, I mean . .
Yes!"

"What?"

"Yes, I'll marry you. . . . . You are actually one of
the few men I have met since leaving the states that
appealed to me in any depth, You're a real man,
Allan." Then she reached out with both hands to
hold his face with one on each cheek, softly, turning
on a subtly sweet smile and said, "To tell you the
truth . . you know enough about me, I suppose . .
my head was always in the books. As erratic and
casual the relationship . . I mean the one we didn't
realize we had, You're the guy, too, My guy."

And she just looked at him with those dreamy eyes with the dark brown irises in the center and an elusive sleepy dreamy blank gaze that somehow said the opposite . . that looked into your soul while hiding her own and spoke of depth and wonderment and understanding. But she had been places he hadn't. Not just the African hinterland he only flew over but **being of Africa** outside of Africa . . and then briefly, within it. Then she pulled him toward her and kissed him, then took her hands down from his face, having made the affectionate point.

Ann spoke with a wry smile that turned up more on one side, "You're so damned naive and innocent while being such a capably brave man. I'd be a fool otherwise."

"What the hell?"

"Cute and tough in one package. . . But the particulars, figuring out a life together, that's another thing. We aren't exactly going to be working in the same hospital together. And there will be a lot places we can't go together. . . including back home . . more so back home."

"Right. You won't be marrying a doctor . . . but . . why 'yes'?"

"Ha ha ha ha . . Well, now that's a lack of confidence. . . . I want to take medicine to people. I want to study their health practices and conditions. I want to improve them. You have a plane," said smiling mischievously with a wink.

He twisted in the wind a little as she teased him, played with him, and Ann continued, "Because I've fallen in love with you. We're both adventurers . . we can't stand to be indoors too long . . we want to see the next place . . we're always thinking about what we can do to help someone, and . . . and because I've realized, once you had the guts to say it like this, that I've been falling for you too . . since long ago. There was just a long intermission."

The two American expatriates, so different and yet alike, sat there just looking into each other's eyes, and a wry smile highlighting a resigned look developed on each of their faces, almost simultaneously, as if each had entertained the thought that they were meant for each other by fate.

Carolyn spoke again, "When divergent people marry, it often fails. I can't have it fail. You see what happens to those actors and actresses, each on their own cinema sets around the world with attractive people playing opposite them, and authors, directors, . . famous architects marrying models or singers, you know. They drift away. What does an architect have in common with a model? And we'll always have one difference no matter how much we are alike."

"I love these different cultures I have not only seen, viewed, but have somewhat immersed myself in.

Your different culture attracts me. We will share that. It won't be divisive."

"But there are those who will denigrate you for it. They will say you're trying to be black, or you married me to be different, or to enhance your image if you become notable later for our adventures. Some way they will make it seem you are using me to play at being black or I am doing it. And that we each have done it to say 'look at me how adventurous and daring I am'. They will make your motives selfish. They understand selfish because they are and think everyone is. It will come from the leaders with big egos, some of the lesser men among the activist, not the genuine ones. There will be a new generation of Frederick Douglases, Du Bois, and others now will be followed by more, but there will be a lower echelon, cruder men trading in race like a commodity."

"It's always like that in anything, Ann."

Allan reached his left hand behind her neck as he had on the stairs and, pulling her forward, kissed her long and lovingly in the amorous romantic style of more natural times. He wanted to erase that last thought from her lips and mind. It would never matter to him.

"I may be going on a mission during this war, and I thought to marry you first if you will. I know I can trust you, and rest assured you can me. I thought while I'm gone, our marriage might protect you from ill treatment if people know in the place we settle. You have to get out of here. You probably won't survive it here. If I don't survive, we would have had these moments, and you the memories. There will be some strong heroes to come out of this, and they'll be scarred and need someone. You'll find someone."

Perhaps slightly offended, Ann replied, "I can take care of myself." Perhaps as well, echoing within her and deeply touching her as it shocked as well was the idea of him thinking this would be cut short by his own death, freely seeing and accepting his own death and worrying more for her future without him, even wishing her another good marriage.

"I know that, Ann."

"I've been doing it for years now . . in foreign countries."

He tried to lighten it and said with a wry smile, "Well, there was Africa."

She looked angry and then broke into a laugh. It was the first time she had really laughed since it all had happened, and he took her hands, saying, "I just want you to be treated with class while I'm gone. I meant no disrespect. I guy can't fall for a girl of a different race and ever intend a mean comment even if he accidentally makes one. You have to overlook things I may say. They will never be intended in any wrong context. You were in France all those years.

Now, while I'm gone, you will probably be in Australia or New Zealand. They have not been kind to their own minorities, you know."

"And where will you be?"

"I'm thinking about a mission, to do a clandestine mission, but perhaps safer than most. I need your professional advice and maybe even quite a bit of guidance."

"It won't be in that Aero. You told me about those little Japanese planes. They'll shred your plane to pieces. I'll be widowed for sure. But what's this gloom and doom stuff?"

"I want to go back into the Philippines, sneak in. It can be done there 'cause they're islands. Can't do it here in Malaya. The Japs'll sweep it here. I can hide in the hills, . . my group can."

"'Til they conquer the whole island, and I'm widowed again, a different way. What group?"

"I don't believe they will have the men to cover all the places people can hide and survive. I thought to sneak a medical mission in. Your African trek gave me the idea. Thought you might recommend a doctor. I'll take one and some Army medics or Navy medical corpsmen. I want to request some experienced noncoms who've been around the block. I know you're not from down here, but I thought you might know a doctor or could help interview and pick one. Medical care may be the one thing that will be lacking in the bush where the guerrillas will station themselves. Then we can do other chores: perhaps experiment with truck farming, medicinal alcohol distillation, all that."

"Sitting right beside you."

"What?"

"You know what."

"No."

"Yes."

"No, No."

Jenny walked up at that moment and commented, "Swell, first fight. You guys are quick."

"It's a pilot thing," replied Ann. "They can't slow down."

"I want to take a small medical crew into the hills on one of the islands in the Philippines. You know stay the duration, provide a service to the guerrillas and some of the locals. She wants to go."

"Me too. Count me in. She needs a nurse."

"Oh no. No you don't. I can't take you girls into that risk."

"You're the one touting Russian female tankers. Teenagers. We're just offering to carry on our trade in a war where there is need," said Ann.

"… and danger."

"They're already there you know," put in Jenny.

Both looked at her, and she said, "American nurses, Army, Navy . . they're there, they're trapped."

And both looked on with a paused blank stare of realization. They hadn't been there; they had been in the air over the Bay of Bengal. They had not received the tidbits of news from the Philippine Islands.

"I believe some will get to the hills, as I believe the men will, some of them."

"That's a rough life, a rough existence," commented Allan.

Jenny responded, "You fellas want us safely stashed somewhere, maybe Australia, where Ann may or may not be allowed to work, while you go play hero and women are already suffering like hell. This is our war too. Ann and I aren't housewives," said with a knowing and friendly, almost sisterly nod to the doctor. She was being blatantly open now in these new friendships. She continued, "There are American nurses right now up in the Philippines.

They won't all get out or to the mountains. They'll be interned in Jap prison camps."

"Only our God knows what will happen to them and hopefully protect them. True, I never know how each country, or hospital facility is going to respond to me. It isn't just my race. Women doctors are still a rarity except for female health issues . . even then."

Allan spoke with more equality of purpose now, rather than acting in a commanding way, as he was desirous of tying himself through marriage to a woman whose whole race was used to unfair rules from his race.

"Ann, Jenny, I do not think I should take my new wife and this young pretty nurse into the hell that could unfold there."

"Whoa Nellie!" Jenny exclaimed softly. "You two **do** work fast."

"Yeah, you almost missed it all, but you're here for this," and reaching in his pocket, he took out a small, square jewelry box, which he opened to display an atypical engagement ring with a small yet appropriately sized glowing Australian opal, holding it near to Ann.

She reached her left hand up onto the table and raised the ring finger a little above the others. He slid the ring of quite some quality on her finger and leaned over to unabashedly kiss her. He had correctly guessed the size on one of the long flight legs by comparing her left ring finger with his smallest finger on his smaller left hand, while she was sleeping. Then he went down a size and a half. He knew it would not be too small; and, if too big, that would be easier to resize.

Jenny walked around to her and leaned over to give the almost obligatory, sisterly hug and kiss on the cheek. Then she sat in the empty third seat. As he had placed it on her and both women looked closer. It was apparent to them that this was an exquisite example of the beautiful gem associated somewhat with the Pacific region they were now in and Australia in particular. It was creamy white with a green glow near the center surrounded by a hint of tan, like beach sand; a little rust brown shown on one side, and a blaze of blue all around faded out to the dominant whitish pearl. In sum, it looked like an island in a sea of blue, surrounded by a dreamy cloud, as if one were in a plane peering through the clouds to see an island far below. As with many, if not most, opals, all the details were dreamily blended in a fog, and yet atypically and mystically, the little island seemed to sharpen enough to be noticed.

"So, you still agree," Allan commented with a subtle smile.

"We're engaged, not married. We'll close this deal when the particulars have been sorted out about what we both do during this big war. Like Jenny said, my skills, degree, and license may be undervalued. You, however offer not only love but employment, though it may be in a voluntary capacity. At least there will be food. . . . and romance."

"Maybe. That is one of the many problems, many hurdles. Nevertheless, let us just enjoy this evening and new friendships."

"Not to belabor the unpleasantness, but this war is the elephant in the room. Those Brits I left a while ago were all in shock at Allan's news about the two big ships. And, when they asked about the photo, I couldn't speak, but Elinor described it and another nurse teared up just from the description. I'll not stay here. I'm going where I can do some good and not get killed at the beginning. They will be hiring nurses for military duty. They'll have hospital ships like in the Great War, and I have heard they plan to put us into the military more officially, maybe with commissions, officers' commissions. Some now are Red Cross nurses. But you offer real service in the middle of it, yet not out on a battlefield like the male medics have to face. I'll leave it now for your benefit on this joyous night for you two, but we have to talk Allan. I want to do it. I've been a surgical nurse. I can assist Ann. Right now, that young naval officer walking over is coming for a dance. Everyone in here can tell you two are out of circulation. You couldn't slip a thin piece of paper between you right now."

127

Turning toward Ann, as Jenny walked up to the officer, Allan asked, "Would you like to dance?"

"I'll await the slower ones. You've set that type of mood for this night with your proposal. Now, I'll leave it too. We'll keep this evening happy. Who knows, maybe not one of the three of us even gets out of Singapore alive. Before, I'm quiet, just remember: you need a doctor with field and jungle experience and in dangerous settings; you need youth and people used to this heat and steamy humidity like I faced a little in Africa; you need adventurous people to even consider going with you; and you have two capable, trained medical professionals who happen to be women who left comfortable lives to travel to exotic places and face challenges, like I did from the beginning in school in Paris. You have two women right here, a medical surgical team. We're lighter and smaller than most men and will eat less of our precious supplies and reduce the amount of foraging when supplies dwindle later. I'm a green thumb gardener, by the way . . since a little girl. Grampa had horses too. You know I can ride."

White Cliffs of Dover suddenly began from a little house band that was quite good. The male singer was one of the musicians and wore British RAF attire. He played the clarinet on songs in which it was dominate or soloed. His clarinet style reminded Alan of Benny Goodman, and his voice was not unlike Sinatra's. The woman singing now with a satiny mellow, not too sharp of a voice was a little native girl from which ethnicity in the region perhaps no one knew. All around, Indonesians, Malays, Filipinos were all partly Malayan. She was dressed without Western European accessories in a beautifully colorful batik sarong that came straight across the chest revealing a tastefully subtle bit of cleavage between her breasts, apparently well-formed and firm though like most in her race not large. The material left to the eye coffee colored satin skin from there up to her raven black hair that was put up in the French way. Her mouth, opened wide with song in the properly taught studio way, functioned on an exquisite example of the classic Malayan woman's face. Without the hair flowing down to frame them, the Oriental, and especially Malayan, round face and high cheeks, beautiful as they can be, sometimes appear exaggerated. In this case, the people present that night just realized that, visually and audibly, they were being serenaded by a Malayan angel. Months and years later, as he sweated out his own survival chances, the pretty petite singer was among the ones Allan would pray survived and maybe even got out of Singapore. You don't forget a moment, a song, or a woman like that, even as you were falling deeply in love with another.

The moment the song began, Ann stood and took his hand. Sad as it was, it was among the war's most beautiful, and they melted into each other's arms and danced like two people in love on the cusp of a war. Both danced well, and mixed couple that they were, they drew a little positive attention, smiles and the like. It was a foreign British colony that was a bit of an enigma, as was America's Philippines, and this was a friendly cafe and watering hole. No one cared what color a pretty girl was and they stared for the beauty. That was all.

The evening and the night went like that: eating, sipping, dancing, and occasional casual talk. Then it became slightly less crowded and most tables still occupied seemed to accommodate lovers or those who thought they were. Ann and Allan sat close holding hands at their table in the back, watching the ever more popular Jenny dance. With those looks, charm, and her dancing, she was the belle of the ball; and, when it took some effort getting away after the last dance, Allan stood up at Ann's request. Jenny succeeded breaking with the man, an RAF fellow and, before she could leave alone, Allan waved her over.

Jenny sat down, excusing herself, as she had seen their deepening display of affection for each other. Ann said, "Don't leave alone. You have too many admirers. The drunk ones might act in ways they might later regret, and there are always just a few bad apples."

"Okey dokey, Mom," Jenny teased.

"We need to talk soon, ladies. I have no immediate contracts, Ann isn't supposed to start yet, and I understand you are on vacation for a few days. Let's meet tomorrow. I will have to fly out before my plane is destroyed in the bombings or people get desperate and try to take it."

"What about in particular, Captain?" Jenny spoke in a more formal manner. "What is your agenda?"

"Getting you girls safely out of the Indies before they fall, and planning this mission, . . or just deciding if it is practical."

"Getting us safely out of the Indies?" repeated Ann.

"I'm not committed here; you are. Beau and I could fly out tonight."

"I see, I see your point."

"What about the planning and evaluation?"

"I'll need you both for that."

"But you don't want us," commented Jenny. "That's a bit cold to ask us to help plan it for you."

"We've much to talk about. I don't know . . it could go very bad . . Planners do not always go on missions, but that's beside the point. I know you both meet the qualifications."

"Well we'll talk about it tomorrow," Ann said wanting to avoid a divisive issue on this special night. He had indicated a softening, and she sensed it would be wrong to push it right then.

It was a different era, yet lovers often rendezvoused when the cafes and bars closed, with all that concept implies, as they had all throughout history. Some just held to their religious belief and morals, and Allan knew enough about Ann to not even suggest they sleep together on their engagement night. If she had changed a little over the years, she'd let him know.

Several hours later the three friends sat in a meadow a bit out in the country having a picnic lunch. Such scenes would soon be impossible in that region, but now a basket was opened revealing a bottle of red wine and various delicacies they had picked up with a careful selection to appease the two he had burdened with angst, who needed no appeasement.

There were egg rolls and sandwiches, some other breads and cookies. For the health of it some fruits were included as well, particularly mangoes.

They ate quietly with only a comment on the wine or the mangoes, accompanying smiles, and an occasional laugh. And few men could have had a better afternoon, that of the company of two women of such quality. Having found his true love, Allan would have enjoyed even better honeymooning with her alone. In a rogue moment within his stream of consciousness he mused, that, as a man who had not socialized with the fairer sex tremendously since

132

leaving home, he surely had managed to discover women of quality to become friends with. Ann, Elaine, and Jenny were actually the only young women he knew well.

"So, let's do it this way. Jenny has an agreement with the hospital, but I do not think it is impossible to beg out of. Now keep in mind as I say this: In a pinch, with bombs falling and the plane's survival and ours in doubt, we will just leave, permission or not. They won't shoot us down. Hell, sadly, by then, they'll have no planes. But for now, because we need to leave now, let's start seriously planning. Things always get worse and it's tougher to do things when one waits. The only ones who do are required military people and police and such, and the journalists that stay as long as they can for the story."

"… and the medical staff," added Jenny with a suggestion perhaps of guilt or cowardice.

"No. don't think like that. And this is why. First, you're Americans and not bound to the British Empire. Secondly, what they're doing here is irresponsible and they are blind to it. I've talked to some military men, though I could see some of it myself. They are reckless and will get their people killed and enslaved. You do not owe the British that. Thirdly, Ann has no final agreement. I mean she hasn't signed the contract. But finally, you will have no embarrassment because it will be known that we are going into service elsewhere when we leave. It cannot be made known, the specifics can't, but the general idea can."

"And that is?" Both had spoken simultaneously.

"What I told you all. I ran into the naval officer at the hospital, the Navy Lt. Commander my contacts mentioned. He says it's doable. He's nervous about it, about you, but says he'll consider it and help set it up in some form when we're all in Darwin. I suppose if we plan things correctly, we can minimize the risks and keep operations far from enemy territory. But we do not know the level of Japanese commitment. We could end up inside the hornet's nest."

"In some form?"

"He may not get approval for you to go. Then we'd be on our own. How would we get back into the Islands without submarine transport?"

"What changed **your** mind?" asked his fiancé quietly but audibly.

"Respect. Respect for your skills and courage . . both of you. I'm sure somewhere inside me, that African trek won me over. I mean that had to be part of it. If you marry a girl for the mutual adventure, you can't cut her out of the tough ones to protect her. And well, Jenny here, well she's just crazy," Allan teased. "The Islands will be full of women. You won't be the only ones, but discovery will involve enormous risk for us all. I just want to do my part and maybe achieve more than dying on some beach with hundreds of others. I know those guys . . they're important; I'm just seeking to make a greater impact where nobody thought to do it. I never thought you would want to go."

Ann didn't react with a kiss on his cheek or a lingering one on the mouth as the scene would have played out in the cinema. She calmly looked down and it was obvious to the other two that the man in her life, her new lover had moved her deeply.

Presenting the depth of the horror they were contemplating; he chose to do so obliquely in the manner of Christ with his well-known parables. And, knowing they were medically trained and each had seen much, he held no detail back. "In the old days in Texas . . . I believe it was the most dangerous situation for women in the Indian wars because Kiowa and Comanche both stole 'em. They stole 'em for breeding stock 'cause they didn't breed prolifically, at least the Comanche didn't. Maybe they lost some stillborn because of being on horseback so much when pregnant while they were moving. They lived a very nomadic life. The tribes dragged these captive wives and sex slaves (depending on their perceived worth) all across the middle of the country, sometimes to the high Rockies of Montana or up near Canada and back. It depended on the Indian nation and their territory. You see the others did it too, the Sioux, Cheyenne, and all. They were nomads, you see, and the white girls and Negro girls weren't used to that, weren't made for it. They caught Mexicans too. And so, they died young. Then, in raids, if they didn't need slaves, they just brutalized them as a terror tactic, killing their men in front of them, naked sometimes . . and them stripped naked too. Sometimes they would mutilate the men sexually first. Then they'd gang rape the girls and women . . until they died from it sometimes. One way an enemy shows its complete domination of a people is to prove they can do whatever they want to their women, the one thing the men are sworn to protect and care about the most. Your kids may be rebellious and go of in a wrong direction in life, but a good wife in a good marriage . . that's supposed to be everything until you die. It is a way to totally destroy a man and then possess his woman or destroy her too. Men who knew what they were doing, if they traveled that country with their women or had to live far out, you know on the frontier line . . well. Well I mean . . they saved a bullet or counted how many they needed, with daughters and all, and they tried to stay alive long enough to kill 'em before the warriors got to 'em, got to the girls. My uncle is married to a half Navajo adventuress. I met her in the Philippines, where they live now. She told me that her white father always saved a bullet for her Navajo mother, in that way, because they were often in tough situations in Comanche lands. The two, her parents, fought the Comanche and were friends with their famous war chief afterwards. This war out here could be like that."

136

He had said it looking down at his clasped hands as he sat on a little folding camp type stool, and he never looked up, for the embarrassment of it. But at the end he did, looking straight and calmly at both of them. And as he broke the gaze and looked down to take a little nibble and some wine, the two women sat speechless with blank gazes in their eyes. Ann knew Allan had Texas ties and had spent summers there. It hadn't been that long ago, the last of it, the Red River War in 1874, only sixty-eight years before, and he may have heard some firsthand stories.

When the three returned to the city, and the couple were alone at the door of Ann's room and were contemplating dinner plans, she took his left wrist and dragged him in, shutting the door with her foot, embracing and kissing him passionately. It lasted long meaningfully emotional moments.

Leaning back only slightly, still embracing him, the intuitive woman said to her lover, "I have seen the longing in your eyes, and your patience speaks of the deepest respect that defines true love. I am as impatient for the full rewards of it and believe we need to get married now, even if it is only in the Church and defies British law, whatever that may be. The Church is what really matters. Let's go find Jenny again, and see if she knows a priest. Your friend Jake can be best man."

Two evenings later, Allan and both women had dinner with Jake Pierce, and his companions, including the U.S. Naval Lt. Commander, David 'Buck' Shaw, who had initially signed off on Allan's medical war mission proposal.

Jake opened the conversation after everyone had taken a seat. "Thanks for the help the other day, folks. Well, Allan! . . a doctor, a pretty one if I might say. You're just full of surprises."

In the quaint yet vibrant café and lounge, where the two lovers had first danced together, the officer said, "It is definitely not for me to say, I suppose, but then it may be within my bailiwick. I put agents into such situations all the time, and just recruited these patriots here for a mission. Nevertheless, I'm gonna have to run this up the chain of command a little, what with putting female personnel in harm's way and such. Well, not really 'up the chain' but consult with my partners in crime, my equals." He knew he would be going back into the southern Philippine Islands in Jake Pierce's Grumman Goose (now the Navy's property) but didn't offer it, knowing there would be no way to bring Allan's idea to fruition in time. It was also clear the Grumman could neither carry all the personnel he intended nor the equipment, and certainly not both. He had decided that he could make the decision but wanted the other men in Australia on his level, who would be involved in his absence, to know and perhaps sign off on it too. It was a respect issue.

Continuing, Lt. Cmdr. Shaw suggested, "An entry by submarine is your best bet. When they go, they'll be taking needed supplies to the entrapped and to guerrillas. When surrender comes, and it will, even if everyone is ordered to, some will hide and fight. It is just in them . . ingrained in some Americans, like the way you folks are thinking. Any missions planned already won't allow for you to go, no time for proper preparation. You have to let this be official, or I don't see how you'd ever get in. If you tried by small boat, there would be bodies of water you couldn't get across in the night. Zeroes or float planes would catch you in the daylight out in the middle of them. The main issues are whether someone is going to balk because you're women and whether the subs can get your group and enough supplies in on one trip. Deciding where to post yourselves is important too . . and security. Not all Filipino guerrillas are going to be nice and friendly or helpful. Times like these, chaos, . . it really is a time of lawlessness. That's the problem taking women in. An organized community would be your best bet. Maybe a mixed group of American and Filipino freedom fighters. Second best is a secluded well protected aid station."

"Otherwise, I'm useless out here, Lt. Commander. I don't think I'll get into a military hospital easily."

"You might be surprised. In an emergency when the bombs are falling, people will worry less about who is trying to save their life. But in general, unless they have segregated units, you might be right. I'm sorry, Ann. You understand how it is; you mentioned it."

Unspoken and maybe understood by most present was the weight on the heart of the true love of the denigrated person like Carolyn in that era, in this case Allan. For the person in his fiancé's shoes had, sadly perhaps, become aware and prepared to be treated rudely on occasion, whereas the lover's heart breaks each time for them. And there can be many incidents in which he can do nothing to mitigate it. He had chosen her for the many reasons that define love, and she him. One task he readily accepted was just to be there for her when she faced such insults. Any husband could have done it, black, white like him, or a man of any ethnicity. Racism was the wound but race was not the cure or even the salve. Love was, and it was colorless.

Ann spoke up, revealing her wealth and worth of knowledge, thinking power, and, now, experience, that of a woman, who sometimes was heard and then not. Maybe she wanted to impress the Lt. Commander, to sell her role in it. "The important supplies are the basics based on need and common sense: medicines appropriate to the common diseases there and to war injuries; medicines that make sense because they don't need refrigeration sulfa pills and powder, chloroform, laudanum, morphine, quinine, etc. We'll need bandages and such materials, because in the Philippine bundok, fabric will become a premium item in a prolonged conflict, disinfectant: boric acid, alcohol and the means to produce it, portable stills; antiseptics for wounds, the sulfa and such; fire starting tools; enough rugged but light weight clothing and shoes for ourselves for a war's duration. If we end up in too deep of a tropical jungle the humidity and the mildew and rot it brings will just eat the clothes right of you. Leather cases and holsters will rot away and fall apart. I studied that for Africa, though we chose a different region. Much of that, what we need will be light, though heavy in volume when multiplied. Now, with a still to make medicinal alcohol, we need the tubing and such. Presumably we can get bottles and cans. Weapons and ammunition will be the heaviest items. Liquids of course are heavy. For disinfectant purposes, alcohol can be distilled, as I said. Local wines may help as mild anesthesia, but a supply of ether and laudanum will be necessary. When treatments for infection and anesthetic is gone, serious surgeries will be horror stories. We'll be back in the Civil War era."

Ann paused and looked at the Lt. Commander and then her husband, both of whom sensed more from her and remained quiet. "We faced violence in Africa. If we're in those island jungles and mountains without weapons, real firepower, or if ammunition runs out, we will be doomed. As a doctor, I still must say, I won't see my friends and colleagues prisoners and abused. We must defer to our defense capabilities first and our medical abilities second, though that is the purpose of the mission. I would like to suggest some type of gun that is lightweight with ammunition that is not too big to carry enough, and then perhaps we need at least one big powerful one with quite a bit of the ammunition for that one."

"Off the top of my head, I would say Tommy Guns and a couple of BARs, wouldn't you agree, Lt. Commander," said Allan.

"The old westerners tried often to carry a long gun and pistol of the same caliber to only need one small cartridge type," put in Jake Pierce. "A .45 Colt cartridge was a small but powerful rifle shell but a very powerful revolver bullet."

Lt. Cmdr. Shaw added, "If this plan takes off, Allan, Ann, I see a second mission that will keep you from being obligated in an intense combat area. I will suggest it to my colleagues in Darwin, the ones I know are there now. It would be very important and be in an area where the Doctor here could practice her trade with the people."

"We don't want to be sheltered," stated Allan.

"You want to do your duty and accept the risks, but you want to have an important duty and limit the overall risks to these ladies who will be with you. My idea may achieve all of that and you all come out alive."

Jake Pierce, an outdoorsman from the California Sierra added, "And take enough of your basics or know where you can find 'em: sugar, salt, coffee, tea. In the Philippines, something might be plentiful but outside your reach. But each of those can be done without, and sugar may be plentiful if still grown. You can collect seawater and let it evaporate to get small amounts of table salt."

Finally, as they all seemed to want to leave the war alone for a while, the discussion slowed to a stop and all, new friends and old became quiet.

Then Shaw broke the quiet solemnly and with a soft voice said, "Allan, before I ask permission from the both of you to dance with your fiancé, I'll tell you, I will authorize your mission when I get to Darwin, but I won't be there when you get there. I work independent of them, but the resources you need may not be available or someone may balk at the women being involved, or honestly, Ann, . . let the color issue get in the way. When you get there, you report to this Marine officer," said handing a slip of paper to Allan. "He's the best they have, and here, Doctor, you hold this. This is my personal letter of recommendation that you head this from the medical side. I typed this up right after Allan asked me about it, just to be ready if we had to part ways quickly. It also says that I've interviewed you all and know of both your qualifications and recent contributions."

Eyes widened, and Shaw elaborated, "I've been in the Southwest Pacific and the Indies since '30. I was concerned about the Japanese since they murdered our naval officer in Vladivostok a decade before, when I was young officer. I moved my family out here. I do my homework. I knew who you both were when we met. You both have files with us and the Brits."

Voices were soft now as they had taken their que from him. No one was a round them and he was opening up to the two. Ann just sat with her mouth slightly open and her eyes still a bit wide, as Alan inquired, "Are you serious?"

"Allan, the plane north of Shanghai in '37 was full of technical documents hidden between layers in its construction . . all smuggled out of Japan. Information about their war machine. Everybody almost died when they learned you risked it all flying into that mess in Nanking. Someday communication will probably be much more instant and you'll have people screaming at you through headphones if you do such a fool thing, while the commanders just have heart attacks standing by. We found out later this time of course. But, I'll tell you, you made some fans with that foolhardy little jaunt. To a man, the people in intelligence I talked to questioned whether they would have had the guts. Now, the pretty doctor here had people with eyes on things down here wondering, suspicions you know. But I kept telling everyone, she's just a dedicated doctor looking for a greater cause. I kept pushing the point that she had to fight chauvinism in the medical world and the color barrier too. When you alone got out Ann, with Allan and Beau's help, I won my point and then some."

He paused, took a sip of his drink, and then said, "Now, if you're sure about it, you two tie the knot sooner than later. If there's any issue about legality, citizenship, race, local laws, let me know, and I will personally get the marriage set up and legal as American citizens. I think we can sell this mission to Marine Colonel Alexander Jenson; and, as to anyone who might give him a hard time about it, best if you're a legally bound couple. They won't see some guy who wants to go off for the duration in some tropical islands with his girlfriend and asking the government to pay for it."

"We are married in the Church. We could no longer wait," Ann reported unabashedly, to spare Allen having to. "We would appreciate the rest."

A day later, a coded message was sent to Australia. A supply emergency had arisen in the mind of the creative Lt. Commander. A new weapon was just being manufactured enough to reach the military, and the Pacific was low on the totem pole, but not naval intelligence officers.

Col. Jensen.

Urgent. Will speak directly soon. Secure one dozen each: that little carbine, Thompsons, 1911s, large supply ammo/each. Sub transport for 10 men. 2-3 radios, crank generators. Try with all diligence re. carbine w/ammo. Re. our Am. Pilot friend.

Shaw

Australia, December - February

Jake Pierce, and Lt. Cmdr. Shaw had left for
Darwin. Pierce and his copilot Steven, another
O'Brian Company employee, had taken along one
of the Malayan girls they had told of rescuing from
prostitution and the wife and child of a British
major. A long war held danger and love for Jake
Pierce, but readers will have to seek those in other
volumes. The Aero would soon follow; there was no
reason to stay. When Allan, Ann, Jenny and
Beaumont reached the small Western Australian
outpost of a town, they could not know that the
Goose with Jake, Steven, and Lt. Cmdr. Buck Shaw
aboard was headed toward the Philippines and
might already be there, a sturdy little plane with its
own patriotic mission.

Only two days later, after verifying that Jon and
Maya had left on the *Star of India* hospital ship,
Allan and Beaumont had lifted off with his wife and
a few Americans who were fleeing. Of course,
Jenny was aboard. An important British official or
two and an officer were aboard, and it had been
Allan's connections with British intelligence that
had kept British military hands off his plane and it
still in his possession.

The morning after Christmas revealed the gift of an
invitation, worded almost like an order, for the the
four individuals, three Americans and one

Frenchman, who made up the apparent, current crew of the Aero. Thus, mid-morning found them sitting before the scowl gravitating toward a mischievous smile on the face of a reasonably handsome, early middle aged, bulldog of an American Marine Corp colonel. All of them sat stone-faced yet tending toward a pleasant expression out of unknowing nervousness and minds full of questions.

After letting them twist in the wind a bit, the gruff yet pleasant man said, "Shaw left this on my desk. I'll get him back one day when he least expects it. He runs around all over the South Seas and Indochina like some afternoon movie idol adventurer, what with his secret license that nobody knows what all he's allowed to do. If he weren't such a good and loyal husband, with his good looks, there'd be little mixed Asian kids all across the Indies by now. He's been here forever, but rushes to her in Sydney whenever he can. Best damn man in the Navy for my money.

I am Colonel Alexander Jensen. Shaw and I are in the same business; but I, the single guy who appreciates the ladies in this tropical world and wants to settle down after this enormous dust up, gets stuck behind a desk while he gallivants like a matinee idol and isn't even looking for a partner."

He was gruff yet warmly friendly and always to the point as he said, "Allan, Doctor, if we all get out of this, we'll have dinner in Sydney, and you two can

147

tell me if and how you've made it work so far . . I mean, 'to that point'. I mean to marry a Malayan woman, probably a Filipina . . for the faith and language and all . . and the food, Oh heavens the food! They're Malayan mostly, you know. I know I probably can't take her home, but, hell when have I been back myself?

Now, the idea was for me to look at this and send it up the line, but it would die there. Most would brush it off, what with all that's to be dealt with now. Many would give it a nod but say to themselves either it would never get approved or that you folks are dreaming . . or crazy. What I saw, when I looked at it, and after he mentioned, off the record, the Doctor's gender and race, in addition to her experiences, was something deeper, more of the gut, visceral. I've heard about you two fliers too, Allison. I've been the man behind some of those calls in the night that led to some clandestine flight of yours over the last three years. You weren't always working for the Brits. You warned these girls, didn't you? Shaw said you were in Nanking in all that."

"Visceral?" inquired Carolyn Ann, perhaps not knowing if she had been insulted or not. It was a derogatory term in some usages.

"Ma'am, Doctora, I see the four of you reacting reflexively, yet with thought put into it . . a 'gut reaction', if you will, but from the heart too . . and guided by the brain. You're three Americans caught out here in this mess with some skills and experiences . . and raw courage, and you want to contribute the best way you can. And I figure, because I can see such things, none of the four of you would fit well in a uniform, metaphorically speaking. It would look good, especially on you ladies, but it would never be comfortable. . . I mean, I'll have you in uniform. But, well you know . ."

He talked like an educated man, because he was, though he had been in it the thick of things, in youth and through the ensuing years. Revealing medals decorated his chest for Belleau Wood and elsewhere, a few described, in vague presentation citations, missions between the wars that were not supposed to have legally happened.

The colonel continued, "Doctor, what people miss about your failed experience in Africa is that it was not a failure. I know all about it. It's my job to . . to know about every mission out of the ordinary in the last ten years from the Mediterranean Levant and Caucus to right here where we sit and south of the Chinese-Russian border down. You sent yourself out on a six-month mission and it succeeded for five, falling apart because of bad men and outside aggression, the Nazis, by the way. I mean bad intruders and an evil warlord who cared not for what was best for his people. The other five aforementioned months are a helluva good notation on the resume of a young woman fresh out of medical school with only a year of work in a hospital before the safari. I might add that I see your race as an asset too."

He had been addressing Ann directly and looked up to the broader group. "Now we need to talk generalities for a few minutes and then plan to get down to details later today. Times a wasting.

Now I think this will work and has value. Most people there would like to be out, especially women. It's not that they're disloyal, but know they can't do much and will end up in camps and prisons. Now we have to ask ourselves: Why send you; why take the risk? What can you achieve beyond birthing a few native babies in the hills and patching up a few guerrillas? Otherwise, you get down in it and could get these ladies in grave danger."

"Colonel, I might be useless here. There could be restrictions, and my only option could be a government job on some Aborigine reservation or whatever the Australians call them. If I go home, if I could even get home, I'll end up the maternity doctor in a Negro hospital somewhere. My race may not accept a woman surgeon easily either. My only option to really contribute may be something like this. I have experience few male doctors will have going in with our troops, however they are planning to do that. Most military doctors not already in the services will probably be right out of school. But you and I both know that a military hospital is not going to accept a woman doctor, my race aside."

"You're right in several ways. They're probably not going to give a valuable berth on a ship going home to a Negro female doctor, and I don't see them giving you a military medical assignment either. It's not the race issue, it's the gender issue . . that and race." Then looking at Allan the officer inquired, "She's your pretty wife. You want her to do this?"

"Unfortunately, she's tailor made for this. But we need a clearly defined goal. I believe we can have enough cover on Mindanao or Panay. Negros Island might be the other option, but I don't know that island as well. It scares me a bit. Every island will have its resistance fighters and there is cover in rugged terrain on all of them. But there may be some bandit types who take advantage of this."

"A lot depends on how many garrison troops the Japs commit. I believe there will be a resistance on the three islands you mention, maybe even little Cebu. For hiding, the best bet is Mindanao, but there's probably a hundred ways to die there in the jungles, and then there're the Moros."

"Moros?" inquired Jenny

"Moslems we've been fighting almost since right after we took the Philippines and defeated the Christians that didn't want us there. Forgive me stating the truth, but either one of you uniquely

151

attractive women would be a prize for some prince's harem. Let's adjourn till this afternoon around two and all of us spend the interim time making sure we have a viable mission to risk you all on. All of you think about these things. Look, I want you to weigh the risks, focus on them, on the bad . . get that part out of your system. But try to weigh it intellectually within the total picture. If any of you are going to have a job in this war, it will be unpleasant.

Now we plan, if you ultimately decide to do this, to give you multiple tasks. There are American nurses and doctors there who will surely make it into the hills and serve the guerrilla movement medically. We will put you in where you can help the people in a given area, help the guerrillas in that area, and work for us as observers of the goings on within your view on high ground and as coast watchers. It is needed and will help the war effort, especially when our forces counterattack and return, and justifies the risk and cost, the supplies, men and the submarine."

"Spies get shot or hung, Colonel. Coast watchers are sort of like that and 'observers' even more."

"To the Japs, it may not matter. They may kill anyone. We've reports from escapees that military men in uniform are being treated badly but the American women so far just incarcerated. I can't think about them being treated like the Japs did the Chinese. I would never sleep and be no good to anyone. Now you all need to think about this, the

152

risks. But as to officially spying, you'll all three be in uniform. I'm giving you direct commissions like some of the celebrities who travel to visit the troops get. You two will be Navy lieutenants, like a first lieutenant in the Marine Corps, and Miss Barkley, you will be a Navy ensign.

Now Allan, if your plane is left here more or less unattended, they're gonna confiscate it, commandeer it. They may anyway, but if you leave Beaumont here to hire a copilot and fly for us, I may be able to keep it out of military or other government agencies' hands. Now you all need to go talk all this over, and see if you're still serious."

Allan and Carolyn went to a little cafe and ate lunch alone. Ann had tipped Jenny that they needed to be alone and that she did as well, to think things out for herself. They were a couple now; she was not. Ann told Jenny she would be available to talk it out later.

As they ate silently at first, Ann looked up at him and said after swallowing a bite, "Allan, Darling, do you really want this?"

"I never want you at such risk. Newborn babies in Aboriginal towns need the best care too."

"I mean the marriage. It brings so much baggage for you. I'm used to it; you're not."

"What? I'm okay."

153

"What if we go home?"

"We'll cross that bridge."

"Said cavalierly."

"I'm not shallow, Ann. I accept this . . you, and whatever comes with this marriage. I've been aware of a feeling for you for a long, long time. When we were down by the river that day . . after graduation . . on the last picnic. I wanted you then, but thought it just my teenage lust. But I knew it was more, deep down it was more, but it was complicated."

"Exactly." then she paused and said, "Complicated might be a mild word for it. It's complicated now."

They were sitting across a small table and the fire of love might seem to have cooled a bit, but it hadn't. They had married quickly in Singapore and had a few passionate nights burning the midnight oil of years of pent up sexual desires and emotional feelings for each other that somehow deep down they may have always been aware of, 'visceral' as the Colonel had said in another context. Of course, they had been enjoying each other for a few days and nights before that day's meeting began.

They were sitting as romantic adversaries yet still close across a small table. Oddly they had chosen it, walked up to it in spite of the several slightly larger tables they could have chosen and sat side-by-side.

154

Were they already unconsciously censoring their own behavior for others' sensibilities?

Looking at her for those long moments, with his eyes intentionally grabbing her when she finally looked up again, he said, "You are worth it. And I'll handle each situation as it arises."

She looked at him and smiled softly and had a faraway look in those dark eyes. It was as if she was looking deep into him and through him to somewhere else at the same time. And he avoided any typical thought or teasing comment one might say out of racist thoughts back home or just speculation about the supposed special attributes of the native peoples that a white didn't understand . . because she wasn't that. She was a Southern small-town farm girl just like the boy he was . . had been. No, the stare was concern.

"You're thinkin' what happens down the road when the new's worn off, and the honeymoon's long over. You're getting skittish after the fact. . . . maybe thinkin' annulment. You're thinking that it will get harder and harder to face things as the unique couple we'll be when we're tired of each other. But I'm never going to get tired."

Her stare had disappeared with a blink and she was looking now with more intensity and love and he said, "I'm not letting your color get in the way; don't you let mine. And I'm not letting the glow dim, even after the newness is gone."

After lunch and the time to think and consult each other privately excluding the colonel, the group met again with the officer, who had a reasonably good-sized project table in his office to the side of his desk, forming a conference area. Lists had been made of supplies needed, those that could be attained or produced on site in the islands, those that were most essential, those that would wear out fastest, and the ones that would be consumed the fastest. It seemed expected that the chore would be done, and this part of planning would be done that day, except for finding out what was going to be available in Darwin and what must be shipped from Brisbane or Sydney.

Then the colonel explained that the next day would be map day and everyone would study the maps together, even Jenny. For in the future, any one of them might end up alone for the rest of the war's duration. There was still the probability that Beaumont would remain behind and run the flying service. That remained to be seen. Entry into the Philippines by air was seen to be almost impossible. The colonel informed them that Jake Pierce and Lt. Cmdr. Buck Shaw were at that moment engaged in what might end up being one of the last attempts to get in that way for months or years. The little flying boat had an advantage the Aero did not, many landing possibilities in an emergency. In fact, to stay out of sight and travel only at night, one refueling had been done in the open sea at night.

Jenny looked seriously at one point at Lt. Colonel Jensen, and when he next paused inquired, "You ask for a reason, you've not asked again."

He looked at her blankly as if maybe overworked and confused and she restated it, "You asked us to spend lunch and after thinking why . . deciding if it was worth it . . I mean..."

"I know what you mean. But mostly I wanted to see if you came back. You see, you are correct, you might all be wasted here. I just wanted you to think about it and not report back, if that was your choice. You're expendable, you know. That's why I can send you if you really want to know."

"How so, Colonel," asked Allan, feeling responsible for the other two of course.

"No one will miss you or complain. When this is over, only your parents might ask questions; and, if I'm alive and asked, I'll just say they volunteered. If this lingers and you die, and we learn of it, you could become inspirational heroes and help the war effort that way. We could lose this game, you know."

"Well, thank you for your honesty."

"Nurse Jenny Barkley, what is the goal in your opinion?"

"To save lives. To do our job while Allan does his and protects us. If we save twenty lives it'll be worth it . . or one, if we save one."

After the second day, the first working with maps, Ann found herself alone in the room with the tough yet intelligent Marine officer, and she inquired, "Why is my race an asset?"

"You blend in," he replied matter-of-factly as they had spent hours in discussions of mundane details.

"I'm a minority here," she replied, hiding any feeling of resentment at his possible thought that all dark people looked alike. After all, when the Americans invaded the Malayan-like populated Philippines, they called the people Negroes and even 'Niggers'. Filipinos just thought it a friendly nickname at first.

"You are correct, but the Indies are a melting pot of mostly colored people, where whites are the real minority. And there are many people here like you, who are not of the Malayan type people or Chinese, Melanesian peoples like those from New Guinea. There are more ethnic groups here than I can count, and quite a few of African or Melanesian descent, like you, are dark. You can lose yourself here. You're very appealing to the eye, but so many of these women are. That's what happens in a melting pot."

She was quiet and he paused, then said, "I'm sorry for how it is back home . . and even here with the British some. The Dutch mix a little more, but they have their problem with the Muslim people not totally embracing them. Things will be better back in the States, and elsewhere, someday. People like you will be the reason. You prove that dark people are not simple-minded primitives, just because some live the old ways in their native lands. Many stupidly think that and maybe fear it a little. Maybe that defines the lower evaluation and even occasional hate."

"I think it's more than that."

"I do too, but I doubt even you and I know exactly what. But I'm sure there are some academics, psychologists and psychiatrist, who would be glad to tell us, and they'd be the least likely to know. Then there are those who wonder at your ancestors' possible 'wild' roots, while they themselves may be descended from Vikings who raped and pillaged half of Europe. Life isn't fair Doctor, and right now less fair for you. But I'll tell you this, that pilot of yours made a good choice when he proposed to you, and you did in accepting. You're a pair matched by God, no doubt. You have to win the little battles in these matters, Doctor Allison. That's how one changes things, good honest choices and courage."

In an era where Western nations attempted to protect their women, not put them in harm's way, this project was innovative and out of line. Though not a racist, the good Col. Alex Jensen may have figured he could pull it off because the woman in harm's way was a Negro, or to many 'just a Negro'. That didn't allow for the nurse's determination however.

Following Lt. Commander Shaw's coded request from Singapore, reiterated when he arrived in Darwin, Colonel Jensen decided to see if one of the pig boats headed in harm's way with supplies could take them and their supplies. If they were bringing people out, they would want enough room for them to bring as many as possible. Perhaps a few less torpedoes and a slightly smaller crew would allow his mission to squeeze in among supplies going in.

So, the four prospective participants engaged in physical drills for stamina and strength and studied maps, off shore sea charts, supply lists, jungle survival books, Philippine climate, and on and on. Both young women were athletic, performing sports skills like men not like women. In other words, they didn't throw a baseball 'like a girl'. Everyone saw the desired bonding with women daring to accept similar dangers to these fighting men. Perhaps it would continue with American and Filipino guerrillas encountered in the Philippine bundok (rugged jungle, mountains, and bush). There they would find the Filipinas often leading their men.

Allan was on his way back from checking out the acquisition of weapons and ammunition. He had been running the numbers for various combinations of weapons and ammo to see what combination would allow for substantial fire power and the most rounds in reserve. This required detailed analysis because certain guns were accurate at longer range and certain ones were effective close in. Rapid fire was important, but that expended ammunition rapidly, and the Marines, already knowledgeable in small arms were practicing more with spraying an area with a smaller burst and training the medical group to do so as well.

Allan, in a khaki uniform now, with his lieutenant's bars, walked across the airfield from the armory and gun ranges to the headquarters building. As he walked, he thought he had discovered the best option: a BAR with a pretty good supply of ammo, a .45 caliber Model 1911 sidearm for each member of the team of twelve, which included the civilian Filipino guide. There would be only ten each of M1 Carbines and Thompson submachine guns. He continued to agonize over dropping the Browning Automatic Rifle and the weight of its ammunition in favor of two more each of the smaller long guns and more ammo for them.

Nearing the edge of the field, Allan was approached by a man in a light business suit who appeared to have come from the main collection of buildings.

With no outstretched hand or other sign of greeting the man came quickly to the point, "I just saw Doctor Carolyn Ann Davis here in uniform."

"And you are?"

"Doctor Hiram Suffolk the Third, of St. Jerome's Hospital in London. I'm out here for the time being. What's she doing in uniform?"

"And your concern?"

"Waste of resources; Ann is brilliant, . . a mere lieutenant? . . uh, no insult intended," said with a glance at Allan's collar device.

"None taken. Lieutenants and doctors each have their place, but sometimes they come together. I believe it is a normal entry rank for them."

"Ann needs to be in a hospital and eventually research. Are you responsible for this?"

"For Ann? Ann does what she wants."

"I heard you and she are involved in some sort of dangerous operation that no one will tell me about. They said you were in charge. Did you drag her into this? What did you promise her?" The man was getting invasive now, and added, "I care for her. She is a colleague and was a student of mine in Paris."

Becoming knowledgeable enough now to push back, Allan informed the man who was now inserting himself into their lives, "My involvement was creating a mission that the military accepted, and inquiring from the best doctor I know, Ann,

162

who I should take with me who might be in Southern Asia. She, being interested in working in the field, would not take 'no' for an answer. That's all I can tell you due to secrecy."

"Well, she needs to get out of that. I can get her a good job here in Australia."

"She might be concerned about the racial environment here, and I don't think they take those lieutenant bars back just because you change your mind."

"She will be treated correctly here as long as I'm around," revealing perhaps the flame of a more personal interest that Allan thought it might be time to pour some water on.

Glancing to his right where he saw her now, as she walked their way, and looking back at the man he said, "Ann makes her own decisions and made this one. I did my duty, as a childhood friend and husband, and tried to point out every risk. She chose her professional medical interest long before the two of us met again in recent years and has been adamant about her medical focus out in the field with the common people. I'm sure you know of her African medical safari. I had nothing to do with that. She was equally adamant about joining this impending military operation. If anyone is using the other to get their way in this relationship, it's Ann. I'm her transportation and experienced muscle . . and . . if a man wants a happy marriage, he must honor her as much as he wishes to be respected by her. My father, who is not a weak man, taught me that."

Looking to her, stopped twenty feet away, he turned back saying, "But I have to go; we have work to do." And Allan reached out his hand, which the man took weakly with eyes wide.

As Allan trotted over to her, he was surprised that Ann turned away and chose not to greet the doctor, who had obviously been important in her past, at least professionally.

Walking along the short distance together, she was quiet and within the conference room continued that way. The room, as muggy as it was, seemed to become cold in every way except actual temperature.

"Okay, what is it? Come on out with it."

"Nothing."

"Yeah right . . I had nothing to do with that Ann. I'm not manipulative. I'm not that kind of husband. When we made that first decision together, that night in the cabaret in Singapore, we were equals from then on."

"About me going?"

"About a life together. I just met the guy. He just walked up to me."

She looked up sort of down in the face and nodded agreement, and he said, "What is it then?"

"I don't know, just that it happened. That people want to run your life, you know. With me, now, it's some colleagues. It may be..." and she paused.

"... that you are thinking some people think you have a duty to carry the flag for your race, and that they need not be the decision makers for how or even if you chose that role."

"How insightful, Allan! You make me feel better."

"Yeah, well, I wonder how much of their concern is for you and how much for them, their ego, guilt, reputations."

Ann walked around the table to him and up close; and, taking a look around, hugged Allan and planted a long kiss on his lips. The careful approach had been wasted, as the colonel strolled in, arm full of folders as usual and commented, "That's what I need, commitment. Now, considering where you're gonna be, you just need to work on avoiding surprises."

He had his final say at a meeting with the team a few days later. "You folks know that Lt. Cmdr. Shaw and Petty Officer Jake Pierce are on their way

back to the Philippines in that flying boat. I doubt
we will get reports from them soon enough but
we'll wait a while and see.

I am sending you with orders I have issued that
prevent your use by commanders there in combat.
They will not be allowed to order these women into
danger following them around on the run to perform
combat medical duties. Yours will be a static yet
portable field hospital. Any other such call will be
yours, the three of you in the field. You are under
this command, and when unable to reach this
command, are answerable to no one else. But I, as
the authority assisting you to get into a combat area,
I am ordering you, . . because of our involvement, I
am ordering the three of you to protect the mission,
which will involve medical aide to a certain chosen
area, providing detailed intelligence from that area,
and coast watching duties there. The 'combat area'
is vague, because the commander MacArthur left
behind, Wainwright, may order a complete
surrender of the forces under his command in the
Philippines. They won't all do it of course, You see
the confusion. You are not of the original command
left to Wainwright. A surrender order does not apply
to you. If safe in the bundok, you are not to obey a
surrender order. If you ever surrender, it is your
choice as circumstances require. You are also an
independent command. An intelligence mission sent
in by this command, and not assigned to the
guerrillas, who are forming, or anyone else. You
will have multiple copies of these orders so stating.
I will supply you with multiple copies of multiple

166

level authorizations and orders that you are to operate independently and in such a way as to guarantee the safety of your two most valuable human resources, the doctor and her nurse, and two most valuable missions, the medical and the coast watching and surveillance. Allan is in command, and the orders so state. You will have two radios because Guerrilla commanders may try to take yours away if they have none. They'll need them. If you thusly lose one through attrition, refuse to give up the other. The written orders state that as well."

Finally, the officer firmed up the command structure, the order of battle so to speak. "We have decided on a five-man squad of Marines with a First Sergeant in command, and a sergeant under him. The other four will be experienced corporals and all are highly trained for this. One was a Navy hospital corpsman who transferred to the Corps when the war began. He will carry both ratings, and give you ladies a valuable assistant. We Marines have no medics. Their corpsmen are ours. I took him with me two years ago in China, when I was there as an observer. He saved me from losing my foot from shrapnel."

When the plan had begun to develop, Allan kept thinking about the very personal logistics of it, and a man essentially going on a very dangerous working honeymoon could not imagine staying away from his wife. Ann had been having similar thoughts, and at the next meeting Allan finally spoke up.

"I want to talk to the volunteers this afternoon, man to man. We have women on this trip and one married couple. That could be hard on young men in an isolated environment. Things could go wrong in several ways, especially with the native Filipinas."

"I had wanted to address this myself, but the actual talk to the men should be done by my husband, I suppose."

"I'll set it up for you for this afternoon, Lieutenants."

After lunch, around two, the delicate discussion began. The five men listened calmly, perhaps too embarrassed to say much, what with the commanding officer who would be with his spouse on the mission being the one talking to them.

"Gentlemen, you are the ones handpicked by First Sgt. Morrow. I know why he chose you and why you are the best. You were all in the Corps or the Navy before this started, and you weren't in there hiding from anything. You will have to be special men for this job. Special in many ways. Now you have been told that my wife is the co-commander on this mission, and we have a pretty nurse along. We may end up with a female native woman or two being trained as nurses as well, Filipinas. Now you fellas will have to deal with that, being on constant duty with no real shore leave, and there won't be any cat houses. We could be in country for a year or more. I've heard wide speculation, but I'm certain this will take at least a year.

Now you will have to treat these two officers with respect at all times, as officers and as women. But you may develop jealousy for my situation, and I don't know how to prevent that. Lt. Ann is a fine doctor, and we've been married about a month. I'm not gonna sleep in a different hut across the camp from her."

He smiled and the whole room laughed respectfully, young single men in their middle to late twenties, possibly Marine Corps 'lifers' away from home and trying to imagine being that close to a new wife but hands off.

"Here's the bottom line. When we meet folks up there, and we will, you treat those girls right. They won't be sailor's whores or bar girls. They'll be village girls and town women, who are generally very religious. There will be native mountain folk who live very simply, and you may not share the way they do things, and the men may be very protective of the women. But most are Cebuano speaking Visayan people up where we'll be, so most'll be the Filipino version of farm and small town girls from back home.

You already know I wanted men for this who have no problem with the color of a girl. You marked that on the form. But it's her color and this part of the world, because if you knock one of these little

169

Catholic gals up and sail away when this is over, you ruin her life. Some of these little villages will shun her or put her on the low end of things forever . . for the rest of her life. She may leave and become a bar girl and worse when it wasn't meant to be in her life. That will have been one half your fault, and St. Peter might bring that up at the Pearly Gates. Now there's a thing called 'miscegenation', and it means marrying outside your race, and its illegal in a lot of our states back home, maybe most of 'em. So, you have to think about that.

Look, I've been in these islands awhile. Even these small town girls are smart and a lot of 'em are pretty. When we are around them, the towns and villages and such, and you're talking to them, if their daddies allow it, don't mess up. Treat them correctly like you would a girl who's a lady back home. If you start falling for one, handle it right. It should change your life if you're a real man and a gentleman. Because you might have to think how you're going to take her back, where you'll be able to settle, or can you take staying here and farming or going up to Cebu or Manila and starting a life together. I know fellas who have done it and they're happy. Your dollars spread well down here and these young women are keepers. You get too close to her, and you end up with a kid and walk away, you ruin her life and you'll be setting holding your white kid some day and wondering about the one down here and his mamma. And I won't feel good."

No one asked questions when he paused, and he summarized it, "I won't stop you fellows from getting together with those people but, first, think of them just like you would a white girl back home, with the same feelings as them. Second, you be gentlemen, because you are and because you represent the Marine Corps. Third. You put some part of your anatomy where it doesn't belong, be prepared to make it belong there legally. Lt. Ann and I will approve it then, for the man who man's up and takes responsibility. But we'll be writing you and hounding you for the rest of your lives if you walk away from her and sail away."

When Allan asked for questions, one man's hand was raised. It was neither shot up nor timidly raised, and when acknowledged, he simply asked, "Are you suggesting we fraternize with the Filipinas with our commanding officer's permission? That seems to be what you're saying, Sir."

The 'Sir' came of slightly disingenuous, but nothing was disrespectful and there seemed no attitude in his manner. These men had been fully briefed and knew their commanding officer was not regular Navy, or even properly trained 'Navy' at all. Allan, Ann, and Jenny had been reading various manuals that any officer in their shoes would know well. Allan decided to address the point of experience. "Corporal, Lt. Ann and I co-command, and you know we are both greener than an ensign who skipped the Academy and was rushed through office's school for this emergency. Generally, being

Navy, an old weathered, salty Chief is required now, but that old leatherneck in his thirties over there will have to do," Allan replied, pointing to 1st Sgt. Morrow and avoiding an immediate answer.

The group broke into hearty laughter, Allan's goal, and he continued on to the answer, "We will be in the back country in a serious on duty state, but possibly reasonably without constant risk, for at least a year, in my opinion. You need to know that, though the doctor is primarily with us as a doctor, she has seen combat in Africa as a private citizen. She acquitted herself well, had to kill, led well, and only lost her people because of overwhelming odds and a surprise infiltration by professional enemy agents. I was there at the end and rescued her, though she was doing a pretty good job on her own.

In an extended deployment of troops in a civilian area with long periods without combat, men are going to have off duty time, just like on a base at home, but with less freedom to go far from base or camp. It would be unrealistic to expect you to have no contact with the local people who may become a part of our daily lives, and those particular people include petite, attractive, young women with charming personalities. I know, I've lived there. Some American men speak disparagingly of them, probably because they just prefer white girls, but I've never met an ugly girl in all the Indies, . . just some less attractive than others. There's something about that cherubic Malayan face."

He took a long pause, and looked slowly from man to man and straight in the eyes of each. Then he made a conclusion, "First Sgt. Morrow picked you for your character along with everything else. You will have down time, and these ladies will be around, and they and their families and daddies take things, take life seriously. See that you do. That's all gentlemen."

Later, the newlyweds sat at the conference room table with after breakfast coffee mugs. They shared a corner for the closeness of it_ affectionately and to share sketches, maps, and tables of numbers.

"Ann, Honey, we can distill tubâ, the native wine. It really isn't wine . . more like rum. Then we need to know what the jungle won't destroy, I mean medicines, soft materials. Eighty proof may be too weak to kill germs. They distill it twice and get it pretty strong, over the hundred and fifty you'd need. Beaumont's fabricating a steel charcoal fired oven for an autoclave. That'll save space and weight."

"Okay, if we don't have to take a lot of alcohol, we can take more pills, food, and ammo. Seventy-five percent will be enough, and we'll take boric acid powder instead of alcohol in bottles."

Ann paused in thought as they sat catty-cornered across the tables corner, each with their own clipboard full of lists. "It's going to be hard isn't it, like the weight on your Aero? But space on a submarine may be worse."

173

"No, the sub is bigger of course. You know that. So, it can carry more weight. It's just that we do not know if we're the only cargo and passengers. They have to get supplies in. We're still trying to hold the Philippines. Hand guns, Tommies, the ammo for them, the BAR, knives, basic tools, grenades, and some canned goods to make sure we don't starve. That will eat up a lot of our space and weight allowance. We'll have basic mess kits and a few metal pans and coffee pots. We'll be camping again after all these years, but I won't have to hold back my teenage lust for you."

"Was it that bad?"

"You know teenage boys."

"So, it wasn't noble egalitarianism?"

"There go those big words again. No just pure lust, and admiration."

He paused and said more solemnly, "It's going to be real rustic, Ann. We can take two big tents about 12 feet by 12 feet, and a couple of little ones for you and me and Jenny. The marines will share one big one, along with equipment storage."

"And the other's my hospital."

"Yep. Even that is enough to draw a lot of attention to ourselves. Everything I have described plus your instruments, surgical hand soaps and gloves and what food things we can squeeze in is all we will have. Oh, and we are taking those radios and a portable radio."

"I'm worried about the ammunition."

"You?! You never cease to surprise. That's my job."

"A .22 for hunting food would be so light and we could carry so much."

"I'll see if I can get one and some ammo. It is good for food in the pot and defense at close range. I do not know if we'll find one out here. Maybe in the Philippines. They're popular with us Americans as you well know."

Then he added, "Well, it's certainly possible to get one, but who are you?"

"What?"

"Ammo's not your field, dangerous African safari aside."

"I just think about everything, all possibilities, and the worst ones." She said it looking down and writing on the clipboard again.

"The worst of it is we're mostly all dead and you're the only Negro comfort woman in this big Pacific war."

"What?"

He shuddered, as he now had to explain it. He had thought she was familiar with it. "The Japanese take a small percentage of the conquered women for military prostitutes, forced and without pay, of course. The only kind thing I can say about it before you slap me is that, you would probably seem an exotic fine wine to them. I don't suspect they've seen many African women firsthand."

Staring blankly back in a cloud of calm subtle thoughts of horror, Ann said softly, "Oh, my God . . I'm not offended though. You're being honest."

Then changing the subject, Allan said, "Do we take the BAR or not? Heavy, big shells, but powerful fire power. Much more sensible than a mortar."

"The weight and the weight and space taken up by the ammo is a concern. Is there another option for a heavy weapon? We need some pseudo-artillery to stand them off."

"The big words again, though couched within logical insight."

"I studied in Paris," Ann theatrically explained, with a faux air of elegant snootiness.

"Let's take all this to Jensen this afternoon."

And decisions were finalized with that meeting. "Well, folks, we have past experience and evidence coming out of the Philippines, Central America, and elsewhere where your ranges will be short due to the foliage, and you can seek such cover when out ranged by the enemy, unless they're lobbing artillery in on you. There may be some scenarios in the mountains involving the need for a long shot. Allan said he will take his Springfield. That 30.06 is big ammo, but we can send enough for one bolt action rifle. But I'm ruling out the BAR, with your agreement, I hope. It uses that same round and gobbles it up. As you know, you will have a reduced squad with you. I'm issuing a M1911 .45 caliber pistols, and an .30 caliber carbines to every one of you, every man and woman, and two extras. Those are lightweight and have good range for in the mountains or anywhere in the open. The Marines will each have a .45 caliber Thompsons, and your headquarters unit will have one. There will be you three officers; 1st Sgt. Morrow; Sgt. Adams: four Marines; and Julio, our Filipino guide. The other Filipino is not going. Then you have more weight and space allowance. Ten personnel; ten .45 pistols; twelve carbines; six .45 Thompsons. It is recommended that the latter are held in reserve for need of heavy rapid closer in fire. Those boys have been trained to shoot correctly to conserve ammunition, as you know because they have been training you in that important skill. The pistol and Thompson share the same .45 ACP round, and the Carbine fires a .30, both effective, both small and lighter weight for shipping than the Browning

Automatic Rifle. The main thing about ammo is it's consumable and we can't do this without it."

"Lt. Allison. You might have the coast watchers choose pistols, leaving more long guns for your arming of Filipinos you recruit. You might give them that choice."

Pausing and looking at his clipboard, as they each looked at him and waited, having memorized everything on their own clipboard's stack of papers.

Finally, he said, "I'm proud of you folks. You're brave Americans thinking how you can maximize your abilities and therefore your roles, thinking of ways to do that. You are all three correct. You're just like everybody else, deserve no more in all this mess, except that you are unique in skills and courage. I agree with you; we need to maximize your footprint. I will try to get as much gear and supplies on that pig boat as I can. Medical care to the natives in the region, support to the guerrillas if you contact any, spying on the Japanese in that important area and those passages, coast watchers . . That's enough for starters . . enough if that's all of it. But that coast is important. We could be sneaking Marine Raiders or Army Rangers in there in significant numbers, when the big push-back begins. Those are groups being created now. Well, the Rangers go back to Roger's Rangers and beyond. The Japs won't expect it. Your information will be invaluable."

"Then you want us to go down overlooking the Straits around Surigao and such?" Ann expressed inquisitively.

Her husband just held back and listened, taking it all in. Allan had the same thoughts but by now wanted to listen to her, the sound of her voice and the insights about these 'manly' matters. He knew to let her loose to run with it as she grasped each concept of the mission beyond the medical and the danger. The more she knew and conceptualized, the more she would know and blindly conceptualize if he wasn't around and she faced whatever… like Ann and Jenny somehow ending up alone in it, through some quirk of fate.

The Marine officer just looked a moment and then said, "It's like you're planning a complicated surgery the night before isn't it?"

"Why yes."

"Those straits around Surigao may become very important someday. I'm not sure when. I will tell you, while you still have time. This war is gonna be longer than everyone thinks. We'll win it, but it will take years. You think about it before you folks get in there and start expecting a child or something.

Now, of course if you encounter the guerrillas, you may have to support them. You'll be in the Wild West; you won't know who to trust unless it is an American organization led by clearly official officers. Don't easily trust all Filipino bands. I love those people, but some are prone to banditry in wild lands. You will very possibly be better equipped than they are and you have good men. Chose the terrain and fight 'em off if they are bad or unusually domineering and authoritarian. Sergeant, you train these folks on the job so they can function tactically if you get knocked out of it.

If you are forced by the enemy's actions and disposition to join a strong group and so choose, you are free to share supplies and work with them. But we want you there doing what we've discussed. Tell them those are your orders and that you are ordered to maintain your ability to do that and defend your selves, unless the enemy forces you away from Surigao del Norte."

~

Allan and Beau stood beside the Aero, which the Colonel had protected from confiscation by claiming its importance for the mutual use by the Americans and British as a private plane with Beau at the controls.

"Are you really comfortable with the Aussie, Beau?"

"I've known him longer than you, next to you, he is my best friend. Your plane is safe. He is tough. But for his gimpy leg, he would be in their military and at the point. He ees tougher than nails, and got the gimp saving my butt."

"'Our' plane. I told the Colonel to get you back west if possible, India and Africa. Nobody on the other side is going to get carriers in there, though the Japs may try to sortie into the Indian Ocean. That worries me a bit, for Elaine. She is headed by plane for Trincomalee, Beau. Go see her, dammit. Be the playboy you claim, but don't play her. I'd never forgive you."

"Eet ees a beautiful harbor."

"Yup. It 'eez' a pretty woman. That's my point. Now look, you're in charge of our plane and business. Please keep to our standards and guidelines. But you make the decisions now for the duration. I don't know your feelings for deep danger, but if they want her back in the show . . back on stage . . you might team up."

The Frenchman nodded. He had become less comical and more pensive and serious recently, probably due to it all, just everything they all faced, the whole world faced, death, separation, distant love, torture, ...

"Beau, we may all get out of this, we may all die, but in life nothing, even a good long, true marriage . . nothing lasts. You might as well face it together and die together. A girl like that, she's gonna run to the chaos, why not be there to protect her and just deal with the bad stuff, the pain together. That's what I'm doing, what I've chosen to do."

181

"Allain, if she gets called into too much danger, and goes, I may park the plane somewhere safe, and tag along."

"Listen, Beau, yes, Elaine is more important than the plane. By all means go with her. If you get to Trincomalee, check on Jake's friend, Jon and that girl Maya. Lt. Cmdr. Shaw had them get married civilly before the *Star of India* left. He left it all in the care of a British major whose family he flew out in return. He asked the Brit to witness it and sign on the marriage certificate. And he, Shaw left a letter tying the two in with our intelligence people. Make sure they got there and see if they need help. There can always be racial issues, and one never knows when those things will pop up out here. She, Maya is Jon O'Brian's wife, he an American citizen and operative as a pilot like us. If he is healed well enough and you can afford three pilots, you might employ him. It will make the watch standing better. George says Elaine has friends there, maybe she won't have problems and can help Maya."

The two shook hands, shared a manly, brotherly hug, stepped back in unison, and saluted each other seriously, as if they were in the military. But private commercial airlines had their protocols too, which included officers and saluting.

~

"I've . . we've, made up our minds what to do with you brave folks, . . uh, where to put you. It will be on the northeast coast of Mindanao, on the Philippine Sea, somewhere around Carrascal Bay I suspect. There are a couple of good-sized islands we can use if necessary, close in to land if you have to paddle.

The Japs took Davao first and there's fighting around Lake Lanao and Central Mindanao. We believe Filipinos and some of our people who refuse any surrender order will gather in the mountains there and resist, as we talked about. Do not talk about that, surrender, outside this room. You folks be discrete, about that possibility when you are in public before you leave for this mission. You are government operatives now, keep quiet in public and privately speak only among yourselves in secure locations."

Looking briefly down at his papers and ever so slightly moving them, Allan thought perhaps in discomfort, perhaps embarrassment over what he was about to say, Col. Jenson looked up and said clearly yet solemnly, "I don't think we can keep the Philippines. We cannot resupply them, and we have no battle fleet. We can only resupply with submarines, a few planes that have gotten through, a very few blockade runners. Those are not likely to get through much longer . . . too much time in daylight in enemy patrolled waters."

He was interrupted by Jenny with a slight emotion in her voice, "I left some nursing sisters in Manila.

Pray for them. All the more I want this now, this mission."

The briefing ended with detailed discussion of the terrain of the whole area, the people, who were mostly Visayans, speaking Cebuano and the region's natives whose Surigaonon language was similar to Cebuano.

The Colonel added, "There are two hill people, hunter gatherer types who you are unlikely to meet because they are more to the South and West of your assigned area. However necessary movements could draw you there. The professor knows them. I study indigenous people a little. It is what I do when I can get a long leave in peacetime and go back up to the Philippines. It is why I want to marry and stay out here. You could encounter Mamanwa speakers near Lake Mainit. It is in your area. They are Negritos who are found in the Philippines and Malaya and some other scattered areas. They are small and dark, thus the name. The tribal people in the Philippines are cultured in the sense they have good family and societal structure and the have a certain level of fashion, intricate weaving and clothing. There are some primitive cultures, but I do not think you will encounter them where you'll be."

As the group stood, the Colonel asked Ann to stay a moment, explaining, "Allan, I have a quick point to cover with your wife, she can share it; I just want her personal view first."

The husband left, closing the door and slightly wondering, and the Marine Officer turned to the medical professional and said, "Lieutenant, I toyed around with giving your husband top rank and you a lieutenant JG, uh, junior grade, but I believe you should rank equally, you being the experienced jungle doctor and all. Now, I know you were in the savanna, but I mean, you're the one with experience with a nation's native people in their own hinterland environment. You're the one who organized and led an expedition. Your husband has the tactical skills and some of his unknown exploits have become legendary among those who know. With your Marine Sergeants and Filipino guide, you will be a well-rounded group. Now, Miss Jenny will have a medical load to carry . . because you will have a share in command beyond the medical. I mean you and Lt. Allison. I've known you a little while now. It doesn't take me long. I know people and how to evaluate them for these types of roles. It's my job."

Interestingly, as she absorbed his words in her mind, there was no: ' . . *so are you ready for this,'* no Girl Scout pat on the back like in the old movies of the Great War, War Between the States, and others, . . just business, a superior officer to a subordinate officer.

She was in uniform but not at attention. It was casual and she simply nodded, saying, "Yes, Sir.". . trying to reveal no particular emotion and remain professional as in her residency days as the new doctor being educated by the old pros.

He added, "Your rank will get you more respect, so wear it. Men in that environment, guerrilla officers, white or Filipino, may be shocked at first . . a female Negro officer, but they can't ignore it. When you're dealing with them, especially the hard-assed ones, let them know it's from Naval Intelligence."

As she turned to go, he said, "Lt. Allison, . . Doctor."

She turned and waited and he said, "When you're out there, don't take any crap off of anyone. I don't want you alone and dragged around by some guerrilla command for their medical purposes. That's why I'm putting you in a useful place on the fringe. And I'll explain more about that when we go down to meet the skipper of the submarine this afternoon. But . . and you listen clear: You are not to be incorporated into their command, unless of a war necessity, and it is your decision. You are to medically assist when necessary and they are operating close to you. And you do not take disrespect from subordinates or superiors. If you are disrespected by a subordinate without an apology, request a court martial for the man. Within your command and your husband's, it's not a request, you order it. If by a superior, file a complaint and carry my name and Shaw's."

Smiling slightly, as if in agreement in principle, and in military obedience, Ann replied, "Yes, Sir."

That evening, the five met at the building housing Col. Jenson office, just outside, for him to take them down to meet the submarine skipper, his executive officer, and the Chief of the Boat.

Jenny's room was next to the couple's, and walking over to meet the colonel, Allan commented to the two women, "The right choices have been made, but I want to enhance security. We have to have a well-guarded perimeter."

"And people on it we can trust . . if we recruit the locals," added the ensign. "We cannot have double agents."

"I regret having fewer fully automatic weapons," he said.

"Dispersion," responded the doctor.

"What?"

The nurse explained, "Dispersion, like in our hospital duty. The basic supplies and equipment, those tools that are mobile, are at each nursing station, in each procedural room, and some in every ward or patient's room."

The doctor then elaborated, "At night, when we bed down. There must be enough men on the perimeter and the machine guns must be scattered around in various peoples' tents or huts, so that there is one near for use at each side, all the way around."

Then the intelligent nurse added, "But do not give them to the sentries. In a sneak attack, if they are overpowered, we've armed the enemy . . and very effectively so."

"You gals have been watching too many movies, westerns, cops and robbers, the Great War . . thank goodness."

The doctor added, "Keep one of the six at the headquarters tent or hut or whatever; have four stationed around each night evenly with sleeping marines; and the sixth with the duty Officer."

"Welcome back Gentlemen and ladies. We'll get right to business because we've got to get you up there before the enemy puts too many patrols in and over the sea lanes. We've got to get rolling so I'll just tell you before we drive down there, be ready to board the sub at 0300 hours Thursday, so early in the morning. Your equipment will be aboard. Others do it differently, but my missions go out at in the wee hours in an attempt to avoid prying eyes.

We've beat this issue of consumables to death. Ensign Barkley had a suggestion late yesterday. She looked for you two but couldn't find you, so she and I discussed it. She has suggested that, because consumables could define the success of this mission, that we drop, eliminate more heavy items in their favor, namely one of the big tents and cots. She suggested taking only the cloth cot covers, and screws with wingnuts, and then using the wood you find or harvest there. A lot of ammo rounds and some more medicines can be accommodated if you do so."

Ann added, "The Ensign and I had discussed this a bit before; it had slipped my mind. The tropical climate portends many parasites in the ground and on it. We are going to want to sleep at least slightly elevated."

"Yes, and as she reminded me, the natives make pretty nice raised houses out of local materials. I've seen them too of course."

Jenny added, "We won't need many blankets on the list in that climate either, even in the mountains, just the lighter ones and sheets, which can become material for emergency bandages. Why not take half of the full cots, to have some immediately, and take the cloth and hardware for the others. We will have to stand watches immediately, probably with half of our compliment on and half off, anyway."

Standing in the twilight of the Northwest Australian coast, Col. Jensen brought up something never mentioned in any meeting, "Should you see fit to organize, . . for whatever reason, based on whatever analysis of the landscape, . . if you see fit to form your own guerrilla movement. You're free to do so. Remember, your position there in Surigao could be crucial as we fight back up that way."

Pigboat to the Philippines

Subs were called 'boats' rather than ships. The 'Chief of the Boat' was the the chief petty officer who was the highest-ranking enlisted man on the sub. The rank itself was the highest enlisted rank in the United States Navy at that time. More recent decades have seen 'senior chief' and 'master chief' added. Those present from the official mission command were Allan, Ann, Jenny, and Marine Corps First Sergeant Harold Morrow. The Filipino guide, Professor Julio Ortega came as well. A unique man, he was of humble roots from the Surigao area and yet had gone on to become a professor.

Walking along the pier, Col. Jensen stated, "Captain Stuart, his exec Lieutenant Montrose, and the chief of the boat have been apprised of your unique team's makeup. They are aware that two of the principles are women. I'm sure none of that will be a problem or would have been, except for the initial surprise had he not been able to brief his crew. The main issue is that submarines are small, cramped, and submerged for long periods. If tensions flare, one cannot go out on deck for fresh air. Nor can they relieve themselves in a private moment over the rail. Pardon me ladies, but bathroom facilities aboard will be sparse and shared as well. You are medical personnel. I felt free to be direct just now."

He commented no further, knowing the captain would figure out the bathroom issue.

Ann immediately picked up on Chief of the Boat, Sam Walker's tough exterior and strong Georgia accent, and as she reached her hand out to offer it to him, hiding her tentativeness, he grasped it with a warm grip, saying, "You two ladies are quite courageous, ma'am. I hope ya'll come back out safely." As they released each other's' hands he added, "It'll be an honor if the *Bangús* is the pigboat to pick you up and return you to base, wherever that might be, if we're still alive to do it."

"Thank you, Chief. The name is unique and sounds of a foreign origin."

"Yes ma'am, Lieutenant. Most subs are named for fish. Most American ones are. The crew was formed before she was named and many of us, including the captain, had served in the Philippines quite a bit. We requested it. It is their name for the very tasty Milk Fish. It contains many fine brush bristle bones, and has to be deboned to be eaten with any ease. If your still in the Islands when this is over, order it fried with a glass of *San Miguel* Beer."

Ann was warmed with a shared camaraderie as her brain processed the knowledge that in some way the war leveled and united people. She had entered the boat expecting a coldness that never materialized. As well, the war would result, years ahead at its end, in a lot of mixed-race marriages, mostly in countries where white, black, and other American men of other ethnicities had fought to save brown people and their ultimately marriageable daughters. But all would not be well with respect to race, and in Port Chicago, California black sailors would be prosecuted for refusing to be the only sailors to have to load a dangerous munitions ship after an earlier explosion had killed many. In the Marianas, in the Pacific, white and black Marines would violently clash over dating rights to native women, including the Chamorro of Guam, who carried a similar beauty and charm to Filipinas on similarly petite and graceful frames and who seemed to want to date both races.

Captain Stuart commented, "Ladies this will be a new experience for us all, but the unusual is becoming commonplace. Submarines are the only way in and out for now. And we've been bringing women out for weeks . . at least over a month. It will be cramped and you may get tense. I have been told you have been warned about this, but nothing but the tower up at Groton, Connecticut can replace being a hundred feet down. Bathrooms will be a bit of a problem. If you are anything like my wife you require counter space."

The doctor replied, "Captain, do not worry about that, Ensign Barkley and I will require very little, only the bare necessities. Ensign Barkley uses little makeup, having a natural beauty she seems happy with; and, as one can see, God has graciously negated my need for blush, or lipstick. I managed to snare this poor fella," grabbing Allan's arm just above the elbow.

With a chuckle, the submarine officer replied, "We will probably simply assign our officers head for you folks and shorten the crew a little. Then I'm going to do what we've done when bringing women out, and put you two ladies in my cabin. It will be crowded but is the best option. We are working the problem now to see how many we can do without and still function safely. We're carrying fewer torpedoes but enough for self-defense. Your gear and supplies will be everywhere. We'll all just have to remember to step high and climb. We received it and the crew packed it carefully and compactly."

The next three days included a lot of range time and simply rest and conversation. During one moment of the latter, Ann confided in Allan, "I hope Jenny is going to handle this trip with all these men in this thing that seems not much more than a small over used capsule. We've inconvenienced these men already and we haven't left, what with all our gear. You know we were stumbling over it the other night and they're not even finished."

"Well, you did insist on the level of ammunition stock of an army base. They're probably stacking in the spaces behind the toilets, ur . . 'in the heads' as we speak."

". . . and just those two tiny heads. I'm just glad I don't have my period."

"It will be okay."

"There are two of us different intruders."

"Ann, subs are pulling people off now as much as they can. Some are families, some women are pregnant. This is a crisis, 'all for one and one for all.' Just imagine if you were one of these American mining engineers' wives, maybe pregnant, maybe with a teenage daughter or two, and maybe he stayed behind to fight. These boys will be gentlemen, even the ones who generally aren't. People rise to the occasion."

The voyage was completely under the ocean surface in daylight with surface running at night to charge the batteries that ran the electric motors when submerged. They were charged by the diesel engines that propelled the boat on the surface where those internal combustion engines could breathe air. This was the same as the method of charging a car battery with a gas engine powered generator in that era and alternators in more recent times. While still closer to friendlier territory and least likely to encounter an enemy plane or ship, the three of them were allowed up on deck very briefly for fresh air and the experience.

Once, several days outbound, in the Celebes Sea, during the last chance for the passengers to be on deck while the sub was running on the surface in daylight, a plane was spotted, and in a sub, in wartime and near enemy controlled waters, you do not stay around to verify friend or foe. Tough Sergeant Morrow was below, having made runs like this before and the three officers on deck heard the dive alarm, the submarine's iconic *"ahooga"* blast followed by the repeated command to clear the decks. Running to the forward hatch that was nearest and near the bows, the three, Allan last, disappeared into the forward torpedo room as the commands came through the boat on the com system and were answered in conformation. Once the forward torpedo room had reported the hatch closed, the command "Dive, dive" was heard.

Their hearts were pounding less with fear, though it was present, but more with the excitement and the respect for the men manning the little courageous vessel, one that the Germans called an 'Iron Coffin' because of the many they lost with full crews. As naval officers now, ones who had legally cheated to get there and had religiously studied the manuals on regulations and protocol, they felt they belonged. And this being their first and maybe only voyage in Navy uniforms, the felt it deeply. The three even watched themselves to not be overly 'Navy regulation' in a corny way. They wanted to fit in, knowing many sailors were not serving at sea, and thus, their positions were normal.

~

The Aero touched down in the night just after sunset was complete on the little secondary field on the outskirts of Trincomalee and Beau felt a pull he had never felt before. All it had taken was to know . .

the validation, odd for such a suave man with the ladies. Maybe the nerves kicked in when It was important.

He went straight to the hospital and learned that Jon O'Brian was there and healing, that he couldn't see him now because of the time, and that his Malayan wife had not been in to see him in two days and had missed work that particular day. She was working in the hospital, and the staff and Jon were worried about her. Next the two, Beau and the Aussie, Arnie, went to the bar and cafe district and asked around about both women of concern to them. She wouldn't be there of course, Elaine, but they would know, . . a woman like that. Everyone told them to inquire in the Chinese businesses about Maya. Rather than seek rooms in these tumultuous times they went back to sleep on the plane, for the security of it.

The next morning, cleaned up at a public shower and dressed better than flight clothes, the two men went to grab breakfast. Beau planned to have seafood coffee and biscuits, the former seeming a bit odd perhaps, but they were sitting in one of the world's most beautiful and peaceful harbors and one, then unspoiled by growth. To make it more breakfast appropriate, especially given his years of often sharing his American boss's habits, Beau also had his heart set on fried fish and chips. He would calm himself and find her after a good morning refueling with high octane coffee to steel the nerves. He at least had a good reason now, for she could surely help seek out Maya and sleuth the problem if she was not able to be found.

To achieve this breakfast, guided by the locals, they found themselves in a very nice little cafe for the purpose with a patio by the water, and lo and behold, there sat Elaine by herself at the far edge of the breezy outdoor dining area just in a corner closest to the sea. Looking around the light morning crowd of generally well-appointed folk at least above the lowest crowd, Beau noticed what he expected, every male in the place, even those with a woman, kept stealing glances at the exotic Oriental at the distant corner table.

As Arnie sat and he was still standing he spoke softly saying "Let me go speak with her alone."

With a soft chuckle the Aussie nodded, and Beau turned toward Elaine's table and the observant woman waved 'hello' and then 'come over', and the Frenchman was the instant envy of every male in the place. Approaching the small round table, he was surprised maybe only slightly that she stood and embraced him in the way of good friends and family. They were the former and somewhat the latter. Troubles, and certainly those on a worldwide scale, drew people closer.

"Eet ees so good to see you again, Elaine. I thought South Africa would be the last time for a long time."

"Me too, until Simpson told me of Allan's plans. Then I expected you back, unless he took your plane away."

"I hope we weel be near more often."

"I as well, Beaumont. I have wanted to talk with you for some time."

"Of what, Mademoiselle?"

"Everything." Then pausing she added, "What thankfully brings you here now?"

"Ees there a problem?"

"Loneliness. I know no one here. My friends have left on an assignment. They are language teachers too. We are a commodity right now, especially if we know Japanese and German or those of any of the captured and occupied lands."

"I have a problem in which you might be able to help. The girl Maya, of which you may have been informed, is missing. I assumed George might have told you of the couple."

"Beaumont, these are my students," the woman said as two men walked up. "They are friends of Mister Simpson. But it has been so long. I will dismiss them."

She stood, walking up to the two men approaching her table, and spoke briefly and quietly; and, with a smile, the men left, having coffee elsewhere on the patio.

Returning Elaine elaborated, "They are Simpson's men. Our course is done. They only need some final advice and the like. Then I am done and bored until the next."

"Thees ees a good place to be bored, one of the world's most beautiful ports."

"When you fly out, I will only have a few acquaintances. I am used to being surrounded by friends back home, some almost as good as Allan and you."

He glanced up from his coffee and then back down, so as not to show her. He had known her as long as Allan had, yet had not become really close, although a closeness develops with one you see often, speaking or not. The contact had been there afterward, as he often answered her calls to Allan over the year or so since they had been in the Philippines less and therefore Indochina less.

"So, Beaumont, what of your copilot?" she avoided 'boss'.

"Married and doeeng things I cannot speak of yet. That ees Arnie over there, my copilot for now. Allain left me in charge. I need your help. I'm looking for a friend of Allain who should be here." Then Beau told her all he knew of the young couple affected so by the war already.

"I saw her, perhaps her, in the Chinese shops a week ago. We will inquire there. We have all day after we eat. Let us go."

"What makes you think eet is her?"

"She is one of few Malaysians here and she spoke of her American Navy husband in the hospital."

"Certainly, let us go then. After we eat. Shall I order now?"

"Oui, I have already."

Their food came one after the other but close and both ate silently, as words are not as necessary as many think when close friends are together.

At one point, the pilot looked up at her, his coffee cup in hand, and said, "You would not be lonely if you flew with us. The Aero ees a comfortable mobile home, and we stay in good hotels otherwise, better if a lady ees weeth us. Eet ees an interesting life and you could be our manager, taking some stress from just two pilots. Arnie is an old trusted friend, and safe. I knew him before I knew Allain."

"Do you travel with ladies often," she teased.

Turning red, he replied, "Eet was speculative, Mademoiselle. But we flew the African American doctor to Singapore and Darwin."

It was learned in the tiny Chinatown that Maya had been asked to consider a part time job for a few weeks as an English teacher to the children of a rich Chinese businessman. She had told a friend, a shopkeeper that she was wondering if she could do it and still handle the nursing work, since the teaching would only be for a month. Maya hadn't been seen since. It was small as ports go and a less developed time all over the world. Information came quickly, because there was less of it.

Searching there could pass quickly as well, and an hour later found the three before the door of the man. Inquiring of the maid, nothing was learned but denials, which countered earlier information.

No one spoke as the three, including Arnie for more support if anything went wrong, had taken a taxi up to the fine house of the business man.

Earlier, nearing their destination, Elaine, who had been thinking it all out, said, "Who takes a language course for a month, especially children? Such courses are usually refresher courses for adults, possibly prior to travel. Who is traveling very much now? Trincomalee is a British port. Everyone here speaks English, their own language and English."

With that analysis, the three tried not to reveal their suspicion as they walked up to the door. That lasted only until the Chinese maid adamantly rebuffed their every polite request about Maya and to see the man of the house.

"I demand to see the owner!" Beaumont surprised everyone, even his companions, with his near arrogance.

The Chinese maid vacillated between anger and trembling in fear, and was off. Soon an angry, portly Chinese man came to the door in his silk pajamas. It was early evening, by this time, as their sleuthing had taken up the day.

"What do you think you are doing," the man said while trying to exude to the intruders the same level of importance he saw in himself.

"Looking for a girl?"

"Well this isn't the bars district and I see you have a fine one already." Then, being rude to make a point, he inquired, "What does she charge?" A woman appearing to be his wife was now present and he didn't spare her feelings.

"Thees ees a woman who came here inquiring about employment and has not been seen since. She ees the wife of a military man, so of importance to us."

"And who is 'us' Frenchie?"

To which Beau pulled out a leather breast pocket wallet from inside his vest, it being too warm for a sports coat or dress jacket. Opening it, he revealed an American FBI identification that appeared official in every way, though of course it wasn't.

"You're French."

"An immigrant."

"You have no jurisdiction here?"

"We have agreements between allies for now that our men are deployed in each other's lands and territories, the emergency, you see, and I have thees," and reaching to his belt on his right, he slid forward the holster and its .45 Government contents.

The man was the arrogant type one finds among some of the well off in any culture, a type that neither defines the culture, ethnicity, nor people of wealth, the latter who are often some of the world's most generous. He still looked back in anger and doubt, yet doubt both ways, and the daring pilot added, "Have you seen any American gangster movies my friend. I listen to thees [patting the gun] and my heart, and a woman is in danger. And I am French . . as you say." Catching the man's continued glances, uncontrollable as any man's near Elaine, Beau added, "Yes, she ees an agent as well."

203

The man still blocked the door, hesitating, and Beau said, "I'll drop you where you stand and your wife and maid. The only unfriendly witnesses will not be alive to talk. I have a gun for their hands too, as for yours."

With the obvious inference of he and his women being seen the aggressors, in this shakedown and not being alive to do anything about it, the man stood aside and thought to grab Elaine as the threesome entered. But the Aussie stopped and stood with him, saving him from dying on the petite woman's stiletto.

Turning to the man, Beau suggested, "We can make this simple, produce the woman. I have a writ of habeas corpus in my pocket."

"My wife is calling down to the government offices as we speak."

To that Beau held up a piece of what appeared to be the home's telephone wire.

"You're not official, you wouldn't behave like that, cutting a wire!"

Playing on the importance of the airline and Elaine to the government as his ultimate backup, Beau continued his charade, "We would to prevent a problem with our small force against your servant staff, which I weell wager are from old Chinese gangs in Shanghai. But we are official in a deeper

sense than you want to know or deal weeth. There is
a war on. Now produce the woman or we weell tear
your house apart. I guarantee that anything we do
weell go unnoticed . . we are that official."

Maya was produced from a back bedroom, and her
hands were bound at the wrist.

To that state of affairs, Beau, smiled and said,
"I thank your stupid servants for this piece of
evidence." And he raised the Leica dangling from
his neck and snapped her picture with the Chinese
businessman just behind her in the frame.

"Now, sir, you weell come with us to be processed.
Your husband weell be back soon, Mademoiselle.
This is on a different level. Do not call the local
authorities from a neighbor. It weell cause more
trouble for heem in the long run."

In the cab back down the slope, with the cabbie
appropriately bribed, Beau, said to Elaine, "Let me
talk to heem."

"Pull over here, driver."

Taking the man into the field in the darkening
twilight, dangling cuffs he had not yet threatened to
use, he wanted to maintain the man's dignity for
possible future use and to blunt repercussions at that
moment and soon after. But at that moment, still
unsure of how official he was in custody and at the

205

hands of whom, fear of impending execution seeped into the businessman.

"Listen, sir. We are een a war now, all of us together. I don't care what things you have your hands een, but as a man now, we must stand together against these Japanese, who have temporarily lost their minds. Eet ees your country and your women they are raping wholesale. That girl, she has a name, 'Maya', and your treatment of her, had you proceeded, would be as bad as the damn Japs, . . only perhaps less brutal. Eet is only a saving grace, that you were holding her unteel she weallingly complied. Sir, eef you do business here weeth prostitutes, please hire ones that want eet, but do not force others." Then stereotypically revealing one of the positives of his French nature, he said, "What else do we leeve for."

Pausing he looked in the man's eyes, and the businessman said, "I am angry at my treatment; I have a small force of 'servants' as you say," emphasizing the faux label.

"The taxi will take you up the hill. Tell your wife the affair will be forgotten. She is a beautiful Hmong; treat her as she deserves. They are a fine, proud people. Treat a woman well, and you weel only need one. . ." Reaching his hand out for a handshake, which the man reluctantly and tentatively took, Beau evaluated the situation, "You have six 'servants', from the Shanghai group that controlled that city for decades, even held it

206

together at times. I have dealt weeth them and worked weeth them and fear them so leettle that we will now stroll slowly home and give you the prepaid car. I have always been welcome among them and bear a tattoo to facilitate such."

Still holding the Frenchman's hand, the businessman looked up with some surprise he now could not hide. Looking back with uncharacteristic cold, unblinking eyes, his adversary said in a monotone, "Three followed us in your smaller car, the Austin, one clinging to the boot. They are trying to stay out of sight around the last bend on the hill there, but the last glare of sunset is lighting up the bumper like a searchlight over London in the Blitz last year. I trained with the Legion a decade ago."

Beau reached out his other, left hand, and as much as it detested him, laid it on the other's shoulder. And just at that moment the scoundrel also looked toward the car, obviously at the one thing of interest there to any man's eyes.

Beau calmly replied to the unspoken question, "She ees a government assassin, but I can't tell you for certain which ones. But for the action of my copilot, you would have died on her blade back there in your entryway." It bothered him not to say it. He figured they would be gone soon and said as much. "We may be reassigned, but we leave companions behind. Leave our American sailor and hees Malaysian wife alone."

~

It was very dark; however, there was some unwanted moonlight due to delays. The submarine could not come in close due to the depth, and she sat offshore about forty yards and ferried the supplies to shore with her little launch. Everyone whispered if they spoke at all, as they went through the routine as briefed. The farm girl in Ann wanted to help lift and carry, but these sailors knew their work, as they had been doing it through three supply voyages to the Philippines now. Wind was whipping up and there was concern as the launch with its low freeboard was a bit hard to handle now in a slight chop. Allan had set the order of offloading and it led off with personal packs and weapons. There followed in order; ammunition, small arms; Ann's surgical tools; basic medicines; more key medical supplies; food; tents and bedrolls. As fate would have it, the chop increased enough to play a role just as the bridge reported a possible vessel in the distance. The order was quickly whispered to get to sea.

Something created an almost exaggerated sense of urgency in the seamen, and Ann could feel it and realized these brave men might be thinking they could lose their boat on the surface in this impromptu 'port of call'. She watched now in near horror as the launch attempted a quick course change to return to the sub and was caught by a suddenly larger wave than the chop they had been fighting. It foundered, and the cargo shifted, sliding overboard and sinking. Meanwhile the sailors, fully dressed in jeans and light blue shirts pulled with all their might to swim ashore, the *Bangús* being too far and already beginning to turn seaward. Ann and all of them had been warned of this, and she watched some of their precious canned goods and the tents head to the bottom of the little bay. Luckily it had been the last load.

Moments later, Allan consoled her, "We have our instruments, bandages, ammo, medicines, firearms . . all the important things. But if we're undisturbed, we will dive for it tomorrow. All that was lost was replaceable food, tents, and alcohol. But I think we can retrieve it all. Even with tents, we'll build shelters."

"Dive?"

"It's only about 15 to 20 feet."

Semi-embraced, each holding the other's upper arms with both their hands, she replied, "Tell me again why all those food supplies were not in the first boatloads and our tools in the one that went down."

"...because we would be standing here now with no way to build anything, shelter, and all that. Survival in a wilderness and a war zone comes first, then the assigned duty. Without the tools we couldn't prepare anything, we couldn't even chop firewood. And, the canned goods are safe there for now."

The sub had pulled away and they had heard her submerge out in the bay in the darkness, heard the rushing sound she made as her tanks filled with the ocean and her massive hull pushed the sea out of the way, displacing it as the gray lady sank down to go to battle.

In the slight glow of moonlight, they saw the conning tower drop out of sight and it all seemed so eerie, even ghostly in the tropical darkness of an enchanted land in the middle of a massive worldwide historical upheaval. Ann shivered and thought briefly of the many legendary stories she had squeezed in between the readings for her medical degree, the Arthurian legends and the Trojan War, even Treasure Island. Magellan's and Columbus's encounters with new tropical lands had been among her wide readings as well, the former's having not ended well right here in the Philippines.

For some long while everyone stood in the darkness, barely lit by the moon, and watched seaward catching occasional flashes of moonlight on low waves. Suddenly the horizon, close due to their low point of view, lit with orange and red, and moments later the rumbling thunder of a significant explosion on the surface of the water hit their ears. Everyone sighed with relief, assuming the destruction of the submarine would at least have been a muffled submarine (under the sea) explosion, if light from it reached them at all. Apparently the brave and well-trained submariners had completed a periscope sighting, a target solution, and a kill, in spite of the defective torpedoes that were only now being discovered throughout the Navy's supplies in the Pacific.

They stared for long moments, and then there was an eruption of surface gunfire, which they could just see flow back and forth, some flashes nearer some far.

She gasped and put her hand to her mouth with the tiny bright explosions and the violence of the sound even so far away. And he heard her whisper, "I caused this."

Standing behind her staring, hands on her shoulders as in a cinema scene, yet not melodramatically, as they both stood and stared seaward, Allan said, "You can't think like that. It's not your fault. This is not my fault, and the mission was my idea. They were coming to the islands anyway. It's what they do; we don't know if they're losing out there."

"But not right here. This is because of me, . . us."

"You and I could not have known."

"That's not what you said in Africa. You tried to talk me out of it. I lost them too."

"It happens, it just happens. I never said the African expedition was wrong; I just didn't want my girl hurt on it. If those boys out there weren't fighting here, they would be somewhere else. It's their job."

A long quiet moment ensued, and then the husband said, "A leader, an officer cannot shoulder the blame for each man lost. Good wars, necessary ones would never be fought. Crap just happens."

There was a flash on the water far off, and then a big distant noise came toward them.

"Now you can worry less. I think they got 'em. That was too far way to be the sub. They do not make that kind of headway underwater. They're surfaced now in a gun battle and closer than that explosion."

The two abandoned sailors awaited the ship's return through the night, and in the morning their forlorn look was apparent.

"Come with me, Ann, let's speak to them."

"Do you think they want me, will respond, I mean..."

"You're an officer and one of the commanders here. Get into the role now. No more time for doubts. We're here." Smiling he joked, "Those two swabbies are awfully young; don't forget you're a woman too."

The two of them walked up to the two sailors who were sitting forlornly on a fallen coconut log and talking quietly, probably discerning their future and absorbing their fate.

"Sailors," Ann addressed them first after her initial hesitancy.

They looked up at her, dressed in everyday Navy khaki. She had decided on it when she arose that morning from a brief nap, figuring there would be little chance to dress such in the future. Her officer's insignia was apparent, and after a moment's pause, the two jumped and saluted.

Returning their salute, she said, "At ease, I wore this just to keeps us all connected to the service in this far, wild place." Turning to Allan she asked, "How do you think last night might have turned out, Lieutenant, since they did not come back?"

"I believe there is a good chance the *Bangús* won that, but they could not risk remaining here and coming back into the shallows. Maybe there are several Japanese units patrolling and they didn't want to push their luck. I think the first and last explosions were torpedo kills."

With his pause, one of the sailors replied, "Sirs, . uh, ma'am, the captain said as much to us. That it could happen this way. He said any man caught ashore would become part of your command, which is Navy too."

She continued, having taken the hint from her husband and taken a motherly roll. Both sailors were about twenty. "We all know what you are feeling. I believe they are fine. That was clearly a distant explosion, too distant to be the sub. They must have won the battle. With such a display Capt. Stuart must have decided he must leave this area before enemy forces gathered."

Allan, interjected, "They're alright, surely, and you are as well. We will welcome you in our small force. It is risky here..."

"As it was in your former berth," interjected Ann.

"Yes, sailors. The Lieutenant is correct. Now what are your ratings?"

They spoke in unison, one indicating medical corpsman and the other a seaman and deckhand. The latter was training as a gunner's mate.

"Well, until they return and if they do not return, we'll reassign you: you with the doctor here and you with the me. I could use another gunner with me, so as not to draw from the marine squad's manpower. I know naval gunnery is a very different thing but the concepts are the same." Corpsman, what is your rank?"

"Petty officer second class, sir."

"Well, we'll raise that to first class, and, Seaman, you to Petty Officer third class."

Ann spoke to the corpsman, "Petty Officer, First Class . . ?" looking inquisitively.

"David Johnston, Ma'am."

"...Johnston, when you feel ready, report to Ensign Barkley, our nurse, you know."

"Yes Ma'am."

"Gentlemen, you take some time to get yourselves together if you need longer after that wild night. But don't take too long. we've a camp to build and work helps."

Things were peaceful so far, and they knew they were probably not in immediate danger. Their companions were trustworthy and the landing point was far from the war. Now, they had to carry everything inland and upland and protect it. Then, when a location was found, they had to set up where they would be unable to be seen from the air and ready to function.

As the day began, following the guidance of Julio Ortega, the professor from that region, the leaders shared the load and helped the supplies to be transferred up the hill to the first base. Three stages were planned to protect all of the gear, three chosen camp sites, one to be achieved each day, though finalizing them would take time. Day one was to get the gear to a temporary base camp. Day two was to move most higher and safer, leaving the original camp as a coast watching outpost. Day three was to move extra supplies to a safe hideout type of camp. This might seem like a rushed plan to those not familiar with the preparation: however, sites had already been picked out in Darwin by Professor Ortega who was from the local area and had family ties to some of the hill people who still lived their native ways. He was *Surigaonon*, the modern native people of *Suriga*o, not an ethnic minority, but his family roots were very rural and his studies had led him to the *Mamanwa* people around *Lake Mainit*, one group of *Negrito*.

Each camp site had been preselected well for the reasonable expectation that moving the supplies could be completely each day by the available personnel. Therefore, at the end of the third day, the team was in their permanent location with all of their supplies. Care had been taken the first morning, and after that, the patrol boats the *Bangús* had battled did not have companions who might land soldiers to attack them.

The chosen primary camp was in an area of former native habitation and was not in an overwhelmingly, thick jungle. It was secluded, from the air, but in livable forest.

Also, the commanders, with Julio's help, knew where they would retire to in retreat and where beyond that; their escape route back doors from each; their ammunition stashes at each; and the two planned lookout positions for their coast watching activities.

Ammunition to be stored was packaged so as to be protected from the humid environment, which required a brown waxed paper cover and tins. Each of the three officers was delegated an area of expertise and control beyond their main specialty. Thus, Jenny was in charge of the supply chain from storage to be transported out by a sailor or marine for use within the camp, requiring her to monitor amount in use at the beginning, depletion rate, resupply rate, amount of time from retrieval from storage, preparation, and depletion of stock.

Ann, granddaughter of farmers was tasked with planning and supervision of production of natural foods, Allan tasked with controlling all scouting and exploration of the area around them, and Sgt. Morrow was in charge of defense. In the beginning, Julio was tasked with contacting of trustworthy locals and recruiting some worthy local men who could add to their force and increase the command's eyes and ears. The plan was to be able to grow the command's force by increments of five up to fifteen locals if needed by the presence of a significant enemy force. With the force of ten that landed, that would make a total of twenty-five. The two sailors from the *USS Bangús* increased the U.S. personnel to a dozen and the planned total to twenty-seven.

A large lean-to for speed of construction had been built at each base up from the beach for emergency shelter, with a front closure and a lower back wall instead of none, thus decreasing the extreme roof pitch. Bamboo poles made into pipes helped devise water collection devices from the rain runoff.

They were settled in, and the camp looked well organized. The men of the marine squad with them were as good as there were at that point in the war, and they were volunteers and men who knew the islands. Three had been born there. Ann and Jenny had finished setting up their medical stations: an examining area, an operating area, and a delivery area for native women and American women refugees. Defensive concerns had been addressed as well. Ann had walked the perimeter, ducking into the forest at times, seeking the wistful spots of sunshine poking through the heavy cover. The canopy was high in some places and always impressive, and she was overwhelmed inside though calm without.

At first, none had thought of food on the first day after identifying the location, for they immersed themselves into their work. They ate late. In the early darkness of the tropical evening, Ann sat now in a hammock, her forearms on her thighs and her legs dangling over the side. Her hands were together, and she looked off into the night across the little camp. There was little to show a camp because that was the plan and there was only a lantern light inside each tent, well shielded. To her it seemed dreary and and tensely dramatic.

Allan walked through the empty, almost nonexistent courtyard coming near her perch without seeing, yet sensing her presence near him. Ann was brown not the near black of some Africans, but she was several shades darker than most Filipinos. Thus, he was near her, sensed her, wanted her, and could not tell where she was. Just as she reached to push his shoulder and play the trick that had become hers as long as it was random enough to be unpredictable, Allan saw her shapely tawny leg and foot and turned to embrace her.

The two, tired now as everyone, sat side-by-side in the strong hammock. Not a word was said for the longest time. For an interminable time, perhaps an hour, they contemplated the night, their purpose, the situation they had put themselves in, and the peace of the tropical forest night in the midst of war.

"I'm scared . . it's natural I know. Like you said, the reality of the dangers are in front of us now . . and around us, all around."

"You've been there. That's why I gave in."

"Why am I scared?"

"Because you've been there and you're going back, and such women and men do scary things because they have to, because if they don't, they won't forgive themselves for not stepping up when their country and humanity called for it. But the most courageous are afraid."

She turned and looked at him pensively in the night.

After long moments, Ann said, "You know it is the unknown. That is the basis of fear. Certain risk is too, but it is the unknown."

Allan avoided 'I told you so' and said, "Ann you're the one to do this, you were right in demanding to come. You are the person for this job. It doesn't lessen my worries, but it is the right way."

"I'm not that afraid, Allan. I want you to know that. I'm afraid like I was in Africa . . once I got there. It is a natural fear. Don't you worry about me. I won't let you down."

"I know that."

They sat a while not talking and at some point, he broke the silence, "Well, look at you now, anyway: hospital director, medical director, chief surgeon, your own nursing staff with no rotations, . . ."

"And corridors of green."

"As is your doctor's coat," Allan said, smiling cheerfully.

Looking down, she replied, "Olive drab in the sunlight. They labeled it correctly. Nothing cheery about it." As the tropical wilderness at their current elevation had taken on a slight chill of night, the woman had thrown a long-sleeved fatigue shirt on.

Contact with organized American and Filipino guerrillas was the next order of business, for Allan and Morrow both had very beneficial Philippines experience. They were having coffee and conferring one afternoon at the rustic outdoor dining table some distance from everything else for the diners' privacy.

"People know we're here, obviously." The speaker was 1st Sgt. Morrow. "We cannot control who they tell, but we can assume they will be prudent. Supposedly they have proven themselves already up to this point."

"...no one can predict what happens when our presence is known."

"Right, Lieutenant. Word of it can stir the enemy's ire and cause disloyal Filipinos to report our location and movements. The Japanese are preventing crops from being grown in some lowland areas. That can only be to make people suffer. They surely won't shorten their own rations. They are very strangely brutal conquerors. Since we have been here, we have heard the stories of the Japanese brutality."

"It is the underlying story here and wherever they conquer. We cannot just be a medical sanctuary; we have to be a part of the fight but remain somewhat protectively isolated."

"This will be harder than I thought. I do not mean we have to become actual soldiers. That could endanger our mission. Allan, Sir, you have our orders that make that clear, don't you?"

"I do."

"We are ready now for defensive emergencies? I noticed Jenny's . . Ensign Barkley's simplicity. Her family . . they're all campers."

"We were raised that way." the speaker was Jenny, as the two women had just walked up with coffee. "I still do it with like-minded nurse friends. I have everything set up so we can move quickly and take all the essentials. I had a meeting with the marines, which I rather enjoyed. There are a couple of good lookin' fellas in this group. It was kinda swell instructing them and hearing the 'Yes ma'ams' and such. Very respectable fellas. I had sorta forgotten my lieutenant rank until they started replying to me as an officer."

"You know, this is all new to them. There are few women in the military . . any branch, and fewer officers. I believe doctors and nurses are the only ones, but I heard rumors before we left Australia that there may eventually be women's auxiliary units," Allan commented.

"I intentionally let my guard down at the end . . they had been so respectful to me and my rank."

"How did that go?"

"Young corporal Benson offered to leave everything behind even his mother's picture, if he could carry my pack for me. Sergeant Adams, that big strapping handsome guy, said the only thing he considered essential was us two gals and he figured Allan would take care of you, Ann, and he could carry me. But he said the agreement must ultimately end in carrying me across the proverbial 'threshold'."

"Well, you asked for it," laughed Allan.

1st Sergeant Morrow chuckled adding, "I may have to speak to Sgt. Adams, chain of command and restrictions about fraternizing with officers, you know."

~

Beau and Elaine sat on the patio at the same cafe' as always and summed up their state of affairs.

"Beau, you must protect your plane."

"But I do not want to draw attention to ourselves. Positioned oddly eet weell do so."

"I'm telling you now. Listen to me."

Looking up from his coffee that he had been staring into with some surprise, he inquired, "Elaine?"

"I hear things, Beau. Things not of my concern, but things the British may not give credence to. I'm telling you, get the Aero off of the field and under cover, natural cover."

Later in the day when they had taxied it over under a very far patch of trees, the move was explained by their desire to both sleep and work on the plane for an extended time out of the way of all others and in the shade.

A some few days later, planes roared over: carrier bombers over the airfield and fighters circling for protection. The Japanese fighters engaged by their British counterparts, defended the bombers, and, noticing resistance waning, joined the attack by strafing targets. Elaine had won him over now and he would forever take her advice as seriously as any other, no matter from whom. Trincomalee's harbor was a scene of destruction, and the Allies around the world were shocked at Japan's arrogance and projection of power into the Indian Ocean. Would the little island nation try to drive the other, historically powerful, little island nation, from the Indian Ocean? Colombo had been hit as well.

The next day, the two were on the phone with George Simpson's man in New Delhi. "Austin, can we leave without getting shot down?"

"I cannot give tactical information, and I have none anyway."

"But we just want clearance, notice of safe passage."

"And you know I can't give that because I do not know it. One must be on our ships to know it, and from hour to hour their information waxes and wanes."

They thought that was not true or that the British truly had lost the enemy carrier force. That was possible because they did not have as many planes as the Japanese carrier force, that the Laotian woman had predicted to Beau days before.

"Geeve me something, Austin."

"I can't. But I should not expect you until the end of the week. Let us confirm tomorrow. Perhaps the weather will clear, at least north and west of us."

The next morning, the two were quiet as they finished the first cup that had accompanied a light breakfast; and then, as he ordered a second for them both, the pensive woman summed up her thoughts out loud, but quietly.

"We should go. . .We should go before another attack comes and we are the last plane left and confiscated."

Without looking up, as the fellow took his coffee delicately fashioned with just the right combination of cream and sugar, Beau said, "Eet ees risky. I keep thinking we may have flown over that fleet coming here. We know not when they entered the Indian Ocean."

"The Japanese are far from their bases. They have fuel issues. Even if they stay in the Indian Ocean a while, I doubt the will go west of Ceylon."

"That would be to go west of India. We'll gamble."

"We will be gamblers, Dear . . as long as we are in this war."

He had not yet acted in any demonstratively romantic way toward her, yet the warmth of the friendship had quickly stoked and the casual term of endearment warmed him.

"Beau, we could be stuck here or wait and then struggle to get on a steamer and face the U-boat risk."

"Elaine, that does not worry me. We need to be een India, just across the channel. My worry is losing the plane and having to walk there and having no business when we do."

"Oui, but the RAF lost Blenheims yesterday. Before they think of it, we have to get out of here with your plane."

"Our plane. Allain's, Ann's, yours and mine. Call Austin, Elaine. He said he would be near the phone thees morning. Tell heem our plan and ask for clearance these boys here cannot override. I weel geet her ready. Geet clearance for Jon and Maya O'Brian. Then go and see them, try to geet them to agree to go."

When the Aero took off in the wee hours of darkness before midnight, with clearance, a second team to face that current world crisis was perhaps loosely formed. For if personalities and current needs of the potential members meshed, and also matched the needs of those who might hire them, there would be a certain symmetry a certain completeness. With Jon healed, the plane would have a three-pilot rotation, plenty of muscle for cargo handling and any combat scenario, an onboard fight nurse in the person of charming and quiet Maya, and a language specialist with espionage experience and more deadly skills. On a whim and without clearance with Allan, Beau had taken the spare parts, tools, and two spare engines from the hanger in Darwin. He figured Allan was leaving the airline to him and his hands were capable of the task. The Japanese might reach Darwin, and then what would they do. Perhaps the experienced and worldly-wise man sensed the creeping doom of the Imperial Japanese military and instinctively realized he might not be able to get the Aero back to Australia. If so, he was correct as the enemy conquest almost seemed to follow the fight of the plane down through Indochina to the Bay of Bengal and Andaman Sea, as it also spread eastward through the Dutch East Indies to British New Guinea.

Looking back later, historians might have realized that Axis victories that had been denied in North Africa and on the Horn and an invasion of Ceylon that failed to be carried out would have drawn an Axis clamp or pincers around Asia and Europe, with the tips of the pincers being held apart only by Southern Africa and India. And, even as the Aero flew across the channel to India, as the British planned a future invasion from northern India into enemy held Burma, that enemy was planning to return the favor, even to succeed first and then possibly conquer India. Britain, alone among European nations, could have been left on the outside looking in, as Russia (the allied Soviet Union) was being choked within the pincer from the Arctic to the Arctic on east and west. The world, everybody, would have then been waiting and watching to see what help might come from the two American continents.

~

In the mountains of Surigao del Norte, the next level of activity was to become a medical aid to the people around them, who would also become their eyes and ears in return. They realized that any mountain peoples may have fled their arrival. As to villages, the leaders realized that they might have to go lower in elevation to find larger towns.

With the trust the commanding officers had in the men they had selected they left them behind and went together to better evaluate matters. Often Jenny remained as well. The goal on any such given day was simply contact and knowledge from lower in elevation than their immediate surroundings.

On the second such exploration the command group came across a former domicile, a small plantation as it were that had apparently succumbed to the war. However, there had been no Japanese encroachment that high that they were aware of. All the leaders were present including 1st Sgt. Morrow, Professor Julio Ortega, and Jenny. Sgt Adams 'held the fort'.

Entering the clearing they saw partially burned buildings of native material and store-bought wood. Walking deeper into the meadow, they saw debris scattered and the look of violence. Then the women saw it, saw them and ran to the bodies. They were burned, some of them, and they had been dead for a few hours. The wood of the buildings was still slightly smoking. Ann and Jenny were strong women, and they were yet overwhelmed. They were life savers and there was nothing here to be done, and both, with hands to mouths dropped to their knees over the women victims yet professionally controlled their urge to cry.

Allan and 1st Sgt. Morrow walked the property, concluding there was essentially a family wiped out. They counted an elderly woman, a couple in perhaps their mid-forties, a young man and two young women, one perhaps a teen. The females had all been violated and not burned, as if left as trophies. Going through the buildings, one obviously the home, the evidence revealed Japanese culture. The faces of the young women, who had not been burned like the men and the old woman had, revealed them to be Japanese. The Japanese settlement of parts of the Philippines, and especially the 'frontier lands' of Mindanao, as the Cebuanos and other Visayans had done during the American Colonial period, was known history. Whether the Japanese were planted agents or sympathizers with the current military government in Tokyo, were just loyal to their homeland, or were happily American colonial subjects at the time the war broke out, who could have known without investigating and interviewing each one?

Obviously, the perpetrators were not Japanese and apparently those in command of the attacking force did not care for proper procedures, whatever evidence they might have garnered. Raping and murdering women was not proper method of operation with any American force or on any crime procedural list in any civilized law enforcement office in the world.

Bodies were buried, prayers were said, the buildings were torn down and the wood stacked off the ground level for the future use of the medical intelligence team or others who might come by before they used them. The patrol had included one Marine for more firepower if needed, and the six of them pitched in and got it done, the two female officers with the same effort as the men, as frontier women or peasant women in any culture would have. With the work done, they called it a day and returned to camp.

The Marine patrols soon reported a camp just down the westward slope and to the south. The men there appeared rugged and were armed. Thus, they were watched by one marine at all times with a rotation, so that, when they finally approached the temporary low camp of the naval mission it was no surprise. Reporting back the marine returned to watch the strangers' camp to be aware of more movement, though it appeared empty.

Twelve of the unknown Filipino men walked right up to the Navy camp revealing that they were aware of its presence or just lucky scouts. One, declared himself the leader and said, "We are fighting the Japanese in our land. You must join us and share your supplies."

Allan looked the man in the eye even at the fifteen yards and said firmly, "We have our orders, we're not to work with other units nor supply them." The Sergeant and the professor were visible in green fatigues, and Allan and the two women were showing themselves and were in their work khakis with insignia.

"You will," and the man turned to leave, perhaps with the hinted threat he would be back with force.

As he revealed his back, the American saw a short Japanese sword on his belt that he knew not the name for. It was not military but one that might be a family heirloom or just from a personal collection. Little if anything of the Filipino revealed any real military membership.

"Wait a minute," Allan spoke in a commanding way. And, as the man turned back, he inquired, "Were you the ones who wiped out those Jap planters?"

"Yeah, they are Japs. They are the enemy."

Allan stepped closer, and stopped, hands on hips, asking, "The young girls and women . . the old one, all the women?"

"They are Japs. Look what they have done here Americano. You damn Yanks left us."

"No. they're dying right over there a few miles," and Allan pointed with his left hand out toward Zamboanga and his right still on his hip. "And I'm right here. I just arrived. We've come back."

"Well, we killed them."

"And the women. You had to do that to them."

"We killed them."

"You did more than that."

Resigning himself to the truth and feeling dominant anyway, the man moved, as Allan had hoped, up close, within three feet. He had a snarling look about him and wore a turned down Fu Manchu like mustache like some Mexicans and had a bit of a Hispanic look as well, as many Filipinos did. Allan felt he was in the middle of a bad Western movie at the moment. His own Sergeant Adams standing nearby, in spite of his last name, was part Mexican American.

"The old one was a waste, but the young ones tasted good," said with a snarling lustful grin.

The flier and now commando had seen that grin on the border during his Texas year, He last saw it on the raging face of Carlos Orlando, a look that was fierce and unnerving. But then Carlos was on his side in that cantina brawl and was now in medical school unless the military draft had pulled him out of it.

Allan took one casual, slow, long step, and they were almost toe-to-toe, nose-to-nose, and he took his hands from his hips and placed in back as one would lock fingers or stand at a casual parade rest, appearing vulnerable. He had assessed and computed the situation completely now.

Ann watched and wondered, tensing ever so much. She had not met this Allan yet, and she thought she was going to lose him this early in the mission.

233

Her husband, looking sternly in the man's eyes, had somehow developed the ability to not blink. Maybe Nanking did that.

The bandit accepted the challenge and breathing it out into Allan's face said slowly, rolling his words, "We feasted on Jap women ..." . . and lightning fast the blade of Allan's knife came out of its sheath on his belt in back, around his torso in his right hand, and was guided forcefully up and under the sternum and into the bandit's heart. As he did it Allan grabbed the piece of scum by the collar with his left hand so as to prevent him falling rapidly and backward. Thus, he kept a moment of protection in front of him, . . long enough for his men to bring up their various weapons, which included a Thompson or two, and cock them. One bandit, for that is what they were, stepped forward to raise a weapon and a carbine was suddenly shouldered and spoke twice, driving two rounds into that man's chest as quickly as the Marine holding it could pull the trigger. It was so quick that Allan wondered how the semiautomatic mechanism could have kept up with the experienced marine's hand.

The Doctor thought to step toward the wounded man. The leader before Allan was dead. Her husband took her hand and said softly handing her his 45, "Check him standing and with a frown on your face. You cannot show weakness. We have not controlled them yet. Don't show you care. His heart is destroyed anyway."

The woman got the message and, pulling the slide back on the sidearm for the effect of it, played the role. She could never kill anyone, unless in combat, not even a mercy killing, but as she stood over the man and told herself he was dead without kneeling to check vitals, she sensed the evil around them and computed the carnage to come if a firefight ensued. Calmly, for the image it would impress on the others, she put a bullet in the corpse's head. Her father taught her and she had a wiry strength, and she held it out in her right hand, firing without producing a dramatic recoil a weak woman's wrist would have, possibly causing the firearm to jam.

Allan hollered not too loud in a commanding way, "Whoever wasn't there or did no harm to those women, prove it to me."

And at the moment, two men, a marine and the second-class petty officer stepped out from their flanking position behind the bandits, each holding a Thompson at the ready, half raised.

There were ten left, and none realized what was coming and they spoke not a word. And Allan explained, "If you did no harm to those women, prove it. If you did, you'll be held responsible."

One man spoke up and said, "They Japs."

"And you had proof of their siding with the Jap army?"

He was met with silence, and clarified, "A lot of Jap's have lived here for decades. Maybe all are not bad. You know nothing about those girls. Do you?"

"They abuse our women. We have seen it."

"Yes. To terrorize us," another said strongly.

With his arms held out in an interrogative gesture, Allan inquire sarcastically, "Those girls, and the old woman. . . They do that?"

Three younger teenage boys raised their hands. And there ensued a long investigation of interviewing and cross checking the claims of every man. All were taken into custody, and it was concluded that two of the younger ones had joined after the atrocity and the third had been there and was still a bit in shock at what he had seen. His story that he had been teased by the men for not taking part seemed legitimate as well.

Allan talked for a moment with Sergeant Adams and then said, "We're gonna bind you young fellows for now. Just so you won't go running off. The rest of you gentlemen will be hung."

The seven condemned were heavily bound and tied sitting down under various trees at some distance. Julio showed no emotion about the decision. Moments later Allan and Sergeant Adams talked with the Filipino, with Ann standing and listening, a part of it but contributing nothing. Hanging was generally to save bullets, but they decided to use rifle fire instead. They could use the lesser rifles of the bandits with a caliber of cartridge unusable in their own weapons. No one really had the stomach for it, but the sergeant had seen it in his career. 1st Sergeant Morrow was away with one marine scouting to the north. A moment later the two commanding officers were alone in the meadow.

Looking up at him, wanting to grab both of his hands and squeeze them yet knowing she couldn't, the woman said, "Execution, Allan? Isn't there something else?" said looking in his eyes and searching. Then looking down at the ground, Ann said softly, "Damn, we were picnicking in Singapore just months ago, now . . . I wish I was delivering Maori or Aborigine kids right now."

"What do you suggest Lieutenant? We can't guard them. We can't tie them up unless we want to baby sit them. They have to relieve themselves with some regularity. We can't feed them or take them with us when we move, and they'll consume our supplies. . . . And, they murdered and raped those young women and the grandmother. It isn't simply punishment. What stops them from doing it again. We can't get them to any authority. We don't even know where any American authority is or if it exists. In fact, we're it right in this spot, at least for this moment. We **are** the authorities. We have no jail and no jail staff, and even if the Jap men were spies or saboteurs, . . those girls, it's a death penalty offense. But I'll confer with Sergeant Morrow with

237

his long military experience. The bottom line beyond their guilt is that they would ruin our planned maintenance of our supplies balanced against the consumption."

It was quiet for several moments as they just stood, not looking at each other so as to not pressure each other's thoughts in any way. Within hers, Ann had been aware of Sgt. Adams's easy manner throughout the whole horrible affair, though tense with the duty of it. She guessed correctly that he was used to such dramas, peacetime soldier or not. It was all happening quickly for her, this education, though it was spread out over many weeks and months. Africa, where she had to kill, the submarine battle with the patrol boats, being at risk; then watching one's own companions fight; then seeing this atrocity close; now shooting someone herself as she unexpectedly had in Africa, and this one dead though he may have been, and now party to a hanging.

"No, Allan. The 1st Sergeant's a noncom. And we would have to await his return. They made us officers for a reason. He's our adviser and leads our muscle, our fighters. You have discussed it with Sgt. Adams enough." Turning her head sideways and looking up at him standing off to the side just a bit, Ann said, "We have to make the big decisions, and you've done that. There may be worse ones ahead."

"You're an officer in the medical service branch. Your oak leaf and acorn designate that."

"Yes, and I'm co-commander with you. Col. Jensen made that clear to me. I can't leave it all to you. I would be shielding myself and shirking my duty."

Sergeant Adams stepped up and stated, "They have some almost useless guns and a little ammo. Those lever guns are useful and the young prisoners say there is significant ammunition at their camp. We can arm five more men that way."

"And the useless ones?" inquired Ann.

"Three old bolt actions with a few rounds, just what was in each rifle." A marine in that era, he would never call a rifle a 'gun'.

The husband said, "Enough for our executions?"

"Two short."

"Hang the two roughest characters; those boys indicated they were the most vicious with those young women, them and the two dead leaders."

The execution party went to the scene of the small massacre and atrocity. There was really no way to soften it for the guilty and the officers wanted to keep as much stigma away from and off of their camp as possible. Since they had contacted other Filipinos, they were able to get a priest from the countryside who would be discrete and give confession and last rights to those brigands who welcomed it. Ann meant not to go, and Allan did not want her to. Then she thought about it and realized she was as responsible as he was for the decision. To not have gone would seem to have put it all on him. Jenny insisted that she hated it, agreed with it, and should make sure she experienced the worst of their war experience along with the good. Both of the commanding officers objected but did not command her to stay in camp. There were no patients. Sergeant Adams objected as well.

Allan and Adams offered to shoot with the three marines and one sailor, so there could be one firing, relieving the tension in the second batch that had to watch the first. The corporal said it was inappropriate and Adams agreed and told Allan so. Thus, they were shot in two lots, four and three with multiple reports, following Sergeant Adams's command, that sounded almost like one big bang with a ragged edge. To save ammunition, as mentioned they used the bandits own hunting rifles. For their own preservation of sanity, they decided they could waste two bullets and the Marines used the American lever action rifles taken from the bandits to execute the two evil leaders, thus saving themselves decades of bad dreams later perhaps watching men slowly dangle and strangle to death. They were not about to waste time building a complicated trapdoor gallows hopefully to never be needed again.

With each of the shots, or rather firing of shots, Ann softly jumped as if surprised by it. That in turn surprised and unnerved her, and she realized it was

240

the unconscious reaction of a man being killed and that he could not fight back, a justified situation or not. And the woman worried, doctor that she was, that all of this surrounding the case would place a stigma on her husband within her mind. Would she see him in a different light, think him the monster she did not know she was marrying and so on. Instinctively, she knew better, and it would be proven with his tender moments with native children and wise decisions she wondered sometimes from whence he found them, and of course it was from within, from his character . . the character of Allan Allison, Sr., his father, who had played casual interracial matchmaker in a racist age and place, but not necessarily a racist population.

Incongruently, and almost irreverently, walking back in solemn thought to the camp, from somewhere within and visceral, all she could think about with vivid mental imagery was how much she longed for their next moment together in bed, knowing that was one side of her real husband that would help erase the sharpness of the current images from her mind as the rest of him, the depth of him would erase most of it from her soul. And she started to pray as she walked so that they might survive to know and enjoy each other for decades to come.

The bandit camp was checked out and found abandoned, and, because there were supplies remaining, the officers determined that the entire group probably consisted of the twelve as the three young survivors claimed. After much grilling the boys were sent off, because it seemed they were not villainous and were truthful in that they thought they had joined a guerrilla outfit prior to the brutal massacre. Once the Filipinos in their teens were calmed enough to feel less threatened by the Americas, Julio and two female health professionals were able to determine that the one seemed traumatized by what he had witnessed and the others had not been present. It was not felt they should be punished or forced to stay, and they chose to leave. Throughout the war Filipinos were generally loyal to their countrymen and America, even if some strong nationalists might have been reluctant, because all were united in a very logical hate of the Japanese at that time.

The events of the previous few days may have filtered out through the boys, and two young Filipino women had appeared one day about a half hour past noon when the second group always ate. The personnel were split into small midday messes at 11:30, 12:30, and 1:30. The women, in their mid-20s walked up to one of the Filipino men, who had joined the camp and was known to Julio, and talked quietly. He then brought them to Jenny. Then the three approached Ann, who was writing notes about meals and nutrition based upon what was readily available locally.

The nurse began intentionally formally, "Doctor, these young ladies want to help. They're asking if we can train them on the job."

242

Ann looked up having already made the decision to be positive about the request if possible. She did not want to turn people away but could not too casually and easily collect mouths to feed.

"What brings you here with this request?"

"It is just our desire to help," one replied. She was shorter, revealing a typical shyness that the group had been prepared to expect from younger rural Filipino women, yet more outgoing than the other and perhaps most young Filipinos.

Looking in the other's eyes that blinked yet looked back, Ann said, "I think it is more than that. This isn't easy."

"We are stuck here, and want to help. We have nothing else to do but sit at Janice's tita's . . uh, auntie's house and sew or work in the garden and also cook." The spokeswoman used a common English word for aunt. Maybe she wanted to impress the English-speaking American women.

"Those are worthy pursuits. Can you grow things?"

"Yes," said the girl. "But we want to learn about fixing people."

"It is rewarding, tough, dirty work," the doctor said as she looked from one to the other staring briefly in their eyes.

The two looked back and then down shyly almost in unison. Then they raised their heads back up, the speaker looking back more directly than the other, slightly behind the other at an angle, with a tilted head and a sideways stare as if looking into the sun.

Ann read a natural shyness of the the young women of the Orient, more of the Spanish, which combined in these girls. It didn't lessen them and she knew that.

"We can train you slowly, and if stuck here long enough and we see enough medical work we can certify you. But when it's over, you will have to be tested at the very least and maybe attend more classes. Are you that serious or just want to learn first aid?"

"We want to do the best we can."

All the while, Jenny had played the role of the dutiful nurse, perhaps setting an example, and stood beside her superior medical officer. Such behavior would speak to the traditional young ladies from a matriarchal society. There was a moment following the more vocal girl's declaration when no one spoke, a sort of weird brief pause when everyone was in thought perhaps.

As the official decision or at least approval had apparently been given by the doctor, Jenny broke the silence, saying, "Why are you stuck here?"

The second young woman now spoke, "We came to stay with my tita awhile and help her after my tito died."

The two naval officers breathed a sigh of relief that the second girl was not handicapped by shyness.

Then the woman added, "We cannot get home, we are so worried for our families."

Jenny walked around behind the two, and, as the two in unison looked up and back at her, she inquired, "Do you have sisters there?"

Each said, "No."

The one who was the niece of the local woman added, "My younger sister came and is with Tita. That is all."

Looking down at the shorter girl who had been the original spokeswoman, Jenny, who had a reassuring hand on a shoulder of each, asked, "So, you have no sister?"

"No."

"Well, you can relax a little and concentrate on your work and studies if we train you. The greatest risk from the Japs is to young women."

The two young Filipino women exhibited the energy of their industrious race and went to work, not minding the initial crude common chores of nursing and similar health related careers.

Ann had asked Jenny of course; and, though busy, she worked their indoctrination in to her schedule. They met at meals often to save time, and the first discussion or orientation went smoothly and revealed their aptitude.

That same evening, the married commanders sat together eating after everyone else was done. Intentionally the common mess table was away from any work area or comfortable rest area and was off limits for relaxing snacking or drinking during mess call hours. The purpose was privacy, and Allan chose to take advantage of it now. It was for privacy to eat meals away from work and everything else unless a discussion came up at a meal, and it was, for that reason, a separation of personnel during meals. Jenny and the Filipinas, ate together the marines ate in two groups together, and Ann and Allan together last. Another purpose was for the casual command discussions of the latter two.

"Ann, as you know, within our overall mission, we have those sealed orders. I want to open them now. The Colonel said to get the camps set up first and feel some level of comfort before we do this. But he said no more than six weeks and really better if sooner. We're well within the six."

"Well, he may have wanted it immediately and realized that would be too hard without being organized. We aren't combat raiders. I defer to you, equal as we are, because you have the experience of action and observation of actual war."

"Here goes," he said opening the envelope. "We are to search for, rescue if alive, and tend to medically a Colonel Jeremy Scott, USMC who is an intelligence officer last heard from in this area. If he is dead and it is possible, we are to recover any and all documents in his possession and notify the Navy."

Sitting in low sunlight of the Philippine rain forest clearing, thoughts went through both their minds of another more peaceful time.

"We might as well be setting in a simple picnic area in the woodlands of Tennessee contemplating which fishing hole is best."

Looking up, Allan replied, "Perhaps God is telling us just how to approach this then. Treat it like everyday stuff and accept the danger like in everyday stuff."

"People drown, fishing boats turn over . ."

"Yep."

"That is how I learned to do surgery. I was scared, but I had a steady hand. Mind you, I don't want to do the delicate stuff I'll bet they will do someday.

I'm just talking about stitching a clamped artery so it holds when the clamp is released. It's heady stuff, Allan. I just told myself one day, after my mentor told me I was thinking too much. I told myself 'Study it, know what to do, know what can go wrong and what to do then. And then just do it and not worry about the consequences. Fear kills."

"Well, let us send out feelers and the Marines. We will have to be careful who we trust among the locals and work through Professor Ortega. He will be able to best evaluate informants."

"We need to know what the Japs have so we can plan to protect ourselves from that."

Finally, a break came in the form of a native messenger, one of the many seemingly humble yet capable men. 1st Sgt. Morrow took one marine with him and two Filipino scouts.

Colonel Scott was discovered with his aides after a two-day hike through the brush in mountainous terrain northward into the peninsula toward the Strait. Wounded originally in the early fighting on Bataan, he had been sent south and survived a boat sinking and other trials. The man, a bit old now for war, had been tasked with getting out through the southerly escape route used by many . . successfully by some, down through the archipelago and then to New Guinea or Australia. Had he achieved the point of departure by sea in a small boat from Mindanao, as some had, he would probably not have survived the voyage this late. By then, the enemy was everywhere. After Morrow passed rigid grilling by the colonel's three aides, he was allowed to take the colonel's papers and notes to the safety of *Camp Bangús*, a name voted on by all.

The man needed attention and his mission carried the importance of his head full of knowledge about the islands and the enemy, and thus the marines came back for Doctor Ann. Seemingly safe and securely hidden and protected with his three military aides, Ann would go with Jenny to make him able to travel. Two Marines were tasked with escorting Ann safely. At the last minute, Allan decided they should not be apart. Intuitively he ordered extra personnel and took Sgt. Adams along with the two and the Filipinos scouts already there. Some insignia had been brought for ranks up through sergeant, and eventually a formal Filipino Scout unit would be formed at *Camp Bangús*.

A runner had been sent ahead with the news of the medical situation, with even a description of symptoms. Thus, two days later the larger party which now included Ann, Jennie, and Allan approached the colonel's camp. Unfortunately, a second runner met them on the trail reporting the discovery of the hiding place by the enemy and the presence there now of some fifteen soldiers. Ominously and expectedly, rough voices were heard as they approached. The Americans' numbers were deficient and it would only get worse.

The Filipino scout, Arturo, spoke softly, "There are many Japanese there, at least fifteen but more. They are questioning the old man roughly, though he still lies in his bed."

"How are they deployed?" asked 1st Sergeant Morrow. "Do they have sentries?"

"Yes, sir," the leader, Mario replied. "They have men in each direction and the fifteen within, mostly kneeling in a prepared way. We face twenty or more."

Arturo had almost immediately become a favorite among the Americans for his obvious thoroughness, his trustworthiness and charm. A handsome young man he looked to be a teenage boy as most Filipinos held their youthful looks well, but some among the working classes, depending on their time in the sun, aged more quickly. They called him Artie.

"How did you see this?"

"They are in a hollow. It is visible from fifty yards away, a high place, rocks that appear hard enough to climb that most would not try. I found easy hand and footholds. I believe someone cut them there long ago, maybe our ancestors. They had a sentry there and nearby. We slit their throats. It is clear to observe from that place."

"And the nearest sentries?"

"Too far, it is high. They won't miss the two until they move and recall them."

Reaching the point, the little patrol climbed to the perch and sought good cover from which they could observe. The runner was sent back to the camp with orders to prepare an ambush for the Japanese if they were followed on their return.

Quietly the four, Arturo and the three officers climbed to the overlooking perch from which they heard harsh voices. Then Arturo went down to be their lookout for any surprises. Looking through the binoculars each carried, they could see a Japanese officer harshly questioning the older man on a pallet style bed. He slapped him several times, causing them all to grimace. Two officers with the colonel were on their knees and had their hands tightly bound behind their backs, folded backward as one might cross one's arms in front across their torso.

"Sirs, we don't have enough personnel to engage these Japs unless we had set up the perfect ambush, such as in a controlled bottleneck," Sgt. Adams climbed up and said. "They have the numbers to just out flank us on the trail. And they must not see and follow us. Your whole command could be lost and the girls taken if they survive."

"What if we're seen, we're too close now."

"Maybe a rookie mistake, Sir. But maybe not. We freeze and stay quiet or slowly back out. This is so

251

much higher than the ground around, and our escape path is fine and guarded, by the Filipinos."

Before anything could be decided and as their whispers seemed like shouting in Allan's worried mind, their chances to move quickly were diminished. A small enemy squad approached from a trail to their right from behind. It was not directly behind them, but unnervingly increased the sense of danger. Ann saw it unfold, cluelessly at first; but, like the doctor she was triaging a patient, she saw the complication that suddenly arose.

And Sgt. Edgar Earl Adams saw it too, "We're safe here," he whispered. "Right here, in this spot. Look, Arturo chose it well, Sirs. We're elevated, off the trail, in a morass of brush, with no logical reason to attract a search. It appears there's no 'here' to be."

"We have to be quiet then."

"Yes."

"You might not like what you see, ma'am."

"I know."

As they viewed from well protected cover over the scattered deployment of enemy soldiers, unable to move closer, or to affect any attack, they watched the man and his officers being abused. To fire with their effective automatic weapons would have led to an assault on themselves, outnumbered as they were, and the captives would have died anyway. Words could not be distinguished, but it was clearly English salted with some few Japanese words. Anger and force filled the man's voice. At one point he raised his hand, and another soldier, perhaps a junior officer, raised his sword and beheaded one of the two who were kneeling, the head falling and turning once on the ground, the body remaining a moment and then fell forward and sideways. The other was not gagged, and a moan was heard, perhaps as he contemplated his own near fate.

Ann gasped quietly, bringing her binoculars in her left hand down and countering with her right coming up and covering her mouth.

"We can do nothing," Edgar turned and whispered to Ann and Allan. "Ma'am, you might want to move back the way we came a few yards. Arturo and Corporal Cole can accompany you. Please stay close though."

"I'll stay here, Sergeant. It's our war, all of us. We all have to tell of it later. The more witnesses the better."

"I don't want you to see thi..."

"I'll be fine."

"You must contain yourself, Lieutenant."

253

"Yes, Sgt. Adams."

Finally, it became apparent that the man could not or would not answer and the Officer seemed to look and point his sword at the other, still kneeling and demanded something. When he did not reply or maybe said he knew nothing, The sword was stabbed in the patient's stomach, causing a weak but demonstratively painful vocal reaction. The kneeling man screamed, "We know nothing!" And slowly and very theatrically the Japanese officer raised his sword and severed the patient's head from bis body. The bed was only a foot or so raised from the ground, and the head fell down to the earth and lay there. With a nod of silent command from the officer, the other American officer was beheaded.

Ann was wide-eyed and just stared as Allan grabbed her arm and commanded quietly, "Let's go! When they start to move, they'll search for their sentries."

The retreat was easy, and Arturo and his companion guided them through grass that might leave evidence of their passage but no tracks. Back to the trail they followed the Filipinos along a meandering route through the bush to throw off any who followed. It was believed that the Japanese buried their victims, but in this remote place perhaps not. Perhaps the bodies would be left to terrorize the natives, of which the Japs were somewhat afraid. Also, once the missing sentries' bodies were discovered, no one knew for sure how the enemy commanding officer would react: anger and search and destroy or fear and retreat from the area. In time, they finally rested safely on a sloping earth. But for safety, the Filipinos eyes had every possibility covered.

Ann lay back with her gloved hands back under her head, her training always prepared for the jungle's parasites. She was staring out still wide-eyed with shock. The doctor and the woman's mind in her head thought of those poor men, her countrymen. The girl in her, the inner child we always carry, the one crying for their mother as they die on the field of battle . . . thought, 'What have I gotten myself into?'

Taking every precaution, the whole team arrived safely a day later in the morning's wee hours. It was certain that they were not followed.

As long as the laudanum, chloroform, sulfa, and morphine lasted, the medical mission, primitive as it was, could function. Each was used sparingly and alcohol, which could be created by double distilling tubâ, could aid with fighting topical infection, and the tubâ or rum could assist in temporarily relieving pain. The hot sun could sterilize washed linens and gowns, and they had brought the stainless sheet steel portable autoclave of Beaumont's design. It assembled into a hot box that was powered by a charcoal fire beneath. Like other peoples, who, though modernizing, were still in touch with their past, nature, and the earth, Filipinos had used homemade charcoal for centuries. The autoclave's seams, where the somewhat portable box was assembled for use, were almost air tight, assisting in the heat, and the firebox below was alternately vented just right. Somehow, Allan knew not how, Beau had known just how to design the box's shape for maximum heat intensity.

Allan wished his unique copilot was with them, but he knew Beau would use the plane well, serve the cause of winning while still earning at least enough to operate it, and do his best to keep possession of and maintain the hybrid 204/304 transport/bomber. Left behind in Darwin unattended, the plane would have become military pretty quickly.

Minor combat occurred between Filipino Guerrillas in the area of *Butuan,* the port in the next province to the west, *Agusan del Norte,* across *Lake Mainit* in the coastal plain. That province together with *Surigao del Norte* and *Surigao del Sur* saw low action during the war, with some exceptions. The region itself was significant, guarding the south side of *Surigao Strait* and forming the mountain walled, somewhat sparsely settled Northeast Coast of Mindanao, creating a good place to infiltrate into.

When they last had moved, the new position gave access to eagle's nest viewing over nearby areas of the Philippine Sea portion of the Pacific. Scouting north produced others closer to Dinagat and Surigao Islands and Surigao Strait. Finally, some combat wounded came to the little canvas and nipa hospital at *Camp Bangús.*

256

Looking toward the soft sounds of disturbed brush and the low voices, Corporal Dodson went over to greet them and help the one walking the least well with support. He, like other *Camp Bangús* personnel, had begun to develop the sensitivity to sounds of an American Indian scout. Guiding the four men, the uninjured one inquired, "We just heard of you from the locals, where in the hell did you guys come from?"

He was in a khaki Navy officer's uniform looking sort of downward as he helped another struggle along and jerked his head up in surprise when he heard Jenny's soft voice correct him, "Guys and gals, Lieutenant." All the men had some semblance of uniforms of various service branches, two Americans and two Filipinos.

She reached to help him carry his load and her sweet perfume, which she had maintained with Sampaguita, engulfed him. They turned as they walked slowly along, looking at each other past their human load, and Jenny elaborated, "We're a special Navy medical and observation mission."

He just stared in wonder and returned her smile.

Later the healthy officer, a Lt. Harold Davis sat and talked to Allan. Allan had just finished filling in information in a sort of informal report.

The guerrilla officer explained as well, "We're a mixed bag, Lieutenant, just collected here and have contacted the more organized fellows to the west north of Lake Lanao and nearer the central region. We stay in contact with runners, and it has to be sparsely so. We can't get to them easily, so they told us to hunker down and act independently, but to mostly observe."

"So, you're to report to them?"

"Yes." He refrained from saying sir as they were both lieutenants.

"I believe those in charge don't want aggressive raids stirring up trouble for these Filipinos."

"Correct, I would say. We've seen and some have heard harsh things when the little Jap hornets get stirred up. More like yellow jackets really. Fierce. You look very organized here, Lieutenant Allison."

"We are new in country here. Fresh off the boat many weeks ago. This more permanent camp is weeks old."

"That seems a special purpose," stated inquisitively.

"Do you have any papers, Lieutenant?"

Glancing up a bit surprised but not demonstratively so, he replied, "I lost almost everything but what was in my pockets. Here's Naval ID and Virginia driver's license. Something secret goin' on? . . Oh wait," and he pulled his wallet out full of photos.

"We're here to provide some expert emergency medical care for whatever Americans we could encounter and the native people nearby without having to roam too far, and to watch the coast of Mindanao here and up to Surigao Strait. We cannot move with a large guerrilla band and compromise our second mission, intelligence. We are also tasked with recovering any intelligence officers still alive and get their knowledge out to Headquarters."

"How many doctors and nurses?"

"One of each. You've met the nurse."

"So, the Negro woman is the doctor?" Ann was the only one with Jenny in the medical tent with the wounded men, and he said it with a bit of surprise.

"Yep, a jungle doctor with six months experience in Africa leading a medical mission alone, the co-commander of this mission, and my wife. We're newlyweds. This is the honeymoon. Everyone here is a volunteer. Marines almost fought each other over the chance to go. I guess they'd all seen a few Filipinas."

"Oh . . Well then, Congratulations," the other said with his hand held out.

Taking it, Allan said, "Thank you. We won't be under guerrilla command. Our orders are strict, from Naval Intelligence, though we are a medical mission, too. We are to assist the resistance as much as possible and practical, but are not to leave our assigned area unless driven out by circumstances. If you are in contact again with any headquarters unit in the future and we're in the discussion, you might make that clear. Of course, we can be their eyes and ears here too, like you, as much as possible. Is there an overall command? Who's in charge?"

"Colonel Fertig. American. A businessman with military experience, I think. The American commanding on Cebu is a mining engineer. The Filipino leaders recruited him out of concern they would let their many personal animosities handicap any of their own who tried. I thought that rather honest and mature of them. He's actually part Filipino, Colonel Cushing."

Allan had thought to not mention the executions but changed his mind when he was asked if he knew anything about the burned homestead and the new graves there with simple rock markers and no inscription boards.

Lt. Davis finally said, "I'm concerned about what happened there. You don't have any information do you Lt. Allison?"

"Not much. I was waiting to see what you knew first. It is a confused situation, them being Japanese and the nature of the crimes . . and the concern of these Japanese settlers being spies . . or not."

"Crimes? All we saw were graves and used lumber . . Japanese? Spies?"

"Yes. Crimes," Allan said strongly and let it sink in. Then he elaborated, "We came upon the scene within hours. They were all brutally killed . . viciously. The women had been gang raped. It was a family of Japanese settlers, farmers in this case, which are common here and elsewhere in the islands, especially here in the South. Only files we don't have might suggest any spy activity. Otherwise, they are American subjects of the colonial Philippines. Apparent victims included a granny, mother, and two daughters, one a teen and the other in her twenties . . brutally gang raped. The men had been burned."

"And the extra graves apart?"

"We caught and grilled the bandits who did it. They literally stayed around through the night so each of seven men could have a go at each woman and girl, killing the men last so they had to watch it. It was like the Comanche, maybe like the Japs. I saw some of it in Nanking."

The other's eyebrows raised and he inquired, "How did you get such confessions?"

"After the initial confession from their leader in a detailed boast, they feared him dead after he and I fought and the others talked under repeated, spaced interrogations. We wanted to know who was guilty

among them. It reached a point after over a day and
night, when we could relieve all pressure and still
get agreeing tales from them all. The guilty are dead
and buried and the innocent were freed, young boys
who returned later to work with us."

"Allison, someone needs to give an official report,
you perhaps."

"That's impractical, but first and foremost, I report
to Naval Intelligence directly and can provide that
documentation for your superiors. We can't be
running nonessential reports back and forth across
this big island through enemy lines chancing
capture of messengers, torture, and our positions
and strengths revealed. I'm confident. It was my
call."

"Still, an investigation is normal."

"This isn't normal Harold. Nothing's normal in the
world right now. But I can tell you, and you can tell
Fertig: we were stationed here by Naval intelligence
to do our jobs and to answer to no one but our
superiors in Australia or wherever headquarters
moves to, and we have the paperwork that
specifically says as much. Perhaps you need to
concentrate on the war and trust all of our officers
on this island. I'm sure Fertig chose well. So did my
superiors. Some might go native . . crazed with
homesickness and inability to handle the survival
level life and dangers here, even the climate. But

most of those won't get to command level, even lower command level.

The men we executed were bandits threatening us with not too subtle innuendo, and the leader freely admitted everything before attempting to threaten me further. Lieutenant Davis, the rapes were a crime under any circumstance. Obviously, the murders of the women would be even if the men were thought to be spies. One of the girls was clearly under age, and it is a crime and a sin to get revenge on your enemy by repeating his crimes on his people wherever you find them."

"They may send me back. Col. Fertig is strict about military behavior."

"As am I. But we are not directly under his command, and have a mission. Let Fertig talk to Australia himself."

"Nanking, huh? You mean '37. How was that?"

"Unpleasant. Like the newsreels. But the rapes weren't in the newsreels . . wholesale rapes and gang rapes, then murdered . . . Still have nightmares."

~

"You're embarrassed. I'm sorry. I am too . . to be the cause of that. Maybe we can share it, since we have to. I mean share the embarrassment."

The shy Filipina looked down a moment with his first words and then looked up with slight surprise she couldn't conceal. She wanted to run into the trees and hide, but Jenny's training was taking hold enough for the body's physical and chemical manifestations of the embarrassment to not totally erase the lessons. In her mind as she looked down again were the visions of the two medical workers who had made such an impression on her in the last few months. And they were women like herself. Women who could do such important things and even order the men around when it came to their health. She had seen it elsewhere. It existed in her culture where the family matriarch had powers as well. But, besides certain scenarios in the Filipino home, it was not a common thing.

"Share?" she inquired softly, looking up at him.

"I've been in this before Carla. I broke by coccyx when I was a kid . . in a fall while I was hunting. A nurse had to do everything for me. She saw my embarrassment and told me the patient just has to realize there's no choice. She said the nurse does it already in her training. I mean, she realizes it's part of the job. It's what makes you gals heroes, Carla."

Again, she looked down in shyness, as anyone does when they are the subject of the discussion. But it was brief and she was feeling less weak in her limbs, and she looked at him again. The man was a ruggedly handsome Marine, a former Navy corpsman, and the intuitive young woman had imagined their work, helping wounded soldiers on battlefields and in jungles like this. And now she was learning to be the support nurse in the field hospitals nearby the fighting. Part of her shyness was the feeling developing for this particular young man among the Marines.

"When I can move enough, Carla, I want to take you out. Well, if you will, if you're interested. There's nowhere to go, but we could figure something out."

"Here, there is nothing to do but walk around and talk. We cannot go far, for the Japanese."

The man was encouraged now at the apparent unspoken acceptance of his request for a date and he, added, "They are not in this area. But we must be careful."

He was about four years her senior, not too bad a difference, a career man so far_ becoming a corpsman and then changing to the Marines when the war seemed eminent. Filipinas had a maturity about them for all their girlish shyness in certain scenarios. Their life in the islands was simpler, with less frills like a movie theater on every fourth corner of a big city and a radio in most homes. Their role became more important earlier in life than most American girls, but like some others, like a girl on a Kansas farm or the California hills, like Sarah Willowood who was the dream focus of another Navy man early in this war, Allan's friend Jake Pierce. So, Carla had shopped in the open market for the whole family when she had been twelve years old and had scolded her older brother when he came home dunk for the first time, to have it never happen again. Carla was a girl with a woman's mind like most young Filipinas.

Picking up the tools of her work, Carla said, "We do not have to go far to be together," And, perhaps a little red faced she glance quickly at him, and said a soft, "Goodbye for now."

Corporal Richard Olin Ferris, USMC combining a combat Marine and Navy Corpsman (a battlefield medic) to compliment Jenny, wore the corporal rank and, on his commanding officers' insistence, his corpsman's rating. It was unusual but not against regulations perhaps.

"Ann, she is a medical assistant now but not a Navy nurse. Not an officer. If we directly induct her, she will be enlisted personnel as the corporal is. We should present that to Allan. It gives better legal control over these girls. The Philippines is American territory . . or was . . still legally."

"Your point is that they can marry."

"Yes."

The two of them, doctor and nurse, could not help using first names in private. Already used to the separation of rank as nurse and doctor, in a group and on duty the separation of rank was already in them before their military experience.

"Look, Ann, our two commanding officers are married and naturally and obviously living in a conjugal situation. You two are an example of marriage. We're gonna be here many months, maybe years. I believe at least a year. Allan told us during our last command conference before we left that he had briefed the men right after they were chosen. He told them to be respectful and not expect Hotel Street or Chinatown in Honolulu. We cannot expect these men and women to essentially live together in a community and not have a few fall in love, and we cannot then prevent them from showing and fulfilling it. We aren't just a command; we're a community, a village."

"I suppose it was like this at the old frontier cavalry posts in the old days. I mean there would be farm girls around and officers' families with daughters. Some even married Indian girls."

"Our job is to protect these girls. Boys will be boys and military men are, well you know especially the single ones can be irresponsible . . thinking it just a perk."

"Well, nurse Jenny, you seem to have put some thought into this, how do we do that? How do we protect them?"

"We need to counsel the girls to use their heads and not be too easily wooed by a guy who isn't serious. We told these fellas, your husband did, not to volunteer if they were in anyway racist because they could be stuck here with these girls too long. Those men, these men that we selected all claim to be bias free about that."

There was a long pause in which she looked at the doctor until she looked up and the two locked eyes.

"Ann, you and I need to talk to these men before this goes any farther. The fellas have been talking with Janice too. She seems more innocent, a provincial girl. You and I need to set these guys down and give them 'the talk' . . tell them the girlfriend's point of view. It's not done, but we need to do it. And . . I've seen your faith and how you've rejuvenated Allan's. We need to let these guys know how important their faith is to these girls."

They had both been looking at each other intently, and Ann added, "I see your point and agree completely. No one is completely unaffected by bias. He may want to take her home, but he's afraid of Mama. We also need to talk to any other girls who end up here. It is unprecedented but needed here. We need to let these young ladies know what the men really want first. They want true love, most of them do, but they want the goodies first and then change their minds, never meant to stay with that particular girl, or want a variety of goodies."

~

Lieutenant Maru's small force was a bookmark. A place holder to have something there. Otherwise guerrillas might cluster there feeling safe. And American submarines might supply them on moonless nights. The Japanese enemy knew now that there had been an attempted landing, perhaps successful, for they had lost two patrol boats that night. They thought they had sunk the sub too. There was debris, but subs could be sneaky about that, intentionally spitting up diesel oil and personal effects and such. Maru saw the distant flashes and heard the explosions that night.

Maru had seventy-five men with little to do. So, he set about to pretend to be a kind a liberator for these simple farmers and fishermen. His men helped somewhat, but with no menial labor. These natives must know their place. However, at some point there was a crack in the façade, when his men started making advances toward the native girls. These were not natives in the classic sense of simple, primitive lifestyles, for they were fully Filipino citizens and American subjects, and some had a little education. They could dress like a Polynesian native of an earlier era to work around and on the sea, working the boats, the bancas, and they might wear a shirt and pants with their women in a dress for church or fiesta. When a young

269

married woman with a small child rebuffed the advances of his top sergeant a scene ensued, and at some point in the argument, the child disappeared. Maru became incensed at the woman and the disappearance of his leverage. He knew that he would have to make a point at some moment, and this had been the right emotionally charged moment. He had planned to have the child impaled on a bayonet and the woman be given to his sergeant permanently. The husband would of course be beheaded publicly. At that time the common thing among many uncommon horrors in areas of Japanese conquest was to toss an infant in the air and catch it on the bayonet on the end of a rifle. The Japanese had strange ideas about winning the hearts and minds of the people they conquered and wanted to make their subjects. The Filipinos would be treated well when they realized who was superior and who was boss, and if one of his men wanted a woman, he could have her. After he terrorized the little fishing village into compliance, he put his men to work again otherwise doing some good work. It may have been all for naught however, because he had seventy-five bored men who thought they would be fighting a war, not holding a place.

Maru, uncharacteristically for the average such Nipponese officer at that time met with and struck a deal with the village elders. He was stuck there with no fight to fight and in an isolated Pacific paradise. The woman in question would become his sergeant's mistress, luckier for her than becoming a comfort woman (whore for the whole troop). Maru would let the missing child go, apparently handed off during the argument to the child's maternal grandmother who had disappeared with it. The village would provide four women to be comfort women, which, at Maru's discretion, might at some later time be rotated with other women in the village. The four ultimately grew to six.

What could he do but give his men the women that weren't his to give, but then, in Japanese military culture they were. When some of the women slowly disappeared into the hills, he picked two more to make comfort women and had a little six cubicle prison shack constructed, a brothel or bordello if you will, or considering the forced compliance of it, the harsher, 'whore house.' It had a main room as sort of a bar-café. He had thought out the problem about the child, but he was a smart man, misused by his superiors in this desolate place. He knew when to fight a battle and when to give a little even to someone like these villagers, who he could crush at his discretion. He could kill all the men and have all the women who had not left, but who would secure the food. His guards watched the work to prevent poisoning with something like Puffer fish. The village elders balked at choosing the doomed women, and Maru decided he would personally do the difficult task through the method of product testing.

Maru wondered if there had been a significant landing the night of the little sea battle and then heard rumors of an American presence in the hills above. There was said to be a doctor, a Negro woman in uniform. The Filipino who related the news wanted his daughter left alone for his effort. She had been chosen to be a spare comfort woman if another was needed. When women resisted the chore, their Japanese soldier clients were known to beat them. A particular feisty girl could end up dead.

The better to control the informant, as such a turncoat against his people he might be useful, Maru took the girl for his mistress with the threat that, if the father spoke any intelligence he gathered to any but Maru himself, his daughter would be turned over to the men, and he would make sure she would get the lion's share of the 'work'. With this threat, and enjoying the young woman nightly, Maru sent the man out often as a spy who could move easily among the villages and even right up to the American camp. The spy knew the terrain, as he had been up there before any one arrived. Maru marveled at the American forces intelligence in avoiding his garrison when they landed the group. He determined that his tough eager soldiers could get up the seaside of the mountains to the American camp and attack one dark night through the deep overgrown ravine overlooking the Pacific. He knew from military reports and reports from his fellow officers who had been to the United States that these Americans could get quite lax when they quieted down at night, feeling safe with just a few sentries.

Keeping the young woman to himself, protecting her to an extent and controlling her destiny, Maru could have a more pleasurable experience than his many men sharing six and certainly no true emotion involved, as if they cared. But with the one, scared young woman he could woo and manipulate psychologically until she would be begging to go with him when he returned to Japan someday. He wondered about the black American doctor, what she would be like, and knew the final step in defeating an enemy was possessing his women and holding their fate, both sexual and mortal in your hands. That had been the main point of Nanking.

~

"I'm telling you we did it," Navy pilot, Lt. Robinson emphasized to some skepticism.

"But to lose the "Lex?" responded 1ˢᵗ Sgt. Morrow.

The carrier Lexington, "Lady Lex" had been a favorite before the war, and as the group around the picnic style table discussed the loss, they shared some angst. A rare tidbit of news, from an unlikely source was being mulled over, and its sparse information analyzed.

"I'm telling you, I bet all the brass have big smiles on their faces. The Japs turned around. We got enough intelligence info to know what the higher ups know about that. They're trying to fight over the mountain spine of New Guinea, the Aussies are there and our boys, I believe."

"The Owen Stanley Mountains."

"Yes ma'am. New Zealanders too, probably. They know mountains."

Four days earlier, a Japanese transport had gone down in a storm on the side of the mountains south of the camp some few miles. News arrived and the now standard search team of the *Camp Bangús* prepared and went out. It usually consisted of 1st. Sgt Harold Morrow in command, Cpl. Ferris or Jenny for medical, and three Marines or Filipinos. On that occasion, Jenny went.

As the storm had raged and the visibility got worse for the enemy transport plane that night, Lt. Robinson had told his captors that the terrain at a certain near point was safest to try to land in the hills. They did not believe him and tried the thin beach in the night instead.

His hands were bound, and he was in a rear seat. Knowing something about crashes, as he had raced motor cars a little before the war, he felt his chances were best where he was. A fire after the crash would be the problem, bound as he was.

Battling the surf along the narrow beach and the rising terrain to port and the west, the plane skidded too fast and struck a wing tip first and turned in to the rising land. Both pilots were out of commission, severely wounded or already dead, and the crew, unstrapped, were thrown around. One engine was burning and Robinson, a captured PBY pilot, screamed to be released by the two Japanese crewmen who were alive and moving. There had been a crew of six total.

One laughed and made motion as if to say the American would go up in smoke, but the other admonished him and released the binding on his body but not his hands.

Apparently, when his plane had been shot down over New Guinea, he had been considered important enough to bring to the Philippines for questioning, and now the higher ranked survivor among his captors was proceeding with that plan. As they started to climb, with only their basic kit and weapons, they had to release his hands and put him between them. There had been no choice. The American was no sheltered youth and had hiked, fished, hunted, raced, and been a dare devil, perfect material for that era's flying forces. As soon as the three were high enough and at a precarious point with limited holds, Robinson grabbed on to a protruding rock with all his might with both hands, waited a couple of seconds for the one behind him to close with him, and repeatedly kicked his enemy in the face until the latter could hang on no longer and fell to serious injury or death.

As the lead Japanese turned to look back and down at the sound of the scream, the Lieutenant heaved himself up two more holds, of which he had previous felt the nearest and seen the other in the low light. Closer to the other Japanese now scolding him, assuming correctly his part in the matter, he saw the man struggle to hold on and unholster his pistol to shoot down at him. It was a tough task in those circumstances, but the man was both vulnerable yet confident in his higher position. The Navy pilot, pulling his own weight up with all his might with the one strong right hand, grabbed the pants leg of the Japanese above him and yanked with all his strength again with a pretty strong left arm and fiercely strong grip. In seconds, another scream cut the night and trailed away and downward.

Rescued further by mountain villagers who sent word, the American thought he was in a dream when Jenny and her companions walked into the village.

In an unguarded moment weeks later, the nurse admitted to her commanding officer and supervising doctor, "He is handsome and an officer, and quite desirable. . . So, at the village, when I was attending to his several minor, but as you saw, significant wounds, he of course made a pass. I know what I've got going for me; it was to be expected," smiling between them. "Well, I said respectfully, 'I am flattered, Lieutenant, . . I truly am, but, that Marine sergeant over there, has my heart all wrapped up in storage for when we are out of this mess.' And he teased back, 'Oh you can't do that. No fraternization with enlisted personnel,' with big, exaggerated eyes. So, I replied, 'We'll both be too tired of this when it's over. One or both of us will seek to leave the military.'"

Now, much later at the table the pilot went on about the big sea battle. The first between aircraft carriers and the first in which opposing ships never came close enough for their commanders and crews to see each other, "Now my squadron skipper said that we damaged one of their carriers badly and that the Japs lost a whole shit load of planes, Excuse me, ma'am."

Ann nodded. "What are they calling it?"

"Like usual, the place name, *The Battle of the Coral Sea*. Now we think somethings up, because the Yorktown was damaged and is hightailing it back to Pearl."

In the Presence of My Enemies

Several weeks later, Lt. Robinson had left to join the guerrillas, as it was not possible to get back to Allied territory or the fleet. the Filipina medical assistant and Marine married. Carla, perhaps a true nurse in training fought through her discomfort in treating Olin's wound due to its location but pushed on. More than one serious conference preceded the quaint little ceremony as the two women pushed through with their philosophy of full disclosure to each gender of how the other gender approached sex. Then Allan had a long discussion with the corporal. Then the two officers approved the marriage and wedding, knowing it could open a Pandora's box. Would they end up with six marines joined with local girls in wartime romances that would not survive afterwards? It was of great concern given the racial issue on top of the other issues. But that was a different type of warfare, different activity. It was a community, not a troop of men always on the move chasing the enemy across the island. If the deployment stretched on to a year or more, keeping the sexes apart would be like shepherding kittens and puppies and the men would surely endure any punishment to be with the women.

Ann was returning from her rounds, always followed by a late walk around the grounds that she was just completing, and she was uneasy. Their camp routine had been set and, like hers, become commonplace, even as it related to multiple camps, activities, and duties. Professor Ortega, who would eventually become a permanent coast watcher, was still the main community liaison reaching out to the several villages and small towns he had been welcome in before the war. All behaved a bit more reserved and reclusive than before the enemy arrived, due to their spreading, horrific reputation.

Scared more than she had expected when they arrived and chastened by the events of the previous months, she never felt the security that she had forced in the beginning. The Japanese family, the executions, Colonel Scott's execution and that of his aides, now seemed ages before, and the wedding, a brighter point, followed a courtship of nine weeks. But the elephant in the forest was that there were Japanese nearby in their province of Surigao del Norte, which was a peninsula leaving limited escape routes under cover. The open sea routes to other islands, besides small ones nearby, would be tough to traverse completely under cover of darkness. With those thoughts swimming in her head, Ann had walked the camp in darkness, having left the hospital later than usual. Things had built up lately within her, worries, compulsive planning for anything and everything that might raise the head of surprise and danger. And every time she didn't reign it in, the final scene was that snarling Jap lieutenant cutting of Allan's head after every other man's in camp, before dragging her and Jenny off to sexual slavery. Incongruously, because she had never worn it on her sleeve, yet logical, because it was her history, thoughts of her people's history echoed softly.

Then, as she walked by and scrutinized Carla and Olin's honeymoon hut, she noticed the guard on that side of the grounds was out of sight. Two were posted on each side of the camp and one was always near their hut, away from the others for the privacy of it. A big ravine on that side was a barrier to attack as well, though it could shelter strong climbing scouts of an enemy. Softly, slightly sloping near the top, the chasm dropped and was so deep that treetops of the canopy rising from below were only a little above the roof of the native cottage. Approaching the hut from the right side, allowing some little view behind it, she completed her scan as she passed in front to the other side. Stopping quietly, on a whim . . a feeling of uneasiness, maybe sensed just below the level of knowing you had actually physically sensed something, Ann walked back to the right side of the hut and down its outer wall front to back. By that time in the month, nights were very dark with a slight waning moon, and in the low light, she stopped at the back corner of the hut and peered around into the jungle rising up from the ravine below, holding her breath and listening . . . . She heard whispered voices . . and listening, they were not Filipino, they were Japanese.

Her head, right shoulder, and part of her torso were just around the corner of the shack and looking down, she silently gasped at the way her Navy issue white T-shirt glowed in the low moonlight, picking up that light. And she jerked herself back and pressed herself against the side wall of the hut in fear.

Through her mind faster than it can be told here ".... I have to calm myself..., I can't call out....no time ...." and quietly yet quickly turning back to the front of the honeymoon cottage ripping her white T-shirt off over her head she thought rapidly, as if it was an emergency in her medical field, a bleeding gash and she couldn't find the artery in all the damage. Sneaking up to the hut's door, opening it slowly, in the dim orange of the lantern she saw the two in the bed. They were playfully active and softly giggling, and sensing her, both raised in surprise to see their commanding officer, shirtless and bare from the waist up. Carla shyly covered herself as Ann placed her right index finger to her lips in the common shushing signal and reached for Olin's Thompson. She knew it would be there because she had insisted, thinking he of all of them would be awake most of the night and, though distracted by Carla, the most aware after the first of it. Ann truly prayed that the Thompson was there.

The 1928 A1 had a thirty round box magazine attached and another taped lightly to the stock with white bandage tape. She wanted a one hundred round drum too, though she knew they were harder and slower to attach.

"Drums, drums, Olin?!"

"There, the sack!" he whispered desperately.

The two must have thought their commander had lost her mind there in the door with no shirt on and appearing to want to join their honeymoon with a weapon, and Ann said firmly in a strong whisper, "Stay quiet and get on the ground to avoid strays. I have to check something. Do not come out corporal!"

She grabbed Olin's web belt with grenades and tossed his 45 pistol to him, saying, "Don't follow, stay down very low. That's an order. Lay on top of her."

For only a moment she entertained the thought of recruiting him, but he might be seen and Carla widowed not long after her wedding night.

As she moved instinctively, she planned her sequence: grenades, firing, magazine changes . . with the same mental gymnastics when trying to save a survivable patient with everything going wrong. She knew the drum magazines could jam.

Rounding the hut, she also intuitively realized that she was the one to do this, she was near invisible in the darkness. The suddenly purposeful and focused woman, with the calm mind and hands of a surgeon, crept up the wall of the hut to its corner, knowing timing was everything. Darker than any Filipino in the command, the Doctora stood near the hut's corner but out from it to avoid creating contrast and heard the whispered Japanese in the brush at the ravine's rim. If she was visible to them, she should have been dead by now and the attack would have commenced.

Before rounding the structure, the experienced and intelligent woman had stared at the darkness to let her irises adjust. Now, standing, then kneeling in the open but unlit and dark as the darkness around her, she began to see them form before her. 'Timing' she thought, and 'speed' . . then 'thoroughness'. . . . for the moment the firing started, her companions could run from their huts and tents into a hail of bullets from the enemy. But if she did nothing, they would be attacked and slaughtered anyway, as would happen if she tried to run around in an attempt to silently warn them. No. She was the only one who knew and the only one to know. It was her battle. It was the only way. She had to put fire down the slope on to them.

As she prepared, there was no time for other thoughts or conscious realization of the fear she was feeling, the near terror . . no time.

Thus, without conscious thought, all the tricks Dad had ever taught her while hunting with him welled up and blended with the fears of the evil she now faced . . and she stood there, eyes adjusted to the darkness now, watching them . . their subtle movements . . heard their whispers . . felt her terror . . but like the terror of an invasive cut into a patient in the wilds of the jungle with no modern equipment and all alone . . and she heard more of them behind . . behind the others . . but they could not fire from there, down the gorge.

Only briefly, one final outside thought passed through in her stream of conscious thought . . that what she was about to do, would be the last thing she ever did on the Earth.

Concealed in the night by her beautiful God given camouflage, the scared, brave, doctor stepped quietly up to the rim of the ravine twenty yards from them on her left and looking away from her, ready to assault the camp. And she lay the belt, drum, and Thompson on the ground. Sgt. Adams had taught her about throwing grenades, and she had asked about measured throws and distances. He refused to show his tricks until she said, "Sergeant, I am your commanding officer, this is an order. You can tell my husband if you feel some responsibility, but you cannot refuse my request."

A mere mistake of seconds could kill her. She pulled the pin on one grenade and then another . . carefully juggling the two and praying not to drop them, released the 'spoon' . . waited a long second and threw them one after another in rapid succession a few yards apart from left away from her to the right closer. As the second one left her hand, she pulled a third and fourth pin and tossed them, waiting only an instant, a bit deeper. Those were lobbed in a high arc, the intent being to have them explode just above the ground spraying their deadly shrapnel over the enemy personnel as they lay prone. Two more were thrown, again in a bit of an arc, a little farther toward the rear of the enemy down the slope.

There was gunfire from them now but weaker than expected and toward the camp, and it was clear they knew not from which direction the grenades had come, . . And she stood in an instant at her position to the enemies left and facing them at a forty-five degree angle, . . picking up the Thompson as the last two grenade blasts resonated, and, as the heavy gun pounded loudly, she sprayed back and forth while adjusting range as well . . not the short burst she had been taught to conserve ammo. Empty . . the woman dropped stoically to a knee then flat and, gripping the Tommy gun and the drum, rolled to her right . . over the rim and down the slope, struggling to go only a few yards. She heard the projectiles rip the brush where she had fired from and they had seen her muzzle flash. But a 30 caliber carbine above had begun firing; and, in the din of collective gunfire, the softness of the jungle foliage, and Ann's near invisibility, the Japanese soldiers, as they also fired, did not hear, see, or account for her roll.

Thankful that these weren't the dry Autumn foliage of the Appalachians, where she had hunted deer, and that she hadn't reached the drop off, praying, she changed magazines, without a hitch, to the hundred round drum. Carbine fire was coming from two places above, and with the silence from her, the Japs addressed their gunfire there.

It was much weaker than the enemy force's numbers should have presented, and at that point she threw the other two grenades she had put in her pocket in high arcs at the lowest point down the ravine that she expected enemy personnel might be. Then standing she came from their flank, sweeping as she walked out into them . . angry . . adrenaline flowing . . remembering Col. Scott and knowing of the comfort girls in the village.

She stopped before walking into friendly fire. Deafening before, it was silent now, the carbines quiet as well. But the drum was not yet empty and she fired a sweeping burst down the lower slope.

Standing like some petite, dark version of the new character Wonder Woman on the side of the hill, midst them a few yards and oblivious now to her own safety, she felt something whiz by her left ear and sting it . . then a burning pain in her side at the bottom of the rib cage and the thought …. Not enough …. not enough. She had to be sure . . there were too many . . . Quickly falling flat among the bodies and rolling to her right she opened up the Tommy where the muzzle flash had come from . . And then rising now through the pain for the higher angle as piercing fire hit her, sending fire and force into the left thigh . . a searing pain throughout the leg that knocked her down . . and the fellas' carbines kept pounding again, and Ann, on her knees, opened up the Thompson again at the man with the pistol still flashing at her, the heavy machine gun pounding her shoulder with every pulsing round and her arms aching, but she didn't know it. Other pain seared through her, erasing the soreness, and throbbed now even up to the nerves in her head, and empty, she dropped the Tommy to the ground and fell back.

All was silence, and she heard a moan or two. Even the stoically malicious and seemingly evil enemy soldiers weren't totally beyond feeling pain.

In a semiconscious place and trying to focus, she felt people around her, familiar, and no more gunfire, voices, voices she knew . . and all she could say, could ask them was, "Is everybody okay, Allan is Allan okay, Jenny…."

Running up, Allan and others who had all come out of wherever they were with the first of it splitting the night, some running to the top of the ravine, crouching low as they reached it shining the inverted L shaped boy scout flashlights as far as they could, firearms at the ready. Others, knowing someone of their command had taken on an enemy, ran to Olin and Carla's hut as the sound and muzzle flashing of the Thompson had come from there.

He had looked for her only briefly, running to his duty; and, worried, he dashed to the area behind the hut. He knew it was not likely she was there, but duty also called. Behind it and staring in the light of several handheld flashlights, Allan heard voices and turned to see Carla and Olin over his prone wife, who was laying back from the rim of the ravine, a little nearer their hut where they had quickly brought her from among the dead and dying enemy.

Bleeding from three wounds on her left side, one soaked only the side of her nude lower torso, revealing a significant but not yet deadly wound.

Instinctively glancing up at her face to see if there was a deadly head wound, he saw the small spot of blood beside her, dripping from the nicked left ear.

Next, looking down, Allan saw the pool of blood under her left thigh and an entry wound in front, halfway between the knee and hip, in the middle of the muscle but outward of the bone. Significant but not profuse blood flow underneath also revealed no damaged arteries. The wound's position did, as well. With a sigh he realized that a dying Jap had fired off three rounds too far to the right of his target; and that, positioned as they were externally, outboard of the body, no injuries were mortal. God, the designer, had place the arteries protectively inside the limbs and their bones, on the body side. Every well-trained knife fighter knew that.

"Her abdominal wound?" he inquired with angst.

"She has lost blood, but not too much, and I have maneeged to stop it. Olin, please maneege the tourniquet while I get some alcohol and sulfa."

As Carla stood to go, Jenny arrived with what was needed and the two nurses got back to work. Dutifully, the sentries had remained at their posts around the camp, preventing any attack from other directions. Sgt. Adams and Olin, the latter against Ann's orders, had fired and then gone down the hill into the ravine with their carbines.

In only a few moments, 1ˢᵗ Sgt. Morrow walked up to report.

Allan had just knelt to her, but she was unconscious, and he looked at the two nurses with a worried expression, to which, significantly the younger, now confident Filipina replied in the precise English common to well-schooled Filipinos, "Seer, she has no head wound, and the ground where she fell on the hill is soft; she has surely just fainted from the emotion and blood loss, which ees not life threatening."

"Sir, . . Allan," spoke Morrow, and the officer stood and turned.

"We got 'em all, twenty-five_ a sergeant, two corporals and twenty-two men. We lost Corporal Shelby Scott. They must have assassinated him in the forest. His duty was this side. The men will take it hard. Some Japs are still alive but serious. We should not waste our medical supplies on them. With those wounds, they would die anyway."

"How did we get them all then, the sentry down? Who gave the alarm and who laid down the fire? It looks down there like we ambushed them, not the other way around. This is amazing. We have some top Marines. Maybe an advancement in rank is due a couple of them. I owe them my wife's life."

"Your wife sir. Look at the lieutenant."

With a questioning expression toward the Sergeant, he did and turned back to Morrow inquisitively.

"Beside her."

Looking again and seeing Olin's machine gun, which had been brought up with her by Olin, he turned back to Morrow, processing it but not yet clearly, still confused. The Tommy Gun could have been Olin's, though there was a carbine slung on his shoulder, or she might have walked with the machine gun that night though usually only with her side arm, knowing the sentries were everywhere.

"What?" turning to Morrow. "What are you saying? Did she engage too . . along with the boys?"

"Allan, Sgt. Adams was the next sentry to the northeast on the perimeter after Scott. He engaged with his carbine after all hell broke loose . . finally got in close too. He probably got some. So did Olin. There was no alarm, Allan. I imagine there was no time. She did it all, Sir . . your wife. The Lieutenant engaged them alone."

As Allan turned back to her, Morrow continued, "Just look around sir, look wide and there to the edge of the drop off. There's .45 brass everywhere, a virtual carpet; there's a web belt missing quite a few grenades. I'll grant you there are a few grenade pins laying around here in the brush. I heard ten; Adams says he threw two. There's a drum magazine there on the Thompson, and I found this empty stick down the hill there. The boys said the fire came from the right in the brush and we found her there, five yards or so in among 'em. She out flanked them after engaging first up here from the rim of the ravine. I think the damn Japs couldn't figure where she was and she moved."

Turning back and looking intently at the Sergeant, sharing a knowing glance, then turning his head down and taking a deep breath, he had no words, and Morrow added, "Sir, Earl said he saw machine gun flashes down the slope some yards. She waded into it, Allan. Look at her ear; an inch or so to the right and we'd have lost her. If she hadn't done it though, we would have all been wiped out. They give medals for this, Sir . . big ones, usually posthumously." The husband turned back to look at his wife again, laying peaceful now, and the two strong, tough men shared that truth between them quietly.

Looking down at the brass shell casings on the ground, hands on his hips, Morrow shook his head slowly, and almost to himself said softly, "Damn, the lady sure can type."

There was silence and then a chuckle from the tense husband, "*Chicago typewriter* . . I haven't heard that one for a long time. Guess I've been away too long. Do they still say it in the States?"

"You got me, Sir. Seems like I've been out here forever. . . . . Look, Sir, I've seen some wounds in my time. It's clean. She'll be fine. The men are going to be so much more confident now in this mission."

The Lieutenant turned and looked at the 1st Sergeant, and Harold Morrow continued, "If I may speak freely, Sir. You two have handled everything smooth, even the executions. But combat veterans like my boys? They're gonna worry about the weak link that could get them killed. And with two commanding officers who just changed out of civvies, well . . you see. But the Lieutenant there, she just wiped that concern away. They know now that the one expected to be the weak link, the woman, is not just a looker."

"A 'looker'; they think that? I mean you know, her being not exactly standard issue for this sort of thing."

"Your wife's a dish, Sir; you're a lucky man."

"How bad are they?" Allan said nodding toward the bodies on the slope.

"Severe shrapnel wounds, even large wounds, from the grenades, and machine gun rounds or both."

"We'll let them die. We need no information. We know who and where he is. We can't spare the medicine."

Walking up, Sgt. Adams stated, "The boys found these ropes and straps down the hill there together with some knapsack type bags. I believe the latter were to help them carry off our medicines and Lt. Ann's instruments. I believe the ropes and straps were for captives, especially officers."

Allan added, "Rumors are that the American women who surrendered here may not be receiving that kind of abuse like that, but they weren't caught fighting the Japs. Fighting like this, may get one the same treatment like the native girls they have abused."

~

In the late afternoon on a Saturday two months later, Ann sat carelessly, casually in the hammock with the sunset behind her, because she knew with the combined view, even a Philippine sunset didn't always dominate . . only simply enhance. The perimeter was secure, and they kept a watchful eye on Maru's small garrison up the coast from their original landfall and the *USS Bangús's* battle with the patrol boats. Ann was almost completely recovered, but Jenny was playing hard-nosed 'doctor' and restricting her. The nurse did not want the wound in the side of Ann's abdomen to become a problem leading to a needed incision and possible infection.

As she looked at her ruggedly handsome husband, looking a bit red-faced in the glow of the sunset, he had just sat himself on a fallen log left where it had been dropped by the axes to serve the purpose of a bench for now. He knew not of her presence, as she was a silhouette among a forest of silhouettes with her dark skin and hair and the light behind. The view was not completely open to the sunset as there were trees. But for the cool comfort of it and to tease and please Allan, Ann had her light dress raised above her knees revealing one brown leg on edge of the hammock, with her heel hooked there and the other pretty limb dangling over, bent over the hammock's edge at the knee. She reclined mostly upright on some large homemade pillows. Thus, the sun creeped and glowed around the edges of her form, legs, cheeks, forehead, nose, arms, highlighting the brown there to gold.

Allan, sitting with elbows on his knees and clasping his hands together, looked up and saw her, as if God had punched him in a rib and whispered, 'Look, you idiot, I turned the sunset on and everything.' But of course, they must be exemplary officers in front of their men.

He looked at her legs, so shapely and seemingly long, though she was petite, and all he could think of was, 'what beautiful gams.' Sometimes simple thoughts were deep.

He studied his wife long and hard, and their lingering gaze revealed more than words. For who could have offered and shared such a strange honeymoon for the other as that which the two were experiencing at that moment. Most would not be able to see the 'honeymoon' within the risks of this excursion. Allan knew there was something special about it that he had not yet put his finger on, had not yet grasped. But he would send his words and thoughts in a different direction.

Before he could speak, Ann said softly yet with some strong level of emotion, leaving out the common racial pejorative, "I hate these Japanese like some of your race hate me . . but stronger . . you know, now."

He let it set for the moment.

After a long pause, during which she wasn't looking for an answer or comment, she spoke again.
"It wasn't hating that night. It's how they are now. I had no choice and I had to turn into that different person. You have no choice. The evil. You have to address it; we have to address it . . our country, our duty here. It's the same old story, Allan, Dear. You cannot know. I prepared myself for anything. It's a war, . . but I didn't expect this . . that."

"Address it?"

"Yes."

As matured as he had become, the both of them really, he didn't discuss that further, in spite of any angst engendered by her meaning. And both sat quietly for some long time, the woman, who had pressed herself into a dangerous world, calmed somewhat now by the expression of herself to her husband.

"You haven't yet scolded me. I have steeled myself for it for days on end, but I wasn't going to bring it up if you didn't."

"We were leaving your graduation those years ago. And we were walking to the car, and he said, 'She's going to Europe, to Paris to study medicine.' I just sort of nodded and kept walking. And Dad said, 'Carol Ann's a nice pretty girl. She'll be there a long time, what with premed and all.' And I looked up at him, as we had reached the car. I guess I was slightly surprised, you know. And as he stopped to unlock the door, he stood there and looked at me kind of serious and said to me, 'You said you wanted to take those flying lessons and that license overseas to get work and have some adventures. And I trust you to keep your eyes open and stay out of trouble. If you run into that girl . . uh Carolyn over there, don't be rude, like people can be here sometimes. You treat her friendly and right. We're gonna picnic with them out by the river again tomorrow. In a way, they're family. Her dad and I served together. It was a special duty behind the lines and he got in it, though with the rules he shouldn't have.' That's all he said right then, and we rode home. He was quiet in the car, and I was too, stunned a little by the imperceptible strength in his words. In the middle of the drive, right in the middle of, he said, 'It'll be different over there,

Europe and such, not as tough for them, not like here.'"

Thinking she had gotten the point, he simply continued on the new conversational course, "There was nothing to scold about a U.S. Navy officer doing their duty by taking the only rational option that would have succeeded at the time."

They sat in long pensive silence, and he spoke again.

"I mean Dad could tell a race joke, but not real mean ones. He didn't like those at all. He liked funny ones that made sense and didn't hurt. Every culture and race does some stupid stuff that's funny. Once, a bunch of my uncles were together in the basement den, and they started that. So, Dad said, 'I've got one,' and he told it. Then he said, 'I've got another one,' and he told a Polish one that was a bit cruder. You see, one of my uncles by marriage seemed to be the most racist toward others and he was Polish. They laughed a little at that one. Then Dad started through a whole litany of really good Irish jokes, which he actually thought were pretty funny, and, you see, we're Irish. By then the room was silent except for Dad laughing at his own Irish jokes, or maybe at the way he had shut them up. Then he said, 'I need a beer,' and he got up and went upstairs with all the ladies."

Allan looked at Ann who was slowly forming in his vision as his eyes adjusted to the dark and the low deeper red backlight. She still had the pleasantly alluring look on her face reflecting her love for him, though there was a slight widening of her eyes in subtle, moderate surprise at his tale. Finally, he inquired of her, "You don't think he actually saw us . . you know, together like this someday?"

"I don't know, Darling, but I do know that is a sweet, even beautiful story. I came with my dad a few times when he was working on projects for yours. That was just after the picnics started, and I was just old enough to take notes for him. I was his secretary in the field sometimes, when I wasn't at school and the secretary didn't want to come or was covered with work. You saw me, but we didn't talk because Dad was rigid about my note taking on the job. I think your dad kinda thought he knew me a little when he spoke to you that afternoon. His words were a bit strange. They were too strong. They weren't just, 'Hey, if you run into Carolyn Ann overseas, be nice.' You know, I think your Dad was playing matchmaker."

"He didn't like jokes that made fun of people in a bad way, like peoples features. He enjoyed the occasional one that made fun of a silly practice or a flaw common to a group. Behind closed doors, he made devastating fun of the Klan. And he loved to rip us Irish . . drinking jokes especially. You know us Catholic Irish can put 'em down . . so can the Protestant ones. It's ruined many a family though when it gets outta hand."

298

"Allison isn't Irish."

"I know, but we're strongly Irish in both my parents' backgrounds."

Both looked long at each other, each wishing to embrace and realizing the impracticality of it at that moment. The sun rouged the sky now with a dark blood red and elsewhere save that area it was almost as dark as night. And she spoke softly yet audibly and with firmness.

"Your pushing through with this, Allan, was the best gift you could have given. It is a girl's dream come true. . . . your trust and the willingness to take the risks . . ."

"It's not what men do, are supposed to do. I'm glad it is appreciated."

"Africa was appreciated."

"You know I didn't want it."

"And you allowed it."

"What?"

"You were already acting like a husband then, but you allowed it."

There was a pause between them, she had opened a box and elaborated, "You could have really pushed me not to go. But you knew how important it was. And maybe deep down you knew back then that we were alike, risk takers for good reasons. I know now of your spy flights: Indochina, Shanghai, Nanking."

"My instinct now is to protect you all the more."

"Yet we are here in the Philippine mountains, in an enemy held land."

"So we are."

"The footsteps of Christ, Allan. Satan's legions are on the earth right now. This could even be the end times. What could we possibly be saving ourselves for? I knew I might die or be tortured if Africa went the wrong way. I know it now."

He had reconciled himself to it all: to this woman of courage, to this war that was an assault on mankind, on civilization itself, to what might occur down the road. He had thought it out on the submarine, tense as he was in the claustrophobic environment. It had been such that to dwell on it was impossible because one could lose control, endanger everyone and become a fool. He had been able to calm himself and then both women, and he told them of the civilian and military women that were praying to be taken off and were being brought out on subs. Dozens maybe hundreds of women would thus get out of the Philippines. The submarines of the era were not yet as safe as in more recent times, and boats are lost even now, even in peacetime. To be sealed in, and to know that if something happened, whether an attack or a mechanical problem, never reaching the surface was a more probable result than survival.

It became dark, and they were quiet. As she had relaxed there in light dress in the hammock, it had been a quiet seduction, but there was time for that. It would be a long night. The west became as black as the rest of their part of the world around them. Ann spoke again, her voice coming out of the night softly, like an unseen ghost, saying, "I'm sorry. I'm so sorry I put you through this. I'm sorry I insisted. Now that we're here, your Old West history story has soaked in. I've put such a burden on you."

"Our brave nurse Ensign Jenny Barkley. She came too easily, insisted too casually and matter-of-factly, and thus, brought an inevitability to this. To me, it made your idea seem simply the thing to do, the thing one does in such a global emergency."

She wanted it to end there, on a good note. It was dark now and they sensed each other's presence, he heard her sighs, and both heard the other's breathing.

"Well, while we're still alive, and we're on honeymoon, shall we find our tent in this darkness and honeymoon."

~

"Lieutenants! Both of you, listen." As the two looked up from their breakfast, The Navy Petty Officer, who had become the official radioman, jogged toward them from across the camp in the early gray tinged glow of morning.

"This came in last night. I'm getting more and clearer chatter now from the outside world. They're closer. I just decoded it, based on the codes we were given. I responded to it and they heard me, and I convinced them who I was. I said straight up in plain English with a Southern draw and a lot of slang to confuse the Japs, '...don't give me secret stuff, just common news all the world knows.' I told them I couldn't read their new codes. So, they responded in the old ones."

"And? Let's see, or just tell me. You seem excited to tell it."

"He does look all aglow, though still military," responded Ann with a smile.

"Yes, Sirs, err, Ma'am. We're in the Solomons, fighting the Japs in a place called Guadalcanal. There's been some big night time sea battles there, but they couldn't tell the results of 'em of course. I think we've been in there a long time, months. The Nips could be listening. I have the feelin' it may be touch and go. But the point is we're attacking back against 'em."

"That's well east of here but very significant," responded Allan.

"There's more, Sir. It's no news to the Japs; they know. After Coral Sea, they clashed up near Hawaiya, a big one."

"Hawai'i."

"I know, just forget, Sir. It was a way up north west on the chain. Most folks don't know it's part of the Hawaiian Islands, Midway. Ma'am, Sir, we sank four of their carriers!"

Attentive already but looking back and forth to and from their plates, both looked up open mouthed and nearly pie-eyed, and Allan inquired, "Did we lose anything important?"

"He wouldn't say sir, but just said not to worry and sounded cheerful. I know he wasn't a carrier sir. It would be too risky to chat with me, . . probably a ground station on the island, Guadalcanal, or a ship offshore that was known already to the Japs."

Allan offered a well thought out evaluation, "He was a sub on the surface charging his batteries closer to us. That way he could not only move away from where he was when you communicated, but do so out of sight. He was charged and ready to dive and got the hell out of there in case the signal was tracked. Only a sub like that or a base commonly

303

known to the enemy, Darwin or somewhere like that would do that without someone getting busted."

All three nodded seriously. Rank was being maintained and chain of command, but in such a setting for an extended time, all had become friends. This Southern boy and the Doctor had similar interests in hunting and fishing, as did Allan. The three bonded over that and hunted and fished for food together. Ann laughed to herself at the realization that the intelligent, non-college educated Petty officer would have been marriageable material in her opinion in a different time and place if she were to have crossed the color line as she had with Allan. Make no mistake, he couldn't have beat out Allan for her affections, but she thought the guy actually had a very respectfully managed crush on his female commanding office. Well, in their little microcosmic war world, in a land of brown Asians, with a command made up of white and brown personnel commanded by a white man and a black woman, perhaps everyone was getting an education, especially that woman.

The sailor broke the knowing pregnant silence, elaborating, "That's why we're in the Solomons, Sirs." He said it knowing she didn't really mind the cumulative title. "We couldn't do it unless we had a numerical advantage in flattops." He was an enlisted man because he joined without higher education, but he loved the Navy and was potential material for officer candidate school someday. "I studied it before the war, on my own, just reading.

We started with seven and they had ten. If we've only lost the Lex and they lost four and that damaged one before, we're even up already."

"But we are in a two-ocean war," pointed out the woman.

"The Germans have no carriers or enough capital ships to sortie in battle squadrons of any size," put in, Allan. "We saw that before the war with the Bismarck and Graf Spee, lone raiders and pairs."

"Yes, Sir. Their whole game against our boys in the Atlantic is their U-boats. They have a lot of them, but they're slow_ speed of a freighter on the surface and crawling below it. They can only attack the freighters with any real success, and we will shepherd 'em in convoys like in the last days of the last war. The Brits are handling them in the Mediterranean, the Nazis and the Italians, the last we heard anything before we were cutoff more by bein' here. The Italians have some ships, but I don't know about their commanders. You know_ goin' against the Royal Navy."

India 1943

In such wars, described by the Navy doctor as the possible Biblical end of the world, people around the world in various corners and duties suffer and struggle, as something is happening almost everywhere at once. Daily lives become dramas, small or large. Ships, planes, and men were deciding the early outcome of the war in the Coral Sea (doorstep of Australia), at Midway, and in the Solomons. In Northern India the issues then were many as the Allies tried to supply China with a 'Burma Road", and the C-47 military version of the then iconic Douglas DC-3 airliner was "Flying the Hump" across the Himalayas. The Japanese were in Burma, and before the war would be settled, that would lead to the *Battle of Imphal* between March and July 1944. In the preceding year leading up to that struggle along the border between Burma and India, both sides were active. And the British Commonwealth forces built up supplies. In such environments, secret missions would cross the border and refugees seeking safer ground would as well, and the Allison Command's mission into Surigao del Norte was over a year old.

In India, the Aero was being prepared for a clandestine flight, one of many. In the ensuing months after the flight across the Gulf of Manna, she had become a government contract ship, flying supplies and people here and there. This began almost as soon as her intrepid crew of five landed and deplaned in Maduria. Days later they began flying shipments to the Burmese India border. But others were more intense and dangerous.

Now as the they planned the third clandestine, dangerous flight, the chief pilot and acting company president suggested that the woman remain on base this time. The two friends, the American-Malayan couple, and the Australian, Arnie Sutherland had been working and living elbow to elbow for many days, ever since the Aero had lifted off in Trincomalee. All the time, the Laotian and the Frenchman had grown closer, perhaps proving the intuition and analysis of their mutual friends, especially the company's currently absent de facto president, Allan Allison. Nothing was said; nature had just taken its own natural course. And, thus, many platitudes and terms of endearment passed between them, with an occasional touch here and there.

With his suggested request, the exotic woman neither spoke nor nodded, and sat quietly, almost disinterestedly, studying maps.

Arnie went to work on maintenance and to do a scheduled plane check. Such things were more rigidly completed by this time because the female member had been given the administrative duties and was meticulous.

"Beau?" spoken ever so softly without looking up and then with her head raised slowly. "I believe in equality in marriage, yet when the vote is one-to-

307

one, the conundrum is the lack of a tiebreaker. The solution is to defer, not always to the man in our general biblical way, but to the one more schooled, more educated on the issue at hand. Again, here and now, we have a tie, you the expert flier, I the experienced agent. And I know you have fought and killed, as have I. With such shared experience and training, unofficial or otherwise, we must act as a team. If one goes alone and does not come back, the other will be destroyed for the time being anyway . . . . may never heal . . probably, never heal. We go together, survive a crash and the Burmese jungle together, fight our way out together, die together . . as our lives should be described from this point on, 'together'."

He looked at her and nodded, and they sat quietly working, yet in thought. The woman had just proposed to the man after all.

Standing thirty minutes later to go for a bite to eat, he stepped to her and the embrace happened faster than could be described or the mechanics be figured out to do so. Everything with the two just seemed to happen naturally, two lives that would flow like a convergence of two rivers into one.

A small Catholic ceremony followed a few evenings later, and soon the two and their crewmen were over Burma in the night and headed for Japanese held territory. Elaine had taken to the work and learned every job on such a plane on such missions. Particularly, she had mastered communications and the radios, and the plane now carried a powerful set for her in the area behind the pilot's seat, on the left, complimenting the built-in unit for the pilots. More frequencies could be monitored from her station. Of course, the pretty, multilingual agent was the right person to be in that plane on that night and others over enemy territory. She also had mastered air to ground observance in daylight and in the difficult night, how to adjust one's eyes and the like. And, on her advice, red night compartment lighting had been installed.

The particular night, British and American agents would be dropped, the latter probably OSS (Office of Strategic Services). In the typical 'need to know' basis, the plane crew had not been told. A different British officer commanded this mission.

The drop by parachute went well apparently, and a second drop three weeks later was planned. A cargo plane taking off from a field in northern India was not unusual, especially as it turned south toward the broader country struggling for its independence from its colonial masters while fighting with them together against a greater evil.

The little group of patriots of mixed lineages lifted off and flew deeper into Burma than before and the men jumped to success or doom. The plane crew could not know. Need to know, you know. But this was what that war was about, a world war, and, besides the armies and navies of nations, it drew in the adventurers and expatriates around the fringes of nations' borders and societies so that one mission could be flown by a Frenchman, an Australian, a Laotian, an American, and a Malaysian. In some ways it was a melting pot war.

Coming out of the country, the danger, the no man's land the Aero roared through the night to safety and Elaine said through the stillness, "I have a distress call!"

"What?" asked the British mission commander.

"In Spanish!"

"Ignore it."

"No."

"I'm in command."

The petite Oriental woman looked at him through the dark red light and replied, "It is our plane, and your mission has been completed."

Of course, it was not quite yet a crisis of command and he did not yet know how to react.

The woman broke radio silence and called Simpson, who was monitoring the mission.

The officer back in the plane could not quite hear, and she said, "George I have a mayday in Spanish."

"What does Arnold say?"

"Ignore it"

"Then do it."

"No."

She turned toward the cockpit to her husband just ahead and said, "I have an idea, hug the border if you agree."

The Aero turned north along the India Burma border and Elaine said in Tagalog, "Acknowledge?"

Finally, after a moment, the radio crackled, and a voice, with an accent, as before, said, "Cebuano." Immediately, the consummate linguist eased into perfect Cebuano Visayan, "What is your state?"

"Catholic mission threatened by small Japanese force."

"Reply and continue Cebuano; presumably safe."

"Agreed."

"Escape route?"

"I think they are not aware of us. They arrived yesterday. We might flee to border. One hundred meters."

"Roger, uh, yes, there is a field due west of your location. That is about one fourth kilometer. Are you aware?"

The Cebuano man replied, "We are on a hill. There is a slope and field below, and a grass field to the border. Closest enemy is north in hills, but a threat. I am not sure we are known to them. Who are you?"

"How many are you?"

"Three priests, ten children. Who are you?"

"A friend. Can you make the border, that field you saw?"

The conversation continued in Cebuano, from the Philippines, presumably unintelligible to any Japanese assigned in the area.

"It would take twenty minutes to cross over."

"Darkest clothing possible, but do not waste time. A flashlight if you have it to signal. We will identify by language if necessary when near."

"Salamat."

"We will gamble. Discontinue radio. Go, Go!"

The British officer had edged closer and asked what was going on.

312

Elaine turned to him in the red darkness and said, "A rescue."

"You cannot do it. I forbid it! This civilian plane is valuable to us."

"And yet civilian."

"Do you realize who you are dealing with, young lady?!"

"George, George? Yes. We are affecting a rescue of three Filipino Catholic missionaries with Burmese orphans along the border. Your man disagrees."

"His opinion takes precedence."

"George. You know what I've done for you . . am capable of. Do you value that? The mission's complete. This our plane."

"Elaine?!"

British Major Arnold on the plane put his two cents in, "It won't be civilian for long. If we get back, I am taking it."

"Elaine?!" George called through the radio.

"Beau, do you agree?"

"Of course. Innocent lives come first. Break out the arms Arnie."

313

The copilot left his seat and headed past the woman to the back of the plane. The Mission commander stepped up to the woman intent of taking control in a military way, and the woman, standing now at the radio, had her hands on her hips, thinking fast about procedures.

"Step back with me, major."

"Are you serious, little girl?"

"I am a devout Catholic woman, major. I have killed three men for George Simpson, for the greater good. I still sleep soundly at night, but I want to save some. They're children."

"I have to stick to the mission."

"Your mission is complete. I have innovated in my work for you British. We will beat the little zombie followers of their emperor because we adjust. We fight this war for them too, those children and priests below us now and frightened."

"You little Chink bitch," expressing openly maybe the thoughts he had about who George Simpson chose to work with. "This plane is valuable to us."

They stood together face-to-face in the red light.

She looked closely at him and inquired, "Were you in Saigon in early '36 and Đà Nẵng in 37 just after?"

314

"Yes, What the hell do you care, you damn Chink. Two of your kind tried to kill me. One almost succeeded. But I'm here. We don't need you."

"I killed both of your assassins . . the last one as he aimed that shot at you in the alley. I was playing his confidante at great risk so I could make sure he didn't succeed because of the information you had and your courage. In his dying moments we struggled afterward and he cut my arm here," and she forcefully shoved the cuff of the leather flight jacket up to show the beginnings of a long heavy scar from a deep wound that shown clearly in the dim red light of the cabin. "It goes to the shoulder. I almost lost the arm. I followed your mission there as shadow security invisible to the enemy, just another girl among many hanging around whites for their money or a marriage and ticket to France or England and a different life. But it was a lie; I loved Indochina. You were a hero and inspiration to me. I'm not Chinese. 'Chink' insults them. I am Laotian. We aren't important enough yet to have insulting labels from Westerners."

The officer stared at the Southeast Asian woman and finally said softly, "Land your plane, give me a machine gun."

"In the locker on the left at the tail. Thank you."

No time had been wasted in their debate, as it just gave time for the refugees to get down the hill and across the stream to the edge of the big meadow.

315

The Aero landed softly nearest the expected path of the refugees at the border. Beau had a touch that allowed a slightly shortened landing, and he would be able to get her up with ease in spite of the terror of it for the passengers watching the tree line.

At the hatch, Elaine yelled back up to the cockpit and said, "We might need your gunship. Don't forget me," and she was gone from the plane. The Major looked to the cockpit and then followed her. Each had a Thompson Submachine Gun and a .45 Government, both American arms, with them.

Regretting the turn of events and her instantaneous decisions and actions, the pilot husband roared off the ground and climbed in the night, as his Aussie copilot was in the back making ready. Things had been refined since Africa in '41.

To the two British soldiers aboard he commanded as if he were in their corps, "Help me here and then have those two BARs at the ready and crouch below me on either side."

With their aid, the swivel mount post was set in the hatchway center bottom in a bracket hole at the threshold, and the .30 caliber machine gun was mounted. The height required less than a standing position, and Arnie had a stool for the purpose. Instinctively he had known that Beau would take the northwest course, because he had landed and taken off that way. Thus, he preferred it. And thusly, the gun was mounted in the starboard hatch and the

plane came across the impromptu landing field
darkened and low.

The men in the plane at every position could see the
action playing out below, even in the darkness. An
enemy sentry had alerted to the people crossing the
border after dashing to it, and the muzzle flashes of
the Japanese twinkled in the bush and counted to be
about twenty, probably the little new border
observation outpost's full complement. Southwest
of that they could see the widely spaced flashes of
the Tommies of Elaine and the Major, leaving a
center channel devoid of fire for the refugees to run
through to the nonexistent plane, which was still in
the air. Between the two flickering light arrays of
death were the invisible refugees, wondering how
they would get away, as they had seen the plane
take off.

But below Elaine's screams were joined by the
major calling to the missionaries and their charges,
"RUN RUN RUN!"

The Thompsons barked, and seemed to move
around a bit, for the girl and major wanted to stay
alive by being moving targets, praying for the real
damage to come quickly . . and it did. Suddenly the
thirty-caliber opened up with two adjoining
Browning Automatic Rifles barking as loud and
deadly. Firing over the refugees and two shooters
and targeting the enemy beyond.

There had been clear enough ground for the enemy, so they had spread out for each man to have a field of fire. Thus, as Arnie raked the center of their formation back and forth, each British commando took his end of the line of Japanese, parallel to the plane's fuselage and spread wide to fire at the refugees.

There was no time for the silenced Japanese to react to the fire from above, and the Aero was soon on the ground. The major quickly guided the refugees to the hatch, where Arnie had removed the gun and its swivel post and the soldiers were now on the ground to offer cover fire with the BARs. But there was no need; the enemy was silent.

Within a second of the secure boarding, and as the two soldiers with the big Brownings started to board, the major commanded, "Stay at you posts, men."

She had been the rogue leader of the particular mission, but he was the soldier and officer and continued to act like it now, turning to the dark silent field of grass. A haystack in which to find a pretty needle.

Then, pistol drawn, he ran to the last position of Elaine's muzzle flashes and, finding nothing in the high grass, quickly jogged around that spot in an ever-widening circle, forming a spiral path. A mortar burst short, fifty yards away toward the forest . . and he continued his search in the night . .

another mortar at thirty yards, and they appeared to be coming from another direction . . and at ten yards out and to the south he found her laying in a moderately concerning pool of blood. She sensed him and, opening her eyes in a grimacing face, said, "I can't stand."

As he bent to her she elaborated through gasps of pain, " . . the bullet broke my hip or pelvis. No artery, but too much blood loss . ."

He pulled out a white cloth from a hip pouch and placed it on the wound. Placing both of her hands there he said, "Press as hard as you can; on the plane we'll address the bleeding at the exit."

Scooping her up as a man carries a wife across the threshold or a wounded woman or child, he made sure one hand was on the exit wound in back so that her weight and gravity would aid suppression of the bleeding, and he ran toward the plane as if the 98 pound woman weighed nothing at all . . and a third mortar shell burst closer but near the last one.

Aboard he screamed to Beau, "Get her off the ground. Head straight to airfield nearest that little town we flew out of, you know the bigger field. We've a base hospital near the field. Mortar fire coming near, get 'er up Captain. . .. Your wife . . bleeding, not life threatening, no head, chest, or abdominal wound. Your nurse has it under control. But Hurry!"

Maya immediately went to work on stopping the blood flow and working on the wound. She had stocked the plane with a complete combat medical cabinet. It wasn't a first aid equipped plane; it was the fore runner of a medical evacuation plane.

The Japanese in another near outpost were firing where the muzzle flashes had been. Walking their mortar fire farther and farther away and toward the sounds of the plane's engines. And Beau needed the wind and would have to turn around and run a gauntlet as the fire came closer. Quickly turning and going to the edge of the clearing to the South east, he turned toward the mortars to throw them of. Perhaps they would miss long then. He taxied as fast as he dared knowing he had one more turn to make and couldn't stand the Aero up on the starboard wing.

Passing East toward the jungle and beyond the last mortar blasts, Beau made that turn and, pushing full throttle, the Aero raced forward and into the uplifting forces of the wind. Thankfully the headwind was not intense enough to dampen her headway yet strong enough for the needed lift. The ship lifted, climbed and turned, almost dragging the treetops with her tail wheel.

In the air and on course with Arnie at the controls, he ran back to her as fast as was possible in a cluttered military transport in the dark of night and full of refugees.

She had denied the morphine and the wound had been treated with sulfa. She was slightly raised and taking brandy for the pain, and as he knelt down by her side, she lifted the glass saying, "To the mission and multiple successes."

He took the other hand and said, "I ought to spank you."

"Ooohh sounds like fun, but wait 'til I'm healed. I'm afraid we have a long abstinence ahead of us."

Unabashed they sat there holding hands and kissing often as the plane roared through the night.

Beau had not left his wife's side as Arnie piloted the plane, and Major Arnold was now commanding the missions. At the military hospital, Beau, married to a minority woman in a government hospital in a foreign colonial land with its own share of sectarian angst, prejudices, anger and violence, was not going to leave her to anyone's protection but his own. As a foreign allied national and owner and manager of the one plane airlines contracted to the British service by that point, he was exempt from any military draft. His nation was conquered territory at that point. His wife, due to her work outside of teaching, her work for the British, French, Dutch, and Americans, surely had made enemies. He would be her personal security.

A week passed and the major had been tied up, but with great apologetic feeling in his manner, he finally visited Elaine in the hospital. The three talked long, and, at one point, Beau walked out. He really worried about enemies of his wife and this was a chance for a bathroom break while she was safely guarded.

"So, you were my bodyguard those six months. How many were watching me?"

"Mostly me. They arranged a sabbatical from my work at my school. You were doing important work that, surprised as we have been, prevented worse surprises."

"You seem to know a lot. I mean about this spying stuff. You vacuum up information and see the future."

"Thank you. That means a lot, considering the source. I meant it when I said you were an inspiration to me that night on the Aero. I know there are colonial wars ahead. We cannot expect these people, my peoples, to watch the Japanese cut through the vaunted Westerners' forces like a hot knife through warmed butter and go back to being docile subjects." She said it as if she considered herself a "Southeast Asian" not just a Laotian, as if she was a daughter of that collective small subcontinent. After all, she had meshed into central and southern Vietnamese culture so much that everyone had long thought her to be Annamese.

"You mustn't get involved. With your abilities, you will be recruited. It will be a deadly, dirty business. The last thing it will be on either side is honorable, whether one is defending the empire, which ever one, or fighting for independence from colonialism. One war like this is enough in a lifetime."

"You'll quit the service then."

"Probably. Maybe paint or write."

"As an artist, you'll succeed better without your prejudices."

He looked long and hard at her and finally said, "That was superficial and shallow of me. I don't really think that way. The words were just ammunition that night. This war . . this theater and this enemy . . what Asians can do to each other; the atrocities have left me scarred. Did you know, that mess in the Chinese cities, that barbarism? The Chinese did it first. In a little enemy occupied town, when the Japs had to pull troops to an emergency elsewhere the Chinese did such things to the garrison left behind. It did not involve the terrible treatment of women and girls though."

The pretty, delicate, yet proven woman had turned away just for the comfort of it and he said, "Look at me." The husband had returned and stood at the doorway to give them the semi-privacy of that plus his ability to sneak into it and make it not so private.

Elaine turned, and he continued, "Do not get involved, leave it, and leave this life. There will be so many offers for a beauty like you. There is going to be trouble everywhere. The Russians will never leave the so called 'liberated' lands. Does anyone really believe it? I know you know better. And your Indochina is going to explode. So many will recruit you. You will be the number one choice on so many lists, and you will be pulled, not to the money but to the causes. Leave it to the young, before it hardens you and destroys your marriage to that noble pilot of yours. We fight for freedom and peace. We need to go and enjoy it when this is over."

"I was not sneaking around spying on you every minute, but we knew they meant to kill you. You have a reputation for committing much to memory."

"So?"

"I was with you when you were at the greatest risk. I made the call on that, because I knew all the assassins in French Indochina, and the suspected ones."

The woman smiled wryly and mischievously, which due to all she was, just made her all the more mysteriously intriguing.

He tried to interpret it as he puzzled over her manner. He had, through his work, become a bit astute at such analysis.

Finally, after a long pause gazing at him, she advised, "When this is over, you might look for Linda Shu."

"Linda?"

"Yes, another Southeast Asian girl using a Western first name."

"How did you . . . you weren't . . .?"

"Every minute. I had to be; we thought she was the assassin. I regretted not having popcorn and a Coca Cola, or maybe better, wine."

"I'm not like that. I'm not that kind of man."

"Yes, you are," looking right at him. "But it does not offend my sensibilities. It wasn't casual. You were in love, truly."

"Yes."

"Thus, I know you're not the racist you acted on the plane. That's why she gave herself so easily. I made a point to to know her later. She is not a loose woman. She's mostly Thai, you know. And very traditional in many ways. She's in love with you."

"Yes?"

"I told them to get her out, Major. She was not on my flight, but George promised me. I offered to give up some of my pay."

"Was she an agent?"

"Informant. She taught in an English language school and many Japanese took classes there."

"Where would she be now? That kind of thing is not my bailiwick."

"I asked George to get her to Australia and let her teach there. She knows Japanese and several Thai dialects that might be useful to our boys. I told her that if I got out, I would look for you and tell you she was out. But I am not certain. Ask George."

"I will ask him."

"Don't be all English and uptight. Ask him and tell him why. George is no stick in the mud. He came to Đà Nẵng just to recruit me, all that way, only me. He is personable as well. Linda? she has seen some pain and is deeply in love with you. She told me so."

"Back on the plane, that night . . I didn't mean, uh, I mean I'm sorry."

"I know, Major, it was the angst and fog of war."

~

The Primary camp was still right near the coast, high above but not immediately in view of the water. It worked because they knew Maru's small garrison was their major threat, that he had probably been tasked for it by his superiors. What else was he going to do with less than a hundred men garrisoned on a desolate coast as an observer, like the Americans above him were? From where the American camp sat, they could assist the small guerrilla band they had connected with that saw little action and mostly needed standard medical care. All were awaiting the American and Allied push back that would come someday so they could act without reprisals. On some islands and the central western part of Mindanao, the guerrillas where strong, sometimes even dominate. The medical part of their work could also assist several concentrations of Filipinos around. There were two more Japanese families that they had discovered, met, interrogated and cleared. And they had been able to convince those around that these immigrants to the Philippines from the enemy land were not 'the enemy'.

They watched the Philippine Sea from a perch in the *Kanyagtiw Mountains* of Surigao del Norte, always manned; however, Julio, now a coast watcher, had set up further northward toward Surigao Strait and closer with line of sight to the near waters hundreds of feet below and out to the expanses of the deep blue Philippine Sea.

The attack had been several months before, and they had been on edge ever since. They had come to assume that Maru had not the will or force to attack them again. It had to be him because it had come from his side of the peninsula and its mountains, too far and troublesome for the other garrisons. The Japanese had not occupied all of the area or Mindanao in general, concentrating, as in other islands on population centers and large-scale farming areas, where they often forbade farming as if as a form of slow, long term torture. The bottom line was that Maru had twenty-five fewer men, thanks to Ann, Sgt. Adams, and Olin.

Matters were discussed one evening at the dining table well before anyone was to eat, still during the business part of the day, though military folk in a war zone were never off duty, as Olin had learned one night while enjoying his honeymoon.

Sergeant Edgar Earl Adams spoke at the meeting of all commissioned officers and upper-rank non-commissioned officers: Allan, Ann, Jenny, First Sergeant Harold Morrow, and Sergeant Adams. The sergeant had been asked to prepare a report because he had become the head of their intelligence gathering from the Filipino scouts.

"This Japanese occupation of Mindanao in our area as it pertains to us seems to be almost exclusively in Agusan del Norte centered around Butuan and Cabadbaran on Butuan Bay. The guerrillas in the low country around the Bay have given them some fits in the past months off and on.

The guerrillas are hampered by ammo shortages but their firearms do not use our rounds, and we don't have extra guns. I am sure they would love for us to become completely defensive in nature and turn over everything to them but handguns. But we would be disobeying our orders.

There have been very little reprisals like executions for their few raids on the Japs, so the enemy may feel worried and unsupported down there. We believe the war is turning against them and supply may be a problem. Any beheadings and such have been few and far between. That might explain why we've heard of no reprisals for our destruction of their ambush force. Or that could be because they do not know down in Butuan. He, Maru, is isolated. He has to send a man cross the peninsula right past us or go far around through unfriendly territory, use a Filipino turncoat, or go all the way around by sea, which is almost as risky. I do not believe he can get a radio signal across these mountains.

Well, that's it, Sir, Ma'ams."

"Do we pick up radio chatter?" inquired Allan.

"Yes Sir, and some seems close and very brief. We've never been able to use that direction finder to dial them in. They aren't on long enough. But it is Japanese."

"It's Maru." Allan evaluated. "I mean of course, could be him. He must have a radio stashed up here, maybe long before we came. Or he could have a portable. He sends someone up to man it or has a permanent man and sends runners up. He runs it very little to avoid us finding the signal. He may have found ours, though we are careful and brief. That would not explain the attack though. Different location."

"And he would have taken out or captured our radio, you'd think," offered Harold.

Allan replied, "In a sense, in this tiny spot in the Philippines, the Americans almost have the upper hand. He's almost acting afraid of us. But I do not believe that will last if he has contact with his superiors."

Over a month passed and it was late in 1943. On another clear night with a waning moon, noises carried cross the water as they commonly do and were heard up in the mountains near the primary camp. There was low moonlight, as it was less than a quarter moon with scattered clouds in the sky.

Brazen, as they had little to fear, the voices of the Jap crew could be heard across the water and it was clear that something unpleasant was impending. It was only a distant sharp angled darkness moving long and low in the dark ether of sky and water as a slight breeze pierced the mugginess of the Philippines . . no people no features save the light catching the angles of the steel bow, deck and superstructure, and voices distant and small and a small screech or clank as equipment moved.

There seemed to be splashes, 1$^{st.}$ Sergeant Morrow believed they were splashes, and as he turned to look at his two commanding officers, he spoke in a whisper, "It's time Lieutenants."

Obviously, their previous position had been known, precipitating the attack many months ago. Was this an invasion of larger proportions to the same site, or did the enemy know their new position?

Everyone was near the edge listening for the splashes of landing craft or boats.

"Let's get moving," Allan responded and he and Ann both stood as everyone spoke in strong, audible, careful; whispers. "Who's in rotation for the trail?"

"Eric and Pedro"

Allan turned and the two were already preparing to drag some useless trunks of trees down the dirt trail to the lowlands to make obvious tracks. It had all been thought out, and everyone concluded that the enemy probably didn't have experienced trackers of the type America produced. Japan was a small land for hunting. Hopefully, they would be somewhat easily fooled. The trail might look like equipment sleds had been dragged along.

"We have time to take the tents. It's a long climb up the seaward side if the Japs land marines. Then they still have to get here. Our one small trail through that heavy area is hard to find," Ann called out relatively softly. "We are a small unit after all."

The sergeants were giving soft orders and delegated the ones to collapse the big tents, big by their standards but really only quality canopies with drop down sides for storms and measuring 12 by 12 feet. Each two people took care of their own, except Ann and Jenny, who had medical equipment and supplies to carry. Allan took care of theirs and Jenny's small tent was handled by Morrow. It was the start of a domestic connection that would grow without official or unofficial objection in the little military 'community' . . against regulations or not. There was a small stock of key supplies that they had to move and that was packed each night for just such an emergency. . things used daily because they were important and prepared for escape each evening. This was the method for the moment, until such time as a really safe permanent camp was achieved. In Africa, Ann had pioneered in small portable medical kits and a few key medicines in packs. The women's job was to carry those. Allan collapsed his and Ann's tent and carried it up to the trail to higher ground. Lack of personal belongs eased things.

The arrangement from the beginning had been to have: 1. a camp with necessities; 2. a secluded supply depot or stash some distance away and off any known or obvious trail near the camp, a total disconnection of the two; 3. an escape route to higher ground and hopefully not too obvious; 4. a 'hideaway' at that trail's end, hidden well and with good fields of fire; 5. a fairly obviously logical escape route that was totally fake but could be made to look as if it was the one taken. Finally, if it was possible, evidence of the camp would be erased, but there was no way to eliminate the native pavilion they had constructed, thinking themselves safe already, their only rookie mistake so far. In their favor, presumably, none of the enemy soldiers from the previous attack returned to report trails. That was little consolation because obviously their newest position was known.

As lookouts peered seaward down the steep slope and others down the access trail, everyone started up the other trail which was barely visible. Several men carried the big tent up and hid it well off the trail. Then they retrieved their own personal gear and followed the whole command. The big pavilion was left standing, but stripped of gear, some thrown far into the brush. The two small wooden covered structures were pushed over to reveal fake disuse and the beginnings of decay and one actual partially collapsed. Some but not all foot prints were brushed out.

The submarine voyage had necessitated little personal gear and only a few tiny books had been brought, little ones prepared for military personnel reading_ fiction and poetry and blank note books. So, jungle and medical gear (including half-sized charting clipboards and paper) was all anyone had except a journal if they kept one. Ann had suggested it of everyone.

Thus, on the slope, it was reasonably easy and they got some distance away before none could miss the shriek from hell split the night and felt its shudder through the earth. The burst of hellfire below near the camp was as unnerving and the thud of its original departure from the destroyer's large bore rifle was heard at almost the same time, as the destroyer's guns were, merely a few miles away. Ann jumped up as soon as she realized she could; and, all, realizing they were uninjured, did the same. She had over cautioned them all about the earthly parasites in the tropical soils and no one wanted to lay directly on it too long. Similarly pushing through the jungle in the night they all wondered if the tiny leeches slept. For they had heard that the little vampires could get in your eyes and, through their sucking, collapse them. It was hard to walk through the Southeast Asian rain forest at night with one's eyes closed, but then, who could see in the inky darkness anyway.

A second shell fell farther now as they climbed. And others rained down as they left the camp far behind them. Then sounds of the barrage seemed to trail away more demonstratively down the slope to the south, as if the ship's fire control officer may have known where the other fake trail lay. Hugging the earth Ann was more composed now and realized they were likely safe unless a landing force tracked and found them. She had seen, at a distance, battle with big guns on small ships and large patrol boats the night of the landing, now it was close . . she was adjusting. "Dear God," she said to herself . . "what of those men in battle?" thinking of the men under such constant shelling. Then her mind turned, "I've kept this camp so clean and trained them. What might we live like now?" And she wasn't concerned for comfort but health.

Dropping everything as they ached from the speed of climbing with such loads, Allan stretched and then turned to embrace her. No words where said and each felt the heavy breathing of the other.

"Oh my . . I pray to God that we don't face worse," Ann sighed as they separated. There were no tears. She was experienced now. She would save those for when someone died or the risks were more deadly.

Still holding her hands held down in front of them, he responded, "This was the last thing I expected, bombardment form the sea."

As they had reached the alternative camp (she resisted the word 'hideout' the others used), they avoided lights but made a subtle shielded fire just to be able to see. Higher and not likely in any danger the next day in the evening, they searched for snakes in their previously built raised platform huts. They were airy with windows all around about four feet up. The risk in the islands was the reticulated

Philippine Python, but their numbers helped in that regard.

The two slept beside each other but not together, as they would have in their tent. It was a certain weird dynamic, two married commanding officers, and they did not want it to affect the men too much. The more they thought about it the more it seemed like an overlooked mistake, what with a married couple and a single woman in an otherwise all male operation and both women being attractive. The camp almost seemed to operate like a ranch crew back in America on a cattle drive where Allan and Ann might have been the ranchers going along to the city to shop and Jenny a daughter or sister. But perhaps in older eras, the men were more used to such loneliness. Well, with the marriage of one of the men and a Filipina, a new dynamic was in play.

They spent three nights and days there creating a little better camp for future use or if they had to stay. They cleared a little, hunted, cooked, explored a little, and sat and talked, told stories, played parlor games and waited. The fourth day some of the lookouts came up with news that no Japanese had been sighted at the camp.

"We went down and searched around. There was no sign down the slope to the beach and the ship was gone," reported Corporal Ferris. "Corporal Eric Cole and Pedro did not return. Several shells landed in their path. I believe they may be injured or dead by now."

"We'll search when we get down there."

"Yes, Sir, but there could have been a party landed. We must consider that. We saw no signs though."

"Where would they be? The coast would not be enough. They could have gone around to the northeast and be waiting. There is a lot of risk for them with the guerrillas."

"But we have to consider it, sir."

"Definitely, but my guess is that there was no landing party. Do you hunt back home Corporal?"

"I'm a city boy, sir, but I did on trips to my uncle's place in the Catskills."

"Well, as you may have learned, moving creatures, including humans, leave damage to the land and foliage where ever they go. And the more a human carries, the more damage. When we get back to the camp to gather the hidden supplies and relocate to Camp Two, take the most outdoor experienced man in the squad with you and go search the beach and all around there and any logical way up. But be careful you're not ambushed. He will teach you a lot while you're there."

The trip down for the whole command was a chore but unlike the stress of the night they had gone up.

"These attacks are related and they know we're here," Alan said at the evening meal. "We need a new camp with access to the hideout."

"Or we need to move altogether," replied Sgt. Morrow. "The quick accuracy of that bombardment proved they know exactly where we are with Camp One and Two, probably."

"Yup."

The Japanese lieutenant left things alone for a while and then sent a five man patrol up the hill. They examined the abandoned camp sight and then discovered the escape trail. There every move was followed, and, when they came too close, needing no intelligence information from them, Sgt. Adams and two Filipinos eliminated them. This added a Japanese, samurai sword, five rifles, various knives, and the ammunition for the weapons to the command's armory. Of course, the captured weapons from the failed attack almost a year ago had swelled the armory as well. On both the assault and the more recent patrol, the soldiers had carried extra ammunition, so that helped. As men had joined them, a small well-chosen group of Filipino guerrillas was at their disposal and under their command. Allan and Ann had wanted a group who would not be impatient and spoiling for a fight. They needed people to help defend the mission, not to fight a useless battle with the Japanese and give away the complete reason they were there. If they chose to attack the Japanese before MacArthur's return, when it would do the most good, there must be an urgent reason.

Several quiet weeks had passed after the bombardment, and there had been a few war wounds among local guerrillas treated in the mountain hospital. That group was mostly in position to observe the occupation around the cities and towns. Being too small and impotent to engage the enemy decisively or do great damage, any action would only risk punitive abuse of the civilians. The area around the near provinces was mostly a Japanese garrisoned area, producing no war material or other commodities. For now, things could just rest until the Allies returned in force and the guerrillas could then add to the fight for liberation. Apparently, neither Maru nor any other commander was going to risk men up in the peninsula again soon.

Stung by his lost patrol, Maru knew not who took them out. The bombardment might have destroyed the Americans and his men had been killed by other guerrillas or just Filipinos. He settled into quiet island life with his men satisfied by the women and him enjoying his still reluctant mistress every night. He found it perfect, a young woman he could influence enough to get some little affection from yet still unhappy enough about it to stimulate his barbaric nature toward a woman. He made sure the father saw them outside together; and, on occasion, would give the man an audience to report his spying while he was in bed with the girl.

Filipino babies had been born at *Camp Bangás* to
women from nearby villages, one a successful
cesarean, luckily with no post-op infection. Having
dinner after a rare guerrilla courier had come, eaten,
rested and gone, Allan, Ann, and Harold, were
casually talking in general strategic terms. The
scene, like many in war, was one of peace, with a
sunset to the west and the sea far away below and
spread out eastward before them. A breeze cooled
the humidity a little, and they were generally quiet
between casual comments of strategic importance
dispersed between jokes, comments of home, and
anecdotes about prewar adventures.

"We know now, if we had any doubt, that little Nip
lieutenant down at the coast knows of us," Ann
mentioned. "He sent those men and probably the
destroyer, but his time is limited."

"Before we fled, I had just talked to some of our
Filipino runner friends," Harold said. "Sir, Ma'am,
I'm reporting this late, I know, but it's less urgent,
not bad news . . the Japs have been pulling troops
north because something's up. I think the Navy's up
to something. It appears little Lt. Maru is all alone
down here with his forty or so men, that small
number thank to the good doctor. They are still in
Butuan and around the Bay, but I don't think they
have time for him. It's curious because we've all
thought any counter attack will come up from
Australia through this big island, and I believe it
will. But maybe there are diversions goin on north
of here to keep them thinking."

"Wow, good analysis." exclaimed Allan.

"Another thing, Lieutenant," the 1ˢᵗ Sergeant said turning to Ann. "The courier today brought this," he continued as she turned to him and he held out a small brown paper wrapped package tied with a string. "You were busy with patients and sick call, and I hadn't seen you 'til now. It's personal to you. From Fertig's command."

Very briefly hesitant and then quickly, she took it from his hand, tentatively at first because of the rarity of more than an unwritten verbal message in the jungle telegraph and particularly the military one. Pausing a moment longer, she untied the string and judiciously opened and folded back the creased and wrinkled paper. Before her eyes was a folded note which, once opened up, was revealed to be a piece of time worn Army stationary, such as one would buy in the PX on base.

Picking up a smaller folded paper package that was with the note and studying it carefully yet ever so briefly, so as to get to the note, she handed the small packet to Allan and read out loud. The official letter blended the familiar and the official language that perhaps characterized guerrilla warfare in its less dangerous moments devoid of contentiousness between rival commands or the urgency of important operations. Officers, regulars, reserves, or those newly appointed in a guerrilla band knew some of the lingo but perhaps not all:

To Lt. Carolyn Ann Allison, MD USNR
Lt. Allison,

This is to notify you that due to your record of service as reported to this command, and verified by reports from our wounded served at your hospital and of knowledge of the Filipino civilians served by your 'volunteered' remote U.S, Naval medical unit, and because of the report of your actions on the night of August 7, 1942, whereby, with courageous disregard for self, you saved your companions and command, I am honored to promote you to Lieutenant Commander. This is a standard 'battlefield commission' and is legal and in full force here on these islands in the Pacific Theater of Operations and anywhere in the services until such time as peace time circumstances should change things.

Lt. Commander Ericson here at out headquarters was gracious enough to give you a pair of his extra collar devices.

I know you have a shared command and from all reports handle it better than most couples handle their marriages. I am sure you and Lt. Allan Allison will be able to carry on the same after this advancement in rank.

A request that you be awarded the appropriate medal for valor is officially pending and delayed by our isolation from our superiors and the fact that certain awards were in revision as the war began, however, we here in our isolated duty station consider it deserved. We will hope it is ultimately approved. If it is not, you may consider it official from this command and on this level of operations. We can officially offer no more.

Major Alexander Ellison, U.S. Army
Adjutant to Colonel Wendell W. Fertig
Commander U.S. Forces, Mindanao

Reaching and retrieving the smaller paper from Allan, Ann unfolded it to reveal two small gold oakleaf pins attached to a little card that was obviously not the one they had originally come on. As she held them in her left hand and the wrapper floated to the ground, her right hand came up and covered her mouth to help choke back a vocal cry, but the woman could not completely hold back the tears.

Standing and walking over to his wife and looking down as she opened her hand to reveal its contents, Allan took the card, removed one device and, taking her lieutenant's bars off of her right collar, replaced them with the oak leaf. Standing back and looking, he said, "Now you're in balance." For her medical service branch collar device on the left collar was a gold oak leaf as well with a silver acorn in the center. He then stepped back again and saluted her. Overwhelmed by the moment and honor, Ann cried in his arms.

Lt. Maru, was neither the personable and kind American educated Japanese officer nor the conniving U.S. educated type of which both can be found in some cinema productions. He was a rat, and thus, even with the useful, if brief (only a year), American background, he had not risen above a lieutenant's rank, even in an army that seemed to value distasteful officers. They disciplined their own men by slapping them after all. Extreme mistakes in the higher ranks sometimes unofficially required suicide. The Japanese war machine was not their version of the Boy Scouts all grown up and sent off to a noble war.

Maru was definitely not a boy scout, and probably not a particularly good soldier as far as actual soldiering technique. Thus, he was given the job covering the territory where it became apparent not much was happening, at least not yet. The Allied powers might decide to assault the peninsula upon the return to the islands that seemed now to be inevitable. So, Lt. Maru was there with only fifty men now where he could be useful as an arrogant projection of Nipponese power and a warning sensor of any Allied intrusion.

Surely bored early on, he had flexed his brutality toward the village as noted and had taken the liberty of keeping his men calm and happy with women from the local population. It was a normal Japanese military practice, denied later by many despite the overwhelming evidence, witnesses, and victims. It was often a bit more removed and organized, a place being chosen away from the local populace, but the lieutenant had nowhere else and appeared to enjoy rubbing the locals' noses in his nation's dominance of them. What further revealed the poor quality of this particular enemy officer was the fact that these simple fisher folk and farmers were not of the sort such a rat as Maru needed to impress his power upon. They were hardly involved in the war or even in the mainstream of Philippine society in general. They were known to others but were self-sufficient people who sent a small party across the mountains a few times a year for certain needs, traded with villages up and down the coast, and occasionally had enjoyed similar opportunities with ships that had passed during better times.

But neither Maru nor his nation's leaders and military leaders seemed to care much for native peoples of Asia, even as they claimed to be building a "Greater East Asia Co-Prosperity Sphere". Significantly, the supposed 'racist' whites of America and the British Commonwealth of Nations (former and present British colonies) were dying in massive numbers to save the coffee colored people of Southern Asia and the so called 'yellow' ones of Northern Asia while the ethnic minority Japanese were killing and abusing those same minority people in their own Japanese '...Sphere' of influence. Also, significantly, though many white combatants were abused and even executed (usually by beheading) non-combatant white men and women were less often killed outright and American women captured in places like the Philippines were less often raped than native ones. Obviously, both whites and the Nipponese were confused about the Japanese prejudices, and the war opened eyes for the Allies: They were not as racist as they themselves and others thought they were, while, at the time, evidence piled up that the racial minority Japanese were racist against other minority Asians, yet perhaps a little afraid of whites, too afraid to overtly abuse their women, lest they finally lose the war and have to pay more dearly for it.

Knowledge of the arrival of the small American medical mission, gave Maru a military focus, but they were hard to find and he had limited resources, thus it had become drawn out. He could and did execute the occasional native as a threat, but at some point, he must have been convinced that the small medical mission was too small and remote to even know that threat existed before the raid that Lt. Cmdr. Carolyn Ann Davis had decimated. He knew the younger females of the local population had left the village when or shortly after he and his men arrived; but if he ever needed leverage, he could find enough of them.

The Village

Allan playfully saluted her with his left hand, as he walked up with two coffees, held together by their handles in his right.

"Wrong hand, sailor," was her smilingly presented cryptic comment.

Setting them down on the rustic table top, he simply smiled and nodded agreement, sitting down across from her. He had been subtly teasing her for days since the collar devices and accompanying advancement in rank. It was cute but now becoming annoying, and it had a strange tenor about it beyond the very subtle jovial digs at a spouse and lover.

 "We have to have a command meeting and access everything."

"Okay. Now is fine with me. All officers and Sgt. Morrow, obviously."

"You get her, and I'll get him . . . after the coffee."

They were having after dinner coffee and meant to stay up a while, and he added, "You have some decisions to make Lt. Commander."

"Funny."

"Well there are some not so funny issues: the people, the hidden girls and children, psychoanalyzing Maru, whether he has support, when will our guys arrive in these islands, when here . . . ?"

"I know."

"We'll get you all the information we can. With your permission, I will send men to reconnoiter the main garrison. How many personnel they have there in Butuan may be a primary factor related to whether we act here."

Ann looked at him curiously, but he didn't notice it.

"The wrong move could cause trouble for everyone."

She added, "I can't believe he has regular contact with them. Radios are still a premium in this war, as far as we know. The mountain should prevent his signal if he has one. I'm not sure you're right about him having one up here in the mountains. . And why hasn't he posted up here?"

"You kicked their asses, remember?"

Both sat again in thought, sipping and searching for a lighter evening subject, but they were officers now and there was the elephant in the metaphorical room even in the outdoors. They had come to help and save the innocent as well as their own fighters. And she said, "We have the high ground, Lieutenant," adding the title as they, though in private, often did to tease.

Mostly sitting silently after that the two occasionally spoke away from the topic. The evening was perfect with the foliage, especially the banana leaves . . that golden green they exude at sunset after a rain. Everything was glowing and wet in the low sun and long shadows, and they might as well have been in some garden from a child's book, *Peter Rabbit* or *Peter Pan*, perhaps. The west had started to redden in orange tones and that played beautiful artistic havoc with the greens on the tropical rain forest just yards away from where they now sat. They talked about that.

Then standing, he said, "Think about everything. I know you are. But . . think about them the way I've seen you study within yourself for a surgery the next day with no modern equipment, sitting there at night like you do thumbing through the books in your mind that you don't have here with you. You're more than a doctor now. You must receive a different kind of respect. . . and you may not know it, but you are." And he had sensed that his teasing had gotten under her skin. Even when they had made love the night before she was different, took longer to get into it.

Looking at him a bit long and hard, Ann replied, "Are you joking?" . . to which he offered only that wry not particularly funny smile that twists one's mouth and presents serious eyes.

"'...Different kind of respect' . . Are you serious?"

He looked at her seriously, saying, "They made you a lieutenant commander. Those hardened guerrilla commanders did that."

Staring back now with her own serious eyes, Ann evaluated it, " . . in the Medical Corps."

He had begun to drop 'Negro' a correct term that seemed to him to carry some less respect, like the slur, almost like just a softened 'nigger', as some would say 'niggra' . . all meant to mask a slur and get by with the cruelty, and he put her main ethnic and geographical origins together with her home county, his country. "Do you know what those guys are, what they're made up of? Those units are thrown together of whomever they could gather, but they're mostly tough Filipinos and Americans who can stand this rough subsistence life. The leaders are officers who refused to surrender and tough American businessmen, and some tough Filipinos. Quite a few seem to be American mining engineers. Those are men who know what they're doing . . . and what they were doing when they advanced your rank, you, a woman they had never met in the middle of a mostly man's war and world . . . and they knew you were African American no doubt."

"In the Medical Corp."

"The citation was for that and your leadership, and the combat that night, mostly for the combat that night . . . . clear thinking, solo, emergency dangerous combat in a somewhat complicated situation_ one person thinking it out, securing the weapons without shouts from the couple, arming, timing, and heaving grenades within seconds of each other without losing an arm, and opening up continuous fire_ accurately and spraying a twenty yard, three row spread of enemy lying prone. Hell, standing up there on that edge and spraying down on them. You could have had more holes than a whole wedge of Swiss Cheese when we found you."

As he finished and paused, looking at her blankly yet emotionally as her pretty face wore a similar look, registering shock perhaps, she knew now that he was mad at her for the risk she had taken as he knew as well that she had possessed no other choice. Otherwise they would all now be dead.

"Your promotion in rank was for all that, but your recommendation for a medal is particularly, for the combat part. The medals for valor are for that particular purpose, 'Valor'! Your advancement in rank was for all you revealed to them, to those experienced, hardened military men, the professionals and tough weathered volunteers. It was not a Medical Corps reward, it was a Line Officer promotion," said staring at her now with stern eyes that seemed to express, love, pride and it all . . angry or not, all the positives one could dream up. And he said, "They gave you two oak leaves."

She gazed back with equal seriousness and some level of shock as he added, slowly turning away with the empty cups, "I don't personally know anyone in my many travels who has done anything to surpass you that night. I could have lost you, and you knew it, but you did what you had to do. I'm proud to serve with you and help with decisions now as always, I'm prouder to serve under you." Then before turning to leave, Allan, with a rakish smile, looking all the more effective with his Clark Gable mustache and now missing beard, winked, adding, "Sometimes I like you on top. We're not missionaries you know."

Ann sat expressionless with her elbows on the table and her head, cradled in her hands, thinking.

The meeting was delayed and was held later the next day at the table that was private because of its distant position, their ability to talk quiet and voices that did not carry, and the enlisted personnel's knowledge of when to stay away for security. Lunch was over, intentionally so, with all its friendly banter. Now they could focus on life, death, survival, and mission.

"We requested this meeting to make sure we all know the full picture," stated Allan.

"This is my concern. Now, we know that these Nips have three young women or more that they have turned into comfort women for that little isolated garrison, and we can't do anything about that. I mean we could stop it, but it's been done before we came. My concern is that they will take the rest of the young and middle-aged women from that village. A downed Navy pilot now with the guerrillas said that when they think they are cornered the Japs will go berserk on the civilians in an area. That can result in mass murder and mass rape. Finally: I have four questions_ can we do anything about the village to protect it; should we; would such an act cause more problems; and when should we act if we do. I insist that, if we act, we must be certain of the safety of our own people. We were ordered to do so. Lt. Commander, I yield to you."

"What do we know of the current situation on Mindanao?"

Sgt. Morrow replied, "That the Japanese still have not gained full control and our guys control a large area, and that there is a general belief that our forces will be coming back to the Philippines soon. It is all in the rumor stage, but that downed pilot said that it's all through the fleet, the excitement. What we know for a fact is that the Japs are on the run in the Pacific. Our boys are pushing them up the different island chains. They are using a tactic of just skipping some places like the Western Dutch Indies. They're just leavin' the Japs cut off from their supplies 'cause their Navy's too weak now to fight through."

"We knew that . . that it would go that way . . little country like that." '

"Yeah, Allan. Little scrappers like that, and dirty too .. they gotta land the knockout early or they get beat to a pulp."

"What if they skip us, the Philippines?" inquired Ann. "There might be a blood bath here. In their extreme angst at losing, at being abandoned . . with all their pride at the beginning and their attitude about native women, it might be . . would be Nanking or Nanjing all over again."

"That's why MacArthur won't skip us, he can't," Allan addressed her concern.

"It's a guessing game you know, . . these decisions are," Ann said. "That is how we lose our command . . . how we get wiped out. We could act for those people there in the village . . we almost have to morally, and the Japs in Butuan could send three hundred across the Bay to wipe us out."

He had left it to her when she had received the advancement in rank. It could have been seen as just within her specialty branch of medicine. But she had earned it for their shared command and combat heroism, so he treated it that way. From that point on, he made sure they all saw him treating her as, on occasion, at the very least co-commanding officer, and more often his superior officer, no matter how slightly above him in rank and a non-combat trained woman. After all, he was not combat trained.

Ann replied to her own assessment emphasizing her conclusion, "In my opinion, *beyond our orders*: to maintain our command, to not be captured or annihilated; to observe the East Coast of Mindanao as far north and south from our position as possible, to try and keep an eye of the peninsula up to Surigao; and to provide medical care to the guerrillas and locals, *we have a moral obligation to try and protect the vulnerable among the local civilian population, within our ability to do so*. The Philippines is an American colony invaded by an enemy. Her people are American subjects even though they are not citizens. I did a bit of research before we shipped out on the submarine. Filipinos are, uh were, before the war, the only Asians freely allowed into the U.S. That's because they are our subjects. We have a duty. Since receiving the promotion, and upon noticing Lt. Allison's reaction to it, his seriousness about it. I began to think this all out philosophically. I have started a plan to be presented to all of you for general approval." And all looked at her with those blank stares of both surprise but understanding, . . just the understanding of the unexpected because you never fully know the person.

Continuing, Ann said, "With no active duty now and mostly a passive watching assignment, without disobeying orders, we have a moral obligation to these people, our people. We cannot sit by in boredom in the world's greatest conflagration." Then speaking emphatically as the experienced, weathered doctor technically now in command, Ann explained, "When you all reply to my comments, I want to know up front_ *Am I correct in believing that we can: first, at the very least remove and keep under our protection in a camp (perhaps a mobile one) the vulnerable among the young and otherwise healthy, and can we emotionally suffer through the repercussions which might include many abuses of the Villagers left behind? Secondly, can we instead, given Maru's small force, remove all or most of the villagers and relocate in a fortified location in these mountains? Finally, can we just go down there, or trick them up here and defeat them?* In considering those options, we have to consider the chances of reinforcements and a big attack. Timing with respect to an Allied invasion of these islands and how close it would be to our location would be paramount. The Japanese might be too busy to worry about us."

She then added, "We must keep an eye on the village, a finger on the pulse so to speak, and meanwhile plan a way to distract the Japs and get the people or at least the women and children out, while we also plan a full-scale attack. All our reports have been of a small garrison force armed primarily with rifles and pistols, and of course their insidious swords the officers and some sergeants carry. They think they're Samurai knights, like little boys, . . deadly little boys irresponsibly playing at war."

The two men looked at each other with wide eyes and in a knowing expression, revealing their surprise at her boldness and the logic of it as well. And Sgt. Morrow said, "We do out gun them in a close in firefight; we just have fewer men. But look what the Lt. Commander did that night when she was able to surprise them. I am pretty sure a force that size, originally, in the Japanese Army has at least one medium machine gun. Handled wrongly by us, that could wipe us out."

"We must be hush hush on this," the woman added. "We must discuss and get all of your opinions. If we decide to proceed, we can act with the small guerrilla band. It may require approval from Col. Fertig. If we act alone, it won't."

Allan added a pertinent point that was based on unpredictable events. "As my wife said, they may become the greatest danger to these people if and when our troops land. If they land, but not here, these guys may go nuts and decide to get as much sick pleasure as they can before their code demands they die. In that position, if we hit them, they may not have the support to fight back if punched hard enough."

Harold pointed out, "We have our original personnel. We lost two in the bombardment, but we had added the two sailors. We have acquired Mario and his scouts and ten more loyal men and have two with M1s and the others with captured Jap rifles and enough ammunition for a fight. With the nurses back here protected by five men, Corporal Ferris and Mario and his four scouts, we can still field seventeen people. From the discussions with the witnesses, it would appear Maru started with not more than seventy-five. So, he can have no more than forty-five because we have killed thirty."

Days later Jenny spoke to Ann and Allan. She had been quiet in the earlier conference and just taken it all in.

"What if we could trick them so that we could eliminate the Japs without it seeming an attack? Then there might be no counter attack. I don't know how, but in a storm many things can happen. That is our goal: to neutralize them before they can further hurt the villagers without incurring greater danger.

Maybe we could draw them away on some wild goose chase during a storm and evacuate the village while most of them are gone. We might still be implicated, but the revenge for attacking them would be absent from the equation. There might be less anger and force sent against us."

"I doubt we can mitigate Japanese anger, Jenny."

"There go those big words again," put in Allan.

"Paris," Ann said with a pretended snobbish smile.

Allan, said to Jenny, "I agree with my wife, but you have given me and idea by suggesting subterfuge or thinking beyond the village. Keep this between the the three of us because I believe there may be trust issues with one of our informants. This is officers only, we three. Jenny, you've been a party to everything going on and have a good mind; you're part of our command. Keep quiet.

I believe we can make a carefully planned frontal approach with an offer of some type of deal as a ruse . . make it look really believable that we are trying to trick them. Make them put most eggs in that basket at the trail and the small river it parallels because they know we are not honestly dealing with them. Then we can send some of our best fighters down to the coast about a mile north and a mile south and they can come down the beach in a pincers movement and close a trap on them. They can have most of the Tommy guns and hit them

358

from behind. They might be able to use bancas and attack fast to avoid discovery. If seen, out off the coast, they may look like fishermen.

Don't even mention it to Harold, yet. He doesn't know who I suspect among our informants."

Reports from the Filipinos and the marine scouts were conclusive that some quick-thinking village people had fled at the site of the Japanese. And after the first girl was made a comfort woman, any who returned left their daughters in the hills with friends or relatives. Most had not fled, but girls would slip away or be spirited away by family, fathers, bothers, or boyfriends. It had become a fishing village of older men and women, mothers and fathers, and boys. There existed a certain ever-present blanket of sadness and even doom with the presence at the northern edge of the village of the house, beside the Japanese camp, where the girls were kept to service the enemy soldiers. Everyone around, in the various hill towns and such, including *Camp Bangús* personnel, had to push it into a corner of the mind and wait. To act rashly could get over a hundred good people killed.

~

Ann lay in the grass on the hillside overlooking the village and peeked through the brush with 1st Sgt Morrow beside her. Allan's original intent was to never be apart, his original role to be simply to protect the doctor and nurse. Now, Ann needed to see the lay of the land at least once for herself, with

1st Sgt Morrow to explain the tactical points. Morrow and Adams were the only ones he would trust his wife with, due to their toughness.

"See, Ann. There are no guards. They're that confident."

"And their little house of prostitution?"

"The last hut north, the medium sized one. You now have seen both areas of concern, the little town in the mountains south of here where he surely knows most of the younger ones are and the older villagers and men and boys here. Other kids and girls are scattered with families in the hills."

"The stream bed runs just south of the village. See the little delta? The beach is narrow but supports the fishing bancas landing. They're all over down there."

"Yes, Ma'am."

The three officers and the noncom were on a first name basis except when formality was required. The two now were sure they were alone and no enemy scout or far ranging sentry was around. That was because they were screened by Mario's group of five scouts, who, like British Gurkhas, from Nepal, dressed light and cared only a big knife.

Ann whispered strongly, "With his threats, he must do something. Otherwise he will lose his grip on them. You men talk tonight without us gals around with our sensitivities. But don't put it off. Talk to Allan; it shouldn't always be him and me. You are the one tactically trained, and he's been in more tight spots than I have. Then let me know what you think. If you two believe immediate action is required, start planning it an let me know that it is in the works. If you want to hold off and let him make the first move, Maru, I will consider that, however horrible that is. Plan for our reaction to it if we wait him out. We have to consider that some of his threats are bluffing to draw us into a trap. He had those two infants killed when the Japs arrived at the village before we were deployed here . . just to intimidate them. And he conscripted those poor girls as well. He's capable of evil but has done only one beheading since. Do not leave Jenny and me out of it because we are women. I've changed my mind. Everyone will be needed."

When Ann returned from the scouting mission, she was approached almost immediately by her husband, and thought him behaving too protectively. Obviously, she was safe; she was standing right before him. He took her hand and pulled her aside near their hut and said in a tight whisper, "We have a turncoat, double agent. One of Mario's men learned of it. And the man is hanging around us more now, acting almost like one of the Filipinos in our force, though he isn't."

"Estacio!"

"Yes. his oldest daughter is Maru's mistress, under duress of course. His hold on Estacio is that it keeps her from being available to all the Jap men as long as he spies for him."

"Well, that's why we were located for the attacks. We can prevent his knowledge of details, but nothing will keep him from seeing our preparations. It seems he will have to be eliminated or sidetracked somehow. No, eliminated. Protecting his girl was desirable. How did you find out?"

"Her younger sister is hiding in the barrio nearest us, and told Mario's men. Her father doesn't know."

"Doesn't know she told or doesn't know where she is?"

"Both. She's old enough to understand and fears and distrusts her father because of it."

"Do you think, does Mario think, the father knows of his little band? They seldom if ever appear here. It's part of their mystery and stealth. Hell, Allan, we know nothing about those five but that they would do anything we ask. What does Arturo think?"

"Why?"

"You pushed me to command. And I listened. You're the strategist; you'll figure something out."

~

They had taken out the sentries and no native
runners that might be working with the Japanese
were around. Mario's scouts had made sure of it.
All, even the women, knew the forest now, and the
Filipinos were trustworthy. Jenny's mind was a
sponge and she had grown up an outdoor girl. *Camp
Bangús* was empty. Before the age of personal
communication devices and in the tropical forest
environment preventing direct-line signaling, Maru
was cut off from knowing his sentries lay dead on
the jungle earth. Jenny and Ann were together, for
this was new to them, and Jenny stepped out and
smiled at the Japanese soldier and pretended to
surrender, begging for mercy. Ann drove a rifle's
bayonet in his side and almost through him as Jenny
leaped on him, smothering his mouth and ability to
scream out. Maru had executed the revered village
elder and his wife, the trigger; and, though they
didn't know them, the American force was as angry
as anyone who did. Small town Filipinos could be
as petty as any American small towner or anyone on
the planet in terms of social relationships; and, in
his wisdom, the old village leader had been in
charge so long because he was impervious to that
trait and prevented its employment, by example, by
others in the village. Maru's action signaled a
possible employment of his threat to execute the six
comfort women if fresh additional girls were not
provided. Since the Americans and Filipinos never
intended to give in to any demand, his lack of trust

363

was somewhat predictable. Perhaps he had read their minds. Or listened to Estacio's reports.

They had called Maru's bluff. And, as sweet old fashioned Jenny aptly put it, "The asshole wasn't bluffing." Now, they would make the appearance of seeking a meeting or surrendering to save the girls.

In pairs, Carla and Olin, and Ann and Jenny had just killed the last two sentries.

The threat had said that three of the six comfort girls would be next to be beheaded to be replaced by young women from nearby villages, once Maru found them. If the American medical force would surrender their own women, or make the villages return hiding Filipinas, Maru would kindly spare the three prostitutes and only add a few more for the time being. If not, he would make a show of the three and add any woman he found, regardless of race, to the house to replace them. In his message delivered by a Filipino runner, he said his men were serving the Emperor with great sacrifice and deserved women to relieve their boredom, after all. He said, they were pretty, some of them, and were just fisherman's women, and this would give them a more noble purpose. Tossing out a crumb to the Americans, he had added that he would promise to take the Filipinas back to Japan where they could be respected mistresses for returning hero Japanese officers who occasionally needed breaks from their wives.

Brash, pompous and over confident, well beyond his superiors' negative evaluation, he expected the attack that was coming, and even more full of himself, half expected the black doctor and blonde nurse to sacrifice themselves to him. Except for his brutality, he was as phony as the ring from a pawnshop during one year of U.S. college.

"There's the light machine gun, Jenny. They're so damn predictable, but he's a little wily, where's the second one?"

"We heard the clickers that Allan made; everyone reported. The field is clear to the village."

"Allan's behind us, but you can't look for him. You can't triple click, for 'danger'. We're too close, but when he's up here, he'll see. Let's get closer, Jen."

There was a stir in the village and all the people came out, lining up like a golf tournament gallery. It was a forced audience. The three forced prostitutes were standing in line unbound and afraid to run, dressed up for the sake of the Americans to pity them all the more. He knew the Americans would not let it go unchallenged, and his trap was set. Every gun among the invaders still in the village was trained on the slope. The young victims, willing and wanting to die, had been told that to run would result in shots that would only wound, legs for example. Then, if he let them live, they would just be crippled whores.

The forty-five remaining Japanese were deployed in the village and on the north side in a small gorge running parallel to the stream, an ambush. Thus, Ann, Jenny, and Allan, coming down toward the village, had thirty Japanese ahead of them with a tripod mounted machine gun and fifteen in the gorge to their left, as they came down, with a second one. The gorge was some distance away, and Allan had discounted it as too far. He started to worry about it, but could signal no one at that point. The ball had been kicked; the whistle blown.

Down on one knee, the two American women, watched the scene below, both of them naval officers, if without all the training a man would have gotten in officers' school or at the Academy or the little spit and polish the WAVEs and Medical Corp got.

Each had a role now, and knew, as well planned as it was, they could lose the gambit. Ann and Allan, yards apart had the same thought at the same time, as close spouses often did: could they really trust Mario, as much as he had come through for them, could they really trust anyone in a land invaded by a harsh enemy that employed terrorist like tactics. Mario had been so all important when Colonel Scott was brutally killed; was that just a set up for later.

The Filipinos with the Japanese rifles began to fire toward the village. They lay prone or were behind trees and as well sheltered from return fire as possible. The point was made to start that fire fight well to the south, to the right of the stream to protect Ann until she could be seen by Maru. If he saw her, he would want to capture and would not let her be shot by his men. With the heavy machine gun on the tripod returning fire, the Filipinos kept their courage and lost only one or two to injury. Among the Filipino riflemen, the machine gun to the south took Manual's head off and grazed Morrow.

Ann had taken the rifle from the sentry, taking out the clip, and she broke it across a tree, quickly standing to do so. Then she unlimbered her Thompson and carrying it low in her left hand started down the stream bed, not yet in clear sight of the village. She was the only one with a Tommy Gun on the hill, as she had proven herself, and it had been 1st Sgt. Morrow's call. Timing was everything. As careful as they had been, things began to unfold too fast.

The machine gun seemed to have silenced, but not killed, the Filipinos too soon, so the first 'trick' was employed, as a small group lobbed grenades into the village from the south in the trees. Before his demise, Estacio had warned Maru of this, calling it a big surprise trick play. The target was his frontal entrenched squad with the machine gun, and the Japanese officer thought it to be a weak gambit revealing the weakness of the American force. He had prepared with a group of five who went into the trees to wipe the Filipinos out and never came out. Mario's were not the only Filipinos in the American force who were proficient with the ubiquitous

Filipino bolo. Filipinos fired again at the machine gun post, silencing it. Maru's command was getting slowly whittled away. And the Appalachian whittler was a Tennessee boy named Allan, architect of Ann's assault on the village.

Maru, with his two sergeants stood in the open on the forest side of the buildings, and he made the first woman kneel. He acted brashly impervious to danger, knowing the Filipinos and Americans would not chance hitting the girls, though it would have been merciful. They were without blindfolds, and Ann now a hundred and fifty yards away played her role too well and started running. The women were worn and sad already and, in some ways, had given up on life and the first he struck like the others was sobbing because we still cling to life as much as we can, especially if we have faith and she sobbed out a prayer as she died . . only to herself, God, Jesus, and Mary. And as her body separated in the traditional way of the old way of legal killing, she would ultimately be alright when the dust settled on the story of the universe.

He went to the other . . he had them spaced apart, and Ann, the country girl and athlete, having covered forty five of the yards, screamed, "NO !" . . and Lieutenant Maru turned and seemed to sneer, but at that distance she could be imagining it.

The officer barked a command and two soldiers pushed the second girl to her knees to be ready. She was a very young woman, perhaps in her teens and her arms were folded tightly across in front, against his orders. She was bound at the ankles to prevent flight, the only one of the three, and she had the ubiquitous long straight black hair of the South Seas.

Next as Ares is often wont to do in battle, several things occurred at the same time, at the same instant.

Totally unnoticed by the Japanese in the village, and probably the villagers too, who had scattered from the gunfire of the Filipinos up the slope, the bulk of the few Marines and two sailors under Sergeant Adams's command in two bancas came around the stone jetty unseen and dashed onto the beach at an angle toward the enemy soldiers surrounding and supporting Maru. Following Allan's plan, the canoes had been found in an old fishing village up the coast days ago and repaired.

"North, north, to the rocks" shouted Maru as he realized he had been out guessed and the attack was from the sea. Leaving only the machine gun with two new operators to keep the impending attack from the hillside at bay, he sent everyone toward the sea to the north side of the village. But running to their new position and exposed, they were cut down in the open by carbines and Thompsons in the hands of the Americans dashing rapidly towards them.

Maru, relying on his men and those in the gorge, in his pride, lust, and superiority, raised his sword

369

majestically as if he were some heroic warrior rather than the piece of human sewage that he was. He paused and then swung downward so overly dramatic that one might wonder if he knew he had an audience he could hurt with the action.

At the moment of his pause before striking, fully visible now in the middle of the stream and running, Carolyn Ann screamed, "NOOO . . . ". . and it reverberated down the stream and back up the cutback that the water had formed and nestled in.

Rifle fire suddenly came from the direction of the gorge Allan had worried about to the north and spattered and clattered around Allan, missing him only because it was sparse and he was lucky. He ran through it just behind Ann and Jenny. He no longer saw the nurse, and wondered if an attack from the gorge was imminent.

Ann had too much speed and was affected by the moment, and Allan grimaced as he feared the result of the slight faltering of their plan . . grimaced . . yet blocked her out to save her . . blocked out the Filipinos that might be failing now and cause his own demise . . blocked out all that . . all the sensibilities and there existed just his hands arms the wood the barrel and the tree trunk they rested against . . just what he could see in front of him . . no Ann right now running into death from a Japanese sergeant's bullet . . no Maru with sword raised and a Stateside school ring on his finger like a thumb in your eye or a middle finger tossed arrogantly up.

And squeezing the trigger on the little carbine twice, rapidly, as he adjusted his aim between instantaneous shots, he saw the sergeant aiming at his wife fall dead and the lieutenant fall as his sword struck the girl awkwardly, his aim thrown off. He knew he had put it right through Maru's damn temple and into his degenerate brain. The sergeant lay on the beach sand with a hole in his forehead.

With its downward stroke begun and irretrievable, the sword followed through and struck a glancing blow to the petite neck in an incomplete way as the girl forced her body to fall to her right onto her right side.

Nevertheless, blood flowed, and to any poetic person who would reflect on it years later, there was incongruity in the clear life blood water of the lush green jungle carrying Ann's scream of horror down to where the red blood of life soaking the dark Philippine sand now recorded death.

The drama on the beach had taken two of the three, one more than the American commanders had expected. As it ended, as sad as it did, the least of the six were lost and the further enslavement of the villagers and their daughters was prevented. Men and women were spared who deserved to live as much as Maru's three intended victims. As much as commanders hated it, war . . battle was a numbers game.

The Marines on the beach and the rifle fire from the Filipinos had silenced the machine gun, never trained toward Ann's path down the stream bed and cutback. A predictable eerie stillness spread over the scene and seemingly the entire earth, as surely it did at many places during many such moments during the worldwide war. Several yards ahead, she seemed to trip but not fall once or twice, and once she did fall and athletically stopped herself with a hand down on a slippery rock and continued, hardly breaking stride.

Allan was right behind, and as they approached the village, a Japanese corporal stepped out from the brush and cogon grass on the right side of the stream. Alan's view was blocked by Ann being more to his right and ahead, but he saw enough when placed together in his mind with her soft surprised gasp and scream. Pressing his body's abilities, Allan pushed her to the side and burst past, diving under the muzzle of the noncoms's extended pistol. The naval officer slid on his right side and butt on the shallow stream bed and took the man's feet out from under him. Grasping the soldier's leg to avoid scooting too far, Allan pulled his knife from the sheath on his left side with his right hand in a cross draw, and falling on the Japanese corporal with the full force of his knees on the man's butt and his left hand on the enemy's neck, he shoved his face under the water of the shallow stream. Then he repeatedly stabbed him in the back.

Darting from the stream as it turned right, away from the village, Ann ran through the cogon grass the villagers had cut low at the Japanese command. Reaching the small, sandy plaza, she dropped to the young girl for the obvious reasons. There were the two, one clearly beheaded and the third kneeling low, bent head in hands to the ground sobbing. The neck of the girl she held was severely cut, and her blood was everywhere soaking into the dark Philippine sand. Instinctively the doctora knew that too much of it was gone from the girl to save her, yet Ann still felt the undamaged side of the neck for a pulse. There was none, and Ann went from her knees to a sprawling sitting position on the ground, cradling the girl, whom it would no longer further damage to be moved. And as her husband reached the younger, physically sound young woman, who jumped at the touch of a man at first, and embraced her with soft words, peacefully, Ann slowly rocked herself as her arms embraced the young woman, rocking the stress from herself while respecting the state of the other. From somewhere perhaps beyond the present world, strength was manifested to open the the young woman's eyes, and, before the doctora could surmise it a mere unusual reflex in death, the girl seemed to react visually to the darker face before her. Slightly opened eyes . . and a smile appeared and a hand and forearm reached up weakly as if to touch Ann, who smiling ever so softly, took it and drew it to her cheek tears forming again in her eyes, and Carolyn Ann held it against her own face, and she heard the girl say softly in a last whisper, "*Salamat, Angelita Negra,*" as the life left her brown eyes.

Allan, embracing the broken younger girl, reached Ann's side just in time to catch the end of their moment. He did not hear the words or know the other had spoken, but he saw Ann take the upheld hand and knew it had been freely offered. Ann was sobbing quietly and clutching the hand as he came to them, and he could not understand her few words that broke the soft rhythm of the sobs occasionally with their own rhythm, obviously the same comment or question repeated. But the young Filipina in her husband's comforting grasped pulled away, dropping to her side and, gently touching the face of her now dead 'sister in suffering' gently with her right hand, then turned and embraced the American doctor tightly saying "*Angelita Negra, Salamat,*" sobbing.

Finally, after some quite long moments, during which he gave her . . them . . their time and didn't touch her, she looked up, still in the warm comforting embrace of the one survivor of the three.

"Why did she thank me . . why did she thank me? . . . . I did nothing."

Instinctively, the doctora knew the girl could have died before she reached the beach and maybe realizing further that the loss of blood would have prevented survival even had she been able to push death away for a while. The girl had bled out slowly and perhaps peacefully because her carotid artery had not been severed but had been partially cut by the interrupted blow, interrupted by Ann's scream.

As his love stood to receive his comforting embrace, helping the young survivor stand and with her arms still around her, he offered an explanation, "Maybe she sensed that your scream eased her death . . . I don't know." After the embrace began and while it long lingered, he said softly in her ear, "You could not have saved her. You would not have reached her. She may have known that too. She has seen their power and their evil. We have ended that at least in this little place. Did she say anything else?"

"She called me, 'Black Angel' . . 'Little Black Angel'," and she began to softly sob still holding the living girl by an arm tightly around her shoulders, while in his embrace.

"I think they might call you that here, so she knew it . . knew who you were, the black doctora. She got to meet her heroine in all this mess they've suffered through. She was also thanking you for that, . . . for them."

Softly, still with a soft, subtle, coughing sob, the surviving young Filipina simply said in the local Visayan dialect they now understood, . . "Yes, you are the Black Angel."

When he had dashed to catch her as she dashed down ahead of him, the firing from the direction of the gorge had stopped abruptly as soon as it had started and Mario's scouts had not been seen since the battle ended. The village and battlefield had been policed, and no Japanese had been left alive. None would surrender, so all were killed fighting.

The three officers walked toward the gorge carefully, spread out and using cover. When they arrived at the gorge, they saw the result of a deadly battle to the finish. From the position of the bodies, the Japanese twisted and turned backwards, it was obvious that just as they started to fire across the battlefield on the slope, Mario and his four scouts, who carried only bolos, had surprised them from behind, hacking them to death. Nevertheless, with the numbers, fifteen to five, the enemy had managed to kill or fatally injure all the scouts. Two, Mario and another, had died just in front of the natural ditch, as they had briefly survived their wounds. Their actions had probably insured victory, though everyone's had been almost equally important. They had almost certainly saved Allan, Ann, and Jenny. They had prevented the use of the other Japanese machine gun.

Later that evening at *Camp Bangús*, the three officers sat together at dinner, all picking at their food somewhat, yet enjoying the taste a little. They had learned over the last two years to savor needed pleasures when they could. Sustenance was most important and Allan and Ann were blessed more than most deployed military personnel to be able to be assigned with their true love. All three were lost in thought and trying to enjoy the food.

Allan's voice jerked them all back to the meal table, soft though he spoke. "I was briefed about the bigger picture before we came on this dandy little vacation. I've worked a little with these guys in intelligence as you know and I was already made aware of much, but they gave me a final briefing, knowing we would not get steady news reports. This. These events today . . are not isolated . . . . . or even in the minority. What I saw in Nanjing back in "37, that is a norm as well. We did all we could today, . . for her and the others. I want you to know that, Ann. The thing is, this is going on worldwide in the war, this barbarism. It's as if the damn Japs and Nazis have reverted to the barbarism of their ancestors. Now, we don't need to talk about it here, not yet, I mean with the others, not yet. But some information has come out of Europe, some really bad stuff. It was speculation before we left. But I believe it. You see, I read his damn book, Hitler's, *Mein Kampf*. They're rounding up the people they don't like, that don't fit the Nazis philosophy, and they're marching them to ditches, giant common graves and machine gunning them. It's Gypsy's and some minorities and smaller religions and especially Jews. They did in the Ukraine at *Babi Yar*, but word got out much later before we left. There have been some massive executions with heavy machine guns and such. Some Jews in America and elsewhere are claiming that damn little paper hanger will murder all the Jews in Europe if he can. I just want you all to know. I want you to know, Ann. Because what happened today happens in this war . . everywhere. It just happens. You nor anyone else can save them all. And we need you to be around here as long as possible for those we can save and you, the doctor can save."

With Allan's words, Carolyn Ann nodded acknowledgment and quietly took stock of her life at that point, a naval doctor in the greatest war ever fought. Her individual role in that war was small, everyone's was. But each was important to the whole, and each could give their life at any moment. Ann was a lieutenant commander now in the U.S. Navy, and a jungle doctor with experiences in the Africa savanna and tropical rain forests of the storied East Indies. From her sheltered, Southern American, conservative, segregated youth she had now met and worked with divergent peoples of her own race and others, of in fact what was then taught as the three main racial groups. She had married a Caucasian, which she had never expected nor sought. Nor did she consider it some kind of step up in society for herself, nor did he. Had any one asked her beloved husband, an adventurous, heroic, hunk of a man, he would have regaled them in his pride in her beauty, strength, intelligence, courage, and medical achievements. She knew, in such a conversation, he would say he was the lucky one to have married above his pay grade.

Jenny, who had been quietly listening finally spoke, saying, "I spoke with the girl. She is Marisa Maria. How very appropriate, given it all, and Ann of course. She is the young mother of one of the babies killed so demonstrative a way by Maru to intimidate when the Japs arrived. She was forced to 'volunteer' as a comfort girl by his threat to kill the child's twin. She was widowed by Maru as well. In fact, her husband and child, the other two comfort women, the village patriarch and matriarch, and the one other decapitation victim sum up the village's toll. The young woman paid the highest price, and she is only twenty-three and seems a pretty smart girl for a country girl, a fisherman's daughter. . . not to denigrate that, it's just a simple lifestyle. I talked to her mother and father, and siblings. That is why I was there with them so long and you folks were looking for me. If she so chooses, they will send her and the other child up here with an escort within two days, just in case we move, and they can't find us. If that is her and their decision . . they have their other grown children . . she will join us and I will care for them, her and the child in Cebu. As I'm under your command, and not a regularly assigned nurse in the mainstream Navy Medical Corp, it is my hope you can secure for me the assignment of rehabilitating the young woman . . for a couple of months or so at least. She will have a tough time at a normal life and perhaps trying to have a loving husband again. I believe I can try to help her heal. It will be research for the many others scattered through East Asia. I believe for a young woman with no, pardon me, but no prior romantic sexual

379

experience, recovery may be nearly impossible. I mean to love normally again, because there was no normal first time. For Marisa, she has everything to live for, that child, and normal love to seek, to want to seek because she's experienced it before."

Ann added, "She is very pretty . . not in just a Malayan Filipina way but, I would think, appealing to many a white or black man," using the term the Filipinas had used for her. "She will need a strong husband if she can ever marry; this war is molding them, even as it weakens and strengthens all of us as well."

The young mother was extraordinarily pleasing to look at, even in the constant sadness she currently wore, and it was a natural beauty, even attractive in her sadness. Sometimes the 'ordinary' Malayan Filipino people of Mindanao, in the ethnic mixing bowl it had been throughout the ages, had Moro blood and that of India in their veins producing exceptionally natural looking handsome men and charmingly exotic women. Marine Corporal David Johnston with the Allison Command, noticed that in Marisa. He had been assisting a lot in the little hospital. If she could ever be affectionate with a man again . . she would need a man that the cauldron of the Second World War had melted, cast, and molded strongly and yet perhaps one who had avoided the psychological damage of heavy, repetitive combat. That thought went through his mind as he mulled it all over, including the fact a husband would have to shrug off the several dozens of men of the enemy she had been forced to copulate with for two long years. Thinking to himself, with all the time a man had to think in the pastoral paradise, that if she was strong enough to fight to heal her wounds and could love him, he could certainly cherish such a sweet, strong flower of the South Pacific. He would just observe matters, as long as the posting lasted and the girl was there. As a twice wounded Marine, who had survived a bout with malaria, and seeing all he had seen so far, he knew not to approach the girl in any but a medical treatment sort of way, which could include kindness and conversation. He made the point to do as much of that as he could, and the nurse and doctor noticed and allowed it.

The first night back in camp and their beds, Allan lay there knowing that he was his wife's hero in both her mind and in his actual achievements, and he wore the knowledge well; but, in many ways, he looked up to her as the adventurous scientist, minor celebrity, and hero she had become, and he proudly yet humbly shared that view with others. That night, Lt. Cmdr. Carolyn Ann Allison MD USNR whispered to herself as she lay in his arms, her back to him, "I must survive this for him, I must make sure he survives." That they must still do their duty, which could challenge those other two goals, was unspoken and understood.

The next morning, they evacuated the people from the village. Now they had the Japanese radio, and could monitor the enemy's conversations undiscovered as long as they made no comments over the air. It was resolved to never use either their radio or the Japanese radio to send with unless it was urgent or the war was going better for the Allies and they could send messages that would help or ask for help. They drove a stake in the ground on the beach warning of cholera in Japanese. It might make it look like weakened Japanese survivors fled with all equipment including the radio, maybe dying inland or at sea. It might prevent others who feared the illness from investigating inland or any other enemy troops from landing there from the sea.

During a two week pause with literally nothing to do but relax, Ann was quieter than usual but still her normal kind and cheerful self; however, she reacted to conversations rather than initiating them and was less funny. When it came to the business of her specialty, a doctor and general surgeon of a back country war zone, she was coldly efficient and serious. She could smile at a particularly pointed operating room joke but would never initiate one and never had.

Jenny worked with Marisa, who had been physically examined and given a clean bill of health. Perhaps due to the isolated assignment and perhaps no previous stationing of the green troops who had occupied the fishing village as an outpost, the girl had avoided all but the most treatable venereal diseases. Of course, time could possibly reveal worse. Her heart and the mind were the damaged areas, and Jenny knew they might be able to be healed and might not be repairable, at least not to a really functional state. The quiet young woman doted sadly on her child; and, only with her, could she ever generate a smile. Jenny made a point with subtle, barely spoken clues and hints to let the woman realize she was among good men, the Americans and Filipinos alike, respected and not feared by her, Ann, or the Filipinas working at the field hospital. She made a more outright point that there were no Japanese close; however, should any unexpectedly appear, the entire command would seek safety or die protecting themselves and her. Then she made another point, "We came here partly to save you and your sister Filipinas. We expected to find some of you abused in that way. So, remember this, none of us look down on you. You are a victim and a heroine to those men out there, for enduring what you did."

Two American couples who, because of their outdoor skills honed in youth, had managed to elude the Japanese search patrols for two years finally were able to get to Surigao del Norte from Bohol. They had worked their way across from Bohol, an adventurous accomplishment in itself. But their struggles getting ashore in an early dawn in rough seas at a desolate point on the shores of Surigao Strait had attracted nearby Filipino guerrillas who brought the four in to the tiny jungle hospital. A hike of several days. The husbands were horticulturists and otherwise experts in plants and even fauna, a fact which had aided in the group's long-term survival. Tired, dirty, and bloody from rock and coral the two fairly young couples, whose love had apparently driven them to shared adventure and danger, still appeared to Ann as attractive, and she somewhat romantically poured herself into making sure they would be able to leave her hospital/clinic prepared for recovery.

The problem was that one of the men had taken a beating in the surf as the boat, already leaky when they had set out, had foundered. Capable and daring, yet the weaker of the two husbands, he had been under water too long and slammed into the rocks at that point on the shore too much. The courageous man had required the standard procedure for a drowning victim for clearing water from the lungs.

By the time the four and their rescuers and helpers reached the hospital that particular man was in dire straits.

Wounds were superficial, with a broken wrist and a dislocated kneecap being the worst, but the doctor and nurse were very concerned about his lungs. Of course, the delay and the trip up to them had not been helpful. It seemed obvious that all the water did not get out and that lung infection or damage or pneumonia might have ensued. Surf water churning up sand and other particles and even microscopic life in the shallows could have deposited who could know what in the man's lungs. Ann and Jenny dealt with that more serious first issue, as Carla and Janice attended the wrist and knee. Hoping to prevent the condition from worsening and becoming a bigger problem was the first concern. The man showed no pain other than his wrist, knee and a general soreness in the obvious places. His weak cough was rough.

Carla commented, "I have seen thees things in my old veellage. I lived where men once went out to rough seas, before I moved here with Janice's aunt."

"Go on," said Jenny.

"He could have, as you say, the water taken so," pressing both open hands to her breasts, "and he can have bleeding within. The water can sicken heem."

"A puncture, a hemorrhage from a blow, what?"

"Any of that, . . of doase. We had a man with a rib puncture it. In my veellage, my town. Doase people there, could do nothing. They had no doctor, no knowledge."

Now with the luck of the local knowledge of their new medical assistant, Ann and Jenny started checking and palpating all over the thorax area. Again, he seemed to show no pain and nothing protruded, raising the skin, nor did a rib seem to be missing because it was pressed down and in.

The wife stepped nearer at some point, and said, "It is bad, isn't it?"

Ann turned and stopped Jenny, instead answering herself, taking that responsibility, "He seems worse than he should be for residual water in the lungs. I will not lie to you, infection, pneumonia, an internal injury are all concerns. Opening his chest here, like this is as well. We are a limited facility."

A few days later, Ann and Carla were eating together.

"I love your accent, Carla."

"Really? I don't always notice how I speak. I try to fix it, the words."

"Don't try too hard; it's charming. A certain man told me he finds it so."

The young Filipina blushed and replied, "Theeze things may hurt my desire to be a nurse."

"You are a nurse, by some definitions, already. Some hospitals might care. I don't know. Where you work will have its own language."

"How, Doctora?"

"The regions here, and other countries."

"Oh, Doctora, I will stay here. But I do not know wheech region. Your country has promised independence long ago to come in 1946. I want to help build my Philippines, if Reechard will stay."

"He may. You have a good man, you know."

Blushing again, the petite islander analyzed and evaluated with a hint of pride, "Reechard, . . Olin? My Reechard wants to stay, too." She seemed to exude a sense of comfort with the expressed romantic possessiveness.

The man did not get better, as his lungs struggled, and eventually died one afternoon. He became alert and lucid and they had their farewell. It was made clear to him that his wife was safe now, though that was not certain. It was certain for none of them. And Ann was learning, had learned that war was about death in many forms and not often preventable.

Ann became a little overwhelmed. They had been a young couple who had been through much, from the challenge of life there in the Philippines in a less than comfortably modern era, and the enemy curse, and then to have it fall apart at the last. Ann was overcome by, not her failure, but that in such rustic conditions, a doctor like her was set up for a certain amount of failure.

She went and sat on the old fallen log everyone in the camp used when they wanted to be alone. It was a camp tradition now, and everyone knew to leave the one there alone. When Ann was there, she prayed.

The two women stood arm-in-arm near the body, the widow sobbing softly.

The husband of the other woman walked up to Allan, who stood alone looking at his wife across a wide area of the camp's central plaza which gracefully rose in the center and dropped on three sides.

The man stood there beside him a moment and said, "Pardon my intrusion, but why not go to her?"

"She needs to be alone for a while. So much has built up in her. Like you, we've been in this since the beginning, since a little after Pearl Harbor."

"You volunteered, the two of you?"

"...and all these men. It was my idea. Sometimes I regret it, but it is a duty. Everyone has one now. I asked her to recommend a tough jungle doctor, and she insisted. What could I do? She was right."

"Does she take each death this hard? I'm sorry."

"It builds up in you. I'm sure you know . . knew, even before this. I'm sure you've all been through a lot. A young Filipina died in her arms two weeks ago, . . injured in an attempted execution to get back at us for a defeat and our service to the people and guerrillas here. Ann believes she could have saved her if the Japs hadn't been between the girl and us. We had to fight through them."

~

In late '44, the small field hospital was moved
northward closer to the tip of the peninsula, but it
remained in the mountains. The combat personnel
rotated to small camps near the coast with good
views over the near ocean's surface. They reported
what they saw and never knew if it was useful. The
ships they sighted before *Coral Sea* was fought may
have been the most significant, but they would
never know. There were two such lookout posts and
later a third, and those coast watchers depleted the
camps defense. This was mitigated by pairing only
one Marine with one or two of the Filipino men to
have someone who could better communicate with
more diverse native peoples that might be
encountered. The three survivors, the couple and the
widow, pitched in in every way, and the man's
knowledge and toughness became an immediate
asset. His wife was a consummate cook of a near
chef level, and meals were enhanced as cooks were
relieved for other duties. Jenny became close to the
widow, intending to take responsibility for her
emotional and psychological recovery as much as
would be possible.

Ann had just walked out and sat on the old log, head
down and quiet. Her husband saw her and watched
discretely, leaving the wounded warrior and medic
alone with her thoughts, the best healing possible
when one could not just leave the war that was all
around them. Finally, as she sat so long, he sat on
the log beside her. It was where everyone who

walked out of the jungle hospital sat for long minute when things were tough, and every soul in the camp had become medical personnel at one point or another.

He said nothing nor touched her, not even a lightly touched hand, and long minutes later, she almost whispered, "Nanking . ."

Allan looked at her and she said, "I hate that word . . . . it's a nice name, but I hate it. . . . . . . It keeps me going. With all this . . " and there were tears in her eyes . . "it keeps me going . . Nanking." And she was quiet again. She had just delivered two children, twins, symbolically perhaps a boy and a girl. "I imagined this, but it never works . . imagining what to expect . . those girls at the village . . When it got so bad that night after the village and we couldn't save some and saved some . . . . I just kept thinking of your stories about Nanking and how much worse that was. How can I let such horror comfort me now . . telling me 'this is what you could have faced'? . . How can I be comforted by so much suffering by others, and . . and little girls in Nanjing . . my mind telling me … 'at least you weren't in China'." And there was a long pause, the tears turning to a very slight soft momentary cry and she sat there composing herself, and maybe it was her African features that rested so sweetly perfect on her face, but Ann was one of those women who looked pretty when they cried rather than grotesquely contorted.

390

Now he took her hand and commented, "You're not doing that . . of course the urge to always say, 'Whew, I missed that.' But you're seeking a different comfort from China, the knowledge that you can help prevent Nanking here in our small way. There is always from the depth of the deepest wrong some light of hope. I never told you but as we were allowed to take off, after the girl, the one in the picture, we saw a troop of soldiers marching. The road they were on went straight to a hospital, where someone had hopelessly placed a red cross on the roof. Bombing had cleared the road in front and it was wide enough for the plane. I put her down well ahead of the troop on foot, and we stepped out and just looked toward the building. Our God only knows for sure what was in my mind. We could have been strafed by a Zero or something.

After a few long moments just three nurses in their white came running with five children . . then another with two more, running up to the plane and without a word shoving the children in the plane, seven by then. The four stood by the door a moment, and one turned tentatively back. I kept motioning all aboard, but the one ran back and the other three sort of froze. I took the hand of the closest . . they were all pretty in an ordinary way. I've never met a young Oriental woman that wasn't somewhat attractive. I assumed if there were more children in there, they would have brought them out. The hospital had a name in English, and they looked at me dazed in indecision, and I said in strong, slow English, as I stared in her eyes and had caught the gaze of the others, 'There're a hundred soldiers marching up here and they rape and murder every woman that they don't keep for a whore.'

They stared in a blank horror, and I said, 'They spare only those and the others are raped over and over then killed like you prepare a hog for the spit, . . . Get in the damn airplane!' In unison the three looked back and then down at the ground, torn by their duty. I took her hand again and said as I looked at all of them, 'You cannot stop it or save a single nurse or patient. It is alright at this point to save yourselves and give these children care. You cannot imagine the horror I've seen here.'

They boarded and we flew over the Yangtze and I told you about that, and they wanted to land in Hong Kong, I topped off the tanks there and would not let them out. It became an angry thing for a moment and I grabbed the one whose hand I had held in Nanking. She seemed the dominant personality and I shook her softly and looked close in her face and said to her, 'Those damned demons are going to take Hong Kong, British or not. I don't know how soon.' And she relented. When we got to Manila, I talked to people I knew. I was staying there a week or two. My contacts and friends worked on their immigration, got them lodgings and nursing positions, and military intelligence interviewed them for hours. The girl and I, . . Lin Chou, and I went out every night, knowing it wasn't serious. But we kissed a couple of times. When I flew out with no promises and with certain feelings toward each other, a definite spark, the last thing I said was, 'Lin, this may grow into a Pacific war. America and the British are going to be angry about Nanking. The British and Dutch control Malaya and all these islands in the Indies. If it comes to the Philippines, do not surrender. It is better to die in the hills free and helping fight than as a Jap comfort woman or one more of their abused victims. We know they hate the Chinese most of all.'"

Ann was turned and locked into the story and her tears had dried. Allan concluded, "Who knows how many died in Nanking. I have heard unimaginable estimates, and it was a big city. I saved ten. That's what I try to remember. I focus my thoughts on the three pretty, dedicated nurses and the seven kids I brought out. It wasn't anywhere near half the brutalized population, but symbolically, my glass of Nanking experience is half full. Hell, I hadn't reconnected with you yet, I even saved a girl I might have loved. Anyway, your glass here is three fourths full, with all you've done . . uh achieved."

"We've achieved," she corrected him. "All of us."

The Lights in Surigao Strait

In October, Allan, Ann, Sgt. Adams, Janice, a sailor, and a marine all went north near the Strait but still up in the hills to help a Navy Avenger crew that had crashed and had several serious and less serious injuries among them. All three had survived, not always the case as the combination radio/radar operator and ventral gunner, generally has no way out in a crash, being trapped below. Word had come to them and the report claimed no apparent Japanese search activity. They reached the men in the forest camp of a small guerrilla unit stationed in the generally quiet area of little or no enemy activity. The wounded crew had been brought up from the shore and beach into the highlands just above.

"We saved our radio man; three-man crew on these new torpedo bombers, Doctor. In a crash like this, the man below cannot get out. So, I decided to set her down in the shallow surf. She would fly and I could control 'er. He was my responsibility."

As they talked and the woman triaged calmly as the emergency care had been given by the guerrillas, Ann knew a small walk north through the bush offered a distant view of Surigao Strait, close enough for a reasonable view of its approaches.

She was cleaning his wound personally. There was only Janice and her. The pilot was a strong man and had overcome the shock, and they were there to deal with significant gashes in his leg that just missed arteries that would have left her with only the other crew members. Something about her had made him suddenly open up and the war poured out. He was a TBF pilot and this was his third ditching, necessary ones all, and this would have been the third man to lose in the bowels of the big flying torpedo bomber. But he had seen enough death and had risked himself most of all with the daring landing, saving the vulnerable man below, who was always on the cusp of it.

The turret gunner was struggling to breath and could not move well or very much. She suspected a spinal cord injury, as the plane had flipped, and knew she had no way to deal with it, hoping it was trauma, swelling around it or something that would subside. But she could save this man, this pilot. Oddly perhaps, the man in the belly of the plane, usually the one most at risk, had come out of it fine.

"I tried to set it down gentle like, but there was no way, no perfect way and..."

"Lt. Commander, reliving it helps, but it will always be with you, I can tell you from experience. The one thing to remember in such emergencies is that you did your best, even if you think back and believe a choice was wrong. When you did it, you did your best."

Ann had finished the cleaning of the wound and covered it with a slight dressing. Starting to stand, she stopped herself and placing her left hand on his right shoulder and taking his right hand in hers as she sat back down, she said nothing. Here was a young man who, older than his current crewmen, had been through the war from the beginning.

He looked up, like many a wounded warrior dreamed of and saw the pretty medical professional holding his hand and holding him together. He smiled ever so slightly and seemed to care not that she was African American.

"From experience miss, uh doctor?"

"'Mrs.' I'm a Lt. Commander. We lost four men out of our small command here in the Philippines. I am responsible. I and my husband over there will have to write the letters. I can't just let a telegram from the war department tell it all. Before the war, full of youthful professional excitement and adventure, I took a medical safari into Africa, recklessly perhaps. I lost them all. I am the only one of twenty souls to walk out of the bush, actually running for my life."

He looked up at her, and she had drawn his attention away from his self-blame and condemnation. "You were trained, Lt. Commander. They let you keep flying after you had lost others. So, they had confidence in you. There are new pilots out here by now. Your superiors had options. You did your job better than I did mine. I was advised not to go to Africa."

Now he had to console her. Her strategy wrapped within honesty had worked, and he placed his left hand on the back of her right and said, "And yet you've come here and been successful in spite of losing some. I'm sure you were properly prepared. How did you get out? . . of Africa, I mean, what happened?"

"I am like you in that there were things out of my control, and I **did** prepare. Foreign agents stirred up the tribal natives against us. My husband, the Lieutenant over there rescued me. I called him and his work and concerns for me had placed him near. We were not yet married. He arrived in the nick of time. It was right out of Hollywood. I guess he became Errol Flynn."

Not at death's door yet, he jokingly reacted, "You've given me cause to live doctor. I have to hear all the details now."

They stayed for the men to heal enough to move. The turret gunner worsened and then began breathing a little better. The pilot became more depressed, but learning of the TBF's mission, which had been intelligence seeking, and of its importance, the two officers were able to build him up to some extent. He had tried a risky landing to save one who would have likely drowned in a normal ditching at sea and might lose the one who would have survived. It was war, a numbers game. The detailed story out of Africa did the trick because of the excitement and truth of it and because he saw how duty just failed sometimes.

All the while Ann treated the almost untreatable patient. What could one do_ in a jungle mountain environment with no hospital equipment, and only a knowledgeable doctor's brain with which to diagnose? The man had no paralysis, no sound of fluid in the lungs, and no symptom other than difficult breathing. She knew through bruising and pain to the touch, that he had massive bruising and attributed the problem to badly bruised ribs and chest and back muscles and perhaps pressure on the cord. The prognosis was up in the air, and the treatment was simply waiting. As the bruising eased over a week, the breathing returned closer to normal. Finally, a tough victory without lifting a medical finger.

Then, some days later, about a week and a half, as he seemed better in all ways, the night exploded while the small camp was mostly fast asleep. In the early morning hours, clearly visible distant flashes of light and explosive sounds that seemed like deep, soft tapping had caught their attention to the north northwest. That could have been anything related to the war, even fighting on land on Bohol across the Mindanao or Bohol Sea. But it was straight north of them toward Leyte Gulf. The whole camp, feeling more secure than ever and guarded by an extra ring of Filipinos now, headed through the trees to an open view of the distant Strait. Several, including the Avenger pilot, hobbled on crutches. Some long minutes later, as they watched through the trees from their elevated perch, louder distant rumbling explosions were seen and heard, causing the appearance of a night of much confusion for someone.

As the flashes preceded the sound, Allan said to everyone, "There's a sea battle goin' on out there."

"Definitely," the pilot concurred, and everyone was quiet and focused on the history in front of them, ... history bigger than them but that they were within and intimately a part of, a history that wrapped around the world joining millions of heroes and heroines and otherwise courageous, or at the very least hard-working individuals, sacrificing something, if not blood.

Time passed slowly, when it really wasn't, and then closer into the strait to the north northeast of their location and just below Leyte Gulf, a distant flash of orange and its composite parts reflected off the clouds with a roar that seemed to have too much power for the distance. A resounding booming and rumbling followed and that sequence of fire and thunder was followed by another, then others seemingly overlapping, as if they were little racing, competing violent storms low on the surface.

The pilot, leaning on his crutch and Allan looked at each other and said at the same time, "A battle line."

"Wow," expressed Allan.

"That would be Surigao Strait there. Someone's closing the Strait. They're battleships; I've seen 'em in action when we invade the islands. I know their sound. Never thought the world would see another gunfight like this, and we got free ringside seats."

"Allan?" She was holding his right upper arm with both hands as she stood beside him on that side. They were quite a few miles from the action they were viewing.

"Battleships, Ann. That strong display to the north is a line of them. I'd say at least three but probably more"

"I'd say the other we heard before was a torpedo attack on the enemy's flanks while he was caught coming up through Surigao Strait." the Navy pilot added.

He had flown a torpedo plane of some type throughout the war and knew the tactic, even when PT boats (patrol torpedo boats) and destroyers did his job. "Someone's come through the Mindanao Sea, with maybe a smaller force, cruisers and maybe some battleships, and had the door slammed in their face to the north-northeast there. Little ships are biting their heels all the way through and battlewagons have blocked the way solid. The sounds are different on each end."

"I hope our guys are doing the slamming."

"I'd expect that to be so, Allan." Their rank wasn't too greatly apart and the command in the jungle was casual at times, and he chose to be informal. He outranked Allan.

"Why do you think that?"

"The Japs still control mainland Southeast Asia. West of the Philippines is still sort of their waters for now, . . still even the western part of the Dutch Indies. We dominate the sky, where this war's being decided, but it's dangerous to be over there at night with our cruisers and battlewagons. I guess they are trying to break through and stop our next move. We've all been gearing up to make a move here somewhere. I guess that's what this is about. Of course, they don't tell us nothing but to be ready, but all the guys have been expecting something near the Philippines."

Allan and Ann looked at each other and smiled, as the thought soaked in and the rumbling in the distance continued. Ann wished Jenny could be there to see it, but with Allan and her both gone, Jenny, now raised in rank by their shared decision to lieutenant J.G., then lieutenant was in command of the camp in their absence. On such occasions, either 1st Sgt. Morrow or Sgt. Adams was always left there to help her with tactical emergencies; but though she was medical branch, the two of them trusted her experience and incredible intelligence. For all practical purposes they gave her the task of a line officer, and neither sergeant had complained.

What the people viewing from the forest did not know, as they stood out from the jungle tree line on the hills above Surigao Strait, was that the allies, especially American forces, had landed on the shores of Leyte Island, catching the Japanese completely off guard. The enemy had expected the Americans and British Commonwealth forces to attack up through Mindanao. Documents recovered from a Japanese officer and given to the Guerrillas on Cebu had reached MacArthur, who adjusted the plans to attack where least expected.

The sea battle the officers observed on the night of October 24-25, 1944 was part of the gigantic multi-day struggle during which the United States Navy blunted and destroyed a massive and complicated attempt by the Imperial Japanese Navy to destroy the American landing forces on Leyte's beaches and the supply ships in Leyte Gulf. The overall struggle called "The Battle of Leyte Gulf", the largest in world history, raged across the big Philippine Archipelago from Palawan and Surigao to north of Cape Engaño, and included a weirdly heroic and ironic victory in the unique "Battle Off Samar" (not 'of') fought by day after the team watched Surigao Strait from the hills. The other historical legacy of it was the duel they had watched during the night before, history's last big gun duel between big ships armed with large caliber naval rifles. Significantly for the historical record, that last gunfight, "The Battle of Surigao Strait" was won with the classic "Crossing the T" technique, the best naval tactic in a gun fight and one hard to achieve. Allan, Ann, the pilot, and their companions had watched the sounds and sights emanating from the crowning event of a tradition that had begun with the first primitive cannons placed on ships in the late Middle Ages.

During the night in Surigao Strait the Japanese squadron had been harrowed up the passage and then blocked by a squadron of six American battleships miles ahead. Thus, blocked and distracted by the big ships the Japanese commanders had to focus on, the Japanese task force was repeatedly assaulted by destroyer torpedo attacks, severely damaged, and forced to turn away. The absence of that Japanese force the next day off the coast of the island of Samar allowed a tiny, outclassed, U.S. Navy force of the wrong type of ships to intimidate and drive off a large IJN battle squadron formed around the massive battleship Yamato, one of two sister ships that were the biggest ever built, with the biggest 'guns. Her sister the Musashi had been dispatched to the bottom of the Sibuyan Sea in the Philippines by American planes the night before, in yet another part of the massive Battle of Leyte Gulf. In the *Battle Off Samar*, perhaps the most unlikely victory in history, the American squadron containing no capital ships caused a vastly superior Japanese battle fleet to flee.

Significant in the story of the War and the many factors bringing Allied victory: at Surigao Strait, the Japanese could only sortie two old battleships against six American newer ones; off Samar the best battleship Japan had to offer, the most powerful ever built with 18 inch caliber guns, was shooed away by a vastly inferior American naval task force not even intended for sea battle engagements but for support of land operations.

~

Back at the newer *Camp Bangús*, how ironic it was that, among the original well-prepared group that deployed over two years earlier, the two strongest most capable men were now the ones in need of assistance to survive.

Now, 1st Sgt. Morrow, Jenny, Ann, Marine Corporal Richard Olin Ferris, and the Filipina nurses in training, Carla Evangelista Ferris and her cousin Janice, struggled down the stream bed toward the coast, praying that the intelligence had been correct and they would encounter friendlies, not the enemy. Marisa, the surviving comfort woman and her child went with them, and Marine Corporal David Johnston came along for assistance with the two stretchers which bore the feverish Lt. Allan Allison and Sgt. Edgar Earl Adams. With them and assisting were the American couple and the widow. Sgt. Adams was suffering from a serious Malaria infection. Ann was not sure about her husband's intense fever and contradictory symptoms, and it worried her, though she had suspicions about the cause.

Corporal Eric Cole died with the Filipino Pedro Saavedra during the naval bombardment of the camp; Corporal Scott was the sentry killed by the Japanese whose prospective raid on the camp was spoiled by Ann; Petty Officer 3rd Class Earl Jenkins USN died in the battle at the village; Professor Julio Ortega remained in Surigao del Norte with the radio and Japanese radio and functioned still as a coast watcher and liaison with the locals of the region he loved. The second radio brought in with them had been donated to the Guerrillas some many months earlier. Now Julio, high in the mountains, could listen to the Japanese radio, with the help of a local Japanese farmer, who had been trusted by the locals and spared any reprisal. Important messages received on either could now be relayed by radio to the guerrillas.

The little Navy field hospital staff, secured by Marines, had lost no patient that came to them with a prospect of survival. It had done so partly because it had not received very many serious combat wounds or ill people. The worst had been the horticulturist who died. One cesarean section had been successful when they had the drugs they needed. A second one, late in the campaign resulted in an infection that couldn't be fought without those medicines. It was 19th Century Wild West frontier medicine at that point with similar survival rates. As reference, in the 1870s, in the modern city of Paris, a zero survival rate for the pregnant mother during a cesarean section was not uncommon on any given year. Ann and her team had done their best, and the mother and baby both lived.

Decades later perhaps the Japanese nation would be accepted again, but the behavior of their men on the field of battle, on what once had been called a field of honor, had perhaps destroyed that concept and revealed to the world what war had always been: a horror story that was only honorable to those who were honorable and approached something so overwhelmingly destructive and pain filled with all the honor they could muster. Men had once been able to sometimes treat each other with such honor, but this war had been about good against evil, and the little group struggling down the mountain with dear ones they hoped to save had simply had enough of that enemy for a lifetime.

With the help of the three American civilians with them and the remaining men, they carried the last of their medicines, the only thing that they figured the incoming American forces could always need. The command had lost three men from the sea services and eight Filipino men. The Filipinos they had recruited and helped improve their fighting skills had gone to join the guerrilla forces that would hit back now at the Japanese in the whole Caraga region and especially around Butuan Bay.

At the site of the old fishing village where the battle had been fought, they had been told to await pick up at 1900 hours as it would be getting dark. American carriers were in the general area and covering the skies, sweeping any Zeroes away. There were few of the pesky yellow jackets anymore, and modern American fighters had reduced them to mere gnats by comparison.

The voyage out to the destroyer in the low free board open launch was an experience after they had all been landsmen for well over three years. The fresh sea air and the wide graying sky was exhilarating, and the women thought they saw it rejuvenate the sick men, as well. Ann introduced herself and Jenny to the Officer of the Deck immediately to avoid any misunderstandings. She was African American, a woman, and she was a line officer and unit commander, against regulations or not. She was also the doctor on record for three years of the two patients. She insisted that, though the voyage would be only hours, through the night, the air on deck was not safe for men with violent fevers and diseases that could kill. Ann and her doctor's orders were respected and the men were sent to sickbay. Of course, on the ship, the doctor was an anomaly, almost a celebrity in her uniqueness, and Jenny, while talking to a flirtatious officer, let Ann's heroics slip out on purpose. Later, when the watch changed, the two women had coffee and cake with the ship's captain in the wardroom.

In the mid-morning they disembarked in San Pedro Bay in northern Leyte Gulf and found themselves before the tents and portable structures of an Army field hospital. With the finality of it, the mission, Ann and Jenny, with women's sensibilities remembered their first casualties, Eric, the always dependable corporal and brave, rugged Pedro.

Ann reported, as they stood outside with the stretchers on the ground where patients were triaged, "It appears to be a dual infection on the thinner man, the Lieutenant. We lost one native man to it. I'm worried about these two. The Sergeant is Malaria."

Looking up quickly, the very young doctor said dismissively, "We'll handle this."

Ann and Jenny looked at each other, and the doctora intentionally held back a reply for the moment. To help or out of curiosity, two more nurses walked out and stood watching the triage team do their work.

Standing up, the young doctor, apparently a lieutenant said, "I'm not sure about this."

There was a moment of silence as maybe everyone, medical professionals all, thought about a diagnosis in Allan's case, while some were wondering where the Negro in military fatigues came from. She had the collar devices of rank and the medical service branch on, but they were small and went unnoticed.

"I am almost certain it is Dengue Fever and Malaria, a dual infection. It being masked further by his general rundown condition. It is very rare. He overworked himself at the last." She spoke as she would have to any group of doctors or nurses on duty anywhere.

The attending nurse, an army second lieutenant, said, again dismissively, "Please. Let us do our work . . ma'am."

"Lieutenant Commander," corrected Ann.

"What?" said the nurse and doctor kneeling again and looking up and around, as if another officer had walked up.

Then immediately, Jenny had sized up the situation and seized the moment with a calm, firm, clearly audible voice.

"Attention on Deck!" And she herself came to attention.

It was a sea services command required to be obeyed at sea or on land, and most present were Army. Everyone not standing rose to their feet and all stood at a not too forced or overly dramatic state of attention. They were not of the sea services but understood. Probably all thought Jenny had caught sight of some big brass walking up to them from out of their field of view.

"This is Navy Lieutenant Commander Carolyn Ann Allison, USNR, and an MD, but a line officer as well and our commanding officer," stated Jenny a bit perturbed. "She is a jungle medicine specialist . . and their doctor and has been for almost three years." And taking a chance that, with equal or higher rank than the Army nurses and executive officer to Ann, a Lieutenant Commander, she could get away with a command, she said further, "Take her report, now."

She added after the briefest of pauses, "The two of them, that Lieutenant lying there and my commanding officer are married."

The nurse turned and studied Ann and Jenny. She noticed the white nurse holding the black doctor's arm at the elbow with both of her hands. It was a show of support for a distraught wife who was still, because she was a professional, composed despite the concern for her husband. It was a show of support from a professional nurse who obviously revered this person who was her boss and commander.

"She outranks him?" the nurse asked somewhat incredulously.

"They were lieutenants when we went in. Naval Reserves. Doctor Allison was given a battlefield promotion by Col. Fertig's command. He commands all the Guerrillas on the big island, literally thousands of Filipinos and Americans working together for liberation. Please, Lieutenant, urgency is necessary."

Looking then at Ann, the Army nurse listened intently.

"It is rare. The mosquitoes are from different environs, but I'm sure my husband has Dengue Fever and Malaria. I am worried about Blackwater Fever in the case of the latter. I know that it's too soon to worry, but I have run out of quinine and he has missed doses. With the Dengue, there is no current medicine. Unless you have something new, Nurse. The treatment is just rest, forced fluids, and analgesics. I ran out of those too. We have had too many cases in the last few months. We lost some," said with her head looking down. "He is hurting like hell. They call Dengue 'breakbone fever' and 'breakheart fever' here in the Philippines. The version in these islands can be dangerous, with organ damage. I believe it is worse here than elsewhere."

"We have heard of it. Blackwater Fever."

"The corpuscles burst in the blood stream and the bleeding can damage the kidneys. But Dengue can do that."

Letting her professional and military guard down a bit, she put her hand to her mouth to prevent and hide an obvious, improper emotional display. She realized at the moment that, after all they had been through, she still could lose him. He, the strong one.

And perhaps the realization had set in, the knowledge that it was over, all of it, and maybe she was unhappy with the results and that she could do no more now to make it better. That she had not saved ones she should have and could not be the one to save her own husband now. She would be a patient too now and a doctor on the sidelines.

And weakly, Ann placed her right hand on the arm and hand of Jenny who still held her left arm at the elbow, and slowly collapsed into a crouching, squatting position. Then, feeling it was more ladylike, dropped to one knee, her right. She looked up in a bravely professional way, and said, "I'm sorry, Lieutenant. That was not very professional or Navy. My legs just got weak."

"That's quite alright, Ma'am, uh Sir. We understand."

And as Ann smiled and the nurses looked at her, they could see eyes wet with tears, and perhaps they thought about what might have been faced on the mission these fellow warriors had just come out of.

Commenting to a second, younger nurse coming from just inside the tent entrance and walking out to them, the nurse commanded, "They have obviously come out of a hard ordeal. See that she speaks with the attending doctor. If her diagnosis is correct, we haven't encountered Dengue since we've been here. I doubt anyone on our staff has. And Sue, if anyone doesn't like them being back there, tell them to see me."

"Get him back there," the doctor who was actually not a lieutenant but a young captain said to the orderlies; and, turning to Ann, he asked "What do you recommend? You've been here for three years."

"Quite a bit over two . . yes, about three, treat for both, the Dengue will pass . . the Malaria must be dealt with. May I attend?"

"Of course." Then to the nurse, "Lieutenant, she has full privileges to view, but get her checked out as well." and turning back to Ann, "Uh, Doctor . . Lt. Commander, you will comply of course?"

"Yes sir."

"Do not try to assist. You are much too weak."

"Yes, Sir."

"For what?" inquired the doctor.

"Sir?"

"Go ahead to your husband. I'm talking to your nurse."

"Yes sir." And the 'sir' had been a courtesy, for she outranked him.

"Lieutenant, What did she do?"

Jenny replied undramatically but with the precise language her matriculation at Virginia had given, "Lieutenant Commander Allison there is a forward area combat surgeon. We were a secret Navy medical and Naval Intelligence mission inserted into Surigao del Norte, Mindanao. I am Lt. Jenny Barkley, her surgical nurse. Sir, Ann was in the right place at the right time. She would take a relaxed perimeter stroll after our work day. We had honeymooners, and while she was checking their privacy, she discovered the sounds of an impending attack in a ravine behind our camp that we had thought a barrier. She retrieved the groom's weapon's belt and Thompson, there being no time for a warning, and attacked the ravine single-handedly with grenades and the Tommy gun. Her color camouflaged and her hunting experience back home allowed a quiet, surprise approach."

"My God! How many?"

"Twenty-five men, all dead or dying."

"Coffee, Lieutenant?"

Turning to where she had last seen Harold, he was still sitting on a fallen coconut tree and drinking some juice offered by a pretty off duty nurse. Jenny looked and smiled. She wasn't worried about that.

"Yes sir. Let me inform my sergeant. We're .. uh .. we've followed regulations, but we're close sir," said as she decided on the truth.

"Invite him and my nurse over there. We're not rigid with people coming out of the hell you folks have been through. These field hospitals are a bit relaxed with it anyway. I'm sure you folks were. How could you have gotten along any other way."

"True sir, but we maintained the chain."

"Of course."

After the coffee break, the doctor saw Ann in the hospital tent where Allan was being treated and she had been examined.

Looking at Carolyn Ann and recognizing her from the pictures in the papers before the war, he said, "Lt. Commander, you and your nurse there might think about anything that we might need to know. All any of us know about these jungles and their diseases is from books from back home and explanations by the locals, and we don't know how recently those books have been updated no matter what the copyright. I've actually not met a woman doctor until now, and a woman of color too. Congratulations. I know of your African trip .. and now this? We must talk, you and I. Perhaps your husband will allow us to have dinner while he's briefly bedridden." Becoming a bit serious he added, "You look a bit malnourished and I'm willing to bet you may have other mild health issues. The *U.S.S. Refuge* should be off Leyte now. We'll treat you both and then get you both aboard her. I'll pull some strings if . . pardon me . . your color becomes a problem. She'll get you both to the hospital in Hollandia. You're a hero; I'll get you a berth on her."

Thanksgiving 1945

The war over, three couples were bent on having a Thanksgiving meal in a restaurant in Cebu City. The circumstances involved old friends and some new acquaintances. The two couples from the Allison mission had met the heroic Jake Pierce, now wearing a Purple Heart, Silver Star, and Navy Cross and his more subtly heroic wife, Sarah, at the hospital in Hollandia, where both men and one of the wives had been treated there for war illnesses and malnutrition. All were fairly fit now, and at that moment the three officers and one Marine 1st Sergeant consoled the one younger civilian who felt a little unworthy in comparison. Harold was in dress blues, with a short sleeve khaki shirt due to the climate. Sarah's husband, also a noncom, a Chief Petty officer, just listened.

They approached a large cafe with the ubiquitous ceiling fans and an open-air dining room that spread uninterrupted out on to a large patio. It was not packed, but the song as ubiquitous at that time as the ceiling fans, Mike Velarde Jr's *Dahil sa Iyo*, soothed quite a few men in uniform and quite a few women, some in uniform. The uniforms were of the various branches of service there at the time, and none was particularly dominate. Recorded originally by the male singer, Rogelio de la Rosa, the beautiful song was currently riding on the velvet voice of a pretty Filipina backed by a band of some good quality.

Seeing the mass of uniforms, and though uniformed herself, the brown African American Navy doctor pulled slightly against her husband's hand as he turned toward the steps up to the patio and restaurant door, giving in finally.

As they climbed up the steps of the particular local South Pacific style restaurant, a soldier by the door quietly stopped them with a hand out to Allan, palm out, presumably because of Ann's race, or it could have related to Morrow's or Pierce's enlisted status, as the room seemed reserved for officers. It was a mixed-up time in the islands where many heroes and commanding officers of guerrilla movements had been Filipinos and even Filipinas. But most if not all in this moderate sized room were white American officers of the various service branches. There were available tables and empty seats.

417

Before the man could say anything that might embarrass his wife, however light and cordial, Lt. Allan Allison stepped up close to him to inquire more privately what the point was, though he suspected he knew. As that conversation had begun in almost a whisper, a major at a nearby table with friends stood up with a cane for support and the words, "Wait a moment soldier." He was Army and arose from a table some twenty feet away with mostly Army and Marine officers. Ann, Allan, and Jenny, were in their Navy dress white uniforms, with open collar white shirts to fit the climate. Chief Petty officer Jake Pierce was in his whites. The men's respective uniforms dictated similar head coverings, officers and noncoms alike. Ann and Jenny wore garrison caps with their rank on the right side in front and the small, officer cap device on the left. As Ann had also served as the combat commander of their unit at the last, she wore the oakleaf device of her rank on both shirt collar tips. It may have been the 'Army's room', the guard at the door being of that branch and MacArthur's boys slightly more dominate in the historic return to the Philippines and that dining room.

The Army major spoke just loud enough to be heard by all as he came over quickly, in spite of the cane and a distinct limp. Reaching the party, he said to the private, "Everyone here has been through a lot. Let's not bar anyone in uniform today. It's Thanksgiving." He was a major and to be listened to, but in a room overweight with brass, he was just a major. However, on his chest were the ribbons for the Distinguished Service Cross and the glaring light blue one with stars of the Medal of Honor. The music had stopped mid-song. An observant man, walking up he had caught glimpses of the Silver Star and Navy Cross on the Chief's chest and what he assumed were copies on the civilian girl's navy-blue dress.

Looking at Ann, the man inquired, "Might you be Lt. Commander Ann Allison?"

"Yes sir," and she saluted, as did the others.

Returning the salute, he responded, "I think our rank is equal, Ann. I always get this inter-service stuff mixed up. But please remain at attention a moment. I received this from headquarters, one of them along the line, and I've had my eye out for you. I was on Mindanao too. We're all scattered now, so I guess this is my duty. I am Major Alexander Ellison."

Turning to the room, he asked with a somewhat commanding voice, "Will the room remain quiet for just a moment." To their compliance he responded, "Thank you. I have a quick presentation. Is this alright or should I wait?"

From a rear table where an Army general and Navy admiral sat and had been talking, the deep voice of the Admiral, the ranking man in the room replied, "Go ahead, Major."

"Thank you, Sir. I will suggest everyone remain seated at first, or you won't be able to see this little gal. If you've ever held a Thompson 1928 A1, look at her and listen to this."

Then turning to Ann, still at attention as he had requested, but not rigidly so, he started in an audibly commanding, reasonably loud voice, keeping it short in respect of the diners with food on their plates possibly growing cold and not wanting to be overly dramatic. But the man, who had been through so much himself, was surely enjoying the moment and did the best he could from memory.

"Lt. Commander Carolyn Ann Allison MD, USNR, I am honored to present you with this Navy Cross for extraordinary heroism in action against an enemy of the United States on the night of August 7, 1942, during which you, with courageous disregard for your own life and receiving wounds, did save your command by alone engaging 25 enemy combatants who were poised for a surprise attack of which you could give no alarm, and did, with grenades and a Thompson Submachine Gun, annihilate said enemy force, with the aid of one of your company's night sentries, and another Marine, who followed your lead."

He wanted to keep it short after interrupting the roomful of hungry military folk engaged in a rare moment of inter-service fraternity. The major had read the citation several times to be prepared if and when he met the woman, and he did the best he could from memories of observing such award presentations in a long career.

Reaching, he pinned the Navy Cross, a somewhat simplistic, beautiful medal and ribbon combination on the left breast of her blouse, always a bit of nervous duty for a man in that new era of women in service to America. Thankfully for both parties, she wore a bra. Coming to attention, he saluted her. She returned the salute. Similarly, he pinned a Purple Heart on Ann, and saluted again.

The room burst out in applause, as Ann stood with head bent down and her hand over her mouth, eyes closed to try and slow her somewhat controllable tears. The blue and white reminded her of Mary.

The deep voice of the admiral seemed to burst out even when he moderated it and commanded, "Attention on deck!"

He was surely enjoying the chance to use the sea services' unique command on the Army fellows there, and followed, "Salute!" And Ann, composed and at attention, received the honor from the whole room of assorted warriors and support personnel. Then, the strong applause filled the room again.

For the Navy, only the Congressional Medal of honor was higher, with the similar Distinguished Service Cross number two in the other services. All services used the Silver Star as their third award for valor. The Bronze Star was forth but was awarded for other things than courage, such as exceptional performance of duty and such. Something about the simplicity of name, colors, and design seemed to elevate the Navy Cross in the eyes and minds of many, as certainly the religious hint within those elements did as well. The current primeval struggle across the vast Pacific Ocean, however high tech at times, forever remained in the hearts and minds of many of its recipients and their loved ones. Some earned it during courageous acts they did not survive. A singular fact of the medal was that all who earned it probably, like Ann, expected to not survive the moment that would eventually lead to its presentation.

Turning to the room the major said, "Thank you ladies and gentlemen. I've been carrying that little package around for weeks. It can get heavy when you don't know if you'll find them or if they are still alive."

Turning back to the group he looked at Ann and said, "We have to talk of old Mindanao times though experienced separately. Please find a table with room for me, if I may join you all later."

"We will, Major. Join us as soon as you wish," replied Ann in slightly broken emotional words.

Allan embraced her with openly displayed affection but withheld the kiss he wanted. Racists that might be in the room might have reacted to such affection he had wished to display; however, some knew of them and thus the marriage, and the word soon passed around the room in whispers with no negative reaction. These men and a few women officers, the latter mostly nurses, knew war. For the moment, Ann grabbed and squeezed his hand, holding and not letting go all the way to the table. As the major returned to his seat and the group from the Allison command started across the room to a tortuously distant open table, another softer yet significant applause followed them. All had heard the clearly spoken citation.

They had all the time they wanted, and after a long early afternoon talk with the major, the six of them stayed through the late afternoon with cocktails and talked some more. It was the Philippines in the scattered jewels of the Visayan Islands at its heart, warm, humid, but brushed with a harbor breeze . . just enough warmth and drink to relax them, just enough breeze and talk to keep them awake. The young soldier, with no dog in the racial political fight and only following orders as the doorman, found that the enlisted men and the dark woman were there to stay, even after everyone else was gone save their four companions. He began helping straighten the room as it was a role he had offered the restaurant's owner for the exclusivity of the venue for the military. And at some point, he ended up in long conversation with the six lingering customers before leaving to other duties.

Looking at Sarah Pierce, Ann said, "You're looking at this all wrong, honey. You have done so much as a civilian Navy employ. Don't you realize there are offices all over this world right now filled with sailors who never left their desks? Many never left American soil. You took the risk, and as I see it, you were clearly at risk several times."

Sarah, not spoiled or shallow but younger than the three and never in combat, just felt she was among real heroes and was a bit beneath them all, had not really served or done her part, and she replied, "I know."

Her husband, Jake added to the doctor's opinion, "Look at it this way, almost no women saw the kind of assignment and risks that Ann and Jenny did. Even nurses out here were not too close to it, to combat, and they are older than you, Darling . . because of their school. The WAVES generally served stateside. A few women pilots ferried planes in the States or out here to the Pacific but didn't see combat and were not trained for it."

As her husband, Lt, Allan Allison listened, Ann added, "Except for the gals captured . . you know the nurses in Manila and such, and a few like me, you have done as much as anyone . . really. I mean it, Sarah. You have helped put families together again."

Looking up, as her head had been down and her hands in her lap, the strong younger woman smiled softly and said, "Thank you, Ann. Coming from you, it means so much." And she really, suddenly felt quite a bit better. When her husband, beside her now, went missing a few years before, she had managed, at age twenty-one, to secure a Navy department job in the Philippines helping search for lost men that, according to the records and all available information, shouldn't be missing. Sarah was now twenty-three. The others were in or near their thirties: her husband was twenty-eight, the doctor was thirty, and her husband was thirty-one. Sarah was intellectually and emotionally mature for her age and had inherited family properties.

The four had talked in Hollandia, as Sarah had been their connection to the places and people outside the hospital for the weeks the other three had been rehabilitating. She was still a naval employee and could get information they needed and special snacks and drinks and such, while hospitalized. Her assignment was a helpful position, though she was working independently now but still under her commanding officer's direction.

Sarah spoke now to all of them, "I've asked all the right questions to everyone I could approach here. I radioed Commander Phillips, and he inquired here in the islands and used his higher contacts in the Navy and with the Australians and British. By the way, Jake Honey, your Khukuri was on the *Refuge* with us and I have it now. It was in the office at Hollandia with other patients' valuables.

Anyway, I currently have no leads on anyone: not Lola Sunny, not Beaumont Chastain, Elaine

Chanthavong, nor Lt. Commander Shaw, or Maya and Jon O'Brian. I believe we might consider working together as a team and work thorough this by location. There is a logical travel itinerary that shows no favoritism. My husband's people would cross through areas where Captain Beaumont Chastain could be. I have put in a request from Phillips to have you, Jenny, discharged to come here to Cebu City as you three have suggested," said looking to the nurse and then at Ann and Allan. That is because of the young woman, Marisa. I cannot help with the 1st Sergeant's posting, and of course you two cannot marry yet. I'm sorry Harold, Jenney. Our problem when we search for others would be money. I have some funds I am willing to contribute with Jake's assent."

"Sarah, we cannot use up your funds now that you and Jake can finally settle down."

"Jake won't settle down 'til he knows about them. Neither can I. I had Jake's parents sell part of my land to a company that wants to build a lodge and cabins. I leased my home to the diocese for retreats, scout groups, stuff like that, and I get half of the profits from the grill each month. I gave Eloise a portion of ownership and she is buying more with monthly payments, So I have that as well. I do not believe I can cover everything though and still put a little back. If we can find your Aero that would help tremendously."

"If it is in decent shape," said Allan. "And finding it might mean finding Beau."

"If we find your plane, Allan, would you lease it to us?"

"Jake, if we find it and it flies, I'll share the piloting and the plane for you folks helping with the expenses. We need fuel, costs of any registrations, and food. Oh, and occasional lodging if we tire of sleeping in her or some airport won't let us."

"That's very generous."

"I just want to be back in the air again and spending time with my wife where our work is without constant fear."

Under the table's edge, she had been holding his hand all through the discussion after the meal. He was her pillar of strength and sanctuary of love. And she unabashedly leaned over and kissed him on the cheek.

Ann summed up things more or less, saying, "We've a good team: a doctor, experienced copilots, and an agent who has over two years' experience searching for lost people. It is pretty handy that all of us have significant outdoor experience too. I worked two years in France before all of this happened and sent what I didn't need home. I guess I lost what little was in the bank in Paris. Most of what I kept went into the expedition which was funded mostly by a missionary women's group. Let's get up in the hills here in Cebu and start searching for the people who should be right here in the Philippines, Jake's Lola Sunny and her family and close friends."

"We will have to see if we're all three gonna be discharged or reassigned, too. You as well, Honey," Jake finished the thought looking at his wife.

"That's true. The Commander may need me more than ever now. I don't think the mainland will involve us though. The Army and Army Air Corps were mostly there. I mean . . we have found some soldiers, especially here in the Philippines, but it was never our main focus. I am hoping to be released or allowed to resign since I am not enlisted personnel. I hate to leave him hanging though."

Jake put in, "Well, I would think, after the Philippines, we were assaulting much smaller islands with less cover. Perhaps fewer are lost on them."

"That is what I believe and hope."

"They'll likely not keep me," commented the doctor. "They surely won't know where to put me. Everything will be awkward for them, but we'll see. I want to be discharged for our search."

"You're an officer, and the 'emergency' is over. Just resign your commission. It was a 'Direct

428

Commission' anyway. They're usually temporary for the 'emergency' or 'duration'," Sarah informed Ann.

Looking up at all of them, the young war wife had managed to wrangle her way from the California Sierra to the faraway South Pacific in the midst of a war to find 'him' and do her part in it. Describing herself as well to a degree perhaps, she said softly, "You're all three heroes, really all five of you. I am truly blessed knowing all of you."

Jenny commented, "Marine Corporal Richard Ferris, his wife Carla, and I are asking that Marine Corporal David Johnston be discharged in the Philippines if he so requests. He and Marisa have become friends. I thought the last thing she would do is befriend a guy, but he is a gentle soul. I hope we aren't asking for too much and all get denied. Bureaucracy thinks it knows best for its charges in their private lives without caring to ask. I'm afraid it will now say, 'You boys need to all get home to your mamas.'"

After a pause, looking at the doctor, Sarah said, "You know Ann, you **are** a celebrity, and that African mission should not mar your reputation. With the war over, the truth can now be told about your adversaries there at the time. The Navy might want to keep you and sponsor something like that . . maybe use you for some well publicized relief efforts here, maybe even with the tribal natives in the mountains. There are some interesting groups up in the highlands on Luzon. A known personality in your field and a war hero like yourself . . it would be good for the Navy's peacetime image . . keep them in the public eye in a positive way as we all try to forget the war. You could end up in *National Geographic* or *Life*."

For a while the table was quiet, though the energy there within them all seemed to hum as the war's end sat in their minds with all the possibilities just discussed, fed by the emotion within their individual and collective hearts at the realization that all had escaped death and survived, both old friends and those just recently discovered.

"Oh, my gosh! I forgot. How could that happen?"

"What is it, Sarah?" inquired her husband.

The issues dear to newly acquired friends not as yet floating as high in her mental sea of bureaucratic information and concerns as her work, she had missed an important tidbit.

"Lieutenant Commander, Lieutenant, I did learn that your plane and its crew served in India," the young rather dynamic field operator said, turning to the couple. "There have been injuries."

"To whom?" inquired Ann.

"A woman, the chief pilot's wife was injured in combat along the Burmese border."

"How, where, how is she?" asked with some angst.

"It was a short telegram, and only said the plane and crew were probably still in India. The lines and operators are all so busy now since August."

"If this war has taught us anything, it is the strength of our women in new roles. I mean to say, they have been doing them through all history. I don't want to see it in full blown battles in the field, like the Russians are doing, had to do, I suppose."

The speaker was Jake who had been in Panay's mountains with the guerrillas and seen the Filipino and American women fighters there.

"Yes," said Allan. "The concern is their capture. Guys like us can never figure out how to deal with that possibility, even if serving together . . and also not knowing where she is, who she is serving with."

Sarah added, "Fellas with wives who are nurses on these hospital ships or in field hospitals, must find it hard, even a distraction. Did any of you know that a kamikaze hit a hospital ship? It killed the surgical team during an operation in the night at sea. But, you know, we all know that if they start using us gals someday, they will never put couples in the same units in combat. The Doctor and Lieutenant here were a unique situation."

"They might do it, will do it, in military operated scientific and relief expeditions during peacetime.

431

You know, when the specialists are a husband and wife team," responded Ann.

Some of them, from years in the bundok, weren't used to big meals and had eaten lightly at lunch. They had talked through the afternoon, and a waiter came up and asked if they were staying for dinner.

Ann, who had eaten a light lunch, replied, "I am if my friends are. Do you have live music like you had at lunch?"

"Yes Ma'am. The best."

To her glance around the group, the others nodded agreement. What else could they want to do but talk to loved ones after all of it was over.

Perhaps, the man had watched her receive the medal. Maybe he had been energized by the rare experience of meeting someone of Ann's ethnicity on his job. Being an officer just made her ever so much more a rarity. The waiter, utilizing a common trait of the Filipino, turned on his most polished charm and inquired, "Well then, Ma'am, may I take your order?"

"Yes. If you have it, I'll have Bangús, fried with a glass of *San Miguel* Beer."

The East Indies & Philippines

During the Colonial Period at the Beginning of the Second World War

Surigao del Norte is at the top of Mindanao on the northeast, a peninsula, pointing toward Leyte and Leyte Gulf.

Cities or harbors are indicated with a dot or the point of a directional line. Singapore is the dot at the tip of the Malay Peninsula above Sumatra.

The top of Australia is seen, and New Zealand would be to the right and below it. Knowing that these Dutch East Indies seen here were almost completely conquered by the Japanese, as well as British Malaya, Singapore, and Borneo, one can easily grasp the fear in Australians and New Zealanders. With their men at war in other theaters as part of the forces of the United Kingdom, the people at home were concerned to a greater degree than what might be considered normal.

The Java sea, shown here, was the location of a devastating naval defeat of the Allies at the hands of the Japanese. A naval gun battle. This terrified the people of Australia even more, as did the bombing of Darwin.

The Philippines

South
China
Sea

LUZON

Manila Bay

Manila

Philippine
Sea

MINDORO

Sibuyan
Sea

SAMAR

PANAY

Visayan
Sea

LEYTE

Leyte Gulf

Sulu Sea

Panay
Gulf

NEGROS

CEBU

PALAWAN

② Iloilo City

Sulu Sea

Bohol
Sea

MINDANAO

① Cebu City

Sulu Sea

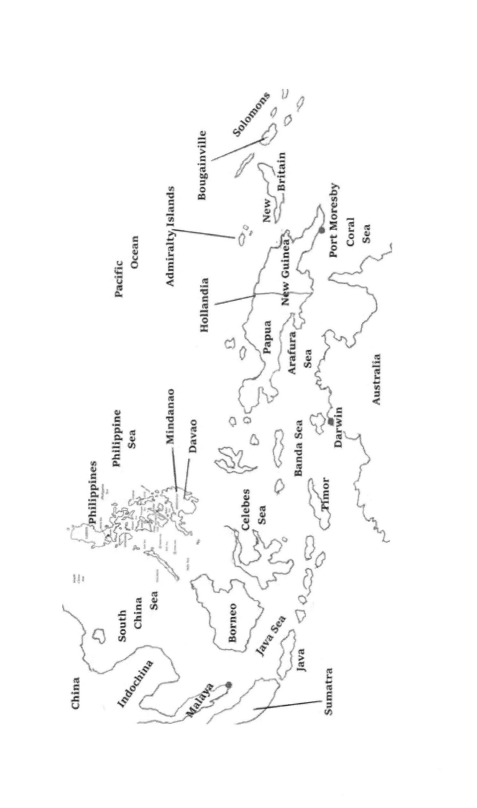

Printed in Great Britain
by Amazon

71179489R00267